Nights of Iron and Ink

Copyright © 2022 Shannen Durey

Cover Design: Whimsy Book Cover Graphics

Map Illustration: Lizard Ink Maps

Edited by Jennifer Murgia and E.H. Demeter

ISBN 9781736645048

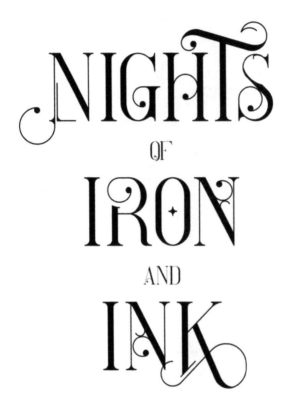

NIGHTS
OF
IRON
AND
INK

SHANNEN DUREY

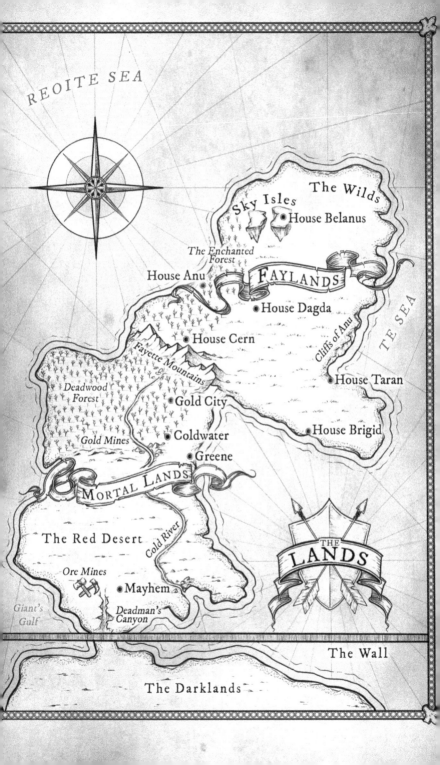

ENCYCLOPEDIA OF BEASTS

Categorized by land, air, and water.

Broken into tiers based on power level: 1-4 with one being the least powerful and four being the most powerful.

AIR BEASTS:

1. Broberie: Appears as a small black bird who moves in locus like swarms to devour dead bodies whole, bones and all. (Tier 1)

2. Flying srphy: Appears as a snake with wings that spits venom. One drop can kill five full grown adults. (Tier 1)

3. Banshee: Appears as a translucent woman in mourning. Wails can burst the eardrum of every living being within a mile radius. (Tier 2)

4. Crua: Appears as a slender figure cloaked in darkness. Controls shadows and uses them as its minions. (Tier 2)

5. Sloaugh: Appears as a skeletal figure in a black shroud. Devours the souls of its victims while it shows them sad memories of their dead ones. (Tier 3)

6. Callitech: Appears as a frozen woman. It freezes its victims, turning them to ice before shattering them. (Tier 3)

7. Fomoire: Appears as a shifting ball of smoke. Turns its victim's greatest nightmare into reality. (Tier 4)

WATER BEASTS:

1. Muckey: Appears as a tiny fish with razor sharp teeth that burrows into its victim's stomach and eats them from the inside out. (Tier 1)

2. Grundylow: Appears as a frog-like creature with fangs that move in schools of hundreds and drag their victims to their death. (Tier 1)

3. Ashray: Appears as a translucent sea ghost that electrocutes its victims to death. (Tier 2)

4. Mermer: Appears as a half humanoid, half fish with fangs and talons. Lures men to their deaths. (Tier 2)

5. Fearga: Appears as a faceless humanoid with excessively wrinkled skin. Dehydrates its victims. (Tier 3)

6. Kelpa: Appears as a shape shifter that shows the victim their greatest desire, luring them into the water's depths to drown. (Tier 3)

7. Treachna: Appears as a three headed serpent with tentacles capable of controlling currents, capsizing boats, and devouring them whole. (Tier 4)

LAND BEASTS:

1. Corth: Appears as a faceless, armless humanoid that spits acid from a hole in its chest. (Tier 1)

2. Abca: Appears as a short, powerful humanoid made of rock with the power to punch through bone and flesh with a single blow. (Tier 1)

3. Failin: Appears as four times the size of a normal wolf with poisonous, retractable spikes hidden beneath its fur. (Tier 2)

4. Bodah: Appears as a faceless humanoid with long spindly fingers that cast webbing to catch its victims and devour them. (Tier 2)

5. Fets: Appears as the face of their victim, temporarily blindsiding them before killing them. (Tier 3)

6. Dullah: Appears as a headless horseman that carries the spine of its latest victim into battle. (Tier 3)

7. Aibeya: Appears as a female playing the harp. Lulls victims into a false state of calm and sleepiness during which time it carves out their heart and devours it. (Tier 4)

Spirit Beast:

1. Pooka: Appears as a shape-shifting creature that is more spirit than beast. Can travel vast distances in the blink of an eye by hopping between the spirit realm and the realm of the living. (Tier unknown)

1

The Red Desert became unnaturally quiet as the last rays of sun dipped below the horizon, but the silence wasn't a peaceful one. It was a warning of what was to come.

With the sun gone, a chill permeated the air, but the tremor in my hands wasn't from the drop in temperature. I squeezed my fingers tighter around the gun I held. I had done this countless times before, and still my nerves were a jumbled mess.

From my perch inside the canyon, I scanned the horizon, searching for any signs of movement. Craggy sandstone formations and scraggly brush cast ominous shadows over the dry landscape. At the edge of the desert sat a massive obsidian wall. It was solid, shimmering in the silvery glow from the full moon overhead.

I tried to convince myself that was good. A solid wall meant the magic barrier in place held, but I knew it would inevitably buckle. It always did.

And they would come.

Any minute now, the beasts would come.

My gaze swept over the dark silhouettes lying in wait

along the top of the high canyon walls above me. Some laid prone with rifles; a handful stood behind hand-cranked gatling guns. All mortals. They were too weak and fragile to fight in the bottom of the canyon with the Rogues—the self-proclaimed free halflings.

Being part mortal and part fae, halflings possessed speed, strength, and advanced healing abilities the mortals lacked. We weren't immortal like high fae, nor did we possess powers like any of the fae did, but our abilities certainly helped when it came to fighting the beasts.

I frowned, my gaze darting back to the horizon.

The wall had thinned and turned translucent. My heart beat furiously in my chest, equal parts relieved and terrified. The sooner the battle started, the sooner it would end.

I peered into the moonlit desert, waiting for the shadows I knew would seek me out like a beacon. The beasts behind the wall were inexplicably drawn to me for a reason I didn't understand and never would. The only being capable of providing me with any answers was a hundred miles away and I intended to keep it that way.

The bloodthirsty beasts I waited to make an appearance were preferable to *her* any day.

Beasts were categorized into air, land, and water. Each category had four tiers with one being the smaller, less powerful beasts and four being the most powerful, frightening beasts. I didn't want to run into any fours tonight. Tier four were the alphas of the beast world. Not only were their powers lethal, but they could also control the beasts in lower tiers.

But no beasts had appeared yet. Where were they? The full moon was as bright as ever. On any other night like this, myself and all the other fighters would have already been knee deep in battle. It never took this long.

"Vera," a low voice hissed my name and I nearly jumped out of my skin, finger twitching toward the trigger.

My gaze shot down to the figure standing several feet below where I perched on a rock jutting out of the canyon wall. At this height, I could see the wall in the distance, but also not break a leg when the time came to jump to the bottom of the canyon and lead the beasts to the choke point.

It was Ryder. The Rogue's second in command and my one and only friend. His sharp features were cast in shadows, but I knew him well enough to read his body language. He was on edge. We all were—and for good reason.

I holstered my gun temporarily before I shot someone. Not that I was opposed to that, but the golden bullets chambered inside were specially made for the beasts and gold was a pain in the ass to get a hold of this far south. I made it a practice not to waste ammo.

"I almost shot you, you idiot," I whispered. "What are you doing here? You shouldn't have left your post."

"What is taking them so long?" he asked. "Have you seen any shadows yet?"

I peered over the edge of the canyon wall. My brows puckered as I saw nothing but sand and craggy rocks. I crouched back down. "No, nothing. The magic took longer to weaken than usual, but the wall is definitely down now. They should be here already."

Ryder cursed under his breath. "Something is wrong. I'll report back to Boone. See what he wants to do."

I watched him jog back to the other side of the canyon, a surge of envy hitting me at the srphy vest he wore. Srphies were flying reptilian beasts easily identified by the beautiful color and patterns on their skin.

His vest had black and white striations with the Rogues' emblem—a red hawk—sewn onto the back. Only full

3

members of the Rogues were allowed the privilege of one. Seven years and many full moons later and I somehow still had not 'earned' the right to a vest.

That was some straight up corthshit.

My make-shift seat started to shake, disrupting my thoughts. I dug my claws in to keep from falling off; my teeth snapped together from the force of it.

Cries sounded above me, and my gaze flew up to the mortals. They all scrambled back from the edge, and I realized the canyon walls were shaking, vibrating with enough force to break off chunks of rock.

A loud crack was my only warning before I crashed to the bottom of the canyon; my spine smacked painfully into the rock I had been sitting on as all the breath was ripped from my lungs. Struggling to draw in air, I saw chunks of falling debris headed toward me.

I tried to roll out of the way, but I wasn't quick enough. A large piece of rock slammed down on my right leg and sharp, searing pain followed. The world around me blurred and spun as bile surged up my throat.

Fuck.

I took shallow breaths through my nostrils until the dizziness stopped, but not the pain. By the time I glanced around, all the shaking had stopped.

What in the lands had just happened?

Quakes didn't happen this far south.

An icy, paralyzing fear took hold of me. Balor, the Lord of Night and Beasts, was rumored to be a giant. He had never left the confines of the wall before so no one could be certain, but a giant's mass was the only thing I could think of as the possible cause.

There would be time to sort it out later. I needed to free myself before the beasts arrived.

I tugged on my leg and hissed out a breath at the nauseating pain shooting up my thigh. No matter how hard I pulled, it wouldn't budge. I only succeeded in injuring it further. It was pinned.

"Hey!" I shouted, hoping to get one of the mortal's attention. A dark silhouette peered over the canyon's lip. A light flared illuminating cropped silver hair—a feature only halflings shared.

"What just happened?" a panicked voice rushed out.

He had to be the Rogues' newest recruit. Vince was a fresh escapee of the Faylands, which meant this had to be his first full moon. First timers sat back with the mortals for both their safety and the Rogues.

Only a newbie would be stupid enough to light a match right now.

"Put that out," I hissed. "They're attracted to light."

The flame vanished. At least he listened well enough.

I licked my lips and grimaced at the grainy taste of sand coating them. "Everything is fine," I tried to console him remembering how terrifying my first full moon had been. "Has anything come out of the wall yet?"

"No . . . "

Relief flooded me. Not a giant then. "Can you come down and help? My leg is pinned."

"Wait—fuck. I see a shadow."

Godsdamnit. *Now* they decide to come out?

I tried to move the rock pinning me with my free leg, but the thing was too massive, even for my halfling strength. Blinding pain followed. My trapped leg was seriously injured.

Shit. Shit. Shit.

Vince's silhouette disappeared. "Hey, wait! Come back!"

Silence.

"Asshole," I muttered. I hoped a failin—a giant, rabid,

5

wolf beast—bit off his dick. No, better yet, I hoped a corth burned it off with acid.

None of the mortals came forward either. Didn't those idiots up there realize I was the only thing standing between them and the beasts?

No, because that would require some sort of intelligence on their part. I knew I couldn't rely on the Rogues either. They were too far away in the canyon to hear me and even if they could, Ryder was likely the only one who would risk his life to come help me.

I sighed. I was on my own. *Like always.*

A bone-chilling growl cut through the night and the hair at the back of my neck stood up. No shadows were visible from my trapped position, but that growl was less than a hundred feet off. If I didn't get free from this stupid rock, I would be beast meat.

Twisting to one side, I braced my hands against the canyon wall and used my free leg to push for all I was worth against the rock. I gritted my teeth, straining under its weight.

It didn't move an inch.

A loud howl preceded paws pounding over the ground. Filthy curses flew from my mouth. We never knew what beasts we would have to face each full moon. They seemed to appear at random. Some full moons we had to battle all the higher tier beasts and barely made it through the night. Other times, only lower tiers appeared.

A failin had come out tonight. Failin were four times the size of a normal wolf with fangs as long as my forearms. Their backs and chest were covered in deadly, retractable spikes hidden just beneath their white fur. Failin were only tier two beasts, but those spikes made them damn hard to kill. They were tipped in poison—one scratch and I'd be dead in under an hour.

I shoved harder against the rock, pushing my muscles past their limits. Sweat beaded my forehead and my breathing turned heavy from the exertion. If it weren't for my halfling strength, I wouldn't have a shot in the dark at moving this enormous rock. Though, I barely had a shot as it was.

My leg muscles were on the verge of snapping when finally, the rock started to shift. I pushed and pushed until the immense pressure on my leg eased. Slowly, carefully, I extracted my limb from under its bulk. Once freed, I saw my leg twisted slightly to the left. There was a sickening lump where the bone had broken under the skin. A muffled cry left my lips at the grisly sight.

The pain had been dulled under the crushing weight of the rock, but now it screamed to life, radiating up my entire body. It was paralyzing, but I had endured much worse.

I had to move.

I lurched to my feet, using the canyon wall for balance, then hobbled forward as fast as I could on one foot, dragging the broken leg behind me. My advanced healing would kick in soon and the bone would mend itself. It would heal at an unnatural angle unless I put it back into place, but there was no time for that.

I had to draw the beasts to the other side of the canyon and slip through the narrow opening where the Rogues waited. It was a choke point, allowing them to pick the beasts off one at a time. As outnumbered as we were, we couldn't defeat the beasts any other way.

There was a sickening crack when the bone snapped back together. I gagged at the onslaught of pain that followed, not daring to slow. If I slowed, I was dead. At least that leg could support some of my weight now.

The growl sounded again. This time it was right behind me. My entire body tensed. Gaze darting over my shoulder, I saw several pairs of glowing purple eyes at the top of the canyon.

"Shoot at them, you idiots," I shouted to the mortals manning the guns.

Nothing.

Useless . . . fucking . . . idiots.

I tried to limp faster, but my injured leg buckled, and I stumbled. I righted myself just as a loud thud sounded behind me. Whole body tensing, my hand slid to the gold dagger holstered on my thigh. I couldn't balance well enough yet to use my gun.

"Please be something easy to kill," I whispered, slowly turning to face whatever beast stood at my back.

It was an abca. Short, no higher than my knees, the beast was humanoid shaped but covered in a hard, nearly impenetrable shell. When they stopped moving, they could pass for boulders. They seemed harmless at first glance, but abcas were insanely strong. A single hit from one of their stony fists could smash right through bone.

The abca tucked into a ball and charged.

I gritted my teeth, forcing my wounded leg to take more of my weight than it was ready to, but thankfully it held, and remained still as the abca barreled toward me, then jumped to the side at the last minute. The abca stopped rolling to reverse its course. Before it could, I leapt on top of it, pulling its bulbous body close to my chest, and sunk my blade into the soft flesh between the hard plates on its neck.

It released a haunting scream I felt in my chest, thrashing in my arms to escape. I bared down more of my weight and the scream turned shriller, then it went limp in my arms.

I was on my feet running again. Abcas were lower tier beasts—little more than foot soldiers. I needed to get to cover before the failin caught up to me. By now, my healing had mended my leg enough to support most of my weight, though I still stumbled periodically.

Several loud thuds sounded behind me. Ice flooded my veins, but I refused to glance back. If the beasts caught me before I reached the choke point, they'd rip me apart before fighting over who got the juiciest parts of my corpse.

The rattle of the gatling guns being cranked echoed through the canyon followed by gun fire.

Rit-tit-tat.

The guns unloaded a spray of golden bullets on the beasts behind me.

Finally. At least the mortals weren't *completely* useless. Just mostly.

I ran faster as the canyon walls narrowed around me. I was a majority of the way across the canyon now. The gunfire was just a faint popping in the distance. Dirt and sand flew up around me, obscuring my vision, but I knew the way by heart.

I was almost there. I could feel it.

The ground shook beneath me as hundreds of beasts stampeded this way. They would be on me soon.

Putting on a final burst of speed brought me to the narrowest point of the canyon. The walls were a breath away from joining, leaving just enough space for me to slip inside. I skidded to a stop, just shy of breaking my face.

The narrow opening was blocked. Fallen rocks filled the crevice I was supposed to squeeze through.

My heart shot into my throat like a bullet.

No, no, no. Stupid fucking quake.

I lunged forward, dragging, and digging rocks out of the way, but there were too many and not enough time. The shrieks and blood curdling growls behind me grew louder.

"The path is blocked!" I shouted, hoping one of the Rogues would hear me, but I knew it was unlikely.

Hundreds of feet of twisting rock columns stood between us.

I was out of time.

And hope.

I spun, ripping out my gun and tightened the grip on my dagger. Thank the Gods I hadn't lost them in the fall.

"Come and get me you bastards!" I yelled at the hoard of silhouettes racing toward me. The ground trembled from their combined mass.

My heart was ramming against my breastbone, begging me to run, but damn the dark if I would be taken easily, or go out like a coward. I would make the beasts work for their meal.

Remembering the gold tips in my pocket, I quickly slipped one over each of my talons. They were sharpened to a wicked point as deadly as my own claws. Once I ran out of bullets, I would use them and my dagger to take as many beasts down with me as I could.

The first silhouette launched itself and took the shape of a failin's snarling muzzle as it came into view.

I shot out one of its eyes.

The beast whimpered, its attack falling short of where I stood, slamming to the ground just a couple feet away. It rebounded quickly and charged. My hands shook as I forced myself to remain still until the last second.

I dropped to the ground like a bag of rocks and stabbed my dagger upwards between its ribs, hitting its heart as it ran over me. I narrowly avoided one of its spikes slicing across my cheek in the process. The beast ran another foot before it fell to the ground snarling. Blood bubbled from the edges of its mouth, dripping down to stain its white fur.

Before I could make sure it was dead and retrieve my knife, something wet and stinging hit my back. It burned through my tunic into my skin. I leapt forward with a yelp, ripping the shirt over my head, and tossed it to the ground.

I spun in a circle searching for the corth that had attacked me. Too late, I noticed the failin stagger to its feet, dagger embedded in its chest, but not deep enough to kill. It launched itself at me.

My head slammed into the ground, stars dotting my vision. I was too disoriented to move before it pinned me beneath its enormous paws.

Hot, viscous drool dripped onto my face from its snarling muzzle as two piercing purple eyes stared into mine. Its massive jaw gripped my neck, and I froze knowing it was over. I felt the ground shake with the force of the rest of the horde stampeding toward me and pinched my eyes shut, praying I was already dead before the rest of the beasts reached me.

The failin shook me, rattling my brain in my skull.

"Make it quick," I growled.

Suddenly, a cold darkness unfurled inside me, spreading through my limbs. Two bright purple eyes appeared in the recess of my mind.

Eye snapping open, I stared coolly up at the dangerous predator above me like it was nothing more than a wayward puppy.

Drop me, you disgusting mutt, before I snap your neck.

The failin whined and released me so abruptly, my head crashed into the ground again. As it backed away, a deafening trumpet call blasted out of my mouth, cutting through the night.

The ground trembled.

I laid still, catching my breath before I sat up and watched the hoard of beasts sprint back the way they came. Every beast inside the canyon disappeared. I blinked slowly with a dazed stare, unable to process what I just witnessed.

I don't know how long I sat there, gazing absently into the empty canyon before voices pierced the silence.

"Why is she shirtless?"

"Where did the beasts go? The sun hasn't even risen."

"Maybe an aibeya came out and played its harp. She could be paralyzed."

"They're tier four beasts. She'd be dead."

"Vera?" A hand touched my bare shoulder and I flinched away. "Can you hear me?"

Ryder's voice, laced with worry, was enough to pull me out of my shocked haze. I blinked a few times and unstuck my tongue from the roof of my mouth.

"I—I can hear you," I rasped. Ryder crouched down, offering his shirt.

"Corth acid," I explained even though he hadn't been the one to ask about my shirtless state.

He hovered nearby as I pulled the fabric over my head. "What happened?"

"Something scared them off," I announced loud enough for all the surrounding Rogues to hear.

"I bet it was the same thing that caused that quake." Boone's deep voice washed over me. He was the Rogues' leader. "Ryder, I want you to get some feelers out. We need to know what that was."

Ryder nodded as he helped me to my feet. Together, we made our way out of the canyon. My gaze periodically darted into the shadows, still expecting a beast to jump out. None did.

They had all willingly returned behind the wall before sunrise when the calling would have dragged them back to their prison.

I should have felt relieved. Everyone else was. The battle had ended before it had ever begun. It was a win for us.

They chatted excitedly around me about how they were going to celebrate.

Instead, this horrible sinking feeling filled my gut because none of them knew what I had done.

I had frightened off a hoard of bloodthirsty beasts.

What in the lands did that make me?

2

I had waited too long to reset my leg. The muscle and tissue had regrown around the misshapen bone. The leg had to be broken again and set correctly. I couldn't do it on my own. It throbbed painfully as I limped down Mayhem's busy streets.

Healing rates for halflings varied based on how powerful their fae halves were. None of us could wield magic like the fae, but we inherited their strength, speed, and healing abilities. Usually, it took an hour of sleep to heal a minor injury and days for more serious ones, depending on the level of damage.

Low fae had similar healing time frames as halflings. High fae healed instantaneously. Except in the case of death. They were immortal, but a snapped neck would take some time to recover from.

Mortal, halflings, low fae and high—I had no idea where I fit in with any of them, especially after last night. I believe I was born a halfling, but *she* had cursed me, changed me into something else; that was an entirely different topic, one I rarely let myself focus on.

Having to make a trip to the doctor's office this morning

was more of an annoyance than the pain itself. I was used to pain, but even after spending the last five years in this city, I still had not grown accustomed to the mortals' fear and hatred of me.

Everyone was out celebrating. They had survived another full moon. The saloons and brothels had opened early. Mortals staggered through walkways strung with tattered, weather-worn canopies acting as a poor imitation of sun protection. At one point the fabric had been a dark brown, but now it was the same yellow as a drunk's rotten teeth and pockmarked with so many holes, it might not have been strung up at all.

Small red bottles dangled between the mortals' fingers. They were drunk on poitín—a fae moonshine strong enough to knock a mortal on their ass after a few sips. Fae were a bunch of self-centered, vain, callous creatures, but they knew how to have a good time.

Glassy eyes and dopey smiles greeted me everywhere I glanced. A couple passed leaning on one another to stay upright, laughing. Their cheeks were sunken and hollow; too sharp to be healthy. They were thin and frail.

At least the alcohol helped them forget how miserable their existences were for a time. Until it ran out and they were sober enough to understand if the beasts didn't kill them, starvation would.

Last month, three air beasts had attacked while the Rogues held off the land beasts until dawn and five mortals died. This time there were no casualties.

How long would it take for word to get around about what happened? Of course, they knew about the quake, but did anyone besides the Rogues know the beasts had returned to their imprisonment several hours early?

Fae magic created the wall protecting the Mortal Lands from the beasts. Their power was derived from the sun while the beasts were nocturnal creatures, strengthened by the moon. On full moons, when the celestial body was at its brightest and most powerful, and the fae were at their weakest, the beasts were able to escape their prison for a night.

When the sun rose and the wall's magic returned to full strength, it called the beasts back to their home. The wall and the land behind it were called the Darklands because with the magic barrier blocking all sunlight, it was perpetually nighttime behind the wall.

The calling unfortunately had its limits, which seemed to decrease with each passing year. Air, water, and land beasts were all locked behind the wall. The Rogues rarely had to fight air and water beasts because they could travel far enough by sunrise to escape the calling and remain indefinitely in the Mortal Lands, which left them to deal with the land beasts.

Not once had the beasts retired early to their imprisonment, but last night they had—because of me.

I shoved away all those thoughts, determined not to examine the deeper meaning behind last night's events. I stuffed it into the box where I locked away the past I refused to acknowledge, idly wondering how much I could fit inside before it broke, and everything spilled out.

A drunken idiot bumped into me. Before I could shove him away, he caught sight of my talons and purple gaze, and his eyes widened comically.

He stumbled back a step, raising a trembling finger. "Beast! There's a beast."

I heaved a sigh.

I rarely ventured into the city center for this reason. When I did, I wore leather gloves, but annoyingly, those had been ruined during the previous full moon. They were custom made. Ordering a new set would take months. I glared down at the black talons winking in the bright sun.

The talons, fangs, and unnatural purple of my eyes were the only things from my past I couldn't shove inside that box, but I still tried my best to pretend they didn't exist.

Unfortunately, they did exist and made me strongly resemble the terrifying monsters behind the wall. My hair was silver like other halflings, but no halfling, mortal, or even fae, shared my other features. Which in many eyes, placed me squarely in the category of beast.

I had *her* and the curse to thank for that.

My gaze snapped to the aggravating mortal as his shouting drew the attention of everyone around us. I tapped a talon against the revolver at my hip. I'd love nothing more than to put a bullet between his eyes, but apparently murdering mortals was frowned upon by the Rogues and I needed to stay in their good graces until the induction ceremony tonight when the Rogues would choose their newest members.

"It's your lucky day, mortal." I stepped around him and gave him a hard shove as I passed. He fell on his ass, too stunned to keep yapping. His wide-eyed expression was priceless.

I smiled, flashing a mouth full of razor-sharp teeth at the gawking mortals. They all scattered like rodents. My sharp smile widened. At least my monstrous features were useful for something.

"I see you're making friends again."

I laughed as Ryder sidled up beside me. "I can't help that I'm so loveable," I teased back.

A loud train whistle cut through the air before he could respond. We both swung toward the sound, then immediately stepped to the side knowing the chaos that was about to ensue.

The mortals stopped what they were doing and stampeded for the tracks just outside the city. Ryder and I watched the swarming mass of people pushing and shoving one another in a bid to get to the train first.

I turned, gazing at his profile as we waited for the commotion to die down enough for us to follow. He was an attractive male with his strong jawline, sharp cheekbones, and chestnut eyes. His shaggy silver hair touched the tips of his ears, adding a boyish charm. The muscles of his arms and chest filled out the black and white srphy vest he wore nicely.

The two of us had arrived in Mayhem around the same time. I was fifteen and he was seventeen at the time and I had quickly developed a crush on him. But Ryder had only seen me like that once two years ago after a mortal girl broke his heart.

We had slept together.

"This was just fun, right?" he had asked afterwards.

"Right."

I had laughed, playing it off, even as I felt a knife twisting in my chest. He wasn't my first. I'd had meaningless sex in the dark with a passing tourist or two just to see what all the fuss was about, but sex with him had actually meant something. Unfortunately, it only meant something to me.

But he was one of the few allies I had with the Rogues, so I didn't let one unpleasant moment ruin our friendship.

"Come on, let's see what the train's brought this time." He reached for my arm, but I stepped out of the way. The train could wait. I needed to get to the doctor.

My injured leg did not appreciate the weight it was forced to bear, and a bolt of pain shot through it. The disgusting angle of the limb was covered by my pants, but I gestured to it anyway. "Actually, I was just on my way to the doctor."

Ryder's eyes darted down briefly. "Right, your leg." I had told him about the rock and the little shit Vince on our way

18

back to the compound last night, but he had warned me against retaliating. I wouldn't. For now.

"The doctor's probably headed to the train like everyone else. I'll take you to see him after."

I nodded in agreement and we followed the line of mortals still trickling out of the city gates. My gait was slow, dragging my right leg behind me the entire time, but Ryder didn't complain and let me set the pace.

Steam billowed out of the metal contraption resting on the tracks. Trains were a new invention in the Mortal Lands, developed only ten years prior. Fae were stubbornly resistant to adopting new technology, clinging to their wagons and swords with a white knuckled grip. I was unsure if their refusal was due to trains and guns being mortal-made, or if the arrogant creatures just thought themselves above the force of change.

We arrived just as the compartment doors were pulled open, the crowd pressing in, all clamoring for a peek inside. The large mass of people kept us several feet away from the train, but I could easily see over every head standing at six feet tall. Ryder was two inches shorter than me, but taller than most of the mortals there.

Wooden crates full of half rotten food were unloaded and handed off to the vendors waiting to sell them in the market. Mortals licked their lips, salivating at the sight. Neither the vendors, nor the gawking mortals questioned the condition of what was supposed to be fresh food.

The train ran every two weeks stopping between cities as it made its way to the Fayland border with the gold mortals traded for fae goods. With the wall leeching all the magic and life from the soil in the Mortal Lands, all the essential goods had to be imported from the Faylands. Without fae goods, the mortals couldn't survive. The only thing of value they had to trade in return was gold.

I wasn't sure why the fae even needed gold. They allowed their runaway halflings to fight the beasts in the south. Gold was a beast's only weakness like high fae and iron. I'd bet they were stockpiling gold as a safety net in case the beasts ever breached their border.

Regardless of the reason, their demand for gold could only be fulfilled by the mines owned and operated by Gold City, which meant it had first access to the goods arriving from the Faylands and controlled their distribution.

I eyed the crates with disdain. "We fight the beasts for Gold City. You'd think they would show a little more gratitude."

Ryder's face twisted to mine, a frown on his lips. "Where do you think we get all the gold for our weapons and ammunition? Gold City's walls protect them. They don't have to give us anything," he explained. "If you want someone to blame, blame the fae for putting us all in this situation to begin with. The wall doesn't bleed magic and life from *their* lands. Only ours." Ryder stepped out of the way as someone with a crate moved past us. "At least we get the best quality of everything brought in."

True. The meals served in the Rogues' housing were the highest quality Mayhem had to offer, even if the bar for 'quality' food here was buried below ground. Unlike Gold City, Mayhem showed their gratitude for the Rogues' service and since I lived with them, I benefited as well.

The last compartment was thrown open and gold nuggets spilled out onto the dirt. Every mortal nearby leapt back, eyeing the precious metal with fear and desire. Just one of those nuggets would feed their family for a month.

That compartment should have remained locked. The precious metal was headed to the Faylands after the train departed Mayhem. The mortals in the crowd threw themselves backwards, attempting to put as much space between them and the gold as possible.

A small boy eyed the shiny nuggets and snatched up one of them in his tiny fist before tucking it into his pocket. The female beside him—I assumed it was his mother—turned ashen. She screamed, lunging for her son. She ripped the gold nugget out of his pocket and tossed it back with the rest.

The entire crowd stilled. All noise cut off.

There were two fae laws:

Do not harm a fae.

Do not steal from a fae.

Or the Enforcer will come.

The little boy, intentionally or not, had just broken the second law. Tension thickened the air, turning it heavy and cloying with the concentrated terror emanating from everyone.

We all held a collective breath as we waited for him to appear.

My pulse revved in my chest, but it wasn't from fear. It was anticipation born out of a dark curiosity.

I had heard stories, but I'd never seen the Enforcer for myself. According to legend, the Enforcer was the boogeyman parents used to keep their children in line, but more frightening because he was real. No one knew how, but anytime a fae law was broken he appeared within seconds. No matter who you were, no matter where you were, he always came.

His description changed with every story. Sometimes he appeared as a giant. Sometimes he was a snarling wolf. But across all the folklore, three things remained the same. He wielded a massive sword, he couldn't be killed, and he always delivered justice in the form of a brutal, violent death.

Rumor had it, he'd slaughtered entire cities before—cities that thought they could outsmart the fae—women, children, livestock, and all.

The Enforcer materialized out of thin air sending a shock wave of fear rippling through the crowd. I immediately understood the source of the giant myth. I had to tip my head back just to see all of him.

He stood two heads taller than the crowd. Turned away from me, I could only make out a set of broad shoulders and the large sword strapped to his back. That weapon was just as infamous as the Enforcer himself. It had killed hundreds, if not thousands of mortals unfortunate enough to incur his wrath. One swing of that deadly sword and fae justice was served.

Most striking was the lack of armor. Dressed in a short-sleeved tunic and dark breeches, he didn't have a single piece of protective clothing on him, even though he stood inside a mob of people armed with only a sword. It spoke to his lack of regard toward us. We didn't even register as a threat.

He *did* have tattoos. Light gray whorls spiraled down each of his thick biceps. I was too far away to be certain, but I thought I also saw a smattering of scars too.

With the whole immortality rumor, I had always assumed the Enforcer was a high fae, but the scars and tattoos had me rethinking that theory. I had seen some high fae come through *her* place as a child, and every one of them was flawless. Porcelain skin in various shades. Not a scar, pimple, or wrinkle in sight. And certainly not an entire sleeve of ink.

The boy's mother fell to her knees in front of him. She raised her trembling hands in supplication. "Please, I beg of you. It's not his fault. He was only curious."

The Enforcer rolled his thick neck side to side, cracking

it. The sound was ominous in the dead silence. "He is your responsibility." His head twisted down to her. "I will take both your lives as punishment."

I pulled out my gun. If the legends proved true, a gold bullet wouldn't kill him, but I only intended to distract him long enough for the little boy to escape. I aimed just to the left of his head—not stupid enough to break the first fae law —and fired.

Faster than lightning, the Enforcer ripped out his sword and swung. The bullet fell uselessly to the ground with a ping.

I stared at the piece of gold. It was cleaved in half.

Shock unhinged my jaw.

The Enforcer's head whipped around, and burning, steel-gray eyes narrowed on me. I tore my gaze from the bullet, lifting it to meet his. The intensity of those eyes stole the air from my lungs. They were hard and merciless.

Survival instincts swiftly kicked in, demanding I run. At the back of my mind, I knew I needed to. Regardless that a fae law had not been broken, an attack on the Enforcer was nothing short of suicidal.

But my legs wouldn't cooperate. I was bound by that deadly stare, pinned in place.

The Enforcer's nostrils flared, inhaling deeply before he released a rumbling growl loud enough to be heard across the distance of people separating us. He licked his lips like a hungry predator.

The action drew my attention to his mouth and the faint scar there.

Warmth instantly pooled in my belly at the thought of how those lips would feel on mine. Soft, but unyielding. His nostrils flared wider at the same time his gaze melted into liquid iron.

He took a step toward me, parting the crowd, and some

sense broke through. That reaction was *not* a normal reaction. What in the beast ravaged lands was I doing thinking about kissing him?

I shook my head to dispel that little bout of sanity.

This man, giant, legend—whatever the heck he was—served the fae. He was the rabid dog they let off the leash anytime we stepped out of line. The only appropriate reaction was to bury a bullet in his skull. Gripping the gun harder, I widened my stance. The moment he pounced, I'd be ready to do just that.

The Enforcer's gaze dipped to the gun in my hand, and I swore I saw his lips twitch. But he didn't come for me like I expected. He held out his hand. Bewilderment drew down my brows.

What was he doing?

Whatever he saw on my face caused his hand to drop. He twisted back, reaching for the mother and son still crouched near his feet, too terrified to run.

I surged forward, but it was too late. The three of them vanished.

I stared at the now empty space. What in the fuck had just happened?

Everyone was silent for a quick flash of time before things returned to normal and the volume rose to what it had been pre-enforcer. The mortals went on with their day like nothing had happened.

Ryder clapped me on the shoulder. Frowning, I glanced over at him. "I shot at him. Why didn't he come after me?" I asked. Breaking the first law—harming a fae—involved spilling their blood. I hadn't gone that far, but from the Enforcer's expression right after he'd cut down the bullet, I expected some sort of punishment.

"Your guess is as good as mine," he said with a shrug. "Next time, aim for his heart."

24

"Next time, take his hand," a feminine voice purred beside us. I turned toward the speaker to see it was Dolly, the brothel madame. Her curly blonde hair was trussed up in a bun with a loose curl framing either side of her face and she wore a red dress that clung to her curves.

"Why would I do that?" I asked, beyond confused by the suggestion. If the Enforcer left with someone, it was to kill them.

"Because he fucks even better than he kills."

I threw a questioning glance at Ryder, which he didn't see because he was too busy glaring at Dolly. I had heard many rumors when it came to the Enforcer, but never anything like this.

"You've . . . been with him?" I asked, looking back to her.

A dreamy expression stole over her face. "He made me take a memory draught before I left, but I still get flashes here and there. And from what I do remember—" she sucked in a sharp breath. "He fucks like a beast. I was sore for days. You missed a golden opportunity, my dear." She sashayed away before I had a chance to respond, drawing the attention of many males in the crowd.

"Traitor whore," Ryder hissed under his breath.

I shot him a disapproving look. He'd enjoyed Dolly's company plenty of times. Call her a traitor but leave her profession out of it.

"Did you know about that?" I asked.

"I've heard rumors that the Enforcer didn't always leave alone. Never seen it firsthand."

"That is the strangest thing I've ever heard."

In my mind, the Enforcer wasn't a man. He was a mythological monster terrorizing the mortals. Just because he did it under the cloak of civility, didn't make him any different from the beasts. One could argue he was worse. Beasts were mindless, violent animals in the simplest sense. Killing was all they understood.

He was a mass-murderer. Who in their right mind would want to bed him?

Cocking the hammer back on my revolver, I chambered the next bullet before re-holstering it and addressed his earlier statement. "Wouldn't have mattered if I had aimed for his heart. He can't be killed."

"Iron dust can."

My brows slammed down. "What are you talking about? He's not fae."

Ryder took in my expression, looking just as confused. "Yes, he is. Didn't you see his draoistone?"

"No . . ."

"I don't know how you missed it. It's huge. That guy is packing a serious amount of power."

Fae magic was wild and difficult to control. The draoistones acted as a conduit, allowing the wearer to channel their magic and direct it. I had learned to identify low and high fae during my time with *her* based on the size of their draoistones. The more powerful a fae, the larger the draoistone they required.

I had been too focused on other things to notice the Enforcer's. Hot, sticky shame swamped me. If that boy wasn't dead already, he would be soon. I might have been able to save him if I wasn't so busy ogling the sick bastard that came to kill him.

What was *wrong* with me?

"I'm an idiot. I should have shot at him again. I . . ." I was too flustered to get out the rest of my sentence; too frustrated with myself.

"Hey." Ryder squeezed my arm. "Don't beat yourself up about the kid. You tried your best."

He knew how protective I was of children. He didn't

know *why*, but he understood enough to know how hard I was going to be on myself about this.

"Why did you mention iron dust before?" I asked. "It's not like anyone can get their hands on some."

Though it wasn't technically illegal, everyone was too terrified of the Enforcer to ever harvest iron from the old ore mines just outside the city. They'd been shut down for centuries. Around the same time the fae laws came into effect.

The mortals had agreed to the laws because what other choice did they have? If they said no, the fae could have easily cut off all trade and let them starve to death.

The fae were basically doing that now. Less food arrived year after year. Honestly, I think the Enforcer was the only thing stopping the mortals from a massive revolt. Generation after generation had been bred to fear his name. It was ingrained in their DNA at this point.

Ryder glanced around, then leaned close, whispering conspiratorially, "Because I know where we can get some." He pulled back, watching my reaction carefully.

This felt like some sort of test.

"Where?"

"The House of Night."

I reeled back in shock. "You mean the crazy cult worshipping Lord Balor and all his beasts?" I huffed. "Yeah, no thanks. They're bad news. Besides, you can't just shoot a high fae up with iron dust, they have to ingest it for it to work."

Ryder sighed. "I know. If a bullet loaded with iron dust was all it took, I would have taken the bastard down a long time ago."

My gaze flitted down to the crown tattooed on his wrist. It marked him as property of House Dagda. Every halfling had one based on the fae house they belonged to. House

27

Dagda was the royal house of the fae and the crown was their emblem.

"You want him dead so you can get revenge?" I guessed.

I knew from Ryder's stories that House Dagda treated their animals better than their halflings. All runaway halflings despised the beings that enslaved their kind on principle, but Ryder seemed to hate the fae more than most.

"Exactly. Killing a fae, high or low, is impossible with the Enforcer around. He always knows and he always comes no matter what."

"You'd risk sneaking back into the Faylands?"

"Of course. The only good fae is a dead one."

"Right," I said, shoving away the memory of how my body had responded to the Enforcer. "The only good fae is a dead one."

3

Ryder accompanied me to the doctor after the excitement of the train's arrival and terror of the Enforcer sighting died down. I couldn't make sense of my reaction to him and stuffed it into that box along with everything else I didn't want to deal with.

We came to a stop outside one of three of Mayhem's two-story buildings. The others were the brothel and Marty's saloon. Drinking, fucking, and getting injured were the top three activities of Mayhem's citizens, thus the larger buildings were required.

After ambling up the three steps leading to a wide porch, we entered through the door with "Doctor of Medicine" painted crookedly across the top. The bell overhead chimed, announcing our presence inside the quiet space.

The first floor was empty except for the handful of chairs scattered over the dusty wooden planks. I had never been inside—I would never ask for help from a mortal unless absolutely necessary—but I assumed the doctor did his examinations upstairs. After a few minutes, a mortal male with sharp brown eyes and short white hair appeared.

He took one look at me and his gaze turned from discern to disgust.

"Get out." He stabbed a finger at the door behind us. "I'm not treating the likes of you. My grandson was murdered by beasts, and I will not help one of their ilk."

I shoved away from Ryder and tried to take an intimidating step toward the doctor, but my right leg protested the movement. I stopped short, gripping the wall for support, and settled for glaring instead.

"I'm not a beast," I ground out.

"I said, out." He thrust his wrinkled finger toward the door again.

My jaw tightened, as rage rang through my bones. I had almost died last night protecting this town, protecting this ungrateful mortal. It wasn't the first time I had come close to death fighting the beasts and wouldn't be the last.

Hand twitching at my side, it hovered right over my gun. It was already loaded. All I had to do was aim and pull the trigger.

An arm wove around my waist. Ryder pulled me back. "Come on," he whispered. "We'll come back tomorrow after you have a vest and he'll have to treat you."

When I still refused to move, he tugged me harder. "V, you've worked so hard for a vest. The other Rogues will look for any excuse not to give you one. If word gets around you attacked a mortal . . ."

Wait . . .

My heart thudded wildly in my chest as I twisted in his hold. "Do you . . . mean I'm getting a vest tonight?"

Ryder grinned mischievously. "You've more than earned it."

A wide smile split my face before I could stop myself. Ryder grimaced at the rows of razor-sharp teeth on display. The one time we had been intimate, he had refused to kiss me because of them. I didn't blame him. I wouldn't want to kiss me either.

I snapped my mouth shut. But the excitement thrumming through my chest remained.

I was getting a vest.

Finally, after all these years.

I wanted to scream and dance, but I tamped down on the impulse. Now was not the time to celebrate. Once I had the vest in hand, I'd allow myself to enjoy it.

My gaze slid back to the giant's butthole standing across from us, watching our interaction with a severe gaze. He no doubt heard the news. Ryder was right. If I harmed one of the beings the Rogues swore to protect, it would only prove everyone's theory I was part beast.

The doctor wasn't worth it.

After giving the mortal a death glare, I allowed Ryder to lead me to the door.

Outside, the mortals gave us a wide berth. I suspected it was more to do with the murderous expression I wore than their respect for the Rogue at my side. I was elated by Ryder's revelation, but the doctor's behavior was an unwelcome reminder of my otherness.

I wasn't sure a vest could make the mortals in this town overlook my beastly attributes.

"You hungry?" Ryder asked as the mortals flowed around us.

"I can eat."

He pivoted, turning me with him and we headed toward Mayhem's marketplace. We stopped outside an unfamiliar stall. I eyed the kabobs of cooked sand snake with wariness.

Ryder laughed at my expression and pulled me flush against his side. "They're good. I promise."

He bought two, then steered us toward a set of stairs so we could sit down and enjoy our meal. Burning sun rays

31

streamed through the hole pocked canopy above, heating my face. This city was one raging inferno during summer. I loved it.

It was easy to spot tourists among the people wandering past us in the street. They were paler and either carried brightly colored parasols, or had their heads wrapped in scarves. Their numbers always peaked just before a full moon. Travelers were drawn here by a dark fascination with the beasts even though they had their fair share in the North.

Mayhem's council had a viewing tower erected on the city's south end just so these idiots could gaze out on a full moon with binoculars from behind the safety of the walls, which weren't all that safe. Plenty had been picked off by air beasts and yet every month, tourists still flooded the city. I think it was the thrill of it more than anything; to stand in the dangerous epicenter of the beasts and come out alive.

Ryder handed one of the kabobs to me, then tore a chunk out of his, and immediately recoiled, fanning his mouth.

"Careful, it's hot," he mumbled.

I bit into mine, unconcerned—I had a high tolerance for heat—and almost spit it out. The snake had the consistency of fish, which I hated, and tasted like over salted chicken. Not a fan.

I forced myself to choke the rest of it down anyway. With how inconsistent the food supply was from the Faylands, I never wasted a meal, even if it tasted awful. Sand snake was a local staple, but eventually they would die off like the rest of the local animal populations without any plant life to feed on.

That damn wall was a blessing and a curse.

Ryder blew on his kabob before taking another bite, and

then hummed under his breath at the taste. I glanced over at him, gaze drifting to his vest.

I fought a smile. Seven years later, and I was finally about to get one of my own. I still couldn't believe it. When Ryder had become the Rogues' second in command, I had outright begged him to help me get a vest on more than one occasion. Each time he had told me if it was just up to him, I would have had one years ago, but it wasn't. Every Rogue voted and their vote had to be unanimous.

"It'll get better once you're a Rogue," he said between bites.

"What will?"

He waved the now empty kabob in the air. "The looks. The fear. Once you're one of us, the mortals will respect you. They wouldn't dare call you a beast."

"Do you think I'm one?" I asked quietly. We rarely discussed my otherness. I knew it made Ryder uncomfortable; probably because he couldn't lie—one of the other things halflings inherited from their fae side.

"I think you're going to make a great Rogue," he said instead of answering.

So that was a yes. It was disheartening, but not a surprise. Part of it was my fault. He probably thought I was born this way, born with these *deformities* because I had never told him the truth. I might as well have been. They were permanent.

"The vest is going to change everything. You'll see."

I turned my face away with a scowl. Ryder sounded confident, but he had no idea. Everyone in this city loved him. He was the Rogues' golden boy. They didn't whisper cruel words behind his back, or stare at him in disgust everywhere he went. And they sure as fuck wouldn't dare refuse him medical care.

One piece of leather wasn't going to change much.

The only creatures that had claws, fangs, and purple eyes like mine were the beasts—the same bloodthirsty monsters that ravaged the Mortal Lands every full moon. The mortals of this town would always see a beast when they looked at me.

A vest might help them hide their hate better though. Even now with Ryder sitting beside me, many mortals who would usually glare or gaze at me with fear kept their eyes respectfully averted because I was in the presence of a Rogue.

The Rogues were the only thing standing between the Mortal Lands and the beasts. Even outside of Mayhem, anyone wearing a Rogue vest was always treated with the utmost courtesy and respect. The Rogues were revered as brave warriors, risking their lives full moon after full moon.

I wanted that acceptance, that respect, with a desperation that squeezed my lungs. Not because I gave a banshee's wail about what any of the mortal's thought of me. No, I wanted, needed, a permanent place with the Rogues. Otherwise, they could force me out of the town at any time, and with nowhere left to go, I would be forced to return to *her*.

None of those thoughts passed my lips. Eager to move this conversation away from me, I glanced down at the tattoo on Ryder's wrist and asked, "How did you escape?"

Every Rogue had their own story of how they had escaped the Faylands, but I had never heard Ryder's tale. He had expertly evaded the question each time I asked. Golden boy he might appear on the surface, but he hid something dark from his past. I knew because I did the same.

His expression darkened, but he only shrugged. "The old mountain pass. Same as every other free halfling."

The Fayette Mountains served as the border between the Faylands and the Mortal Lands. The Te Sea was too treacherous to cross with its stormy waters and beasts lurking beneath the surface, which left the mountain as the only way in or out of the Faylands. The fae controlled the tunnel running beneath it. That left halflings only one escape route —a dangerous mountain trail.

I shook my head. "No, I mean how did you escape House Dagda itself?"

Ryder took his time answering. "I had help," he said vaguely.

I wasn't letting him get off so easily this time. "Help how?" I prompted.

"Where were *you* before you came to Mayhem?" he threw back. "Why don't you have a fae brand like the rest of us."

My mouth flattened. Only Boone knew and I wanted to keep it that way.

Ryder cocked a brow. "Don't ask for answers when you're not willing to give any yourself."

"That's fair."

We left the stairs and wandered further into the street lined with vendors hawking the goods fresh off the train, but the deeper we moved into the market, the more goods derived from beast parts, we saw. This close to the wall, beast goods were Mayhem's most traded commodity. Another reason for the tourists.

Failin furs, musical instruments strung with an aibeya's hair, and leathers made from tanned corth's hide all lined the vendor's tables. I even spotted a jar filled with bodah fingers—the inch long black nails with silk threads hanging off the ends were a dead giveaway for the faceless beast who spun webbing to trap its victims and devour them whole. Even long after their death, their fingers would produce yards of silk.

These items were all procured by hunters. The mortals

didn't hunt the beasts. They only pilfered what they could from the corpses the Rogues left behind on a full moon.

The goods on display were for everyday use, but beasts also possessed magical properties and were often used by witches to cast spells and practice magic like the fae. I had visited my share of witches to undo the curse put on me, but their magic couldn't compete with *hers*.

Mortals could purchase dismembered beast parts in Mayhem's meat market. Some considered their flesh a delicacy, but most wanted it for the paltry magic. With it, a witch could make a potion for whatever ailed their child, or a charm to protect them from an evil spirit. The spells and potions only worked half the time and poorly at that.

There was only one witch with the ability to produce real magic.

The Crone.

She wasn't a mortal playing at magic like the other witches. No one knew what she really was, only that she was as ancient as she was powerful. Only those truly destitute and desperate sought her out because she was equally as likely to help them as she was to kill them.

We passed a stall selling quills made of black feathers and I stopped in front of it, brushing my fingers over one of the soft feathers. It had come from an air beast—a broberie. They were small birds, no bigger than a fist, with a taste for dead flesh. In flocks, they could consume a giant's remains in a matter of seconds—bones and all.

But by themselves, they were harmless, adorable even, with their little jumps and chirps. Their satiny feathers were as smooth as silk and highly sought after for mattress stuffing, writing implements, or for northern mortals with enough coin to spend, ridiculous winter fashion.

The sight of the broberie feather knocked a memory loose from my box. It sucked me in before I could stop it.

I ran through the forest, dead leaves crunching under my little bare feet. I zipped through trees, yipping, and laughing.

On the forest floor, laid a ball of feathers. I rushed over to it, expecting the bird to fly off. It tried, but it couldn't fully extend its left wing. I frowned at the pathetic squawking it made and scooped it into my arms.

"You're okay, little bird," I cooed, stroking its head with the tip of a talon. "I'll take care of you." I raced back to the cabin, hiding the bird under my shirt before I entered, whispering, "You have to be very quiet now, okay? No one will hurt you, but only if you're quiet or else she'll find you."

The bird made a soft trilling sound in response like it understood.

"Good birdie."

I slipped inside and silently made my way up the stairs to my room. I created a make-shift nest for my new friend using a woven basket and one of my shirts. I stepped back to admire my handiwork before glancing at the poor little bird's broken wing.

"I'll be right back. Remember what we talked about. You can't make a sound."

At the bird's silence, I stroked it under its beak, then slid the basket under my bed. I rushed back into the forest to collect twigs and vines I could use to make a splint, the same way I had watched my mama do for me. I had lots of broken bones and they all healed super well with a splint. Sometimes in minutes.

Birdie's broken wing would heal, too, as long as Mama didn't find her first.

I gathered some nuts and berries on my way back to the cabin. Birdie would need to eat if she were to heal.

"Birdie?" I whispered, softly closing the bedroom door. When the bird didn't make a sound, my heart thumped wildly, worried that Mama had seen her after all. I rushed over to the bed and blew out a breath when I saw Birdie safe and sound right where I had left her.

"You didn't answer because you were being quiet. Good girl," I crooned. I set the wing, fed birdie, and watched over my new friend day and night, leaving only to gather more nuts and berries.

The wing healed fast. Almost as fast as I could heal myself. The bird was my constant companion for the next two days. It was nice to have a friend. I had never had one before.

The door to my bedroom opened. I froze, with Birdie sitting in my lap, out in the open for Mama to see. Her eyes sparked with interest, and I curled myself around Birdie, blocking her from view.

"Please don't hurt Birdie," I begged.

"You named it." Her face twisted in disgust. She moved toward us on the bed. "Someone is here for a cloaking spell."

I clutched Birdie tighter. "Mama, no! You can use me. Just don't hurt Birdie."

Mama sighed. "Fine, darling. Come along."

I went with Mama. I didn't even cry when she ripped off one of my talons. It hurt. It hurt a lot. But Birdie was safe. That's all that mattered.

The wound healed and I went tromping off into the forest the next morning to gather more food for Birdie. When I returned, Birdie was missing from her nest. I raced back down the stairs and sprinted to the back of the cabin.

Mama had Birdie tied upside down as she plucked off feathers. Birdie wasn't moving.

Fat tears welled in my eyes. "Mama, you promised!" I screamed.

Mama glanced over at me, emotionless. "I promised nothing, sweetheart." She plucked another feather. "The brobrie was of no use to either of us alive. Useless things must die, you understand?"

I balled my hands into fists. "Birdie was my friend!"

Mama's gaze lifted skyward to the forest's canopy, then back to the bird. *"Don't be so pathetic. You are testing my patience."* She *continued to pluck Birdie.*

"Stop," I ground out. Mama didn't listen. My talons extended, their shadow lengthening across the ground. An ember smoldered in my core; a small flame licking at my insides.

"Or what?" Mama sounded amused.

That flame turned into a raging fire inside me that burned bright and hot as it spread to my limbs. Everything blurred, and I struck. There was only blackness and a burning inferno until I heard someone screaming my name.

I blinked, the memory dissolving around me. Ryder's face swam in front of mine. His mouth moved, but I couldn't hear anything. I jerked my head to shake off the haze, and the world came rushing in. Smoke burned my lungs. Someone was screaming.

Ryder's wide eyes met mine. "Vera, what did . . . you do?"

"I—" A cry cut me off, drawing my attention to the stall of broberie feathers. I stared, trying to piece together what I saw.

Burnt feathers were scattered all over the ground. The table that once held them was cracked in half, scorch marks covering the surface. Behind it, the stall owner was frozen in a fetal position. He was nothing more than a charred husk. Skin had been melted to the bone in some areas, the rest was heavily burned.

I raised my hands. They shook violently, my skin coated black like I had dipped them in ash.

The saliva in my mouth turned acidic. It hurt to swallow. My throat worked as I tried to say something, anything, but all I could manage was sucking in a breath of smoky air— smoky air I created—and it burned all the way down.

My gaze shot back to Ryder. I lunged forward and grabbed his hands. "It was an accident, I swear. Please don't tell Boone," I pleaded.

His eyes filled with pity as he disentangled our hands. "I won't, but it doesn't matter, V. Look around."

As I took in the horrified faces of the crowd surrounding us, my stomach hollowed out. I knew word of this would spread quickly. Within hours, Boone and all the other Rogues would know what I had done. It wouldn't matter to anyone that it had been an accident.

My chance of becoming a Rogue had just gone up in smoke.

4

My stomach twisted into a series of knots as I trailed behind the other recruits through Mayhem's streets, still limping because the bastard doctor refused to treat me. Nervous sweat turned my hands clammy and I periodically dried them on my pants as I walked.

Induction ceremonies only happened once a year. If I was passed over tonight, I would be going on my eighth year without a vest. Another three hundred and sixty-five days of being dependent on the goodwill of Boone and the others to keep my home here.

Without a vest, that goodwill could shift like the sands, and I'd be out on my ass with nowhere to go, but *her*. I'd rather die than let that happen.

I took a deep breath to calm my churning stomach. Living with the uncertainty of it all was taking its toll. I needed a vest. Needed the security of knowing I would never have to go back there.

Vince said something to the other recruits. Forced laughter followed. I glared at his back as he swaggered next to another male and female. The little shithead was noticeably absent the remainder of the night after he had left me to fend for myself in the canyon. I owed him for that, but now was not the time. Boone would be furious enough with me over the mortal's death.

This wasn't the first time my control had slipped, and a mortal had suffered for it. Boone had lectured me for hours after.

'The mortals pay us for protection. They are already terrified of you enough and want you gone. I won't keep covering for you. If this happens again . . .'

Part of me wasn't certain I should even show up to tonight's ceremony, but I held onto a small tendril of hope the events of this morning would be overlooked in favor of all the sacrifices, all the work, I had put in for the Rogues over the last seven years.

Before I arrived, the Rogues pulled sticks every full moon. The Rogue unfortunate enough to pull the short one had to be beast bait and lead them to the choke point. My first full moon, while I had waited on the canyon's lip with the mortals, we discovered the beasts were naturally drawn to me.

If not for my quick actions, every mortal with me would have died that night, but I didn't hesitate to climb into the canyon and lead the beasts to the choke point. Nor did I hesitate to say yes when Boone asked me to do it again the next full moon and the one after that until they all just expected me to be the bait. I was only fifteen when I first started.

All that had to count for something. At least I hoped it did.

I was either walking into the best night of my life, or the worst. I had no idea which. Still, I moved one foot in front of the other, that ribbon of hope carrying me all the way outside Marty's saloon.

I hesitated at the steps, chewing my lip. Raucous laughter and light spilled out through the swinging doors the other recruits disappeared through moments ago.

The Rogues didn't accept every runaway halfling that turned up in Mayhem. Born and bred to serve the fae, some returned to the Faylands, to the comfort of the only life they had ever known—even if it was one of servitude, even if the fae lord they had run away from might kill them on sight.

High fae were known to be mercurial creatures. It was anyone's guess what happened to those halflings that went slinking back to their masters.

Other runaways simply lacked the courage it took to face a hoard of bloodthirsty beasts, month after month. I remembered one fresh arrival fainting at the sight of blood and knew he wouldn't last long. Luckily for him, and many other halflings unfit for the Rogues, mortals welcomed them into their towns. Most ended up working in the gold mines. Their speed and strength made them exceptionally adept at physical labor.

I wouldn't be accepted by the mortals, even in the mines. My appearance was too similar to the nightmarish creatures plaguing the lands. It was why I had stayed with the Rogues so long even after they continuously passed me over for a vest.

Taking a fortifying breath, I threw back my shoulders and marched up the steps through the doors. The noise inside snuffed out immediately like a candle exposed to wind. I stood stiffly in the entrance as every gaze darted my way. Whispers started.

"She killed a mortal."

"*Burned* him alive."

Duke, the Rogues' third in command, with white peppered through his silver hair, approached me like one would a rabid animal. "You shouldn't be here," he whispered.

Slapping on a cocky smirk, I stepped up to him and tapped a talon over his sternum. The male held deathly still. I tilted my head and smiled, showing my fangs. "You going to try and make me leave?"

His Adam's apple bobbed as he swallowed hard. "N—No."

I patted his chest, whispering, "Good man." Then I moved around him and took a seat at the bar. Marty, the saloon's namesake, stood behind it, drying a glass.

He released a throaty chuckle as I sat down. "Never seen a grown man quake in his boots like that."

Muffled laughter broke out over the tables and the sound cut through the swell of nervous tension. The noise of the saloon steadily returned to a normal volume, and I relaxed on the bar stool. Though I never understood why, Marty had always had a soft spot for me.

"Thanks," I whispered. He nodded. "Can I get you anything, sweetheart?"

"Water would be great."

Marty retrieved a brown bottle from under the bartop and popped the top off with a knife. I studied the faded tree with deep reaching roots inked on his wrist—House Anu's crest. His shock white hair had been silver once. As far as I knew, Marty was the first halfling to ever escape the Faylands.

He slid the bottle over to me.

"What?" he asked gruffly at my pursed lips.

"How old are you?"

He chuckled under his breath as he wiped up the trail of condensation left by the bottle.

"*Old.*"

Halflings had double the life spans of mortals, but they

44

lived two or three hundred years at most. That could vary though, depending on how well a fae house treated them.

Marty's skin reminded me of the underside of a failin's fur that had been dried out too long in the sun. Deep creases framed his face, but his light brown eyes were sharp and watchful.

"Honey, as much as I like your eyes on me, you ain't gonna figure it out just staring." He tipped his chin toward the bottle. "Take a sip of your water before it warms."

I blinked, realizing how hard I had been staring. I flashed an apologetic smile, then brought the bottle to my lips and was surprised at how fresh and crisp the water tasted. The town's water supply always had a gritty taste to it from all the sand that snuck inside no matter how many times it was filtered.

"This is delicious."

"It's water straight from a fae spring."

"Really? Who knew you had such expensive tastes, *Martin*?"

He scowled and tried to whip me with the tail end of his rag, but I ducked out of the way, laughing.

"No, but that's what I tell all those touristy northerners coming through here. They're dumb as dishwater."

A Rogue approached the bar, ordering a shot of poitin as I took another sip. Marty poured it for him. His movements were swift and skilled as if he had been slinging drinks since the day he was born. He moved with the speed and agility of someone half his age. Based on his earlier response, he didn't want to say what that was, which was fine. He was entitled to his secrets, same as me.

"I didn't see any tourists off the train this morning," I said once the Rogue had left. Which was surprising. The train after a full moon always brought at least a handful of them to get the beast parts the hunters had collected while they were still fresh. There wouldn't have been any dead beasts last night because of what I had done, but any incoming tourist wouldn't know that.

Marty shrugged, wiping down the bar again, an endearing habit of his. He cleaned it constantly. "I reckon any that were on that train hopped off and turned right back around home after yesterday's quake."

"I thought it was just Mayhem," I said, taking another sip.

"Nope." He popped the 'p'. "The whole Mortal Lands from here to Gold City shook."

I frowned and made a mental note to ask Ryder if he had learned anything. As if my thoughts had summoned him, the Rogues' second entered the saloon. He swaggered down the rows of tables, every Rogue greeting him with a respectful nod or clap on the back. Briefly, he met my gaze with a blank expression before stopping to sit with Duke. I didn't know if that was good or bad.

"Think tonight will finally be the night?" Marty asked, leaning a hip on the bar.

I swiveled back to face him as the sense of dread returned to my stomach. I suspected he had already heard the rumors. My talons clicked nervously together. "I killed a mortal, Marty. I'll be lucky if a mob doesn't come after me."

"You got a good heart, Vera. If Boone can't see that, he ain't fit to lick your boot." He tossed the rag over his shoulder. "You could always come work for me."

Warm tingles flooded my chest at his offer.

I sucked in a deep breath of the saloon's sour air as my gaze swept around the space. Even in the dim lighting, the years of neglect and harsh handling of the building's interior were visible. Candlelit light fixtures hung from the ceiling and stuck out of the walls creating layers of wax that dripped over the edges. Bullet holes puckered the interior, and the floor was scuffed and faded.

I loved this place, scars and all. It had been my safe haven in a city of people that feared me as much as they hated me. This wasn't the first time Marty offered me a position and as much as I would love to take him up on it, I knew I couldn't.

My appearance would send all his customers running. I'd ruin his livelihood. I couldn't do that to him.

"You're one of the few people I can stand in this dusty old town. If I worked behind that bar, I'd end up murdering another mortal."

He chuckled like it was a joke. It wasn't.

Behind us, the saloon doors banged open, cutting our conversation short. I spun in my seat as Boone stalked in, obviously in a foul mood. He dumped a pile of vests on a table near the front.

Wings unfolded in my chest as I dared to hope one of them was for me.

A hush fell over the saloon for the second time, but this one was filled with anticipation and excitement.

The Rogues' leader was bald and built like a bull with a temper to match, possessing a wide pair of shoulders and massive arms. With his natural posture, always leaning slightly forward with his hands in fists at his side, he looked seconds away from charging.

"I founded the Rogues fifty years ago. Back then it was just me and that wrinkly faced bastard over there." He tipped his chin toward the bar.

"Still look better than you," Marty called out. "You can back a broberie off a fresh corpse with that ugly mug."

We all laughed.

Boone glared in return, but there wasn't any heat to it.

47

He shucked off his vest, the leather worn and cracked from age, and twisted it so everyone could see the back.

"Anyone know why we wear the hawk on our vests?"

"Cause we fly free!" Ryder belted out from his table.

Chuckles sounded around the room at his enthusiasm.

"That's right. We fly free while our brethren in the north remain shackled by the fae. We pay a price for that freedom though. Battling the beasts every full moon is a heavy burden. Five months from now is the Blood Moon, and we might not all make it out alive. If you aren't ready for that, don't accept a vest."

The mention of the Blood Moon sucked any pleasantness from the room. It was the one night everyone in the Mortal Lands feared the most. Summer was just ending, but as winter neared over the coming months, the nights would steadily grow longer until the peak of the cold season. For twenty-four hours, the moon would block out the sun, casting the lands in total darkness.

The calling didn't draw the beasts back into their cage for a day, which gave them free reign to travel through the Mortal Lands slaughtering everyone in their path. The Rogues did their best to hold the frontlines, but it was impossible to stop them all.

It was called the Blood Moon because of how much blood was spilled on that night alone.

"Fight free or die trying!" Duke yelled, dispelling the tension choking the air.

Several other Rogues echoed his words, shouting, "Fight free or die trying!"

As soon as the noise died down Boone continued, "The fae want to sit behind their borders like cowards and leave us to fight their battles? Fine, but we're gonna do it on our terms. We're gonna do it *free*. We're gonna do it *Rogue*."

Fists banged on tables in a steady rhythm and a low

chant broke out. "Fuck. The. Fae." It grew in volume as more joined in until everyone was on their feet shouting in tune with their pounding fists. "FUCK. THE. FAE. FUCK. THE. FAE."

Boone let it go on for a long moment before his sharp whistle cut through the noise. The chanting died off as everyone lowered back to their seats.

He picked up the first vest and my heart slammed against my ribs.

"Luke. Get your ass over here, boy."

I forced myself to clap as Luke took his time walking up to Boone. He'd only been here less than six months and was already getting his own vest.

"Jonas!" Boone chunked a vest across the saloon, smacking the recipient in the face with it. Everyone laughed but me. There were only two vests left and five recruits remaining. I didn't like my odds.

"Callie!"

A slender halfling with umber skin rose from a nearby table and, unlike Jonas, she managed to catch the vest before it smacked her in the face.

"And last, but not least . . ."

My pulse hammered in my ears.

"Vince!"

What did he just say? Vince? Fucking *Vince*?

I shook my head. No, that couldn't be right. He had arrived less than a month ago.

Time slowed as Vince got up to receive the last vest. He swaggered through the rows of tables with the most arrogant smile, like he knew he'd get a vest, like somehow, he'd earned it after only one full moon he'd spent cowering on the sidelines.

I pinched my eyes shut, convinced this was all a bad dream and I'd wake up any moment, but when I opened

49

them again, the same scene played out before me. Vince shrugged on the vest. The little shit looked downright smug about it.

An ugly barb knocked violently around my ribs like an agitated ashray.

I slammed my fist down on the bartop."*Him*? Are you serious?" My words sliced right through the applause. Vince jerked his head up, glaring at me for interrupting his moment. "That fucker left me to die last night. You really want him fighting at your backs instead of me?"

The edge of Vince's mouth curled into a sneer. He dragged his haughty gaze over me. "Better me than some half-beast, or whatever you are."

Oh . . . this fucker. He was just asking to get shot. My fingers inched toward my gun.

"He ain't worth it, darlin'," Marty whispered and I forced my hand to relax.

Boone's stare flickered to me and slightly widened like this was the first time he noticed my presence. His gaze instantly darkened.

"This is corthshit and you know it," I said as soon as I had his attention.

"You." That word was punctuated by a sneer. "You're lucky you're even still here," he barked. "I spent all afternoon cleaning up your mess. Get out of my sight until I figure out what to do with you."

Anger and shame burned through me as I lurched to my feet, unsteady, feeling the weight of everyone's stare. All those eyes, all those witnesses to my public shaming burned over my skin. I bared my fangs at them.

"Whatever. I don't need this shit. The Rogues are nothing more than glorified soldiers for the fae." I spun, my gaze skipping over every face. "You all get that, right? The only reason you're all here is because the fae *allow* it. Your so called 'freedom' is a big fucking joke."

"Go!" Boone roared.

I listened this time cursing the stupid, useless hope that had brought me here.

5

I spent the next day holed up inside my room, licking my wounds. The space was tucked away in the farthest wing of the Rogue compound where no one would have to hear me scream at night. It used to be a utility closet back when the compound had operated as an inn. Boone refurbished and fortified the abandoned building shortly after he arrived and founded the Rogues.

As more halflings escaped the Faylands, the more the Rogues' numbers grew. When I first arrived seven years ago, I had a normal sized bedroom, but eventually I had to give it up to a real Rogue. I didn't put up a fight to keep it though. The room had a neighbor on either side, and I knew they'd heard my night terrors.

Although this room was small, it was nice not to be greeted by their awkward stares each morning. If anyone knew what really happened while I slept, the Rogues would have kicked me out years ago.

Something terrorized me in my sleep, but it wasn't bad dreams. It was part of whatever curse *she* had put on me.

Hundreds of claw marks marred the walls on either side of my bed. Then there were the chains I slept in each night.

The Rogues knew about my fangs, claws, and mysterious powers. There was no hiding those things, but the monster I was went beyond the surface.

A darkness lurked inside me. I could feel it stirring at times like back in the canyon. Could see deep purple eyes staring at me, watching me in the shadows of my mind. It woke during the night and raged while I slept, demanding freedom. I had slept in chains for as long as I could remember. I had no idea what would happen if it ever got out.

It terrified me.

A thick layer of scar tissue covered my wrist and ankles from sleeping every night in my shackles. The damage was too extensive for even my healing abilities. I normally wore gloves not only to cover my talons, but the scars on my wrists as well.

The Rogues didn't need another reason to fear me. I knew I had given them another anyway after accidentally killing the mortal. There was no love lost between me and the mortals of this town, but I still felt immensely guilty for what I had done. No one deserved to die the way the stall owner had.

I stewed in shame and self-recrimination, hating myself for both for my actions and being naive enough to believe the Rogues would accept me, until the feelings boiled over and ended at a melted lamp.

I had been imagining Vince's stupid, smug face when my skin ignited along with the lamp I had been reaching for. With a heavy sigh, I hid the ruined apparatus under my bed, then perched on the edge of it.

The fire was another leg of the curse I didn't fully understand. It came and went at random. I had no control over it.

I had no control over anything. I hung my face in my hands, beyond exhausted with my situation.

What was I going to do?

I had spent the last twenty-four hours trying and failing to ignore the ugly feelings stirred by the Rogues' rejection—their seventh rejection. I could beat any Rogue in a one-on-one fight. I risked my life every full moon for them, and yet, I had been passed up year after year for a vest. This most recent full moon, I had almost died leading the beasts to the choke point and *still*, they deemed me unworthy of being one of them.

I understood killing the stall owner, even if on accident was wrong, but felt I earned some leniency considering all the mortal lives I'd saved over the years in fighting the beasts.

Instead, I had been given none, and now a sniveling coward who thought nothing of leaving one of his fellow fighters to die was wearing my vest. Would Boone have kicked up as much fuss over my death as he did the mortal's?

Doubtful.

My hands clenched into tight fists, talons scoring my palms.

No, I had waited long enough. They needed me now more than ever with the Blood Moon looming on the horizon. Either they gave me the vest I deserved, or I'd leave. To where? I had no idea, but I would figure it out if it came down to that.

I shoved to my feet.

With a determined stride, I left my room. This soon after a full moon, everyone would take time off from training, but with the Blood Moon only five months away, no one could afford to. Complacency would get them killed.

I exited the compound to the large patch of desert where the Rogues held their morning training searching for the one male who could give me what I wanted. The meaty thunk of flesh hitting flesh and pained grunts filled my ears.

When I didn't spot Boone among the rows of sparring halflings, my gaze skipped past them to the shooting targets beyond. He wasn't there either.

"Where's Boone?" I shouted to no one in particular.

A few heads turned my way, but the rest remained focused on their sparring partners.

"You're still here? I thought you'd be reunited with your family behind the wall by now," a familiar voice called out. Vince was bare chested, but I could see his vest lying in the sand nearby. Jonas snickered beside him, elbowing his buddy as he muttered, "Good one."

"Oh, hey Vince!" I smiled, waving casually. I bounded over to him pretending like we were the best of friends and hid a grimace at the strain the movement put on my injured leg. The pain would be worth the payoff.

Both males frowned, darting confused looks at one another.

I stopped in front of them, still smiling. "I never got to thank you for the other night."

Vince's frown deepened. "What are you—"

I ripped out my gun and shot him. The bullet tore through his kneecap, and Vince fell to the ground screaming bloody murder.

Tapping my gun against my thigh, I sighed. "Oh relax, would you? It's just a scratch."

His head snapped up as he clutched his leg to his chest. "Just a scratch?" he yelled. "You fucking shot me, you crazy bitch!"

"First you inferred I was a beast. Now you're calling me a female dog." I cocked my head to the side. "You know those are two very different things, right?"

"Vera," Duke said, as he approached us, eyeing me warily. "You shouldn't—"

"Yeah, yeah. I know. I shouldn't be here. I'll leave just as soon as you point me to where Boone is."

Duke's lips thinned. He didn't want me wherever Boone was either.

I shrugged. "Fine, I'm more than happy to keep Vince company. I don't think I've thanked him properly." I raised the gun, aiming between his legs this time.

The third in command sighed. "Check the weapon's room."

Idiot. Why didn't I check there first? Boone always did inventory around this time.

I holstered my gun, nodding in thanks, then glanced down at Vince's trembling form. "You should probably thank Duke here. He just saved you from getting your little dick blown off."

Not waiting for a response, I spun and marched off back into the city and barged into the compound's armory. The faces inside briefly flitted my way, then dismissed me.

A handful of Rogues stood around a long table lined with empty gold bullet shells. The end of the table held a weighted scale Boone was using to carefully measure the exact portions of gunpowder needed to fill the bullets. Ryder stood beside him, taking notes, tallying how much gold casings they would need to request from Gold City and have delivered before the next full moon.

I never understood what they based their calculations on. Each tier of beast required a different number of bullets to go down—the higher the tier, the more bullets required. We never knew what beasts would come out the next full moon so how could they determine the amount of gold bullets we'd need?

Sure, one could stab a beast in the heart with a gold dagger and they would die, regardless of how powerful they were, but that approach was incredibly risky because of how close in proximity you had to be.

Beasts were fast and agile even without their deadly powers. Only the most experienced fighters could hit a vital organ in a single shot. The usual approach was to pepper their bodies with as much gold as quickly as possible to kill them.

Ryder briefly glanced up from his paper. He shook his head, silently warning me not to do whatever it is I had planned.

Fuck him and his advice. He should have had my back the other night.

"Either you give me a vest, or I'm leaving," I said point blank.

The gazes of the five Rogues filling the bullets darted between me and Boone.

He didn't bother glancing up from his scale. He laughed, a mean, ugly sound. "Be my guest," he said dismissively. "Go back to *her*."

I crossed my arms, leaning back against the door frame to take some of the weight off my aching leg. Hiding my pain was a skill I had honed as a child. Right now, I was grateful for it. I didn't want to look weak as I faced down Boone.

"You need me," I said coolly.

Boone pulled his attention from the scale with an annoyed sigh. "Give us the room," he ordered the others. They all left except Ryder.

"You've become more trouble than you're worth," Boone said as soon as they were gone. "Mayhem's council is demanding your head."

Every city in the Mortal Lands was run by a group of elected officials. Mayhem's council had been gunning for me since day one. My gaze darted to Ryder for confirmation.

"We met with them yesterday. They're furious, V," he

explained in a low voice, setting down his quill. "You crossed a line killing that mortal."

"It was an accident," I argued. "You were there."

Ryder shook his head. "Doesn't matter what I saw. Everyone else in the market saw you *burn* that mortal to death, intentional or not."

Some friend he was. It didn't come as a surprise though. One of the reasons Boone had appointed Ryder as second was all the sucking up he did. If Boone took a shit, Ryder would be there to wipe his ass. Boone was a huge reason Ryder and I weren't as close as we used to be.

"They think you're too dangerous inside these walls and I am starting to agree with them. They want you out of the city," Boone added. "So, no, you're not getting a vest. We don't need you tarnishing the Rogues' good name. The only reason you're still here is because you're useful."

My nostrils flared. I grit my teeth to hold in the scathing insults. "I've done everything you've asked of me. I have risked *my life* more than all the other Rogues combined. Beasts kill mortals all the time. What does one more matter?"

Boone shook his head, his lips twisting in disgust like I had just confirmed all the reasons I didn't receive a vest. "Careful. You're starting to sound like a fae."

The comparison grated my nerves. I was nothing like those self-serving, power mongering bastards.

"Heck, maybe you are one of them. I don't know what *she* did to you, but the only halfling thing about you is your hair," Boone continued.

Ryder's brows furrowed. His gaze shifted between us. "What is he talking about?"

"Nothing." I glared at Boone. "You won't give me a vest? Fine. I'll be gone before nightfall." Let the Rogues see how well they fared without me.

I left without another word, slamming the door behind me. I stormed down through the compound.

Well fuck, that had gone terribly.

What was I supposed to do now?

"Vera! Wait!"

I spun as Ryder raced toward me. "What?" I hissed.

"Please come back," he called out, pausing in the middle of the hall. "We want to make a deal."

I narrowed my eyes, suspicious it was a trick. Even if it wasn't, part of me wanted to keep walking, tell them to shove their deal up their ass, but the more logical part reasoned I should at least hear the offer.

"Fine," I growled and followed Ryder back into the armory.

Boone leaned back against the table at my entrance, sizing me up. "What are you willing to do for a vest?" he asked slowly.

"Anything."

He nodded like he already knew that would be my answer. Ryder and he exchanged a look. "Tell her," Boone said.

"Do you remember the quake two nights ago?" Ryder asked.

My leg throbbed painfully in remembrance. "How could I forget," I snarked.

"My sources told me it wasn't natural. Something washed ashore in Greene. People say it looks like an axe of some kind. A fisherman stumbled on it. No one knows what happened for sure, only that his dead body was found clutching the axe and the earth around him had fissured, cracked wide open. It's being transported to Gold City the day after tomorrow."

I had no idea what to make of that information, but

anything involving those selfish bastards in Gold City was bad news.

"Why isn't it staying in Greene?"

"Gold City threatened to cut off any and all trade with them."

I frowned, brows pinching together. "What in the dark do they want with it? They're safe behind their walls."

Boone and Ryder exchanged another glance.

"What?"

"We think they're going to trade it to the fae," Boone explained.

"Those greedy idiots," I hissed under my breath. They were going to hand over a potentially deadly weapon to a race of powerful beings all so they could barter for more fae luxuries to fill their gluttonous bellies while the rest of the Mortal Lands starved.

I glanced between them. "Let me guess. You want me to steal this thing before it ever makes it to Gold City."

Ryder flashed a smile. "It'll be a breeze, V. A wagon will depart Greene two days from now. Just intercept it before it makes it to the trade road."

Eyes narrowing, I scoffed. "If it's so easy, why send the volatile halfling with a penchant for turning things to ash?"

"Because there can't be any witnesses," Boone interrupted smoothly. "If Gold City thinks this was anything other than a random robbery by some bandit, the other cities will suffer for it. This can't lead back to Mayhem or us in any way. The driver has to die. We've protected you from the council because the Rogues have sway here, but if this goes sideways, we can't protect you from Greene or any of the other cities and—"

"And if I get caught after killing a mortal, I'll swing from the gallows," I finished, my words tinged with bitterness. Mayhem's council and the Rogues would disavow ever knowing me. They were asking me because I was expendable.

"The council will pardon your crime. Not only can you stay in Mayhem, but we'll give you a vest too, " Boone said. "And we all know you have no issue murdering innocents."

I ignored his snipe. They must really want this thing if they were willing to offer me a vest for it. Which meant, there had to be more to it than they were letting on. "Do you know what this thing really is?"

"No. Only that it was powerful enough to cause a quake from Gold City to here. That's nearly a hundred miles. Imagine what it can do to a fae or a beast." Boone's face took on a dark edge. "Or a halfling. You really want Gold City handing that kind of power over to the fae?"

No . . . no one did, but that didn't mean I was willing to risk my life either.

"I need to think about it."

"V, the transport leaves in two —"

"What's to think about?" Boone interjected. "It's either this or *her*."

I scowled, jaw locking. As much as it irked me to admit, Boone was right. My ploy to leave the city and return never would have worked. The council wouldn't have allowed me back through their gates.

Nor would any other city. Sure, I could try and fit in, cover up my otherness, but that would only work for so long. The little control I had over the darkness lurking inside was already hanging by a thread. It was just a matter of time before I harmed another mortal and this time Boone, and the Rogues, wouldn't be there to save me.

Boone's lips curled into a slow smile. He knew he had me before I even answered. I would take death anyday over returning to my past.

"When do I leave?"

6

———

Balor's balls, it was cold. The ground where I laid flat on my stomach felt like ice. The leather corset I wore over my tunic covered me from navel to just under my breasts and provided excellent protection against most of the weapons the wagon driver might carry but was piss poor for warmth.

I had forgotten until this moment how much I hated the north. Ryder's intel had brought me to the juncture outside Greene. It was an overnight ride from Mayhem and landed me squarely in the icy buttcrack of the Mortal Lands, otherwise known as the north.

A shiver racked my frame and I cursed. The chill seeped through the cloak I wore, the collar upturned to shield my neck. I adjusted my braid to cover more of my wind-nipped ears, but none of it did much good against the cold.

Gods, how could northerners live like this? Summer had *just* ended. I had grown up in the Deadwood Forest about fifty miles to the west of here, but I couldn't remember it ever being this frigid. Then again, I blocked out as much of my childhood as possible.

I craned my neck down the small dirt trail running

parallel to train tracks leading into the seaside city where this mysterious weapon had washed ashore. Since the train only ran every two weeks, any deliveries or traveling in between had to be done via wagon.

Said wagon path was empty. It had been for hours.

My sighing breath came out as fog in the icy air. I twisted my head toward the scraggle bushes where my horse's black rump was poorly hidden and smiled as Ness munched on the leaves. She seemed to be enjoying herself and not at all bothered by the cold.

Ness had been with me since my time in the forest. In fact, the black mare had been the reason I had escaped. She had appeared outside the cabin one day and I had been so terrified of what would happen if she was seen that I rode her, intending to take her out of the forest to safety, but when she exited the tree line, Ness didn't stop, and I didn't ask her to.

We made our way south, doing what I would do if the blasted wagon ever arrived. Together we robbed the mortals' wagons and trains to survive, stealing whatever we could eat or sell. Thank goodness the fae's gold wasn't edible, or I might have accidentally gotten myself killed stealing it along the way. I only learned about the fae laws once we arrived in Mayhem. Ness had been by my side ever since.

If I could, I'd have Ness live with me at the Rogue compound. She had more loyalty in one hoof than all of those bastards combined. She stayed in the city stables, but when I wasn't training with the Rogues, we went riding through the desert.

Something rumbled in the distance and my head snapped back to the wagon trail. Flattened on the ground as I was, I could feel my heart punching into the dirt in anticipation.

Please, please be the wagon with the stupid axe and not some travelers.

I wanted to get this over with quickly and leave this awful cold behind. Minutes ticked by, slow and tortuous. Finally, the source of the noise came into view.

The wagon was covered in a failin's hide with the black spikes still attached. Normally, those spikes were cut and sanded down as close to their protrusion point as possible. If they were removed altogether, it would leave the valuable furs riddled with fist sized holes.

I eyed the spiked covering with disappointment. This was a travel wagon. The spikes were meant to deter air beast attacks. Those beasts had escaped the calling by flying far enough north by sunrise on a full moon and many now roosted in the Deadwood Forest.

Strangely enough, beast attacks by those freed from the wall were rarer than expected, whether it was due to the fact the mortals knew better than to venture out after dark when the beasts stirred, or another reason, no one could be certain. If a mortal was unlucky enough to stumble into their territory, the beast would undoubtedly attack, but the freed beasts seemed to be altogether less bloodthirsty than their imprisoned brethren.

Still, one could never be too careful, thus the spikes.

The wagon rolled past, bouncing over the various rocks and pebbles lining its path, before it made a sharp left turn at the junction where it headed south to any number of the cities between Greene and Mayhem.

I shifted, propping myself up on my elbows once it was out of sight.

"Where is this godsdamn wagon?" I whispered.

What if Ryder's intel was wrong? Or the transport was delayed?

I pressed my forehead into the cold dirt, desperately wishing I could close my tired eyes.

Ness and I had traveled through the night to get here. I had packed my chains and bed mat, but Ryder could only tell me the wagon would depart from Greene in the morning. I wanted to be at the junction before sunrise in case the wagon departed in the early hours. Now it was well past noon, several hours later, and my lack of sleep would catch up to me soon.

Tired people made mistakes and got themselves caught. I needed to be ready and awake, but it was getting harder and harder the longer the wagon took to arrive. And laying on the ground wasn't helping the situation. At least the cold was good for something. It was the only thing keeping me awake at this point.

An hour later, as I was on the brink of dozing off, I heard the tell-tale rumbling of a wagon. Energy flooded my veins, snapping my eyes wide and alert.

Another wagon appeared, this time with a cloth covering.

My fogged breath tumbled out in an excited rush.

Please be the right wagon.

I held my breath as I waited to see which direction it would go. Gold City sat at the northernmost tip of the Mortal Lands, just outside the Fayette Mountains where the Fayland's border lay. If the driver went right at the junction, I knew I had my wagon.

The wagon turned. It was headed north.

I held still until the wagon had ambled several hundred feet down the trade road away from Greene, then I pushed off the ground and raced over to Ness as quiet as possible. We were off, dirt and dust flying up behind us.

The driver heard our approach and tried to outrun us, but Ness was faster.

An aged mortal with white hair and fierce eyes scowled at me as I held him at gunpoint. "Pull over." I jerked my gun to the right.

The mortal hissed under his breath, shaking his head, but did as he was told.

"Put your hands on your head and step out of the wagon," I ordered.

He dropped the reins and lurched to his feet before hopping out of the driver's bench. I dismounted Ness, keeping the revolver fixed on the back of the driver's head before I stepped up behind him. I pressed the barrel to the back of his skull.

"On your knees."

The driver lowered to the ground. "You're making a mistake," he hissed. "The cargo in that wagon belongs to the fae."

I froze, fear crystallizing in my veins.

No, he had to be lying. It was the one ability mortals had that fae and halflings didn't.

Another driver had pulled a similar stunt on me before, claiming his payload was headed to the Faylands. Drivers often used the threat of the Enforcer to protect their haul from bandits. It was clever, but I wasn't falling for it this time.

I shook off the worry, tightening my grip. "Corthshit. You're just trying to save your own hide."

Ness nudged my shoulder with her muzzle. I twisted around, stroking her once with my free hand, then gently pushed her out of the way. "Not now, girl."

"I ain't—"

I fired and the mortal's body went limp before slumping to the ground. Ness stomped a hoof, snorting, but I refused to feel any remorse. Not when I was so close to getting my vest. Besides, if the situation had been reversed, the mortal would have gladly taken a shot at the first opportunity.

What did it say about me that my horse had higher morals than I did?

I didn't really care.

Ness turned away her muzzle when I tried to stroke her again.

"Oh, stop pouting. We'll be done soon." I grabbed the reins and led Ness over to another one of the scraggly bushes she enjoyed munching on so much, then approached the back of the wagon.

It was empty.

Frowning, I peered into the dark interior. No, that couldn't be right.

Splintered wood bit into my palm as I hauled myself inside. I walked over the wooden planks, eyes scanning every surface. Wood creaked below me and I froze in place. The wagon was ancient and loose wood was to be expected, but that sounded wrong.

Squatting down, I examined the wooden planks where the creaking came from. My hand ran along the wood. Nothing unique about this section of planks; just as old as the rest of the floor. I was about to abandon my inspection when I found the source of the odd noise. The floorboards were spaced farther apart than the surrounding planks, as if they had been pulled out and replaced.

A secret compartment. I smiled, impressed by the mortals' cleverness.

I stabbed into the wood with a talon, and raised the loose plank, then the next one. The process repeated until a wide enough opening formed for me to peer inside, but I never got the chance.

Something clattered to the floor behind me. I spun, eyes

landing on a retreating figure outside the wagon. They moved unnaturally fast, so rapidly they were a blur.

Too late, I realized what they had left behind.

BOOM!

I flew through the air, flesh on fire. My skull hit the ground hard enough it bounced. Air fled my lungs. My vision went in and out. The high-pitched ringing in my ears was deafening and drowned out all other noise.

Everything spun. Smoke burned my eyes and throat. I couldn't move. I could barely breathe. Blood dribbled down my head as I fought for air.

If I wasn't a halfling, that explosion would have killed me.

Terror seized my battered body. Ness! Oh gods, where was Ness?

Please, please be okay.

I tried to sit up to search for my precious mare, but my body wouldn't cooperate. I couldn't do anything until my healing abilities kicked in. Head lolling to the side, I watched helplessly as blurry shapes swarmed the area. They vanished as quickly as they had come.

Slowly, I was able to angle my head more. My gaze swept around the destruction. The images were blurred and hazy, but I saw the wagon was blown to bits. One wheel survived intact, but the rest of it lay in splintered, smoking pieces.

A long, relieved exhale decompressed my chest when I saw no signs of Ness amongst the rubble. My smart girl had run off to safety.

I rolled my head back and shut my eyes. Just a few minutes of rest while my body healed, then I'd force myself to get up. To process what just happened.

The ground shook.

My eyes shot open to find a giant looming over me. I only made out a set of black boots before something sharp pressed into my throat. My gaze climbed up his massive form to his face. His mouth moved, but I couldn't make any sense of what he said with the loud ringing in my ears.

I coughed up blood, trying to tell him that. The sticky liquid spilled down my chin.

The blade disappeared in an instant and the giant crouched down.

His piercing steel-gray eyes were the last thing I saw before everything went black.

Awareness returned in small pieces.

My head ached like I'd been bludgeoned by a giant's wooden club. The pounding in my skull threatened to split it in half. Cobwebs coated my mouth. I swallowed, wetting my scratchy throat. I laid down on something soft, possibly a layer of furs or some sort of bed roll.

A low scraping sounded nearby followed by humming.

I peeled open one eye and found myself staring at the ceiling of a red tent. I tensed at the sight, knowing I had not brought myself here—wherever *here* was. The last thing I remembered was staring at the stick of dynamite someone had thrown inside the wagon with me still in it and the scalding pain after.

The low scraping sounded again. I didn't dare lift my head to discover the source, familiar with the sound of metal dragging over stone. Someone was inside the tent with me, and they were sharpening a blade.

Memories flashed across my mind.

The cold tip of a sword pressed to my throat.

A metallic gaze staring down at me.

Icy panic wrapped around my lungs, choking them. A scream lodged in my throat.

I knew in my bones I laid inside the Enforcer's tent. The driver had been telling the truth after all.

Squeezing my eyes shut, I whispered my confession

knowing he could hear. "I swear I didn't know I was stealing from a fae. The wagon was supposed to be headed to Gold City."

There was a long beat of tense silence where all I could hear was my pulse pounding in my ears.

Then he spoke.

"Oh, Little Thief, you didn't steal from just any fae. You stole from *me*."

7

The Enforcer's voice shocked me almost as much as what he'd revealed. I had heard him speak back at the train, but it was different being this close to him. His voice was deep and sensuous like the most decadent fae treat. It touched me in places it had no business touching. I hid my scowl—knowing he could see my expression—annoyed with my body's ridiculous reaction at a time like this.

My unwanted response was easy to dismiss as the weight of his words settled over me. Not only had I broken one of the fae laws, but I had also tried to steal from the very being tasked with enforcing them. It wouldn't matter that I hadn't been successful.

Inwardly, I groaned.

Stupid didn't even begin to cover it.

"Why am I still alive?" I croaked, not ready to sit up and face my fate. Because he would kill me. Of that I was certain.

"Look at me."

"Make me."

I covered my mouth, horrified those words had slipped

out. Now was not the time to be a stubborn ass. But by the dark, I despised being ordered around.

Knowing he would kill me anyway, I didn't take it back, or apologize. Whether he killed me now or minutes later didn't matter. I had sealed my fate the moment I tried to rob him, and I refused to go into the dark night begging and crying for my life.

Emboldened by that thought, I tensed, ready to attack as his heavy footfalls moved toward me. The male was smarter than I gave him credit for. He stopped just a hair out of striking distance.

With me prone on the ground and his substantial height, the Enforcer really did appear as a giant to me like he had after the explosion. I shoved to my feet, greatly disliking how vulnerable the height difference made me feel. Even standing, I was still a head shorter than him.

My injured leg protested the weight, but the rest of me felt surprisingly refreshed given someone had tried to blow me up. I must have been asleep for a while.

Why hadn't he woken me? Why was I still alive?

I looked to the only person who could give me answers.

I had never traveled north far enough, but I suspected standing in front of the Enforcer would be like standing in front of the Fayette mountains. Their full size was incomprehensible until you were right in front of them.

Though I could have easily tipped my chin back to meet his gaze, I made a point of refusing, and stared straight ahead at his chest instead.

It was a poor choice in hindsight. I could see the swell of his massive pectoral muscles peeking out the open v of his sleeveless tunic and part of a tattoo inked beneath his collar bone. Even in that small portion of visible skin, I observed several scars, the damaged tissue slightly lighter than the rest of his sun kissed skin.

Something cold touched just below my chin and my head was forced up by the end of the Enforcer's sword. I hadn't even heard him draw it; I was too focused on his chest.

Idiot. Idiot. Idiot.

His mocking gaze, the same color as the blade under my chin, stared into mine. He leaned forward whispering, "Made you."

I glared even as my stomach clenched at the sound of his sensuous voice. "Going to slit my throat now?" I challenged.

He drew back slightly. "No, not until you tell me where the godstone is."

My brows dipped down almost touching. "Godstone? What's a godstone?"

"You don't even know what you were stealing? What kind of thief are you?"

Not a very good one apparently, otherwise I would have known who I was stealing from and avoided this entire situation in the first place.

"I didn't rob you. I mean, I was going to, but another group of thieves got the jump on me and took it."

His penetrating gaze on my face felt invasive. It dipped to the column of my throat and the layer of dried blood there, tightening my skin, before moving back to my unnaturally colored eyes. He stared so hard I could feel him peeling back layers of skin to see to the heart of who I was.

Could he see the darkness lurking there?

The sword dropped. "You're telling the truth."

"Halflings can't lie," I reminded him.

"No but lies can still pass your lips when wrapped in partial truths. But the eyes, the eyes can never lie half as well as the tongue," he said. "Fae have made honest deception an art. I assume halflings are no different."

I bristled at the comparison. "Halflings and fae are about

as similar as beasts and mortals except neither enslave the other," I snapped.

Ignoring my outburst, his gaze lowered to my wrists. "While we're on the subject, where is your fae brand?"

"Is it against fae law not to have one?"

"There is no precedent—"

"Then it's none of your business, *Fairy*."

"Little Thief, I have lived and battled for over a millennium. You will need to try much harder to provoke me into striking distance with those lovely, but deadly, weapons on your hands."

I growled under my breath, infuriated he had seen right through me. It was a long shot thinking I might incapacitate him long enough to escape. Really, I just wanted to die knowing I had spilled the Enforcer's blood.

My mouth opened, on the verge of explaining that I didn't have his godstone and I had no idea where it was so he should just get it over with and kill me already, but he stopped me with a raised finger. A finger I wanted to bite off.

"Hold that thought. Finn?"

A figure, whose presence I had been completely oblivious to, peeled out of the shadows and approached. He wore a long-sleeved tunic, but I could still see his neck and face were a rich black that made his cerulean eyes appear even more startling. He had smooth, dark hair, pulled back into a low bun that accentuated his high cheekbones.

"Yes, My Lord?"

"Who was responsible for coordinating the godstone's transport?"

"Fealor."

"Send him in."

The Enforcer moved deeper into the tent as Finn left. His exit allowed in a gust of cold air from outside. The temperature, and the fact that the Enforcer had brought me to a tent and not a fae house, told me we were still in the northern Mortal Lands.

My eyes darted toward the flap.

"Go ahead, I love a good chase," the Enforcer said absently, perusing through a set of papers stacked on a table.

I shot him a dirty look though he didn't see it.

"I know whatever face you're making right now isn't pleasant." He turned over a paper.

I scowled. Did he miss *nothing*?

I understood why he hadn't bothered tying me up. The Enforcer would know I was planning to run even before I did, he could read me so well.

A new fae entered the tent, the blue-eyed one following close behind. Finn returned to his position in the shadows while the new fae stopped beside me. His gaze slid to me a moment before dismissing me and addressing the Enforcer.

"Lord Taran, you called for me?"

One blink and the Enforcer faced us, armed with his infamous sword. Suddenly, all I could hear was the blood pumping in my ears.

This is it. This is when he finally kills me.

My instinct screamed at me to take a step back, but my stubborn pride wouldn't allow this fae an inch, even in the face of death. He raised the sword, the steel gleaming in the sunlight streaming in, and struck.

But not at me.

The Enforcer cleaved Fealor's head right off. Only years of fighting and training with the Rogues made me quick enough to duck a split second before, or the tip of his sword would have stabbed me in the side of the neck. Blood splattered my clothes and skin.

My eyelids stretched wide as the head rolled toward my

feet, my heart slamming so hard against my ribcage I was certain it would break through the breastbone.

Weapon sheathed, the Enforcer returned to the table, now facing me and the freshly made corpse. He resumed pouring over the papers as if nothing had happened. I stared in shock at his casualness. There was a head sitting inches from me, blood still sputtering from the severed neck.

Once the stupor wore off, something in me snapped. "You almost took my head off, you big oaf!"

I froze, bracing for a blow. When none came, I dared to peek up at the Enforcer's face.

He stared with a severe gaze. "I didn't 'almost' do anything. If I wanted you headless, you'd be headless."

I swallowed hard. Warning received.

"Now you have five seconds to convince me I shouldn't take your head too."

I could only stare. "You're not going to kill me? I thought breaking fae law was an automatic death sentence."

"I am the judge, jury, and executioner. Your fate is entirely up to my discretion," he explained. "A perk of the job, if you will." The last part was said sourly.

So he never had to kill anyone. He chose to.

I wasn't Miss Morals or anything, given I'd killed before, but his death toll was in the *thousands*, and he didn't discriminate. He killed everyone, innocent children included. Even I had limits.

I was too shocked and disgusted to respond.

"One," his deep voice intoned.

"Five seconds isn't—"

"Two."

My mouth clamped shut. Arguing would not keep my head attached. In my peripheral, blue eyes shined in the shadows like a beacon, enjoying the show. I glared.

"Three."

Think, you idiot! Think!

"Four."

Head tilting to the side, I studied him. The Enforcer stared steadily back, not a hint of his thoughts visible. He knew I had not stolen the godstone, but that wasn't why he was keeping me alive. I had asked the wrong question.

"Why is it that the mythical Enforcer who always seems to know exactly when and where a fae law is being broken can't find the real thieves?"

The Enforcer's gaze brightened, looking impressed. "They're blocking me somehow."

"A halfling with brains. How unusual." This came from the blue-eyed figure in the corner. My blood heated. Typical fae, assuming he was better than everyone.

"Why don't you come out of the corner and say that to my face?" My talons clicked together.

The Enforcer read the threat of violence in my expression. His face darkened to a frightening degree. He leaned his mountainous frame forward, hands engulfing the table where they spread.

"It is my duty to punish those who spill fae blood, but when the blood spilled is one of my own, I take that *very* personally. You understand?"

Goosebumps broke out over my flesh. Menace dripped from every word.

"I just watched you cut off one of your men's heads," I pointed out.

"He was a traitor and his actions have caused irreparable harm to my House. Let that be a warning."

"Don't harm your people. Noted."

My words seemed to pacify the Enforcer.

"Good, but you still haven't convinced me to spare your life," he said. "Five." The Enforcer straightened to his full six-foot-six height, gripping his sword and was in front of me in one movement.

"I can help you find the godstone," I blurted out, hopping back. The sticky splat that followed told me I had stepped right in Fealor's blood. I grimaced.

He stopped. "How?"

My throat tightened, metallic saliva pooling under my tongue. I worked my throat as I struggled to speak. I had the answer he required, the answer that would save my life, but it was the last answer I wanted to give.

"I know where the All-Seeing Eye is."

"Everyone knows the Crone possesses it. Try harder."

I ground my fangs, thankful for the surge of anger. It helped chase away the lingering discomfort even if I also wanted to stab the Enforcer in the eye with one of my talons.

"I know where the Crone is."

Interest flared in the Enforcer's stony eyes. He leaned forward. "And how is that, Little Thief? No one finds the Crone unless she wants them to. Hundreds have tried. Or better yet, what is to stop me from leaving an offering of my own for her?"

"You could try," I conceded. "But you said it yourself. The Crone is highly selective about her clientele and *if* she chooses to help you, she requires your most treasured possession. Are you willing to pay that price?"

The Crone liked to collect hearts both literally and figu-ratively. If she couldn't have the organ, she demanded the thing a person loved most in the world in return for her services.

"Are you?" he shot back.

If only he knew . . .

What's the only thing a child could offer anyone?

Their unconditional love. Their innocence.

I had given mine endlessly, tolerated many awful things, all in the hopes *she* might someday return it. She never did.

I love you, Mama.

Your only value to me are the bits and pieces I can chop off for my spells. Keep that disgusting emotion to yourself.

I couldn't help the small, anguished undercurrent riding my voice. "I already have. More times than I can count. Once more won't matter."

If I lived, I still had a chance at a vest. At a place with the Rogues. If I had to tolerate one last visit with her, so be it.

The Enforcer scrutinized me with an intensity that might have made me squirm had I not spent my earliest years with the Crone—the notorious lover of Balor himself.

"Very good, Little Thief. Give me your palm."

I eyed him warily, keeping my hands at my side. "Why?"

"We are going to make a bargain." His tone brooked no argument.

I argued anyway. "The fuck we are!"

A fae bargain was irreversible, short of the bargain creator's death, and given this fae's immortality, I would be magic bound to fulfill it. I would have to hand over the godstone and any chance I had at earning a vest along with it.

I jerked back too quickly and my injured leg buckled. The Enforcer grabbed my waist, stopping me from falling right into the pool of blood.

He frowned. "Are you always this clumsy?"

I glared down at his hand, so large it not only covered my hip bone, but part of my stomach too. I batted it away, snarling, "Don't touch me."

He gripped me tighter, pulling me close, and threw my words back at me. "Next time I should let you fall. Noted."

I tried to jerk away again. "I'm not bargaining with you. I'd rather let a dullah rip out my spine." The headless land beast liked to carry the spine of its latest victim as it rode into battle and would be preferable company to the Enforcer.

"Then you aren't any use to me alive."

His voice held no malice. He wasn't reacting to my sharp words, just stating a fact.

I blew out a breath, attempting to calm down. Anger was clouding my judgment. Another inhale, another exhale. I needed a clear head. My pulse started to settle.

The Enforcer had me by the throat. It was either accept the bargain or die by his sword. Even knowing that didn't make it any easier to agree.

"Fine," I gritted out. "Bargain it is."

"You will find what was stolen, accompanied by myself, and in return, I will spare your life. Do you agree to my terms?"

Was there a choice? This fae was just using me like everyone else in my life.

I thought I would be used to it by now, but it still stung.

"I agree."

8

The Enforcer pulled a dagger the size of my forearm from his belt and drew a line across his palm with it, blood pooling in its wake. He gestured for my hand next, and I stuck it out, grateful the long sleeves of my tunic covered the scarred skin on my wrist.

"This will be unpleasant," he said almost . . . apologetically.

Pain was nothing new to me, and besides, the Enforcer had just been ready to kill me. What did he care about my comfort?

"Just do it."

He cut my palm, then pressed his bleeding hand to mine, meeting my gaze. Those hard, gray eyes softened, shifting between mine. I schooled my features, ensuring he'd see none of the fear or anxiety.

"So I swear," he said.

"So I swear," I repeated.

A burning sensation started where his hand pressed against my skin, traveling down, growing hotter as it went. By the time it reached my toes, it felt like my skin was melting. I clenched my jaw to contain the scream working up my throat. When I glanced over at the Enforcer, he stared at me, seemingly unaffected by the magic burning me alive.

"It will be over soon," he whispered. His reassurance was oddly comforting, but also frustrating. I didn't want any comfort from him. He was the reason I was in this situation in the first place.

Instead, I studied his face for the first time to distract myself. The Enforcer was too rough, too masculine to be considered pretty like most fae males, including the one who watched from the shadows.

He had a sharp, square jawline dusted with day-old stubble, and a slightly hooked nose. With his hair sheared close to his head, I could just make out the blond coloring. Now his lips—those I would call pretty—were much too full and pink for a male like him. As if someone else had agreed, a jagged, curved scar stretching from his chin to his right ear sliced right through them.

The longer I stared, the more scars I saw. Raised puckered scars interrupted smooth, sun-darkened skin all over his face and neck just like I had seen on his chest.

Even more curious than the scars, were those whorls of light gray ink tattooed down the thick column of his throat. The ink disappeared under the collar of his tunic and reappeared, branching out and down his large biceps.

One of those biceps had a gold band cinched around it containing a bright blue gem the size of a fist—the draoistone I had missed before.

"How do you feel?" The Enforcer's rich voice tore me from my inspection.

"What?"

"The bargain is sealed. You shouldn't feel any pain now."

Lips pursed, I flexed my muscles, testing what he said. My leg ached from standing on it so long, but the other bone melting pain was gone just as he said.

"I feel fine."

He nodded. "Good. Finn, watch over her. I need to make arrangements for our journey. And you." The Enforcer's gaze cast my way. "Sit there and don't cause any trouble." He pointed to a stack of furs I stood on top of.

My nostrils flared. "I'm not some dog you can order around."

Two strides and the Enforcer was in my space, looming over me. The scent of leather mixed with vanilla and amber-wood hit my nose.

Damnit. Why did he have to smell good?

He angled close with a teasing grin. "You'll learn to like when I give you orders," he whispered, then stepped away before I had a chance to react. I glared at his broad back as he disappeared through the tent flap. He was messing with me.

I considered remaining on my feet purely out of spite, but my injured leg screamed for relief. Reluctantly, I plopped down on the furs.

"If you so much as blink in a manner that displeases me, I will make you suffer," Finn snapped the moment I sat.

The Enforcer's steward, at least I assumed that's who he was, wore a gold circlet around his bicep embedded with a draoistone. His stone was half the size of my fist, confirming my suspicions he was a high fae.

On the surface, he appeared of little consequence. He was slightly shorter than me and packed with lean muscle. If he were a halfling, or even a low fae, I could easily over-power him, but the size of his draoistone warned this fae was dangerous.

Even still, I couldn't stop myself from provoking him. I opened my eyes comically wide and blinked slowly several times like a startled owl.

He advanced on me but stopped short when the tent

flapped open. The newcomer acknowledged Finn with a nod, then strode over to the decapitated corpse. I had almost forgotten about the dead fae. After sending me a seething look that promised retribution, Finn took a seat at the table and watched me vigilantly.

They didn't even tie me up. If the Enforcer thought I would sit here like a good little captive, the male was not as intelligent as he appeared. While the Enforcer was distracted with our journey arrangements, I needed to escape.

I might not have another opportunity like this. If I fled and got my hands on some iron dust, I could kill the Enforcer and end our bargain before it ever began.

My right leg was still partially swollen. I wouldn't get far on foot, but all I had to do was find a horse. There had to be at least four nearby based on the number of fae I had seen. I had no idea where I was, or how outnumbered, but I had to try.

The newcomer disposed of the head, then returned for the body. I waited until he had a grip on the legs before I barreled into him, knocking him to the ground, and fled the tent.

The dull throbbing in my leg sharpened to a piercing pain as I ran. There were only a handful of tents in addition to the Enforcer's. The horses were tied off in an outcrop of trees only a couple yards off. With a burst of speed, I closed the distance between me and the horses.

I threw a glance over my shoulder when I realized I hadn't heard Finn shouting behind me. He hadn't even exited the tent. Maybe he had slipped in the pool of blood in his haste and knocked himself unconscious. I frowned. That explanation seemed unlikely.

A low warning tingle shot down my spine, but I ignored it. I couldn't afford to stop.

I chose the closest war stallion, untied its reins, then swung myself onto its back, riding off into the dusky light of the rapidly approaching night. I had been unconscious longer than I thought if it was near sunset.

Flowing water filled my ears as I rode. The Cold River had to be somewhere nearby.

I got about two miles away before I slammed into an invisible force. Pain radiated up my face and neck. It felt like someone had punched me in the nose.

I blinked and found myself back inside the tent staring up at the Enforcer. On my knees.

Balor's ball sack. It had to be the bargain magic.

"You run with the grace of a flailing worm," Finn said.

The Enforcer cut him a look. "Leave us," he ordered. His steward's lips puckered sullenly, disappointed he wouldn't get to witness my punishment. He offered a curt nod and left.

The Enforcer stared down at me with an inscrutable expression. "Get that out of your system?"

I growled under my breath, releasing a string of filthy curses. No wonder they didn't tie me up. The bargain would drag my ass right back to him.

"How exactly does this bargain magic work?" I asked, feeling a little stupid I hadn't asked more questions earlier.

"You are bound to me until I release you, or your end of the bargain is fulfilled. The tether linking us is under my control. Think of it like a leash. I can shorten, lengthen it, or drag you to me at any time. It has its limits though. I can only give you so much rope before it will become incredibly painful for you to be away from me."

Leash? This bastard had me on a *leash*?

A humiliated flush crawled up my neck as I scrambled to my feet and tipped my chin up to glower at him. My right leg buckled, already strained too far during my escape, and

I fell right back to the ground, thankfully this time on my ass.

I didn't bother trying to get up again. I could be just as infuriated and indignant on the ground.

After a moment, he crouched his massive frame down in front of me, frowning. He tapped a finger on my knee.

"Did you hurt yourself trying to escape?"

"No," I growled, shoving his hand away.

The Enforcer became unnaturally still. His nostrils flared. The tendons in his neck were stretched taut, on the verge of snapping. He seemed to grow in the darkness. "Who. Hurt. You."

I stared at him, bewildered.

He took one deep, controlled breath at my continued silence. "Little Thief." His tone was calm but strained. "If you do not give me a name right now, I will lay waste to every single soul in the Mortal Lands to ensure whoever dared to lay a finger on you comes to justice."

I was too shocked to deny him. "A rock," I blurted out. "A rock fell on me."

All the tension melted from his bones in an instant. The change in him was startling. Fast enough it made me light-headed. I scrambled back on instinct, but I didn't get far before the Enforcer stopped me.

"The bargain was for both of our benefits. You are under the protection of my House for its duration. If anyone dares to harm you, they will answer to me."

His House?

I didn't know much about fae hierarchy, but I knew the basics. The fae were divided into Houses based on their powers and each House was ruled by a lord or lady; they answered to the fae king.

"You're a fae lord?"

I recalled the dead fae addressing him as Lord Taran but

hadn't thought much of it. There wasn't much known about the mysterious Enforcer. Knowledge was power. The more information I could gather, the better prepared I would be when I found a way out of this bargain.

"Yes." He sat back on his haunches and unlaced my boot before removing it and rolling up my pant leg.

"If you're a fae lord, how did you end up as the Enforcer?"

His gaze skimmed over my face before returning to my leg. "You are awfully curious for someone who just tried to run away," he said. "How did you end up trying to steal from me anyway?"

And further incriminate myself, or potentially the Rogues?

"Pass."

He gave no reaction, focusing on my leg.

I watched him gently prod around the swollen lump with an odd sense of numbness. His behavior was strange.

So was mine. I should have been snarling and shoving him away, but I couldn't muster any of the indignation this fae's touch warranted. He examined my leg like we were familiar, like we weren't enemies, and I hadn't just tried to escape him.

His fingers were calloused and warm against my skin. The Enforcer's touch didn't make my skin crawl like I expected it to.

It was almost pleasant.

That thought was like a splash of poitín to the face. It brought me back to my senses. I kicked his hand away with my good leg snapping, "Back off, fairy."

He didn't listen. Lord Taran restrained me with embarrassing ease. He had my good leg trapped between his thighs and my hands pinned over my head in a flash. I snarled, trying to dislodge his hold.

"Calm down. I only want to look at your leg."

I fought harder.

"Gods, female, are you always this stubborn?"

I bared my fangs. Fangs. Why wasn't I biting him?

As if reading my thoughts, he grinned wickedly. "I like it rough." His warm breath fanned over my face. "You bite me, and I will want to do a lot more than look at your leg."

I forced my face into a mask of disgust, ignoring the heat spiraling through me.

"Get off me, you brute, or do you make it a habit of forcing yourself on females you claim are under your protection?"

The Enforcer moved off me so quickly, I thought I might have burned him. But I knew that couldn't have happened, or I would have felt my power stir. He rubbed his jaw, crouching near me.

His gaze flickered to my throat, to the area he'd nicked. I'd caught him looking at it earlier too.

"Has that healed?" he asked.

"For someone whose job it is to literally *murder* people, blood really bothers you."

Tight lines formed around his mouth. He didn't respond, rising until he towered over me. "I didn't bring my house healer with me. We'll leave for Gold City at dawn. One of the mortal healers will have to do for now."

"That's not necessary. I'm fine."

"You are not fine," he said in aggravation. "And you need new clothes."

As he moved away to rummage through a trunk, I glanced down at myself. There was a hole in my tunic around the collar bone area. The rest of the shirt was covered in various tears and singe marks from the explosion. And Fealor's blood. I grimaced.

"Do you wish to bathe?"

"Yes," I said, over eagerly.

He approached with a folded set of clothes. "These might be a little large on you."

I frowned. "I'm not wearing your clothes." They would smell like him.

He raised a brow. "Well unless you have a fresh set magically hidden away somewhere, you don't have a choice."

Yeah, that seemed to be a running theme in my life.

"I'll be sure to pack an extra pair of clothes next time I'm kidnapped."

"I did not kidnap you," he said adamantly.

He really believed that, or he couldn't have spoken the words out loud.

"Do the fae have another term for when someone is brought somewhere against their will and not allowed to leave?" I asked sweetly.

Something flashed across his expression too quick to catch. He was quiet a moment before demanding, "Do you want a bath or not?"

"I already said yes . . ."

He glared.

I glared back.

"Follow me," he clipped out and briskly left the tent.

Apparently, kidnappers didn't like it when you called them kidnappers . . .

I took my time wandering out after him. There were three other tents set-up near the Enforcer's, but none of the occupants were outside. The sun had fully set, but only four days after a full moon, the waning gibbous provided ample moonlight.

Lord Taran grunted when I finally caught up to him, then took off toward the sounds of the river without another word. Amusement filled me. Who knew the *big scary* Enforcer was so touchy?

89

I trailed behind him, limping on and off.

Abruptly, he stopped, spun around, and charged. I was tossed over his shoulder before I could process what was happening.

I beat on his back. "Put me down, you bastard."

"No. You're too slow."

"Because I broke my leg!"

"How did you manage that anyway?" he asked, casually like I wasn't screaming and thrashing in his grip like a wild banshee. "Rocks don't just fall out of the sky."

Frustration burned through me.

"I was fighting the beasts while you and all the other fae cowered behind your borders," I snapped.

"So, you're a Rogue?"

I froze. I hadn't meant to share that. If I implicated the Rogues, there was nothing stopping the Enforcer from going after them.

"No," I said carefully, thanking the Gods for once that was the truth.

I was put on my feet again and saw we had reached the river. I quickly backed away from the Enforcer. He tracked my movement with a frown. "Then why were you fighting the beasts?"

I ignored his question, gesturing for the clothes in his hand.

He held them away. "You'll get these as soon as you give me an answer."

I shrugged. I hadn't wanted to wear them to begin with. Changing back into my blood splattered clothes after washing was a bit unsanitary, but I'd gladly do it to prove a point.

"Let's get something straight, Lord Taran—"

"You can call me Ronan."

It would be a sunny day in the Darklands before I called my kidnapper by his first name.

"As both a fae lord and mass murderer, I'm sure you are accustomed to getting your way, but I don't answer to you. You don't get to make demands and expect me to jump to fulfill them. It's not happening."

When he only stared, still keeping the clothes out of reach, I sighed and moved over to the river. Fed from underground springs in the Faylands, the water was chilly year-round. I dipped a hand in and withdrew it with a hiss. Technically, the well water in Mayhem had come from this river, but by the time it made its way into the Rogue compound it was room temperature.

It had been years since I had bathed in this river. I had scrubbed dried blood off myself many times in this water. My back ached in remembrance.

With my important bits covered by my tunic, I wiggled out of my pants and undergarments, opting to keep the shirt on. It had nothing to do with preserving my modesty. Spending the last seven years sharing a bathing room with a bunch of sweaty, disgusting males would do that to you. Besides Ryder, none of them had ever seen me as a woman anyway. I was something *other* in their minds.

It was my back I was concerned about. I slipped into the river, teeth clenched at the temperature, and forced myself to duck under the water so my body could adjust to the cold quicker.

I popped back to the surface, shivering. The river's current was slow and halfheartedly tugging me with it. It was shallow enough for me to touch the bottom while still having my shoulders and everything below submerged. With the water taking most of my weight, I was able to balance on one leg and keep pressure off my injury.

Boots crunched over the ground behind me. I spun as Lord Taran lowered beside the riverbank. He removed his shoes and rolled up his pants. I saw a flash of his massive calves tattooed with the same ink as his upper body before he dipped his feet into the river, not even flinching at the cold.

The action was so very . . . mundane. Not something I ever imagined a man like the Enforcer doing. It was a bit disarming.

"What?" he asked gruffly at my staring.

"I've heard so many stories about you. You've always been built up as this larger-than-life myth in my head. As this dark boogeyman I should be afraid of, but you're just—" I gestured to all of him. "You're just a man, or fae, or whatever."

He inclined his head sideways, appraising me. "Why *aren't* you afraid of me?"

I didn't even have to think of the answer. "Because I've met much scarier monsters."

"You think I'm a monster then." He seemed . . . disappointed by my response.

Jaw tight, the Enforcer jerked his head toward the pile beside him. "There's soap and a drying cloth. Get yourself cleaned up."

He stood roughly.

"And Little Thief?" He glanced down at me. "You're foolish not to be afraid. I am every terrible story you've heard. There is no separating the man from the myth."

He left me staring after him as he marched back to camp.

92

9

I found the bar of soap he mentioned tucked between the clothes. It was vanilla scented, just like him. I scowled at it. There should be some universal law that mass murderers weren't allowed to be attractive or smell phenomenal. It was damn confusing.

I vigorously washed away all the blast residue and blood from my skin and hair, then moved onto my clothes, hoping they could be salvaged. As I scrubbed at the numerous stains, I thought of the Enforcer's warning.

I had a high fear tolerance. Being raised by an evil witch had that effect. There was only one thing I was truly afraid of in this world, and it wasn't the Enforcer. He was powerful and could kill me at any moment so I would need to proceed with caution until I figured out my next move.

I left the river feeling better than when I had entered it. I dried off and changed into the clean clothes the Enforcer had left.

They were laughably oversized. I had to roll the pant waist down six times just to get them to stay on my hips. The tunic dwarfed me just as much, but thankfully it had long sleeves.

I felt ridiculous, like a child playing dress up in a giant's clothes.

I waddled back into camp, clutching the waistband of the pants in one hand and the dirty clothes, soap, and towel in the other.

I hesitated outside the Enforcer's tent. Should I knock?

No, fuck his privacy. Kidnappers didn't deserve any.

I stormed through the flaps.

The Enforcer held a scrying mirror. It was all black framed with intricately carved designs. Scrying mirrors were two-way communication devices operated by magic. The caller's face would appear in the mirror on the receiving end and vice versa.

He was talking to someone on the other end. His conversation cut off at my entrance. "I'll keep you updated," he said curtly and set down the mirror, then gave my new attire a cursory glance. "You look—comfortable."

"Careful," I said flippantly. "Might make a girl blush."

"I could," he offered in a low voice that had my stomach tightening. I mentally chastised myself for it.

Kidnapper, remember?

"Where am I sleeping?"

"There's room in my bed." His voice was a purr, but his gaze was flat and disinterested. Bored even, like he had done this song and dance a hundred times before. Was this some sort of fucked up test? I didn't understand what was going on.

"Not interested."

"You are. I saw the way you reacted to me outside the train."

"Is that why you offered me your hand?"

"Yes. I wanted to fuck you. Still do."

He stared expectantly.

What? Did he expect me to get on my knees and start sucking his cock or something?

"Are you attractive? Yes. Do I want to have sex with you? No."

"No?"

"That's what I said."

He looked perplexed, which made me even more confused. This was getting weirder by the second.

"Women throw themselves at me. They all want to know what it's like to get fucked by a monster." The last part was said with a hint of bitterness.

Dolly had been telling the truth. I hadn't given much thought to her story because of how ridiculous it sounded. What woman in their right mind would willingly leave with him?

Unless . . . "Are they all willing?"

Fury flashed across his expression. "*Very*. And I don't appreciate the accusation."

I shrugged. He made it clear he wanted me to know what a monster he was. He had no right to get upset when I assumed just that.

"Well again, not interested."

His brows slanted down, stare hardening. "I don't understand you."

Man, the Enforcer really wasn't used to being denied. Maybe it was some sort of thrill for the women, like the tourists who visited Mayhem on a full moon drawn by the danger and excitement of it all. I could see the appeal of having the full attention of this muscled, tattooed, and lethal man solely focused on me.

Except . . .

"It's pretty straightforward." I started ticking off things with a hand. "You kidnapped me, threatened me, and forced me into a bargain with you. And yeah—that about covers it."

He was silent a long moment before he pointed to the stack of failin furs I had woken up on. "You may lie there."

"Where can I hang my clothes?"

"Burn them. I will purchase you a new wardrobe in Gold City."

Accepting anything from him irked my pride, but I also didn't want to have to spend anymore time in his clothes than necessary.

I tossed the tunic into the small fire contained within a brazier. There was no salvaging it. The pants were better off. I laid those out near the fire to dry along with the towel.

The Enforcer had a coil of rope in his hands when I finished.

Perfect. My chains were lost with Ness anyway. As much as I would love to wake up and see his face shredded like my walls back at the Rogues' compound, I couldn't risk it. I had no idea what that darkness would do if it were freed, even for a night.

Just to keep him on his toes, I offered my wrists like a good little captive after I sat down on the furs.

"I can't allow you to roam freely while I sleep," he said, but didn't move. His gaze jumped between my wrists and the rope, hesitating.

"You took all my weapons," I pointed out, though I had no idea why. I *wanted* him to bind me. Some small, idiotic part of me enjoyed provoking him.

"You are always armed." He lowered himself beside me on the furs, gaze fixed on my talons. "I have never seen a halfling like you before."

The edge of my lip curled back in disdain. "Guess I'm just special."

"Do they make it difficult to grip weapons?"

My gaze snapped to his. "Are you mocking me?"

He was taken aback by the accusation. "No, I've never

seen a more deadly weapon." His expression was curious, thoughtful even. The lack of trepidation or disgust made me suspicious. Uncomfortable. I didn't like it.

"You're right. You can't trust me. I'll use these—" I waved my talons "—to slit everyone's throats while they sleep."

His gaze darkened and the unsettling heaviness in my chest lifted. "Go lay down over there," he growled, tipping a chin toward the pole in the middle of the tent that kept the fabric from sagging.

So I wasn't sleeping on the furs then.

I allowed him to tie my wrists without complaint, not even when the night turned exceptionally cold. It took hours, but eventually I drifted off to sleep.

When I woke in the early morning, a failin fur had been draped across my shoulders.

Confusion filled me as I stared down at the covering through heavy lidded eyes. The fur had not been there when I had fallen asleep. Casting my gaze around the tent, I found the Enforcer asleep on a palette of furs and a bitter heat filled my belly. This was his doing.

He wanted to be the villain. Fine, but he didn't get to be the nice guy too.

With a frustrated growl, I kicked the stupid fur off. Cold air slapped my skin and I shivered against the pole. My ass was numb, and my arms ached from being tied behind my back all night. I flexed my wrists as much as the rope would allow in an attempt to stretch, then surveyed the tent for the first time.

It was four times the size of my room at the Rogue compound, but simply furnished for a man of the Enforcer's stature. There was a table covered in linen, candles, and unfinished food. The half-eaten plate screamed how privileged he was; how unconcerned he was when he would see his next meal. I rolled my eyes at the absurdity of it.

Adjacent to the table was the bed where Lord Taran slept. Movement on it caught my eye. The Enforcer jerked in his sleep, pain contorting his features briefly before evening out.

Bad dreams. Good. I hoped all the lives he'd taken weighed on his conscience, but who knew if a man like the Enforcer was even capable of remorse.

He was bare chested, his whorls of gray ink glowing in the soft morning light. Against my better judgment, I let my gaze linger over the hard planes of his chest, and wished I was close enough to read the lettering tattooed below his collarbone.

My tongue darted out, wetting my lips as I continued my inspection of his torso, then upward along his strong jaw, his lips parted slightly in relaxation, and then to his eyes.

Eyes that were open and focused on me.

His lips tipped into a lazy, knowing smirk and shame burned through me. I'd been caught staring.

Baring my teeth at him, I dropped my voice to a threatening whisper, jerking my head toward the discarded failin fur. "Next time, let me freeze to death. It's a better fate than being stuck in a bargain with you."

Humor lit those steel gray eyes as he sat up, stretching. His muscles rippled with the movement. "Good morning to you too," he rumbled. Whatever strange mood he had been in the night before had passed. I ripped my gaze away with a scowl.

There was nothing good about this morning. The thing I was supposed to steal was out there, Gods only knows where, and I was stuck with this insufferable male until I found its location, or a way to kill him. Neither of which would be an easy task.

I needed to get my hands on some iron dust and quick. I

had no idea where to find the Nighters and even if I did, I wasn't sure I wanted to.

The Enforcer approached. He wore a loose pair of breeches slung irritatingly low on his waist. A gray whorl covered each hip before disappearing below his waistline.

I caught sight of the dagger in his hand, and tensed.

"I'm not going to hurt you," he said with a frown. "I told you, you're under my protection for the duration of our bargain."

I stuck up my chin, glaring. "Yeah, I feel real protected right now, bound up like this."

He kneeled, that frown deepening. His gaze briefly flickered to mine before he focused on cutting the rope. "You threatened my people. I had no choice."

The Enforcer had given *me* no choice, but whatever. I wasn't going to waste precious energy arguing with him.

The pressure of the bindings fell away and I breathed a sigh of relief, rubbing feeling back into my wrists. I was careful to keep the mountain of scars there covered with my long sleeves. My skin was slightly chafed from the coarseness of the rope, but I had slept surprisingly well given the circumstances.

Something akin to guilt flashed across the Enforcer's face as he watched me, but that couldn't be right. I had to be imagining things.

"Are you hungry?" he asked.

I shrugged.

"Little Thief," he said sharply, and my gaze jerked to his face and the stern expression it held. "The bindings were an unfortunate, but necessary precaution. While we are bound together, your wellbeing is my responsibility, and I will see to it that you are well cared for. When you have a need, voice it. Now tell me, are you hungry?"

I wanted to say no out of sheer stubbornness, but in

truth, I was hungry. I hadn't eaten since someone tried to blow me up the day before. Speaking of which . . .

"You mentioned the thieves blocked you from finding them. What does that mean exactly?"

The Enforcer stared.

"We're not friends, Enforcer. You want to know something. So do I. Let's make a trade."

"What I want to know is entirely for your benefit."

I shrugged again. I could go days without eating. I *had* gone days without eating. "How important is my wellbeing to you?"

His eyes narrowed. "You are more stubborn than you are smart," he murmured, then stared for a moment longer. "I can sense when the fae laws are broken. My magic teleports me directly to the culprit. Some dark energy interrupted my teleportation this time and sent me to the scene of the crime instead."

"You can *sense* when the fae laws are broken?"

So little was known about the Enforcer and how he always knew when and where a fae law had been broken. It was fascinating to be able to peer behind the curtain and learn more about this enigmatic fae.

"Yes. Always. It is like a tugging on my soul. Except this time. I could not sense the true perpetrators then, nor have I been able to since."

Brows shooting to my hairline I asked, "How is that possible?" He was supposed to be the all-powerful, all-knowing Enforcer.

His expression darkened. "It shouldn't be."

Wonderful. He had no idea who or what we were up against any more than I did. His answer made me rethink my plans. The Enforcer would ultimately have to die—I'd never be able to bring the godstone home otherwise—but it might be good to have some backup until that time came.

Well, a deal was a deal.

"I'm starving," I said answering his earlier question.

"Good." He stood and offered a hand to help me do the same. I ignored it, standing on my own, which earned me a smirk. "Your fearlessness toward me is a breath of fresh air."

"Yeah, I couldn't give less of a shit."

My gaze scanned the tent, but I couldn't find what I was looking for.

"Where's my cloak?" If we were going farther north, I'd need something for the cold. I had been wearing it during the explosion, but when I woke up inside the Enforcer's tent, it was gone.

"You weren't wearing one when I found you."

It probably came off when I went hurling through the air.

"When you kidnapped me," I corrected.

He said nothing to that.

I grabbed my dried pants, wiggled out of his with the long tunic covering the important parts and pulled them on. I turned toward the Enforcer, offering the pants.

Hungry eyes were riveted to my legs. He tore them away, clearing his throat, and accepted the pants with a nod.

Voices sounded outside. The Enforcer tipped his head in that direction. "Go on. They'll have breakfast ready for you."

I strolled out of the tent. Three male fae stood over a campfire, the Enforcer's steward among them. Their gazes swung to me, staring curiously. Except for Finn. He glared at first, then his lips stretched into a mocking grin. "How's your face?"

Bastard had let me run on purpose. Slamming into that magical barrier had *hurt*. He must have known it would.

"Still better looking than yours," I taunted.

The fae on his right with light, playful gray eyes winked at me.

"Don't wink at her," Finn said aghast. "She's a prisoner. And a rude one at that. Glaring and scowling only."

I chuckled under my breath. I knew he wasn't intentionally being funny, which is probably the only reason it *was* funny.

The flirtatious fae's gaze dragged over me. "She doesn't look like a prisoner."

"That's because she's not," Lord Taran announced behind us.

Two of the fae bowed in unison to the Enforcer, murmuring, "My Lord."

Finn interestingly did not.

Sarcastically cocking a brow, I looked to Lord Taran as he approached. "Oh, yeah? What am I then?" This ought to be good.

"My business partner."

He was delusional.

I scoffed, crossing my arms. "Partner implies I had a choice."

"You did," he said simply.

I dropped my voice, attempting to imitate him. "Bargain or death."

The flirtatious one burst into laughter. Lord Taran sent him a look and the sound immediately died in his throat.

The Enforcer's gaze cut back to me. He smirked. "I never said they were *good* choices."

The absolute arrogance of this fae. Let him mock me all he wanted. I'd have the last laugh when I slit his throat.

My murderous expression had his smirk dropping. He frowned at me before turning to his men. "Get my guest some breakfast. Give her a double portion."

Double portion?

"You're too skinny," he said at my questioning look.

I fought the urge to glance down at myself, growling, "My weight is none of your business."

That smirk was back in full force. "Are you always this feisty first thing in the morning?"

The fae, the one who had been silent all this time, stepped forward offering a plate full of food I didn't recognize. "Roasted seaweed and dried venison," he explained in a toneless voice.

I snatched it out of his hands while glaring at Lord Taran. "When I've been kidnapped? Absolutely."

I stomped off a distance, plopped on the ground and immediately dug in. I tore off a piece of the seaweed with my fangs. It was surprisingly good with a crisp, salty taste and subtle sweetness. The venison was manna from the Godlands. I couldn't remember the last time I had meat like this.

The Enforcer ordered his men to break down the camp and the tents disappeared in a flurry. When I was certain his attention was elsewhere, I glanced down at myself. My hip bones stuck out and my pants were a little looser around my waist than they should be, but I wasn't terribly skinny. With starvation running rampant through the Mortal Lands, I was considered a healthy weight by mortal standards.

I had just finished my last piece of seaweed as the horses were readied and Lord Taran beckoned me over.

"Do you require any more food?"

"No."

He nodded and handed over my gun, holsters, and a dagger.

I stared at the gold blade. Its handle was black obsidian with a snarling wolf carved into it.

"That's not mine," I said in confusion.

"I'm not returning this poor excuse for a weapon." He

pulled out my dagger and snapped it on his thigh. The gold blade broke in half. He tossed the remnants to the ground. "This," he explained, extending the second blade. "Is a taranis dagger. My House makes the best weapons in The Lands."

I stared at it, then lifted my face to his, cocking a brow.

"I might not be able to kill you with that, but I can still make you bleed."

His lips thinned into a grim line. "I hope for your sake you do not try."

Because that would be breaking the first fae law.

I snatched them from his hands, buckling the dagger sheath around my upper thigh and the gun holster around my hip. I jammed the weapons inside. Their familiar weight eased a tightness in my chest. It felt like I was missing a limb without them.

His men swung themselves into their saddles. "Finn, you are in charge while I am away," Lord Taran announced. "Scry me only in the event of an emergency."

The steward inclined his head, then steered his horse away from camp, the other fae following close behind.

"What happened to the horse I stole?" I asked. The bargain magic had snapped me back to him, but not the mount.

Lord Taran whistled sharply and both horses trotted over to him.

"I called it home," he explained, then ran a speculative eye over me. "Will your leg be able to handle the journey to Gold City?"

"Handle? Yes." Would all the jostling in the saddle be painful? Absolutely, but pain I could handle.

He frowned and said nothing else as I approached one of the horses and swung myself onto its back. The movement pulled painfully on the injured leg, but I was careful to mask my reaction. If he didn't think I could uphold my end of the bargain, he might kill me before I had a chance to kill him first.

The Enforcer mounted his horse and we started north. There was nothing to see on the ride. The landscape was barren, just a long swath of dirt occasionally interrupted by an outcrop of sickly trees. Way off in the distance, the peaks of the Fayette Mountains bit into the sky.

An hour into the journey, the constant motion of the horse began bothering my leg and the ache flared up with a vengeance.

Just three more hours until we reach Gold City.

I grit my teeth against the shooting pain and adjusted my seat in the saddle to alleviate some of the pressure. Not that it did any good.

"Let's give the horses a break," Lord Taran announced where he rode behind me.

I glanced over at him, frowning. "What are you talking about? It's barely been an hour."

Our mounts were a powerful war breed, made of muscle and intended for speed. Their black manes were braided into three cords and threaded with red strings that hung over their silky dark fur. They were even tall enough to accommodate the giant Enforcer comfortably.

They could go an entire day without rest.

"I know my horses better than you."

"Okay." Whatever. My leg needed the break anyway. I steered my horse slightly to the right, then dismounted and plopped down in the dirt, stretching out my leg. The relief of being out of the saddle was bliss.

A cork popped. Lord Taran sat down, sipping from a leather bladder. He offered me some, but I declined. He beat the cork back into the bladder with a fist and we both sat in silence as the horses got their 'rest' until the Enforcer broke it.

"You ride well. With the trains and wagons, mortals have lost that skill. Where did you learn to ride like that?"

Leaning back on my arms, I peered up at him. A light layer of dirt dusted his thick neck, blending with the swirling gray markings. His eyes appeared softer in the early light and those pretty pink lips were relaxed, not mocking, or frowning at me for once.

"Why does it matter?" I couldn't hide the suspicion in my tone. This felt like another attempt to learn how I had ended up trying to steal from him.

He smirked. "I was simply making conversation."

"Well, *don't*."

We weren't friendly companions traveling together. He had kidnapped me, threatened my life and then forced me into a bargain. We were enemies working together toward a common goal. Nothing more. Nothing less.

I rose, ready to return to my horse and hid a grimace at the uncomfortable pressure. The Enforcer's sharp gaze missed nothing, but thankfully he didn't ask any questions, returning to his horse as well.

We stopped four more times after that. I wasn't stupid. I knew what he was doing. He wasn't stopping for the horses. He was stopping for me.

Lord Taran was only concerned about my well-being because he falsely assumed I would operate less effectively finding the godstone. My worth was tied to my usefulness. Just like with the Crone. Just like with the Rogues. I had suffered many broken bones growing up. The dull throbbing in my leg was nothing new. His concern was unnecessary ... and annoying.

"We're not stopping again." I strangled the reins in my grip wishing I could do the same to his neck, then added, "I can complete this bargain with or without an injured leg if that's your worry."

He threw me a strange look before glancing away. "I'm sure you could fulfill our bargain even if you were missing both your legs, stubborn as you are," he murmured.

I took that as a compliment.

The Enforcer didn't try and stop us again and when the shining walls of Gold City came into view, I had never been happier to set eyes on the vile, greedy city.

10

Gold City was named after its walls. I marveled at the gleaming slabs of pure gold. Rumor had it, at the peak of summer, the walls created a glare strong enough to blind a person. We had arrived a month too late to discover if the rumor held any truth as summer was ending.

Mining all that gold must have taken years, but the gold also made it the safest city in the Mortal Lands. The walls kept the beasts away, leaving the citizens of Gold City protected and unaware of the horrors the rest of the mortal cities faced every full moon. It also meant they were damn picky about who they let inside.

The line for entry was a mile long as we approached. When we reached the end, I pulled my horse behind the last mortal. Lord Taran continued past.

"Where are you going?" I hissed. "This is the end of the line."

"You're welcome to wait," he tossed over his shoulder. "But I don't have the time."

Insufferable prick.

On a sigh, I followed, reasoning that if he was left to

shop for my clothes on his own, I would end up looking more ridiculous than I already did in his dress sized shirt.

A small girl with big brown eyes tugged on the sleeves of her mother as I passed. "Mama, how much longer?" The female peered down at her daughter with a smile. "Not long, baby." When the mother raised her head again, her smile had disappeared, replaced by tight lines framing her mouth. I knew what little chance they had of being allowed inside Gold City.

I stared at the little girl in her moth-eaten clothes hanging off her much too thin frame. The other mortals in line weren't any better off. Many of their bodies were near skeletal, their faces hollow and sharp. They were starving.

A gruesome image flashed through my mind; a memory of a child laying in the dirt with her stomach ripped open, some faceless beast feasting on her intestines. Nausea rolled through me, and I jerked my horse to a stop.

She was the first dead child I had ever seen. I had seen plenty since.

Starvation or beasts, either were cruel deaths.

I forced myself to continue toward the gate, keeping my gaze averted.

"Is everything alright?" Lord Taran asked as I caught up to him.

I knew my expression was just as dark as my thoughts. No, nothing was alright. "A third of the children you see in this line will be dead come the next full moon. The beasts always go for the elderly and children first. They're the easiest to kill."

I didn't even know why I was telling him. It's not like he cared. If he cared about innocent lives, he wouldn't go slaughtering them over petty offenses.

Lord Taran's jaw clenched as he stared straight ahead.

"That's what happens in the Mortal Lands while all you

powerful fae hide behind your borders like cowards," I continued.

The Enforcer had the decency to look ashamed. After a moment, he sighed. "I know you won't believe me, when I say this, but children are the most beautiful gifts. I wish I could save them, but I can't."

I laughed. The sound was saturated in judgment. He was an immortal, powerful being. All the fae lords were. I had heard stories from the Rogues of what they could do. I did not believe for one second he couldn't help if he wanted to.

I raised my voice higher than I meant to, my anger getting the best of me. "You're telling me the big bad Enforcer is powerless against the beasts?"

Lord Taran's large stature had already drawn attention. Not everyone was unfortunate enough to have seen the infamous killer in person, but the moment 'the Enforcer' slipped out of my mouth, one of the mortals gasped. Murmurs started, eyes darting our way. Even if they didn't recognize him, that name was infamous in the Mortal Lands and caused a rippling effect of fear down the line. Eyes rounded. Faces drained. Some mortals abandoned their place and fled into the dirt beyond. The rest pressed themselves as close to the city wall as they could.

Despite their obvious fear, there was an underlying anger to some of their postures. I wasn't surprised. Enforcer or not, he was fae, one of the beings that left these lands destitute and at the mercy of beasts while they hid behind their borders, squandering their powers, and demanding half of the gold the mortals needed to protect themselves.

Lord Taran shot me a reprimanding look, which I met with an unconcerned shrug. Alerting the mortals to his presence was an accident. But honestly, if I knew it would garner this kind of reaction, I would have done it on purpose. Making things harder on the Enforcer was my new form of entertainment.

"I am not here for any of you," Lord Taran's deep voice announced, but his assurance did little to ease their worry of the fae they had been programmed to fear their entire lives.

A daring soul stepped into our path, and I stared with interest at the only mortal who did not seem to fear the boogeyman.

"Fae Scum!" He palmed something, ready to launch it at the fae's head. Lord Taran cut him a look, sharp as a blade, and soon the mortal forgot his temporary courage, dropped the rotten fruit, and returned to his place in line.

The Enforcer dismissed the mortal, giving him his back as he continued toward the gates, showing just how confident he was the mortal wouldn't make a second attempt.

I stared after him. He twisted his head back when he noticed I no longer followed. "Something wrong?"

I lifted a shoulder. "Just surprised you didn't kill him is all." He had disrespected the Enforcer in front of nearly a hundred mortals.

"I don't kill needlessly."

"Whatever you need to tell yourself to sleep at night."

Lord Taran rode forward without responding. He didn't check to see if I followed this time either. I did . . . reluctantly. I hated this city.

We dismounted to address the guards. Ten manned the entrance, staring at our approach with wide eyes. Lord Taran didn't even have to open his mouth.

"En—Enforcer, Sir, what an honor. We weren't expecting your visit."

"Tell Lucinda I want a word."

The guard's fell over themselves moving out of the way to allow the Enforcer into their city. I shook my head at the ridiculousness of it all. Gold City's head was so far up the fae's asses, it was any wonder this city didn't smell of shit.

We handed our reins off to a stable boy who bowed deeply at the Enforcer before scampering off.

I glared at the gold painted cobblestone streets. My gaze narrowed further as it shifted to the surrounding buildings made of white marble stone with veins of gold. The yellow metal was everywhere I looked. The mortals bustling within the city even had it painted on their skin.

A woman walked past wearing a ridiculous gown. It had a lavender bodice, a skirt made entirely of black, glossy broberie feathers, and a matching feather hat. The dress swished elegantly over the gold street as she strutted past us. Another mortal, a male, wore a black silk suit with gold trim. Those two outfits alone were worth a year's worth of food in Mayhem.

The longer I stared, the more nauseated I felt. All this greed, so prominently on display, was disgusting. Children were starving just outside their gates.

We didn't have to wait long before a beautiful female approached, curtsying before Lord Taran. Every visible part of her body was painted in gold.

"Good morning, Sir. Lucinda is in a council meeting but will be free soon. She sent me in her place to ensure your visit to our wonderful city is a pleasant one. I am Abigail."

If I had to witness one more person kiss the Enforcer's ass, I was going to vomit.

"You know he kills your kind all the time, right? If you break a fae law in front of him, he won't hesitate to cut your head off," I said. "You don't have to be so polite."

Abigail's freckled cheeks heated beneath the gold paint. "The Enforcer is an honored guest in our city. All fae are," she said, running a disapproving eye over me. "And who might you be? I was only instructed to escort the Enforcer."

I finally understood why we had ridden here instead of Greene, which was much closer to the fae's camp. Gold City's lucrative trade agreement with the fae made it the only city in the Mortal Land's that welcomed his kind. If this were Mayhem, we would have been greeted with hostility, Enforcer or not.

"Nobody and escort away." I breezed past her, uncertain where I was headed, but I didn't care as long as it took me away from all the ass kissing.

The muscles in my right leg were tight and throbbing from riding all morning. I only managed to walk a short distance before the injured limb buckled and left me sprawled out on the city's shiny street.

Seconds later I was airborne and the Enforcer's delectable, but annoyed voice was in my ear. "Your leg is not fine."

I shoved at his chest. "Put me down. I don't need your help, you presumptive, arrogant prick."

The temptation to claw his chest, or bite him when he ignored me was great, but I remembered his warning from last night. *I like it rough.*

"No." His rumbling voice so near amped up my anger.

I punched his shoulder as hard as I could and instantly regretted it. Stinging pain swelled in my knuckles. He didn't seem to even notice I'd hit him.

Gods, what was he made out of? Stone?

"I said, put me down!"

He ignored my protests again, tightening the steely arms banded around me. "Abigail, take us to your mortal doctor."

"Of course, Sir."

Crossing my arms indignantly, I glared up at his stupidly nice jaw line and allowed him to carry me without any more protests. In truth, my leg ached fiercely, and I wasn't certain I could walk the distance on my own. At least this way, I could save a modicum of my pride and not have to ask for help.

He peered down at me, brows slanted together. "Why are you being reasonable all the sudden?" The suspicion in his tone almost made me laugh.

"Wouldn't you like to know."

He dipped his head, lips brushing my ear as he whispered, "I would. I like when you fight me."

My skin tingled where his soft lips touched it and I suppressed a shiver. Not well apparently based on the smirk the Enforcer wore when he pulled back.

"Stop flirting with me. It's weird."

He had just been threatening my life the day before and now he was being playful and flirtatious. There must have been something in his water.

Husky laughter shook his chest, soaking into me.

"I'm serious," I said.

"I know. That's why it's amusing."

No, not the water then. He was just playing games with me.

"We're here," Abigail chirped.

Thank the gods.

"Put me down."

I felt him hesitate a moment before he grunted and set me on my feet.

Abigail primly folded her hands, watching us. "I will be just outside if you need anything."

The Enforcer nodded, then pressed his palm to the middle of my back, heating my skin through the tunic. Huffing, I moved it to my arm to help steady me as I scaled the marble steps leading up to the doctor's office. I moved out of reach as soon as I stood safely outside the door.

The inside was just as ostentatious as the building's exterior. Chestnut wood paneled walls lined lush cream carpeting. Lord Taran had no issue navigating the space with its soaring, arched ceilings. Warm, natural light poured inside from the skylight window.

A female in a tight srphy skin skirt with her dark hair pulled into a tight knot on her head approached. She dipped into a small curtsy. Only her face was painted gold, which made her light brown eyes appear more striking.

That brown gaze dragged heatedly over the Enforcer with a sultry smile. "Welcome to Doctor Sutherland's office," she purred. "How may I be of assistance?"

I wrinkled my nose. Women really did throw themselves at him.

"My companion here needs her leg reset," Lord Taran stated, ignoring the female's attempts at flirtation.

Her smile fell, but she quickly slapped on a professional face. "He will be with you shortly. May I offer you any refreshments while you wait? Perhaps water bottled straight from a fae spring?"

The Enforcer glanced down at me. "Little Thief, are you thirsty?"

The female's eyes flicked to me for the first time and widened fractionally as they lingered on my talons.

"Please excuse me," she said stiffly, then rushed off, disappearing behind a door at the end of the room before either of us could answer her question.

I sighed. "Doctor Sutherland is suddenly going to find himself indisposed. I bet you ten silvers he won't treat me."

He cocked a brow. "Do you even have ten silver coins to gamble?"

"No."

The door opened and the female returned, more cautiously than before. She cleared her throat, not meeting either of our gaze's as she explained, "Doctor Sutherland sends his sincerest apologies, Sir, but a dire injury has called him away."

I stuck my palm out toward the Enforcer. He ignored it.

"Is that so?" he asked in a dangerous voice. Lord Taran drew his sword and stalked past the two of us toward the door the mortal had just come from.

The doctor's assistant blanched, realizing his intentions. "Wait! Sir! Please, that door is for staff only!"

Her gaze darted to me for help.

"Don't look at me. You and the doctor brought this on yourselves."

Any hint of politeness vanished from her face. Her expression twisted into a familiar mask of disgust as it dipped to my talons.

"No, you did this, you half-beast," she hissed, then stormed after the Enforcer.

"If you're going to insult me, at least be original about it," I called at her retreating back.

The door banged open a moment later. Lord Taran dragged out a willowy man, I assumed to be Doctor Sutherland, by the nape. The assistant appeared behind them watching the Enforcer's rough handling of her employer with wide, panicked eyes.

He shoved the male forward, then brought the tip of his sword to the back of the doctor's neck.

"If I have to watch that female limp around for one more second, I will slaughter every last mortal inside this city starting with you, you understand?"

The mortal raised his trembling arms in surrender. "Y-Yes, Sir."

Doctor Sutherland made quick work of re-breaking my leg and setting the bone correctly as the Enforcer hovered menacingly nearby. When I hopped off his examination table, there was none of the aches or pains I had grown accustomed to over the last four days.

"Thanks, doc. Been a real *pleasure*." I gave him a smartass salute before waltzing over to the door, which earned a head shake from the Enforcer, but he was smiling.

"Come, Little Thief. We need to purchase some items for our journey." He gestured for me to leave first.

"You owe me ten silvers," he whispered as I passed.

"Corthit. You cheated."

I frowned at the deserted market district. All of Gold City's shopping was housed indoors along Market Street. The half-mile stretch of stores sold every indulgence a person could think of and was the main entertainment for most of the city's upper class; yet there wasn't a soul in sight.

I peered up at the sky and saw the sun peeking through the heavy cloud cover. Market Street should still be open. Dusk was hours away.

A woman appeared in front of us at the entrance. She wore a srphy skin dress with blue and white striations that clung to her curves and a black velvet hat with white pearls encircling the brim. Her sharp brown eyes were a shade lighter than her hair streaked with white.

The woman's face and neck were painted a deep shade of gold. I assumed the deeper coloring meant the paint was less diluted and had a greater ratio of gold than the other tones I had seen.

She didn't curtsy, merely dipping her head in a slight, but respectful nod toward the Enforcer.

"Good afternoon, Lord Taran."

"Lucinda," he returned.

The newcomer turned and addressed our tour guide. Abigail had led us here after Lord Taran had expressed his great displeasure with Doctor Sutherland.

Since I had made it more than clear I could find the godstone with an injured leg, I could only assume his reaction to the doctor's behavior was out of his obligation toward my wellbeing.

It was strange that a mass-murderer would have such a strong sense of duty to protect others. The Enforcer was as complicated as he was dangerous.

"Abigail, thank you for your assistance, you may go," Lucinda said.

She nodded and left the three of us standing in the empty shopping area.

Lucinda swept an elegant hand toward the street. "I've had the market district shut down for your convenience."

Of course you did.

"Why don't you just wipe his ass while you're at it?" I huffed, rolling my eyes.

Lucinda looked aghast. "Young lady, I am the head councilor of Gold City. You will mind your language."

Lord Taran spoke before I could spew more venom. "I need to have a word with Lucinda in private. Get whatever you think we need from the market." He tossed me a pouch, then walked off with the councilor, dismissing me like I was some errand girl. Like I was just another meaningless halfling he could order around.

Anger flared, but I quickly shoved it away. There was the asshole who'd threatened my life and forced me into a bargain.

Pieces of their conversation carried over to me until they walked out of range.

"What is that ugly *thing* doing in my city?"

"The girl is not your concern."

Yanking open the pouch he had tossed me, I counted the silver pieces inside. I could buy a few of those fancy fae war horses with the contents.

I pocketed half the silver for myself before strolling down Market Street, whistling a merry tune as I pushed their conversation to the back of my mind. Technically, I wasn't stealing since the Enforcer had given me the pouch without instructions on how much I could spend.

The first shop I entered claimed to be a general store, but there was nothing general about the goods it sold. Lips puckered, I picked up a loaf of bread. It was braided and stuffed with what the sign beside it described as some sort of fae delicacy. I sniffed it and jerked back at the awful smell.

"What is this?" I waved the loaf in the air toward the store's attendant. "Why is it stuffed with foul smelling fae shit?"

The slender mortal in an apron rounded the counter and jerked the bread out of my grasp before gently returning it to its wooden shelf.

"It's called ashray tail and the only foul-smelling thing in this store is *you*."

I was too shocked by what he'd revealed to be offended. And at least his insult had been slightly original.

"You people eat ashray?" I said slowly. "As in the same water beast that electrocutes its victims under water so they drown to death?"

"They're harmless dead, but the tail still gives off little zings in your mouth. Wrap it in some lemon filling and it's phenomenal. You should really try it."

These mortals liked to shock themselves on purpose?

I screwed up my face. "Yeah, no thanks. Got any normal loaves of bread?"

"If you want to eat like the poor and desperate, you're in the wrong city, but there is a small section we like to call vermin town. It's where all the pathetic mortals and their kids we allow in our city once a year just to keep all the other cities happy. They've got a seedy little alley market. It's a real eye sore. You can't miss it."

I shot him in the foot.

Lord Taran really should have given it more thought before he returned my weapons this morning.

The mortal collapsed on the floor screaming like a banshee.

"What was that for?" he shouted trying to stem the flow of blood.

"For being shittier than a giant's asshole." I twirled my gun and reholstered it. "Too bad for you I already reached my limit of interacting with pretentious pricks for the day."

I calmly exited the store as some of the other shop attendants came outside to see what all the noise was about.

I hiked my thumb behind me. "Someone might want to call that Sutherland fellow. Guy's a bleeder."

Ignoring their horrified glances, I followed the attendant's directions and found the stretch of dilapidated buildings hidden away at the edge of the city. Rotting wood made up the buildings' structure. Unsurprisingly, the cobblestone here wasn't painted gold like the rest of the city. It was broken, weeds sprouting through the cracks. The whole area reeked of mildew and sour sweat.

I lived in better conditions back at the Rogue compound and many considered me a half-beast. This was how Gold City treated other mortals, although based on the shop attendant's little speech, the poor and desperate inside these walls were also seen as sub-human.

The alleyway market sat in the shadows between the rotting structures passing off as homes. I sucked down the fetid air, relieved there was no trace of the foreign, flowery smells that lingered on my clothes from the market district, and took in the dirty faces watching my approach.

"Anyone got some bread that won't electrocute me?"

Someone laughed. "Vera, is that you lass?"

The owner of the voice stepped out of the shadows, and I smiled at the sight of Orin's wrinkled, mean mug.

"What are you doing all the way back here?" I asked.

Occasionally, I made gold runs to the city when the Rogues were low. Orin was always one of the guards on duty when I arrived. We'd gambled together a time . . . or ten.

"Hiding."

I laughed. "How much you owe?"

"Enough."

I stared down at him thoughtfully. Orin had been a guard at Gold City's gates for years. With all those people coming and going, you pick up things, hear things you shouldn't. Orin used to bet secrets when he ran out of silvers during some of our card games.

"Come here." I hooked a finger. Orin's beady gaze turned suspicious, but when I jingled the pouch of silver, he damn near ran.

My eyes darted around, expecting the Enforcer to appear out of nowhere and strike me down for what I was about to ask, but thankfully he was nowhere in sight. "Got any idea where that looney cult, the House of Night, is hiding out these days?" I whispered.

Ryder had mentioned they were the only ones insane enough to harvest iron dust from the ore mines. I hoped that was true. They were my only way out of this bargain.

Orin reeled back. "What do ya want with them? Those crazy beast worshipping zealots are dangerous as they are loose in the head." He eyed my pouch. "But . . . if you're determined, I might."

I shook the pouch again, letting him hear all the coins clinking together. "Half of this is yours if you tell me."

His eyes narrowed. "Where'd ya get all that silver?"

"Do you really care?" I asked with a raised brow.

Orin stared a beat before answering, "There's an abandoned church about a mile west outside the city."

"What in the lands are they doing this close to the Faylands?"

That was *bold*, even for them.

"Their way of sticking it to the fae I guess." He shrugged. "They're processing iron dust right under their noses and the fae have no idea."

Well, as long as they could help me get out of the bargain with the Enforcer, I didn't care what those crazies were up to.

I handed over half the pouch as promised.

He took it, running a speculative eye over me. "Still no vest I see."

It was just a casual observation. I knew he didn't mean anything by it, but it still stung.

"I'm working on it."

Which reminded me . . .

"Can you get a message to the Rogues for me?"

Boone and Ryder needed to know what happened. They couldn't have known the weapon they sent me after belonged to the Enforcer. It was impossible to steal from the fae because of him. They would never have sent me on a fruitless mission if they had known.

Orin frowned. "Why can't you tell them yourself?"

"I just can't," I said.

"Fine, but it'll cost you."

I glared at the greedy bastard. "I just gave you enough silver to buy everything in this market."

He stared.

"You Son of Balor," I growled, jerking open the pouch and slapping a handful of silver coins into his palm.

"What's your message?"

"Tell Boone and Ryder that things didn't go as planned, but I've got the situation under control, and I'll be home for my vest soon."

He pocketed the coins. "I'll be sure to let them know."

Dismissing that conniving opportunist, I perused the market and purchased some dry food for the journey and a new bedroll for myself. There weren't any clothes or fabrics being sold which meant I would have to return to Market Street. I scowled at the thought.

The gratitude and relief on the vendors' faces when I paid made me feel even better about spending the Enforcer's silver here. The food I purchased wasn't as fresh as the other market, but the food in Mayhem wasn't either.

There was one more thing I needed.

As much fun as it would be, I knew I couldn't antagonize the Enforcer into tying me up every night, and I refused to admit to him I needed chains in the first place.

I spotted a length of chain wrapped around some hand carved chairs to protect them from thieves. The chains weren't ideal. There were no cuffs, so I would have to secure the links directly around my skin, which would only add to the mountain of scars; but, seeing as this was the only set of chains I had spotted so far, these would have to do.

"How much for the chains?"

A large shadow stepped into the alley before the vendor could answer, causing the mortals nearby to shrink back from their tables. I turned just as the Enforcer strolled into the alley and growled in frustration.

His timing was total shit.

"Little Thief, I do not appreciate having to track you down."

Well, I didn't give a banshee's wail what he appreciated.

"Oh good. You can carry all this crap." I lugged the items I had bought over to him and dumped them into his arms.

He frowned down at my purchases. "You bought this here? Why? Market Street sells all these items, and they are much better quality. Was the silver I gave you not enough?"

I stuck a hand on my hip. "If you don't like the way the *ugly thing* shops, do it yourself next time," I said, but he wasn't paying attention.

He was busy untying one of the bundles of cloth. "Little Thief," he growled. "This bread is moldy."

I rolled my eyes. A little mold never hurt anyone. I snatched the bread out of his hands, pulled off the end with the small black spots, and tossed the moldy remnants to the ground. "There, you big baby. All fixed."

He shifted through the rest of the cloth bundled food, grunting, "This is all inedible." Lord Taran dumped everything in his arms to the ground save for the bedroll.

I stared down at the piles of cheese, smoked meat, and bread sitting in the street, now covered in dirt. Hot, molten anger licked through my veins the longer I looked.

Jerking forward, I made to snatch up the discarded food before the insects got to it, but the Enforcer grabbed my wrist before I could.

My head snapped up.

"Leave it," he ordered.

I ripped my arm away, leveling him with a nasty glare. "Are you serious? Half the Mortal Lands is starving, and you just threw away two weeks' worth of perfectly good food."

"Return the pouch," he demanded. "We will go back to Market Street."

There was only a quarter of the silver he had originally given me left. He wanted it back?

Fine.

I lobbed it at his face.

The Enforcer had not anticipated the movement, the arrogant prick assuming I would obediently obey. Not even his lightning-fast instincts were quick enough to avoid it. The pouch hit its mark, smacking him in the cheek. He didn't move, didn't flinch.

Only the sounds of coins clinking together as the pouch landed in the street could be heard in the silent alley.

"*You* go back to Market Street." I spewed the words like srphy venom.

My temper fizzled out as soon as it registered that I stood only a few feet away from a lethal giant, and I had thrown something at his face. His gaze shot down at where the pouch landed, then slammed back into mine.

The alleyway suddenly seemed too small to contain his massive frame. Muscles swelled, stretching out the ink on his arms. Tendrils of black leaked into his eyes, swirling with the silver. His face sharpened into something predatory.

Time stretched into an uncomfortable, heated silence.

I tensed, ready for an attack.

He caught the subtle movement and tore his face away with a harsh exhale. When he looked at me again, he had wrangled whatever I had seen peeking out of his gaze under control.

Rattling sounded behind us, the vendor choosing the absolute worst time to fulfill my chain's request. My face burned.

Understanding flitted across the Enforcer's face and I knew, I just knew, he had seen the scars on my wrist. Dark shame twisted through my chest like a poison-tipped arrow. I would rather he attacked me than look at me the way he was looking at me right now.

I pulled my gun and aimed it at him, needing him to leave. "Go."

The command ripped away the pity in his gaze and hardened it. "Are you threatening me?"

I cocked back the hammer. "I sure the fuck am."

In two long strides, the Enforcer loomed in front of me with the gun barrel pressed against his chest.

"I think you've forgotten who I am," he said when I made no move to shoot him. "Don't make me remind you."

I hesitated a second before I dropped the gun, self-preservation kicking in.

He pushed a key into my hand. "That's where we're staying. Be in your room before nightfall."

The Enforcer leaned in close, whispering, "This is the second time you've pulled a gun on me. There won't be a third." He left the alleyway without another word.

12

The House of Night appeared abandoned. Orin's directions had taken me a mile outside the city to an old steepled church. Its paint was faded and peeling. Part of the roof had collapsed in on itself. Every window was broken, or missing, wind whistling through the open spaces.

Mortals had lost faith in the Gods long ago when all their prayers for protection against the beasts went unanswered century after century. These structures, once symbols of faith and hope, were now nothing more than rotting specters across the Mortal Lands.

I eyed the church, suspicious Orin had either lied, or I had misheard his directions. There wasn't a soul in sight. There wasn't anything in sight beyond the church and the surrounding miles of dirt. I was tempted to keep riding, but I could already feel the bargain magic tethering me to the Enforcer stretched taut. A silent warning not to go further, or he would snap me back to him before I got what I came for.

He had disappeared after giving me a curfew and a key to one of Gold City's premier luxury inns. The expensive accommodation had undoubtedly been secured by the city's head councilor. As for the curfew, I had no intention of obeying. I'd arrive at the inn when I damn well pleased. I would be there before we left for the Deadwood Forest and that's all that mattered.

I had cleaned off the discarded food as best I could and distributed it among the mortals waiting outside the walls. Too embarrassed by my interaction with the Enforcer, I had abandoned the chains and mission for new clothes and come straight here.

In hindsight, pulling a gun on him hadn't been the brightest idea, but I couldn't stand the pity I had seen on his face. I was ugly and scarred. Cursed. I knew that. But I didn't need anyone feeling sorry for me over it, least of all him.

While he sulked, I had borrowed a horse—not one of the ones we had brought with us as I knew that would draw suspicion—and rode to this church.

Set against the dark clouds rolling in, the derelict building appeared even more ominous. The wind howled, kicking up clouds of dirt. The fresh, earthy smell just before rain sat heavy in the air. I greedily inhaled the scent. It was one of the few good memories from my time in the Deadwood Forest. That smell, followed by the soothing patter of fat rain drops hitting the dirt, were two of my favorite things.

A strong wind gust threw stinging bits of dirt into my eyes. Gold City was too far north, nestled at the base of Fayette Mountains, to suffer the great, destructive sandstorms the cities along the Red Desert experienced. But this part of the Mortal Lands was infamous for its nasty storms with hail the size of fists. Being caught out in one could be deadly.

I couldn't risk staying out here in the open for too long with only the rotting church to take shelter in. A crow landed on the roof. It cocked its head, staring down at me, then cawed loudly. The ominous sound sent a shiver trip-ping down my spine.

Then if that wasn't creepy enough, the church door opened suddenly. No one was on the other side.

At first, I chalked it up to the wind, but if that were the case, the door would have flown open, banging against the rafters, not standing perfectly still like some unseen force held it open.

I peered up at the crow. "I guess that means I'm supposed to go inside."

The crow cawed again and flew off.

I hesitated a moment before moving to the two steps leading up to the door. Unlike the rest of the church, they were made of stone and besides being smoothed down from the wind, remained in good condition.

On the top step, I peered inside the doorway. The church's interior was dark. More so with the incoming storm shading the sky. I couldn't make out more than the silhou-ettes of pews and some other discarded furniture.

A candle or torch would come in handy right now. I was unsure where to step, certain the inside of the church was just as decayed as the outside. Extending one foot forward, I tested if the floorboards would support my weight. The wood buckled immediately, and my boot sank right through it.

I leapt back gripping the door frame as a candle appeared.

It hovered mid-air in front of my face. When I went to reach for it, the light moved just out of my grasp. I swiped for it again with the same result.

"Magical asshole candle," I grumbled. "What good are you, if I can't use you?"

The candle touched down on the floorboard beside the hole I had just created. I peered through it. The space below was dark, but I could just make out the glint of sharpened steel. Spikes. There were spikes down there. If I had fallen through, I'd be impaled.

I jerked away. This place was booby trapped.

Who in the dark night were these people?

Little was known about the radicalists other than their extreme views. They operated in the shadows. Once, I had caught a glimpse of one of them while riding through the desert with Ness at night; a lone figure wearing a skull mask and a black robe, but the most disturbing was their hands. Curved bone claws stuck out of their sleeves where fingers should have been.

Just thinking about it made me shudder.

The candle plunked down on another set of floorboards, beyond the death trap. Then it returned to its position, hovering just out of reach.

Warily, I eyed the piece of wood before glancing at the candle.

"How do I know this isn't another booby trap?"

It slammed down on the wood with a loud bang. The wood held. Okay then.

I stretched my leg to the board the candle had hit and tested its sturdiness just in case. It held my weight. I stepped over the fresh hole in the floor onto it.

The candle lowered to another set of boards on my right. I tested them, still not trusting the inanimate object's guidance, then moved to the next. This process continued until I reached the pulpit set on top of a platform at the back of the space.

Some witch must have spelled the light to direct people safely through the church—or to their deaths. It was a neat and disturbing party trick. I don't know why the Nighters were allowing me into their den, but I was grateful they were.

I frowned as the candle touched down on the pulpit, not understanding these new instructions. Obviously, I wasn't supposed to stand on it like the floorboards, but the candle had brought me to it for a reason.

The candle rose and plunked back down on the pulpit with a soft thud.

"Am I seriously getting an attitude from a candle right now?" I shook my head at the absurdity of the situation. This is what I got for seeking out a beast worshipping cult. A creepy church and a saucy magic candle.

"Keep it up and I'll blow you out," I warned.

It didn't move after that, but I could *feel* its impatience. I ignored it and crouched down to examine the pulpit. I teetered it to one side, which wasn't easy—the thing weighed a ton—and discovered some sort of cellar door underneath it.

I kicked the pulpit out of the way, laughing as the candle nearly toppled over with it. In return, it flew too close to my face and singed some of my hair.

"Dick," I muttered, then pried open the door and peered down into the darkness.

"We've been waiting for you," a voice called from the near-pitch black.

I startled back as cold fingers skittered down my spine. The speaker's emotionless tone set my nerves on edge, and I swallowed hard, questioning every step that had brought me here. Did I really need iron dust to kill the Enforcer? Maybe I could—

"Come," it said.

Fuck it. I had come all this way. It would be a waste to turn back now.

"There is a ladder directly to your left," the flat voice continued.

I pawed blindly through the air until my palm

connected with something solid. My hand slid lower and felt the smooth surface of a wooden pole and the rung attached to it. I turned, entering the cellar legs first and carefully descended into the dark.

The trap door slammed shut as soon as my boots hit the floor, sending the space into total darkness.

Panic immediately set in. My heart bashed into bone like a battering ram and my whole body shook. The dark and I were *not* friends.

I forced shallow breaths through my nose. This was not the time to show fear.

"You there?" I asked, careful to mask the tremor in my voice.

"Yes." The sound of their voice, as cold and unfeeling as it was, was enough to calm my nerves knowing I wasn't alone in the dark.

I curled my hand around my gun. The feel of it steadied me. "Got a light?"

"Hold on to my shoulder."

The toneless voice sounded in my ear, and I jerked away hissing, "Keep your creepiness out of my personal space."

"Very well. Your hand?"

Slowly, I extended one hand while keeping the other on my gun.

Something cold and hard touched me and my stomach rolled. They were wearing those bone claws. My hand was lifted and placed on top of something firm, but silky to the touch. It didn't feel like any of the course clothing material I was familiar with, probably a robe.

Applying a firm pressure, I made certain the figure felt the threat of the talons I could easily slash across their throat.

There wasn't a single light to guide our way, but the Nighter navigated the inky darkness with ease. At one point,

I reached out to run my hand along one of the walls. Rough stone scraped against my palm telling me we were in an underground tunnel.

As we walked, low, vicious animal growls could be heard in the distance. A shrill scream sent chills over my skin.

"What in the lands was that?" I whispered to my guide.

"They are contained. You are safe," the voice assured me, but I didn't feel very safe.

"What's *they*?"

The voice didn't answer, and a cold ball of dread formed in my stomach. Everything about this felt wrong and unsettling, like I had walked into some nightmarish labyrinth. If I knew of any other way to get my hands on some iron dust, I would have turned right then and ran back the way I came.

These fanatics believed the bloodthirsty creatures locked up in the south were Balor's creations and worshipped them as gods. The Nighters blamed the fae for the beast's imprisonment, which made their hatred for the fae run deeper than most. Nighters were the only ones ballsy enough to deal in iron dust and risk the fae's wrath.

The Nighter pulled to a stop, and I heard muffled humming on my right. A soft click, like the turning of a knob, and the low chanting doubled in volume.

"She's here," that toneless voice announced, and the sound abruptly cut off.

The accompanying quiet held a sinister weight like I had just interrupted a ritual sacrifice. The hairs on the back of my neck rose. I couldn't see anything in the yawning pitch black. Maybe *I* was the sacrifice.

"Excellent," a cultured, masculine voice with a slight lilt to it cut through the silence. "Light some candles for our guest."

A dozen flames flickered to life at once and I stared into a space similar to the church above, but with less dust and rot. The tension swelling in my bones eased and I exhaled slowly through my nostrils. There was no sacrificial altar.

Pews lined an expansive room carved out of stone. Stuffed into the wooden benches were robed figures wearing beast skulls. Some had crescent shaped horns attached that cast eerie shadows against the walls.

One of the masked figures stood behind a pulpit. He wore the largest skull. It had to be from a failin. A red robe covered his broad frame.

They all watched me with an unnatural stillness, dark eyes peering out of bone.

"I came for—"

"I know what you came for," the speaker behind the pulpit said. He stepped off the dais, his red robe flowing behind him like a river of blood. The speaker walked down the aisle splitting the rows of pews in half and stopped a few feet away. "You want to kill the Enforcer."

Brows tipping together, I asked, "How could you possibly know that?"

"Lord Balor has blessed me with his power of sight."

I hid the skepticism from my face. This Nighter had a few loose screws, if he thought he was some kind of omnipotent being, or maybe he just wanted his congregation of crazies to believe he was.

I bet he had spies in Gold City that informed him who my companion was, and he had put two and two together. If he was able to convince this room full of people to believe his insane teachings, he had to be at least somewhat intelligent.

He extended a hand, wearing those curved bone claws over his fingers. Seeing them up close made me shudder. In his palm sat a glass vial. Its silver filaments sparkled in the low candlelight.

Iron dust.

135

This one little vial wouldn't find the godstone, but it would solve my most immediate problem.

I tried to reach for it, but the Nighter snapped his hand shut.

Idiot.

Of course he wasn't going to just give it to me. There was a price. There was *always* a price.

"If you start down this path, there is no going back," he warned. "All ends lead to death."

"Death is kind of the point," I said dryly, glancing briefly at his masked face. "What's the cost?"

There was a flash of teeth. I could have sworn they were pointed.

"*This.*" He turned to his congregation. "Seize her! Let her serve as a test for our brethren."

Masked figures swarmed me. Hands shackled my arms before I could reach for my weapons.

I was shoved to my knees. I tried to sink my fangs into the closest set of arms and recoiled as my teeth hit something hard. It felt like biting into stone. Mocking laughter followed.

Were they wearing armor under their robes?

I snarled and thrashed in their grip, but there were too many hands holding me.

"Be still. It will be over quick," one of them instructed.

"You're going to be dead by the time this is—"

The threat died in my throat as a robed figure appeared leading an aibeya. They were the most humanoid of the beasts, appearing as a female with long auburn hair obscuring her face. Behind her she dragged a massive harp. The sound of it scraping over the floor set my teeth on edge.

My eyes rounded. Is that what those sounds were earlier? Beasts? They were keeping beasts here? These people were out of their damn minds. I didn't want to be a part of whatever this 'test' was.

"I don't want the iron dust anymore," I said frantically. "Just let me go."

"You have nothing to fear," the leader said. "We just need to confirm our methods worked."

Pure terror shot through me.

I *was* a sacrifice.

I kicked out one of my legs, but the angle was awkward with me kneeling, and it didn't connect with anything. I threw my head back as hard as I could next. It slammed into someone's groin. They grunted in pain.

Hands snatched my hair and wrenched my head back. More hands grabbed me. I was pinned in place.

"Don't try that again," a voice snarled. "We're stronger than you."

The aibeya moved closer.

My heart slammed into a violent race.

This is when I die.

The monstrous thing inside me woke. An ancient, furious voice hissed through my mind.

Let. Me. Go.

The Nighter's imprisoning me leapt away like I'd burned them. They stared in bewilderment. There wasn't time to question it. I leapt to my feet and barreled forward, taking the leader by surprise. I slammed my fist into his mask. It cracked from the impact. I ripped the iron dust from his hand as he stumbled, then bolted down the pews in the other direction.

"Stop her!" he shouted, but no one did as I sprinted toward the door. I charged through it into the darkness beyond.

Yelling and footfalls sounded behind me as my heart clamored in my chest. I raced through the dark without a clue where I was going. I couldn't see a thing. I had no idea which direction the trap door was.

There was an impatient tug on the bargain tether, and I wanted to scream with relief.

Yes! Pull me to you.

The pull sharpened into a jerking sensation. I recoiled at the lash of pain.

"We'll be seeing each other very soon," the leader's cold voice rang out in the darkness just as I was ripped from the Nighter's den. "Do make his death painful."

13

I landed ass first on a cold floor inside a bathing chamber. Breath sawed out of my lungs. I quickly shoved the iron dust into my boot, then bent over, clutching my chest. That had been too close. If I hadn't managed to escape . . .

How *had* I escaped?

I shook my head at myself. Nope. Examining the how meant opening the box and I didn't think I would ever be ready for that. I was just grateful to be out of that place.

Giving a cursory glance around the room, I tried to figure out why the Enforcer had brought me here. Gold tiled walls framed a bathing pool with a fountain at its center. Purple foam and suds covered the water smelling heavily of lavender.

This was a nice change in scenery from the dank, dark Nighter hideout I had just come from. Gooseflesh broke out over my neck and arms just thinking of the hair-raising interaction.

We'll be seeing each other very soon.

Gods, I hoped not.

The pool rippled and I scrambled back as a figure swam

underwater toward me. They stopped near the steps and surfaced.

A delicious expanse of naked, tattooed flesh rose from the water and all logical thought fled. Rivulets of water dripped down, following the lines of hard muscle.

My thighs clenched.

I wanted to lick the bath water running down those abs.

If I peered hard enough, I could see below the water to his—

"I told you to return by nightfall." The deep rumble of the Enforcer's aggravated voice pulled me from my lustful thoughts. At the back of my mind, I had recognized who I was admiring, but for a moment, I hadn't cared. It was a damn shame that all that rippling muscle belonged to him.

I tore my gaze away from the water and focused on his face. He crossed his arms over his chest with a flinty stare. He was still miffed about earlier. Too bad. He wasn't getting an apology for pulling a gun on him.

"Where were you?" he demanded.

Plotting your death.

At least that answered the question of what exactly he could sense through the bargain bond. He could obviously sense how far I was from him, but not where I was.

"Went for a ride. I hate this greedy, gold painted city."

I would try and catch Orin before we left to tell him about the horse I accidentally abandoned outside the church.

"Is that why you spent all my silver on inedible food?" Annoyance flared in his gaze. "As a form of rebellion?"

Yes, he was definitely still upset about what happened in the alley.

Well, so was I.

All my earlier indignation came roaring back and I rose from the tile, hands clenched at my sides. The Enforcer might be nice to look at, but everything else about him was repulsive.

"Or maybe you're just a spoiled, entitled brat. That food I bought would be considered *fresh* where I come from. Have you actually spent any time in the Mortal Lands, beside your little pop-up appearances to murder innocents, or find your next fuck?"

The Enforcer rested his arms on the edge of the pool and stared up at me, unperturbed. "I don't find them, they find me," he corrected.

I scoffed. The arrogance.

"And," he continued, "your concern seems odd considering you shot a mortal in the foot this afternoon."

He heard about that, huh?

"I care about the kids. Less and less they get the chance to grow up and become adults like that snooty shop attendant I shot. And what little life they get to live is awful. Plagued by beasts or starvation. They deserve better. They deserve to be protected."

Lord Taran's eyes tightened. He stared at me in silence for so long, I didn't think he would respond.

"To answer your question, no, I haven't spent much time south of our borders," he finally admitted. "Seeing that line of mortals waiting outside the city . . . that was the first time I had seen how awful things had become."

And yet he had still done nothing to help.

A desperate twitch started in my hands. The iron dust was so close, tucked away in my boot, but even naked and weaponless in the pool, the Enforcer wasn't as vulnerable as he appeared.

His name struck fear into the mortals for a reason, and I hadn't forgotten what I'd witnessed in the alley, the way his face had transformed after I'd hit him with the pouch. Something dark hid behind that gaze.

I finally had the last piece I needed to get out of this bargain, but it would take careful planning to kill him when the time was right. I stormed into the next room before my temper made me reveal my hand prematurely.

"There's something on the bed for you," he called out, which I ignored.

Of course, Lucinda had given Lord Taran the largest room known to mortals, but I had already guessed that since the room came with its own pool sized bath. The lavender scent from the water suffused this area.

Crystal chandeliers, gold gilded furniture, and marble flooring decorated the three adjoining suites outside the bathing chamber.

Everything dripped in opulence. I couldn't stomach looking at it anymore and moved over to one of the bay windows. Rain pelted the fogged glass. I swiped the surface and peered out the clearing. Lightning streaked across the dark sky. A thunderclap followed, shaking the room with its explosive boom.

At least the bargain magic saved me from riding during this storm. That poor horse though. I prayed the borrowed animal had found shelter somewhere and wasn't stuck out in the open.

My heart squeezed thinking of Ness. This was the longest we had ever been apart. As soon as this business with the godstone was finished, I'd scour the Mortal Lands for her.

Another flash of lightning lit up the darkened city below. This inn had to be several stories high. I could see the outline of the walls and gate in the distance. The line of waiting mortals had been surprisingly short when I snuck out to the church. I bet the incoming storm had chased them away.

I hoped it passed through and there would be clear skies

for the rest of the journey. We already had to contend with bloodthirsty beasts and the Crone in the Deadwood Forest; having to make the entire trek with rain and mud would make the journey downright miserable.

Being in the Enforcer's company would make me plenty miserable all on its own.

"What do you think?"

I startled at Lord Taran's voice, turning away from the window. I hadn't heard him come in. He had a bath towel wrapped around his waist. My eyes caught on the tattoo I had seen from a distance back inside the tent.

I am the sword and shield.

The cursive was tattooed in black ink below his collar bone. The gray whorls lining his throat and branching down to his chest framed but didn't obscure the lettering as they flowed around it and covered the rest of his body.

"Well?" he prompted.

"If you want an ego boost, you can ask anyone else in this city."

His lips quirked. "I was asking about the chains."

I cleared my throat and haughtily lifted my chin, refusing to be embarrassed. "Right."

He had said there was something on the bed for me. My gaze darted to the monstrous piece of furniture swallowing the room. It was large enough to fit twelve people, or three of him, and covered in various bundles, probably the 'edible' food he had purchased from Market Street.

I spotted a pile of metal. The chains sitting on the bed were not the same ones from the market. The links were thicker and made of a stronger material. My eyes slid to the cuffs at the end of the chains, and I huffed out a quiet laugh.

There were pink fuzzy cuffs for my wrists and ankles.

I glanced back to the Enforcer. "Where did you find these? The brothel?"

That's where he'd gone off to after our argument. I remembered Dolly's words. 'He fucks like a beast.'

An image of him with a brothel worker flashed through my mind. His strong, tattooed hands gripping her hips. His big cock hammering into her with his face twisted in pleasure.

Gods, I want that to be me.

I blinked, startled. Where did that come from?

I was literally just out getting something that could kill him. Sex with the Enforcer should have been the last thing on my mind.

"Will they work for whatever purpose . . ." his words trailed off, expecting me to fill in the answer.

I refused to look at him, gazing back out the rain-streaked window. My eyes were the color of lilacs freshly bloomed in spring. Gold filaments ringed the pupil. They were unnatural but striking. If I had never seen a beast before, I might even consider them beautiful.

My bow lips were lush and pink, but as soon as I smiled and the rows of dagger like teeth showed, the beauty of my lips was lost to the terrifying display in my mouth. I didn't bother glancing down at my talons. There was nothing beautiful about hands that ended in three-inch, black razor-sharp claws.

The silver hair cascading down my shoulders, stopping just below my breasts, was the only redeeming feature I had. It wasn't enough to overshadow the rest though.

What kind of a person slept in chains? Monsters did.

I could see the Enforcer's reflection too. He stared impassively.

"When did you see the scars?" I asked his reflection. I

should have put it together sooner when he asked about my lack of a fae brand.

"When I first found you."

He fell silent. Waiting.

Rain peppered the glass. I tracked the droplets as they fell. "Go on. I know you want to ask."

He lifted his chin toward the bed. "There's a cloak and new clothes there for you too," he said, then disappeared into one of the other suites. I watched him walk away in the window with a confused expression. Lord Taran never reacted the way I expected him to. He was unpredictable and that would make him even harder to kill.

Leaving the window, I found the cloak he mentioned first. The fabric felt buttery soft under my fingers, and unlike my cloak lost in the explosion, it had a fur-lined hood to keep my face warm.

"Why purple?" I asked when Lord Taran returned a moment later. He had dried off and changed into a loose pair of breeches, but still no shirt.

"It matches your eyes."

I looked at him quizzically, then back to the cloak. It was a pale violet—the exact same shade as my eyes.

I had pulled a gun on him and in return he'd gone and bought me this.

A foreign feeling knocked around in my chest as I stared at the cloak. My skin tightened over my bones, buzzing unpleasantly with an insatiable itch. I didn't know what this strange emotion was, but it was disturbing and left me desperate to scratch off my own skin.

"Return it," I demanded, spinning on him.

I didn't want his cloak. Or this weird attraction. I wanted to be rid of him altogether.

"I can purchase it in another color if that is your issue."

Where was the male who had threatened to kill me? The one who allowed Lucinda to insult me?

"Return them both," I snapped. "We both know if you didn't need me to find the godstone, I would be dead already. I can do that cold and with chains that scar."

"You're under my protection for the duration of the bargain. I won't allow you to suffer unnecessarily."

But I needed him to. This was supposed to be a simple transaction. Help him find the godstone and I get to live. His strange thoughtfulness wasn't part of the deal. It muddied the waters, made this arrangement seem like more than it was.

He was just using me like everyone else. I had to remember that.

"I don't *want* or *need* your protection," I snapped.

"I know you don't, but it's yours anyway."

He stared patiently as that knocking rattled my chest harder and my skin stretched unbearably tight. I was seconds away from crawling out of it. I needed it to stop.

"You're a monster. You murder innocent children in cold blood," I growled. "I need to be protected from *you*."

My words hit their mark. His stare flattened and that knocking eased. A relieved exhale stretched my ribs. This version of him was familiar. This I could handle. It still wasn't enough though. I wanted to rattle him the way he rattled me, so I drove the knife deeper.

"I know you have night terrors. Tell me. Do the faces of all the innocents you've slaughtered haunt you?" I whispered. "Can you still hear their screams?"

Lord Taran flinched, glancing away.

Guilt lashed through my stomach, but it was too late to turn back now. I went in for the kill.

"You are *disgusting*."

The set of his shoulders turned rigid. He remained

146

motionless for several moments. Abruptly, his gaze snapped back to mine, wearing an unexpected grin. It was wicked, promising a thousand dirty things.

Confusion swiftly followed. Then desire.

"Am I?" He whispered and prowled forward, attempting to back me up to the bed. I refused to move, which put us chest to chest.

He lowered his head. His soft lips grazed the shell of my ear. I shivered.

"I'm not returning anything, and if you argue with me about it again, I'll use those chains to tie you up and fuck the stubborn right out of you."

I licked my lips, shaking my head. "I'd rather fuck a beast."

He took a deep breath, then smirked. "I can smell what a dirty little liar you are."

"I can't lie."

He pressed his nose into the hollow of my neck, took a deep breath, and groaned. The sound sent heat spiraling through me.

"Did you know fae's nasal cavities are more sensitive than any other beings?" he asked, nuzzling my neck. "We can pick up on hundreds of scents no other creatures can." His breath whispered over my skin and my stomach clenched.

Shove him away you idiot!

I swatted that pesky voice away, too absorbed in the feel of his lips on my neck. He licked the shell of my ear and I bit down on a moan. My body was stretched taut as a bow, eager for him to put his hands on me. I balled my hands into fists to stop myself from touching him first.

He bit my neck. Just a teasing graze of teeth. This time I couldn't stop the moan spilling from my lips. I tilted my head to give him better access. He took it, lightly sucking on my skin.

Fuck.

"More," I whispered.

He pulled away and I stumbled back a step.

Gone was the wicked grin. In its place was a cold stare.

"I can smell your arousal," he said in a callous tone. "You might find everything about me loathsome, but your body doesn't."

I glared as heat suffused my cheeks. "You don't know what you're talking about."

He stared for a long minute before shaking his head. "Your room is next door," he said. "Get some sleep. We've got a long journey ahead of us."

I left his room, puzzled by our interaction. He seemed almost . . . hurt by my rejection. Even more confusing was the guilt I felt.

This would be a long journey indeed.

14

The storm followed us east from Gold City. Leaning back in the saddle, I tilted my head toward the sky. Directly above, it was clear blue, but in the distance, dark, heavy clouds loomed. We would ride into a nasty storm later.

Nothing to be done about it now. The Deadwood Forest was a day's ride from where Gold City sat near the Fayland border. By the time we reached our destination, it would be dusk and pouring rain.

"Once we reach the forest, how long until we find the Crone?" the Enforcer asked.

This was the first time he had spoken to me since our argument the night before. We had left at dawn, riding in silence. I wore the cloak he had bought for me. It was made of a thick material that kept me warm and comfortable in the chilly climate. I also wore some of my new wardrobe.

He had purchased far more tunics, pants, and undergarments than I would need, in exactly the right style and size.

The purchases were irritatingly thoughtful. He had taken time to carefully select each one based on what he had seen me wearing when he'd first kidnapped me. I couldn't understand why he went through the effort. The Rogues couldn't even remember my birthday.

I almost apologized for how I had reacted to his kindness. Then I recalled how in the short time since I'd met him, he'd kidnapped me, forced me into a bargain, and threatened to kill me, and I'd beaten back that idiotic urge with a fist.

All those barbs I'd thrown at him had been true. Just because he had done *one* nice thing didn't change who he was, or what he had done.

As far as the attraction went, I could admit I was tempted to see if his skills in bed lived up to the rumors— what hot blooded female wouldn't be—but that was a line I wasn't willing to cross.

I had a mission. The iron dust was hidden away in my saddlebag. All I had to do was find the best opportunity to sprinkle it onto some of the ridiculous food he'd purchased in Gold City, and I'd be rid of him. Then there would be no more of the confusing feelings he stirred.

I would be doing The Lands a favor. No one would have to fear for their lives anymore. The Enforcer's reign of terror would end, and I would be free to find the godstone and earn a vest.

Twisting in my saddle, I glanced back to where Lord Taran rode and explained, "We can't bring the horses. We'll need to go on foot, so about four days there and four days back."

He frowned at the mention of making the journey through the woods on foot. "Why not?"

"If a beast doesn't eat them, the Crone will."

He grimaced, then his eyes sharpened on me. "How is it you know so much about her?"

I squirmed in my saddle. Gods, I really hated his questions. The Rogues never pried. I had not fully appreciated their lack of interest until now. With them, I could hide in the shadows. I was comfortable there. The Enforcer was attempting to shine a light on the parts of myself I was desperate to keep in the dark.

"I spent some time with her," I said offhandedly.

"Next time try meeting my eyes and I might believe you."

I flung my gaze to his face. "I have a better idea. Stay out of my business."

"No."

"You're infuriating."

"Sometimes."

I rolled my eyes and focused straight ahead, determined to ignore his presence for the rest of the ride.

Eventually we reached the brewing clouds; the landscape darkened prematurely from their shadow. Dusk was still an hour off. Thunder rumbled in the distance and lightning bolts cracked across the sky in short bursts of light.

The forest's tree line became visible on the horizon just as the air turned heavy with ozone and the first drops of rain fell. The light drizzle grew in volume until fat water droplets hit us.

I nudged my horse into a gallop, racing toward the woods several hundred yards off.

The forest's canopy wouldn't protect us if this storm turned deadly, but it would provide partial shelter from the rain. Hooves pounded the ground alerting me that the Enforcer wasn't far behind.

We slowed once we reached the forest's threshold. The scent of decay hit me first. All the fallen leaves were rotting, being consumed by the forest, and returned to the earth.

Thick, gnarled trees jutted from the soil like arms; trunks contorted at odd angles in a bid for sunlight. Their bark was the same gray as a tombstone, which is where the forest's name came from. With their black leaves, the woods appeared to be one lifeless burial ground except for the various trails and prints saturating the mud from all the animals who had fled to seek shelter from the rain.

Part of the Cold River running down from the Fayette Mountains cut through the forest. The body of water emptied into the Te Sea, allowing water beasts to swim upstream on full moons. The river was teeming with both fish and beasts, but also served as a divider. The smarter animals stayed to the east of the river—the side we were currently on—while the west was largely where the air beasts nested and hunted.

Thunder cracked overhead like a whip, uncoiled. My horse whinnied. Another reminder of how much I missed my beloved mare. Ness wasn't afraid of anything.

The rain turned violent, beating at the canopy overhead until even the leaves couldn't withstand the force. Rain pelted down on us harder and harder until our visibility diminished to our horses' heads.

"We need shelter!" Lord Taran shouted over the din of the storm.

"There's a cave a mile from here," I called out and guided my horse in that direction. The storm would only grow stronger as the sun set, and we did not want to be caught out in the open during the night where the rain made it impossible to see what lingered in the shadows.

A bolt of lightning lit up the entire forest, briefly illuminating the woods. Thunder boomed overhead, so close it was deafening.

Mud splashed beneath me, splattering my pant legs as my horse galloped through the torrential downpour. Branches clawed at my face and arms, the rain making it difficult to see ahead. Swiping the watery film off my eyes, I peered around for any landmarks to orient myself.

I spotted a familiar thin trunk that looped around itself

before shooting up to the canopy. As a child, I had always been fascinated by its odd shape when I passed it romping around the woods.

The cave wasn't far.

Rain sluiced down my face, blurring everything in sight. I urged my horse blindly forward, guided by memory.

Something hard and cold crashed into my head. I rubbed the injured spot as I glanced up in time to witness a torrent of hail. If we didn't reach the cave soon, we'd be pummeled unconscious by those balls of ice.

I forced my horse into a run, flinging cold mud all over my face and clothes.

Finally, the rocky overhang marking the cave's entrance came into view. I jerked my horse to a stop right outside the cave's large maw and dismounted before leading it inside.

Hot, musty air struck me, like a drunken mortal's breath, followed by smells of mud and clay. The front of the cave was high and narrow, but it opened into a comfortably sized chamber. At the back, it branched out into smaller channels, but I had no idea where they led.

I guided my horse to the edge of the main chamber and placed several rocks on the reins to keep the animal from bolting into the dangerous storm. Lord Taran followed closely behind and did the same.

As I passed him returning to the front, I couldn't help admiring the way his damp tunic clung to his body. I could see the outline of his abdominal muscles well enough to count each one.

When I lifted my head, I caught him staring at my wet clothes just as intensely. I cleared my throat and continued to the front.

The toll of riding through the rain registered. The temperature had dropped considerably since entering the forest. I shuddered, soaked to the bone. The drenched cloak

I wore was doing more harm than good at this point. I flung it off and wrapped my arms around myself as I conjured visions of a fire to distract from the chill racking my body.

Lord Taran appeared, and though he was just as wet, he seemed unaffected by the cold. He frowned down at my curled, shivering form. "You're freezing. Go change out of those wet clothes while I get a fire started."

For once, I listened, too tired and cold to muster any indignation at being ordered around.

I returned to the back of the cave and retrieved a fresh set of clothes from one of my saddlebags. They were slightly damp, some water having leaked inside, and even after changing, my skin still felt like ice. With numb, trembling fingers, I unfastened my soaked bedroll and carried it to the front of the cave to dry near the fire the fae was supposedly building.

Surprisingly, he *had* built one.

Fae kept the children they sired with mortals so they wouldn't have to do something as undignified as remedial chores. Back home, he undoubtedly had hundreds of halflings to do those things for him. Lord Taran would never have the need to start a fire himself with all those halflings around, so how did he know how to start one?

With my back turned to him as I spread out my bedroll, I voiced that question out loud.

"The same way anyone knows how to do anything," he said dryly. "They've done it before."

I twisted around and scooted closer to the flames. Holding out my hands, I sighed blissfully as some feeling seeped back into my fingers.

"I believe vagueness also counts as honest deception. If you don't want to answer, then just say so," I said.

When he remained silent, my gaze drifted over to where he sat across the fire. Those gun-metal eyes were fixed on me, narrowed, and assessing, like he was calculating the different ways I might use the information against him.

It was annoying that he didn't underestimate me like I expected. That would make it more difficult to kill him. But it was also slightly flattering that he considered me an adversary worth choosing his words carefully around.

"During the Dark Wars, I spent many nights in the frozen tundra at the northernmost tip of the Faylands. I served as a War General for the fae king. If I had not known how to start a fire, I would have survived, but the many soldiers under my command would not have."

I didn't know much about the Dark Wars, not many in the Mortal Lands did, only that the fae had battled the beasts and won. It wasn't surprising the Enforcer had been alive five hundred years ago—he had mentioned earlier he was over a thousand years old—but it was surprising how much he cared about the wellbeing of his men.

"You're very keen on duty," I commented.

"I don't take the safety of my people lightly."

"How are desperate mortals who steal to fill their bellies a threat to your people?"

He sighed leaning back on his thick arms. "I have my reasons for doing what I do. Reasons I can't share with you."

At least he was straightforward about it.

I didn't ask anymore questions after that. The howl of the wind and rain outside the cave filled the quiet. Lightning lit up the cave periodically, followed by explosive thunder.

Lord Taran rose and disappeared into the back of the cave. He returned in a dry set of clothes, carrying two bundles.

"You need to eat." He offered one of the bundles. I cautiously accepted it, knowing it would be some strange food from Market Street. But when I opened it, it had a small loaf of bread and cheese cubes, both normal looking.

I caught his gaze as he sat across the fire.

"I returned to the market in the alley and asked them to put together some *edible* food."

I stared down at the bread and cheese, annoyingly touched by the gesture. "You didn't have to do that," I said quietly.

"No, I didn't." His words held a weight to them. An expectation.

"I'm not thanking you," I huffed and shoved a handful of cheese into my mouth, all lady-like. I wasn't going to praise him for doing the right thing.

When I finished chewing, I found him watching me. "What?" I asked with my mouth full.

"We don't have to be enemies, you know. This journey could be pleasant."

Doubtful, but I was curious what he meant by that.

"Pleasant how?"

"I could make you feel good."

I choked on a piece of cheese. I coughed, hitting my chest, and finally managed to swallow it down.

He was propositioning me again. Unlike the time in the tent, the offer seemed genuine. I couldn't say I wasn't interested this time because it would be a flat out lie.

"I don't think that's a good idea."

"Why not?" he demanded.

Because I'm going to kill you.

"It just isn't."

He smirked. "You'll be begging for my tongue and cock before this is over."

"That is not happening."

"It will."

He sounded so sure. I rolled my eyes and finished off the rest of my food, listening as rain and ice hammered the forest. Despite the violent storm outside, the sound of the rain and the warmth of the fire lulled me into a state of sleepy relaxation.

I retrieved my chains to settle in for the night. I pulled them from my saddlebag. The accompanying rattling sound echoed down one of the thin chambers.

Lips pursed, I surveyed the surrounding area for any large boulders I could attach the ends to. None of the head-sized rocks lying around would do. They were too light. I glanced toward the entrance of the cave where the Enforcer sat on top of his bedroll with his back to me, staring out into the storm. The rocks in that area weren't much larger.

I cursed, depositing the chains back into the saddlebag. I would have to forgo sleep tonight. It was too risky otherwise. I marched back to the cave's opening. "I'll stay up and keep a lookout in case any beasts come take shelter inside."

The Enforcer stared, those piercing gray eyes seeing right through my half-truth. "This is about the chains." A statement, not a question. It held no judgment, but his perceptiveness was aggravating. I glared at him, waiting to be peppered with invasive questions, waited for the flash of horror at my sleeping arrangements.

"Attach them to me," he said simply.

"What? No." I clutched my hands to my chest, needing some sort of barrier between us.

"Why not?"

"I have bad night terrors. You might wake up missing an eye."

His scarred lips curved into an amused smile. "I've had worse."

"I'm not sleeping anywhere near you," I said, turning out right belligerent.

A mocking gleam entered his eyes. "Why not?" He leaned forward. "Afraid you'll like it?"

"No."

I stomped to the back of the cave and retrieved the chains, feeling the Enforcer's gaze on me the entire time. He didn't look away even when I turned around and caught him staring at my ass and pointedly raised my brows. Instead, he smirked and beckoned me forward, crooking a finger.

I gritted my teeth and approached, knowing I couldn't back down from the challenge he had issued. I had to do this to prove he was wrong; that I could resist him.

My determination lasted all of five seconds when the Enforcer's possessive stare dragged over my body, leaving a trail of heat every place it touched. He stuck out his wrists and rasped in a voice honeyed with lust, "Chain me."

Hot desire spiked through me.

I jerked back flushed and scowling. "I knew this was a stupid idea."

He laughed lightly and gripped my wrist, stopping my retreat. "I'm just teasing you. I promise I'll behave."

I didn't know what to do with this side of him. Mass murderers weren't supposed to be playful.

When I didn't try to move again, Lord Taran released my wrist and remained perfectly still, acting like a model gentleman as he waited for me to decide. Srphies squirmed in my stomach. Every fiber of my being was against this idea, but I also saw no other alternative other than staying awake the whole night.

Tomorrow, we had a full day's hike before we reached the river crossing. Doing that on no sleep would be rough and unnecessary. I could sleep beside the Enforcer. He wasn't irresistible despite what he thought.

I dragged my bedroll over to lay beside his, then kneeled on top of it.

"Give me your hand," I snapped.

Lord Taran extended his arm, and I quickly secured a

pink fluffy manacle around his hand, touching as little of him in the process as possible. The cuff was barely able to close around his thick wrist.

I noticed each of his knuckles was tattooed with those gray whorls. I imagined how sexy it would be to see one of those fingers inside me.

No! Stop it right this second.

Besides the obvious reasons not to act on my attraction —the kidnapping, the mass murdering, the fact that I was going to kill him—his challenge had turned it into a matter of pride. And I was stupidly stubborn when it came to protecting my pride.

I moved on to his ankle next, then attached the other end of the cuffs to me. Once we were secured to one another, the chains didn't allow much room between us. To stay on separate bedrolls, we would have to sleep on our sides facing each other.

We were close enough that I could feel his warmth, his sweet-smelling breath fanning my face. The Enforcer smiled wickedly at me, beyond pleased by our sleeping arrangements for some insane reason.

I stabbed a talon at the slim boundary between us provided by the bed mats. "If you even think about crossing this line, I'll feed your dick to a beast."

He flashed a devilish smile as he answered, "Wouldn't dream of it."

It took longer than it should have to fall asleep. I was hyper aware of how close our bodies were.

When I finally drifted off, pain and darkness shrouded my dreams. Something wanted to rip out of my body. It tore and clawed my insides, demanding freedom. The pain was scalding. My body twisted and jerked as fire roared through my blood. Everything burned.

I screamed, begging for it to stop and suddenly the dream shifted.

Heat surrounded me, but nothing like the fire I had felt before. It was warm and soothing and chased the monster stalking my dreams back into the shadows. Purple eyes watched me from the dark edges of my mind. I knew if this heat left, the cold would return and so would the nightmare.

I settled into that warmth, clung to it, begging it not to leave.

"I won't," it whispered.

15

I cuddled deeper into my bedroll, humming under my breath at the blissful heat cocooning me. The heady scent of leather mixed with vanilla and amberwood filled my lungs and I greedily inhaled it, moaning at how delicious it smelled.

The solid warmth at my back pressed firmer against me. A finger traced the slope of my neck, the rough pad leaving a trail of goosebumps. I shivered, humming louder.

More of that delectable scent flooded my nostrils. I shifted, trying to move closer to its source. A masculine groan followed. The sound sent a jolt of arousal spiraling through me.

The iron band around my waist tightened. "You're in dangerous territory," a deep voice rumbled. I didn't care, as long as I could chase more of these exquisite feelings.

I rocked back again and something hard pressed against me, matching the cadence of my rolling hips. A hand skimmed over one of my breasts, squeezing lightly before trailing down my stomach until it reached the hem of my tunic. The hand slipped under the fabric, splaying out on my stomach as it held me tighter against that hardness. The delicious friction coiled heat low in my belly.

Lips brushed the shell of my ear. Then my throat. I twisted back, desperate to feel them on my own lips.

"Fuck," a guttural voice groaned. "You shouldn't feel this good." The familiarity of that voice scratched inside my skull. There was something I needed to remember about it. About the person it belonged to.

Those lips, those beautiful, scarred lips came to mine and that niggling sensation was forgotten. The kiss was slow . . . exploratory. It sipped and tasted. Teeth dragged over my bottom lip, and I moaned as the tension in my stomach spiked higher.

But it wasn't enough. I needed more. I ached to be touched.

Fingertips slipped into my waistband so close to where I needed them. Just a few more inches . . . I angled my hips higher. The rough pad of one brushed over my clit.

"Yes," I gasped, trying to rock into it, urge it to move again, but it wouldn't.

"Tell me you want me to touch you," that rough voice panted in my ear.

I managed to shake my head. The finger rubbed me again, sending pleasure thrumming through me. "More," I moaned.

"Not until you tell me," the voice growled. "Tell me you want me."

The scratching returned. More insistent this time. It demanded I open my eyes.

They shot open to find a black gaze burning into mine. His expression was savage, on the verge of losing control.

My gaze drifted down to our positions. One of his hands was shoved down my pants, the other digging into my hip.

I tried to tear myself away, but he tightened his hold, snarling low in his throat. I froze. This wasn't Lord Taran anymore.

"Enforcer," I said firmly. "Let me go."

He did, after releasing a measured breath. I rolled away but couldn't get far because of the chains.

We stared at each other. Breathless.

That midnight gaze watched me with an unnatural stillness. The planes of his face were harsher and partially obscured in shadows. Power pulsed from him in waves, prickling over my skin.

"I remember you from the alley," I said. "What are you?"

Teeth flashed. "The killer." His voice was off. Deeper, like the rattle of a gatling gun being cranked. "Are you scared?" he whispered mockingly.

The way he said it, it was like he wanted me to be. But I wasn't. He had nothing on the Crone.

"No. Go back wherever you came from. I need to speak to Lord Taran."

We were going to have some words on how I had ended up in his arms.

A feral grin sprang across his lips. "I like you," he rumbled. The black bled away from his eyes at the same time his face cleared.

I was even more curious now what the Enforcer was hiding. Was he cursed like me?

"Who's your friend?" I asked.

"No one," he said curtly.

"Fine. You *are* going to tell me how I ended up in your arms."

"I pulled you over to me."

I *knew* it.

"I warned you," I hissed, flexing my talons.

"You were having a nightmare," he said. "Look at your bedroll."

I glanced down. The mat had claw marks in it, the stuffing spilling out of the fabric.

My anger deflated in an instant. A hot flush of mortification burned its way through me.

"I—" I snapped my jaw shut, grinding my teeth. I really wish he hadn't seen that. What was I thinking, chaining myself to him?

I should have at least tried to stay awake. Then my shameful secret would be safe.

"Is that why you sleep in chains?" he asked gently. Sympathy shimmered in his eyes. He pitied me. Poor, ugly little monster.

"You had no right to touch me," I snapped.

"If you want to dismember me for comforting you, then be my guest." Lord Taran's gaze darkened. "I wasn't going to just let you suffer."

"What makes you think I needed any comfort from *you*? You're the Enforcer. You've spilled so much blood, it's any wonder you're not drowning in it."

Pain flashed across his face. "This might come as a surprise to you, but even a monster has feelings," he said. "I understand you are lashing out because you are embarrassed. You have no reason to be." He uncuffed himself, then abruptly rose to his feet, and disappeared through the cave's entrance.

Growling, I uncuffed my wrist and ankles and threw the chains to the ground.

He had kidnapped me and forced me into a bargain. Why should I feel guilty that I hurt his feelings?

I sighed.

Because as much as he touted being a monster, he wasn't

one, at least not to me. Outside of the unpleasant circumstances that bound us together, he had been nothing but kind and patient even when I was being cruel.

Which was so *confusing*.

How can the man who had murdered hundreds of innocents be the same one who held me to keep the nightmares away?

Squeezing my eyes shut, I pinched the bridge of my nose. I didn't want to feel this way. I couldn't afford to separate the man from the monster if I was going to do what needed to be done. And I especially couldn't have sex with him. It would make things even more complicated.

I didn't want to think about what I had almost let happen between us but knew I would anyway. The feel of his hardness against me would be imprinted in my mind forever. It was as giant as he was. After one night, I had been seconds away from doing just as he said I would—begging for his cock. It was pathetic how quickly I had almost lost that challenge.

Even more disconcerting was how refreshed I felt. Usually, I woke up exhausted and my ankles and wrists ached from thrashing in my sleep. I had slept better than I had in ages.

After putting out the fire and repacking my saddlebags with the iron dust hidden inside, I removed them from my horse, then did the same with Lord Taran's possessions. Now that the storm was over, it was safe to let the horses go. It would be too dangerous for the gentle creatures to continue any further into the woods.

I slung my bedroll over my shoulders and secured the saddlebags on either side of my hips. Hips the Enforcer had been gripping as he rocked into me.

My stomach clenched.

I shoved the memory away, determined to focus solely on getting to the Crone's cabin as soon as possible. This morning was a mistake. One I wouldn't be repeating.

Outside, streams of sunlight filtered through the dense canopy. Mud squelched under my boots as I guided the horses to the path we rode in on. I slapped both of their rumps and sent them racing toward freedom, wishing I could join them.

I sought out the sulking fae lord, but the brush beyond the cave was too dense to make out much. "Enforcer?" I called out. The river was a day's walk from here. We needed to arrive before sundown to set up camp.

A branch snapped to my left followed by rustling. Lord Taran appeared, lumbering through the brush.

"Where'd you go?"

He ignored me, stalking past inside the cave to retrieve his things.

Lord Taran returned after a moment. Leather straps bisected his tunic-covered chest from where he secured his sword to his back. Strips of ivory cloth were wrapped around each of his wrists.

"I released the horses."

"I saw."

My stomach tightened uncomfortably at his curt tone. He was more upset than I thought and that only heightened my guilt. It was aggravating.

Ignoring his sour mood, I explained, "We need to cross the river. The Crone's offering site is another three-day hike from there."

"Lead the way."

We walked silently through the high grass, but it was nothing like the companionable silence we had shared the night before. Lord Taran lagged a few steps behind me the whole way. His agitation was palpable, biting at the air.

The elevation of the ground rose steadily the longer we trekked west. Eventually we hit a ridge and walked along its edge with a sharp drop-off on our left.

We followed the ridge line for hours, stopping periodically for breaks, until the light pouring in through the trees dimmed and the sound of rushing water filled my ears. The ridge plateaued, then dipped down into a gentle slope. Below, a few yards off, I could make out parts of the Cold River between the trees.

The slope, though not steep, was slick from the recent storm. My boots struggled to find purchase, and I ended up slipping and flailing most of the way down.

Lord Taran leapt off the side of the ridge, avoiding the muddy slope altogether and landed gracefully near the riverbank.

"Show off," I grumbled to myself, but based on the way his lips twitched, I was certain he had heard me. Hopefully, that meant his mood had improved.

As soon as my boots hit solid ground, I dashed off to the river's edge. I kneeled on the bank, noting the river was substantially high for this time of the year. It was also swifter. Water rushed by, carrying a gigantic fallen tree with ease. My gaze followed the trunk until it was out of sight. This was the aftermath of the storm.

The rain had made the edges slippery with mud, and with how rapidly the water was flowing, the river would tear me away in a heartbeat if I fell in.

Still crouching, I stared down the visible length of the river, trying to locate the bridge. If memory served me, we weren't too far from where we would cross. The brush and weeds were denser down here than up at the top of the ridge, so it was impossible to see more than a couple hundred feet ahead.

I spotted a game trail cutting through it, the high grass

stomped down by whatever animal used this area of the river to hunt, and decided to use it to search for the bridge.

Lord Taran's heavy foot falls were close behind.

My gaze scoured the foliage in the distance for rope as we walked, but there were only bare trees. Unconcerned with my feet, I failed to avoid a particularly muddy patch and only the Enforcer's grip kept me upright.

The heat of his palms seeped into my skin. His hands on my waist stirred phantom sensations of the last time he held me like this. I could feel his cock grinding against me, his strained breathing in my ear.

My stomach constricted.

"Careful," he said in a rough voice. His hands lingered longer than necessary.

"Thanks," I mumbled awkwardly when he finally released me.

Then I saw it. Something hung from a tree trunk a little way off. The light brown material stood out against the gray bark where it was tied.

I peered toward the river directly across from the rope, but there was no bridge.

My eyes flitted between the length of rope and the area where the bridge should have been, then toward the other side of the river. Sure enough, there was rope hanging on that tree. I rushed closer, skidding to a stop in front of the rope and lifted it for a better look.

I cursed at what I found. The end wasn't frayed or worn. Someone had cut the rope. Recently too, based on the fresh prints in the mud at the tree's base. My gaze cast up to where Lord Taran loomed nearby.

"Who would have done this? Is it possible someone else wants to use the All-Seeing Eye to find the godstone?" I asked.

The Enforcer's stoic gaze dropped to the rope. "I am certain many will try."

"Why? What is the godstone really?"

His scarred lips thinned.

Still feeling bad about earlier, I played nice instead of demanding an answer.

"How about a trade? I will tell you something you want to know and in exchange you tell me about the godstone."

Lord Taran canted his head to the side, regarding me as he considered the offer.

"Information on the godstone is a strongly guarded secret. I want two answers from you."

"Deal."

I braced, waiting for him to ask about the Crone and how I ended up trying to steal from him. Neither were answers I wanted to give, but it would be worth it to know about the weapon I was after.

"What's your name?"

I hid my shock. Of everything he could have asked, that's what he wanted to know?

"Vera."

"*Vera*." He tasted my name, rolling it around on his tongue. Hearing my name spoken in his deep, decadent voice sent an unwelcome surge of pleasure coursing through me. He grinned. "Strong and fierce, just like you."

I wasn't sure what to say to the compliment. "What's your second question?"

"Why do you sleep in chains?"

My heart lodged in my ribs. I wanted to shrink into the shadows, but there were none. It was late afternoon and plenty of sunlight streamed through the canopy. The Enforcer's penetrating gaze could see everything.

"You're wasting a perfectly good question." I kept my tone light.

"I disagree."

"Ask me something else."

"No."

I scowled. "It doesn't matter."

"Again, I disagree."

"I was cursed, okay?" I snapped.

"Cursed how? And by whom?"

"No. You asked two questions and got two answers. That was the deal," I said. " Now tell me about the godstone."

He stared for a moment before he started, "As you may already know fae are the descendants of the seven gods that once inhabited these lands, with high fae being the most directly related to our divine ancestors."

I had been taught there were eight original gods by the Crone, but I didn't correct him. He was a fae lord. I am sure he knew his own history better than her.

"There are seven fae houses, each led by a fae lord, or lady, who can trace their bloodline and powers back to a god. My house is descended from Taranisin, the God of War. He was tasked with creating a weapon that could destroy anything, including a god."

My brows pulled down. That didn't make any sense. "Why would the Gods want a weapon that could kill them?"

"Balance. Unlimited power corrupts. It is the same reason every fae pays a price for the use of their powers."

I had never heard about the latter before. It was on the tip of my tongue to ask about his powers and their price, but I was not prepared to offer him any more answers. I swallowed the question and waited for him to continue.

"The godstone had been lost since the Dark Wars until it washed ashore seven days ago," he finished.

"So basically, this supremely powerful weapon is out there somewhere in the hands of gods only knows and anyone else that is aware it has been found can use the All-Seeing Eye to lead them right to it?"

News spread quickly in the Mortal Lands. Who knew how many people knew about the godstone already?

"Only if the Crone allows them access."

"True," I agreed.

"It is in our best interest for someone to steal it from the original thieves. I might be able to sense it if they do."

The roar of the river behind us reminded me there was a much bigger issue at hand. I wandered toward it.

I stopped, hands fisted on my hips as I glared at the churning water. A fish leapt out of a white cap, fighting against the current. Either it was too tired or not strong enough and was pulled back into the river and swept away, just like we would be if we attempted to cross on foot.

We had to get to the other side to reach the Crone and the All-Seeing Eye. Without a bridge, that seemed impossible. Farther down, the river channel only grew wider. No bridge meant no Crone, and no Crone meant no vest.

"I suppose we will have to wait until the current dies down." Lord Taran's voice sounded right behind me, and I nearly jumped out of my skin. The male could move as silent as air when he wanted to.

No way in the dark night would I wait around with only the Enforcer as company until it was safe to cross. Not after what happened this morning.

"Can't you just do the teleporting thing like you did back at the train and get us to the other side?"

I had thought about asking him to do that to get us to the Crone's offering site, but I couldn't risk giving him the location. I was only alive because I was useful. If he could find the Crone, he didn't need me.

"That is not how my Enforcer powers work, Little Thief.

That magic only activates when a fae law is broken and even then, I do not control where I go."

Well, that was useless.

I eyed the giant over my shoulder. He was tall and strong, but so was the tree I had seen the river sweeping away. The water would do the same to him if he tried crossing on foot. Maybe he could throw me? I glanced back toward the river much wider than he was tall. It was too risky. If he threw me even a few inches shy of the other side, I was done for.

"Let me think," I said and started to pace back and forth, wearing a line in the mud. Every so often, my eyes darted toward the river like the bridge would magically appear. On the sixth time, something in the distance caught my eye. There were some trees peeking out of the water, unmoving despite the strength of the current. They extended across the river channel.

The weight of the Enforcer's stare burned into my back as I inched closer to the river to see if my hunch was correct. If the trees were in fact growing in the riverbed, they had to be embedded deep enough to withstand the river's current, otherwise they would have been uprooted by now.

I crouched until I was eye level with the tops of the trees. The water was murky from all the dirt and debris, making it impossible to see beneath. From what I could tell on the surface, these weren't floating. The trunks were sun bleached and cracking like they had been in the water for some time. This area must have been part of the forest before the river flooded it.

The trees stood straight up, spread out in the water just far enough that we might cross from this side to the other if we moved from tree to tree.

I whirled around.

"No," the Enforcer's deep voice intoned.

"You haven't even heard my idea . . ."

"I don't need to. We will wait."

Arrogant asshole.

He could wait if he wanted to. I was crossing with or without him.

We set up camp before night fell, several paces from the river's edge. The evening was cold without a fire, but we couldn't risk the light attracting any beasts.

We ate, then retired early, both exhausted from a full day of hiking.

Getting him to digest the iron dust was going to be more difficult than I originally planned. I had to be able to blend it into a mixture to cover it, but so far, none of the food I had seen Lord Taran eating would work. Then there was the matter of his diligence. He was constantly alert, head on a swivel at all times. Slipping iron dust into his food right under his nose would not be easy.

"You're welcome to join me. I'll keep you warm." The Enforcer's voice was practically a purr from where he sprawled out on the ground. He laughed when I dragged my bedroll and chains as far away from him as possible and set them down with an aggravated huff.

I pretended to fall asleep, even selling it with some light snoring.

Sometime later, I heard a muffled sound.

Moving as little as possible, I glanced around. It was hard to see with the scant amount of light provided by the crescent moon. I didn't see any other silhouettes besides the surrounding trees. Not an animal or a beast then.

I heard it again, clearer this time. A low groan.

The Enforcer was moving on his bed roll. What was he doing?

Oh my Gods. He was stroking himself.

His hand was wrapped around his thick member. It was covered in those gray whorls like the rest of him.

His cock was tattooed and almost as large as my forearm.

I couldn't see his face from this angle, but the lines of his body were taut. Wetness pooled between my legs. I squeezed them together to try and alleviate some of the tension. My muscles tensed as I fought the urge to go to him. To sink myself down on that rigid shaft.

The stretch of lowering myself down on it . . . Fuck. I was so tempted to slip my fingers between my legs, but I couldn't risk it. If he couldn't smell my arousal now, he definitely would then.

I clapped a hand over my mouth to keep from making any noise as I watched him furiously pump into his hand.

"Vera," he cried out and then his body went slack.

Holy fuck.

Did he just . . .?

Shock rooted me in place. I don't know how long I laid there, frozen, before I heard his soft snores fill the night. The sound galvanized me into action. I couldn't stay here. I knew with certainty we'd end up together again and I wouldn't stop him this time.

I quietly removed the cuffs on my wrists and legs, then discarded them off to the side. On second thought . . . I wrapped the chains tightly around my torso, under my tunic. I couldn't risk losing a second set.

I left my gun beside my bedroll, not wanting to get it wet. As soon as I made it to the other side of the river and proved my plan worked, I would have Lord Taran toss my things over to me.

I crept down the riverbank to where I had seen the trees. My boots sank deep into the muddy shore. The ground was so slick I nearly fell several times just trying to get into the river. It didn't help that I could barely see either. I managed to get both feet in and sank up to my knees. The icy water chilled me to the bone as I rushed forward, impatient to get this over with.

There must have been an undercurrent. As soon as I launched forward, the river almost tore my feet out from under me. I plunged into the water, the cold suddenly knocking the air from my lungs, and swam for all I was worth toward the first tree.

My hands wrapped around the thin trunk, strangling it, as the water surged around, trying to take me with it. The current was stronger than it looked.

I pushed myself off the first trunk to the next one, paddling hard and fast to keep from being taken by the current. I blew out a breath when my arms hugged the second trunk. Only one more to go.

"Vera." Ronan's thunderous voice cut through the night.

Heart hammering in my chest like a child caught doing something naughty, I twisted toward his voice. He stood glaring at me from the riverbank. His face was cast in shadows, making his murderous expression appear even more terrifying.

"You have five seconds to get your stubborn ass back to shore."

"No, I'm almost there."

"One."

His body tensed and I knew he was seconds away from coming in and dragging me out.

"Two."

There was a loud crash nearby. I whipped my head to the side to see an enormous tree barreling toward me in the water. I ducked under the surface before it crashed into the tree I held, but the trunk was so brittle and waterlogged, it snapped at the bottom from the impact, knocking me into the river's grip.

Splashing sounded. A hand reached for me. I grasped it, raking my talons over scarred skin, but the water's grip on me was stronger. The river pulled me, but the hand didn't let go. It was dragged with me. The Enforcer's face floated above me, then I was on the surface, gasping for air.

I clung tight to him, staring into his wild eyes as the river swept us away.

16

"Find something to hold onto!" Ronan yelled over the roar of the river, spurring me into action. All we needed was for one of us to get a grip on something and we'd be saved. I clawed and scratched at every piece of debris I passed, desperate to find purchase.

My claws sank deep into a small sapling, but instead of stopping me, the entire thing uprooted, and we were pulled back into the center. I tried kicking toward the water's edge next, but the current was too strong. I couldn't swim more than a few feet before I was dragged back into the middle of the river.

Lord Taran made it close to the shore several times, but the river swept him back just inches shy of his goal. Not even he was powerful enough to overcome the force of nature.

We swam and fought for all we were worth, but there was nothing to hold on to except each other. I exhausted myself to the point I could barely lift my arms enough to keep my grip on him. I tumbled underwater on and off, my lungs and nostrils burning.

"I've got you."

Strong arms wrapped around me. The Enforcer gripped me tightly to his chest, keeping me above water, as the river swept us farther downstream.

I clung to his neck, breathing raggedly. I had really fucked up.

We managed to get a hold of a floating tree trunk at one point. My limbs felt heavy as boulders. The only thing saving me was my talons. I dug them deep into the wood, but my arms were growing weaker as my muscles tightened from the frigid waters.

The current knocked us violently around, but as long as we held onto the log until we reached calmer waters, we'd be safe.

It was dark except for a small amount of moonlight streaming down and the glow from Ronan's draoistone. The latter cast a crystalline blue over the surrounding area. If we were in a deeper part of the river, I would have had him cover it, but there wouldn't be water beasts here. And I was grateful for the light.

Now that the immediate danger had passed, the temperature of the river registered. My body shook violently. I could hear my teeth chattering over the raging current.

"Your lips are fucking blue."

I glanced over to where Ronan gripped the log beside me. He was glaring at my mouth.

"O-o-o. I'm s-s-s sorry. L-let me-me magically t-t-turn them pink again."

"Even on the verge of freezing, you still manage to sass me," he said in disbelief. "Come here."

Banding an arm around my waist, he repositioned us, so my back was pressed against his chest with one arm holding me and the other the trunk.

I sighed in bliss as his body heat soaked into my frozen skin.

"You want to tell me what you were doing crossing a raging river in the middle of the night like a madwoman?" The Enforcer said in my ear.

"You want to tell me why you were stroking yourself like a pervert while I was a few feet away?"

"I knew you were awake." There was a smile in his voice.

"That's beside the point, you creep."

"Did it turn you on?" he whispered, tightening his hold on my waist. "Is that why you ran?"

I felt him harden against me.

"There is something seriously wrong with you."

We were in the middle of a violent river for gods' sakes!

His breath ghosted over my neck. "I think you like what's wrong with me." At the same time, his hand moved lower on my waist, just above the apex between my thighs.

"I could make you feel so good right now. You wouldn't even have to beg."

He was a lunatic. And so was I for being tempted to accept.

I jerked his hand back up to my waist. "Let's just focus on getting out of this river alive."

He laughed darkly. "I know you feel this pull between us. You won't be able to keep fighting me for long."

The Enforcer was obviously underestimating how stubborn I was.

"By the way," I started. "Why didn't you just use the bargain magic to pull me to you?"

He was partially to blame for our predicament. There was no reason to dive in after me. He could have just yanked me from the water through our bond.

"I didn't think about it," he said carefully. "I saw you fall into the current and I acted."

"Aww, you were worried about me," I teased.

"I was."

Unease stirred in my stomach. That was not the answer I was expecting.

I scoffed. "You were just worried about losing your only key to the Crone."

He was quiet for a moment, then a long exhale rustled my hair. "If only you knew, Little Thief. If only you knew."

"Know what?"

"Nothing," he said too quickly.

"Tell me," I demanded.

"No."

I angled my face sideways, hitting him with a fierce glower, one that had sent mortals fleeing in the other direction on more than one occasion.

He traced a finger over my scowling lips. "You're adorable when you're angry," he murmured. "It makes me want to fuck you even more."

My nostrils flared, equally annoyed as I was aroused. I slapped his hand away. He was becoming too comfortable with touching me. *I* was letting him become too comfortable.

"What's this around your waist?" His hand moved over the chains hidden beneath my tunic.

"Nothing," I threw his response back at him.

He tried to ask me another question, but I ignored him. I just wanted to get out of this river and his arms as fast as possible.

Dawn cracked through the leaves of the canopy by the time the river spat us out into calmer waters. Ronan released me and I sluggishly swam for the river's edge. My arms trembled as I attempted to pull myself out of the water. I slipped and fell before the Enforcer grabbed my hips and hefted me up.

I shoved away from him as soon as I was safely on the riverbank.

Lord Taran climbed out while I collapsed on my back, breathing heavily. The bastard wasn't even winded. He smirked down at me, then moved passed into the brush.

I made a rude gesture at his back.

Even once I caught my breath, I delayed following him for as long as possible, needing some space to gather my thoughts.

In hindsight, I could acknowledge crossing a raging river in the middle of the night wasn't the smartest of plans. My only way of killing the Enforcer was back with our bags. I still hadn't quite worked out when and how I was going to do it, but now if I saw a window, I wasn't going to be able to take it.

Idiot.

I was rash and impulsive on my best day, but the Enforcer really seemed to bring it out of me. I charged face first into battle every month with terrifying beasts, but for some reason, hearing Ronan whisper my name as he found release was so much more frightening.

It made me want things I shouldn't. I wasn't experienced in the bedroom like the Enforcer. I had only had sex a handful of times. Sex with Ronan would mean more to me than it would to him, and I was already having trouble remembering he was just using me to find the godstone. And that I was going to have to kill him.

He was standing between me and everything I wanted. I couldn't afford to act on this strange, consuming attraction between us.

I laid there in the mud until my skin grew itchy from my river-soaked clothes and insects buzzed around my head. With a heavy sigh, I forced myself to find the Enforcer.

He kneeled inside a small clearing, positioning rocks in a ring for a fire. I left him to finish and continued deeper into the brush to find some breakfast. It was the least I could do since our food and supplies were several miles upriver.

My wet clothes slopped around, leaving a wet trail behind me as I collected blood berries and dug up edible roots. Our morning meal wouldn't be as extravagant as the food Lord Taran had purchased from Gold City, but it would fill our bellies and provide enough energy to walk the additional day our little trip down river had added.

At least we were on the right side of the river now. That had to count for something.

I returned to the clearing with the berries and roots bundled in my wet tunic. The Enforcer had a small fire going.

And he was naked.

I slapped a hand over my eyes. "Where are your clothes?" My voice came out higher pitched than I was proud of.

"Drying."

I peeked between two fingers. His shoulders were broad, twice as wide as me. Every inch of him was packed with hard, lethal muscle. White scars littered his body, interrupting the smooth expanse of sun-kissed skin. Those whorls of gray ink spiraled down his hips and thighs.

I felt the stirrings of desire and quickly shoved it away. Last thing I needed was for him to smell I was aroused at a time like this.

Ripping my gaze away, I dropped my hand and focused on his face. He stared stoically back; thick, muscled legs stretched out as he leaned on his arms. He was at ease, totally naked in the middle of the forest.

Huffing, I marched out of the clearing and returned with a head-sized leaf. I held it out to him, averting my gaze. He didn't take it.

"If you didn't want to see me naked, perhaps you should

have thought of that before you got us lost in the middle of nowhere without any supplies, or dry clothes."

"Please," I ground out. I had never used that word before with him; rarely used it at all.

He frowned at my pleading, but thankfully took the leaf. I heard rustling and assumed he had done as I asked, but I still wasn't brave enough to look any lower than his face again.

"Thank you," I told him. "And we're not lost." I reached inside the makeshift pouch I had created with my shirt and offered him half of the berries and roots I had collected. "Those are blood berries. They only grow in the southwest section of the forest, which means we can't be more than a day's hike from where we were," I explained.

I could tell he wanted to ask, so I offered, "I grew up in this forest." A piece of my past without expectation; it was as close to an apology as I would ever give for getting us into this mess.

He accepted it with a nod and thankfully didn't pry further. Lord Taran popped a berry into his mouth, chewing methodically before he said, "This is better than I expected."

The Enforcer did not enjoy the roots nearly as much, discreetly spitting the partially chewed remnants out. He rose and left the clearing. I snuck a quick glance at his toned bottom before he disappeared.

Taking advantage of his absence, I stripped off my wet clothes, leaving them to hang on a branch near the fire and unwound the chains. Dressed in only my undergarments, I curled in front of the flames, cupping my knees, and ensured my uncovered back would remain from the Enforcer's view when he returned.

He did a short time later carrying a fish speared on a branch in one hand and holding the large leaf over his groin with the other. I pressed my lips together to keep from laughing at the ridiculous image. His gaze dragged over my near nakedness as he resettled in front of the fire and cooked his breakfast.

The stench of its seared flesh made me want to vomit. Fish was the main staple served when I was a child growing up in these woods and I had eaten enough of it to last me a lifetime. The sounds of the rushing river behind us filled the silence as he slowly turned the fish over the fire.

"So, you grew up here," he said, gaze fixed on his meal.

"I did."

That piece of me was free. He wasn't getting any more than that.

The Enforcer didn't ask for more. He surprised me when he said, "I grew up by the sea."

"Is that where you learned how to fish like that?" I asked, gesturing at the handmade spear he'd carved with his sword. I knew from experience, it wasn't easy to spear fish like that without lots of practice and he had only been gone a few minutes.

He nodded. "Because of my powers, I am magically gifted with any type of weapon. If it is capable of inflicting harm, I can wield it expertly the first time it touches my hand. As a boy, I used to cheat and use my powers to spear fish until my uncle caught me." The Enforcer chuckled. "He smacked me upside the head and lectured me on how a man needs to know how to feed himself. He made me stay out by the sea all night until I speared a fish on my own. From then on, that's the only way I fished. Without magic."

I frowned at him. "Why are you telling me this?"

"I told you. This journey doesn't have to be unpleasant."

"I'm not having sex with you."

A grin tugged at his mouth. "I know you believe that."

I didn't bother arguing with him again. My mind was

made up. I was already in dangerous territory with how familiar I'd allowed us to become. It couldn't go any further.

Lord Taran removed his fish from the fire and offered me a piece. I vehemently shook my head. "I'd rather eat mud."

With a shrug, he dug into his meal, chewing with vigor. The fish was polished off in seconds.

I stared.

"What?" he asked.

"Anyone ever told you that you eat like a wild animal?"

A rumbling laughter shook his chest. "I can't say they have." He discarded the branch. "Have I mentioned how enjoyable I find your lack of fear?"

"Yes. You're a big, bad monster and I should be shaking in my boots."

"I'm glad that you are not. I find I can be myself around you."

Yes. Drop your guard so I can kill you.

"What about the women you bring back? They can't be that afraid if they want to have sex with you."

"Their fear is what brings them to me. They come to me to ride the fine line between danger and pleasure. For the thrill of fucking a monster. I give them that. I rut them rough and hard, then send them on their way with a story to tell their friends."

His tone was hostile. There was none of the usual cockiness when he spoke of his sexual prowess.

So he was just a faceless body to those women, and the sex was meaningless. That sounded sad and really lonely.

"It can be."

Shit. I'd said the last part out loud.

My gaze moved to his. He didn't hide the hollowness in his eyes. The Enforcer was *lonely.*

That thought hit me right in the heart. I *knew* loneliness.

I didn't know what life was like without it. Godsdamnit. I didn't want to see this side of him. But it was too late.

His entire body froze.

He rushed over to his drying trousers, hastily pulling them on before he snatched up his sword. "I'll return shortly."

He vanished.

One moment he was there. The next he was gone.

What the . . .?

I blinked slowly, then surveyed the clearing, thinking he must have just moved quickly into the woods. "Lord Taran?" I called.

My shouting scared a small flock of birds. They shot through the canopy, disappearing from sight. There was no answer from the Enforcer.

Prickles of pain spread under my skin. The tingles sharpened into a stabbing sensation. I cried out and leapt to my feet, panicked hands flying over my arms to stop the excruciating pain.

What in the lands was happening?

The bargain tether thinned, stretched. It snapped and suddenly I was catapulted out of the forest. I stood inside a darkened, rocky tunnel strung with bright lanterns.

The pain was gone. I vaguely remembered the Enforcer mentioning something about there being only so much rope he could give me before the bond became painful.

He was nowhere to be seen.

Dressed in only my undergarments, I ran a hand over the rough, choppy walls, trying to figure out where I was. They looked like they had been chipped away. My gaze dipped to the set of tracks running along the ground. I followed them deeper into the tunnel until the din of hundreds of pickaxes being swung into stone filled my ears.

This had to be a mine. The only active one in the Mortal Lands was the gold mines outside Coldwater.

At least the only known active one. The Nighters kept their operations in the ore mines under the fae's radar.

The thin layer of gold dust covering the ground confirmed my suspicions.

Why had Lord Taran come here?

I froze, a pit opening in my stomach, as I realized the answer. Why did the Enforcer go anywhere in the Mortal Lands?

Someone had broken a fae law.

All the clanging from deep in the mine abruptly cut off leaving the tunnel eerily silent. I crept forward, unsure what I was walking into.

Sharp voices pierced the quiet. I recognized one of the deeper pitches as the Enforcer and moved quicker through the tunnel. When I finally reached the voices, I ducked behind a metal cart partially filled with gold nuggets.

Crouching, I peered around the edge and took in all the wary, haggard miners crowded into the narrow tunnel. Sweat dripped off their faces, creating clean streaks through the gold dust coating their grim expressions.

It was easy to pick out Lord Taran's towering form among them.

He loomed over the lawbreaker, but I couldn't see their face from here.

"You dare steal from the fae?" his voice slashed through the quiet like a blade.

From this angle, I could only see his profile, but there was no mistaking the hardness in his eyes, the coldness in his expression. This wasn't the same male who had shared a piece of his childhood with me minutes ago. It was like he had completely shut down that part of himself. This was the legend. The monster to be feared.

The crowd of miners squeezed back against the walls, putting as much distance as they could between themselves and the Enforcer's wrath. I didn't blame them. My legs itched to do the same.

The surly reply that came next was unexpected. So was how young it sounded. "Yeah. I do."

I stretched out further to see the speaker. It was a scrawny teenage boy. His cheeks were sunken and sallow.

There had been a thread of fear in his voice, but he still puffed out his chest and glared up at the giant towering over him. I liked this kid.

"They're workin' us to the bone just to meet your quota —" he broke into a coughing fit— "What do you even need all that gold for, huh?"

Murmurs started among the other miners, discontent washing through them. A few started to close in on the Enforcer, but before they could do anything, he unsheathed his sword, whirling it in his hand. The encroaching miners stopped dead in their tracks.

"It is not your place to question the fae." His statement was directed at everyone. "You know the punishment for breaking fae law?" This he asked just to the teenager. The boy was trembling now, but he said nothing, jutting up his chin and glaring. I expected Lord Taran to disappear with him like he had the little boy. I thought I had time to reason with him, convince him to spare the teenager's life.

"Death," he declared.

"No!" I shot up from my hiding spot.

The Enforcer ran his blade through the boy's chest. Shock filled the teenager's expression. He stumbled back, clutching at the gaping wound before he collapsed.

I bolted over and sunk to the ground beside him. I tried to put pressure on the wound, but there was too much blood. It bubbled through my fingers.

Ice spread through my chest.

"No," I whispered defeatedly, pressing harder. There was the softest intake of air and then he was gone. I gently pulled him to my chest, rocking him.

"I'm sorry," I said over and over again, stroking his hair. Tears slipped down my cheeks. I didn't care about the blood staining from my front, or that I was still in only my under-garments. I only cared about giving this boy the comfort in death he never received in life.

"Vera." Lord Taran stood over me.

I brushed a curl from the boy's face, tucking it behind his ears. He was young. He couldn't have been more than fifteen. And he was so skinny. I could feel his individual ribs.

"Where are your clothes?" The Enforcer put himself between me and the miners.

I kept rocking the boy.

"Who is in charge here?" Lord Taran barked.

"I—I am, Sir."

"Keep better watch over your people, or the next time, you will die with them."

I didn't hear their response.

"It's okay," I told the boy, but it wasn't. Nothing was okay and it never would be again. Because he was dead.

And for what? Trying to fill his belly?

Fire burned away the coldness in my blood.

"He didn't have to die," I whispered, then I was on my feet, screaming and pounding on the Enforcer's back. "He didn't have to die!"

Lord Taran twisted and pulled me tightly against him. Before I could react, the mine dissolved around us, and we were standing in the same clearing as before. He released me.

I tore away and glanced down at myself. My white

undergarments were stained, and my belly was smeared with blood. The boy's blood.

A pressure built behind my eyes, pounding in my skull the longer I stared. That tide of fury grew into a tsunami threatening to obliterate everything in its path.

Damn the godstone. Damn the Rogues.

If the iron dust wasn't back with my belongings, I would have rammed it down the Enforcer's throat.

He turned to me wearing a placating expression.

"I wish you did not have to witness that. The bargain bond had reached its limits, I had to—"

I slashed him across the chest with my talons.

We both stared at the blood dripping from the fresh claw marks.

The Enforcer touched his chest, staring bewilderedly at the open wound.

I had just broken the first fae law.

He dropped his hand as the damaged skin knit itself together. When his burning eyes snapped to mine, I could see some of his otherworldliness peeking through. Black had eaten away all the gray. The power emanating from him was intense and burning. My skin prickled to the point of pain. His predator had come out to play.

A feral grin spread. He licked his lips. "You better run," he whispered. "And you better run fast because if I get my hands on you, I'm just as likely to fuck you as kill you."

I leapt over the surrounding brush and took off into the forest with his dark laughter trailing behind me.

17

Branches sliced across my torso, stinging my skin, as I raced through the trees, but I didn't dare slow for even a moment. Lord Taran's heavy footfalls pounded over the forest floor not far behind. I had the advantage as I was familiar with the terrain, but he was unbelievably quick for a male his size.

I needed to find somewhere to hide and fast. I cursed my impulsiveness. Not for clawing him, no, he deserved so much more. But if I had taken more time to plan before crossing the river, I'd have the iron dust with me and could find a way to use it.

For now, I needed to lose him long enough to find a hiding spot and make a plan. My pride rebelled at hiding instead of fighting, but I was half-naked, weaponless, and up against a being much more powerful than myself.

I steered toward a section of the forest where large, gnarled roots jutted out of the soil in every direction, making it difficult to navigate quickly. Instinctively, I knew where the tree roots were and flew over each one without looking.

A loud thud informed me Lord Taran had not been so

lucky. If I wasn't running for my life, I might have laughed at the image of him sprawled out on the ground.

I pumped my legs faster.

My speed stalled when I didn't hear Lord Taran thundering behind me. Good. If luck was on my side, he hit his head when he fell. I slowed for a second to catch my breath just as something barreled into me from the side.

The Enforcer twisted us at the last minute, taking the brunt of our fall when we slammed down on a large collection of roots. Our bodies bounced, separated, and rolled off opposite edges.

I landed on a pile of moss, breathless and disoriented.

Get up! Get up!

Wheezing, I forced myself to stand, swaying with the effort. I took one step, then yelped as a hand grabbed my ankle and dragged me back down. My head slammed into the ground.

He tried to yank me to him. I crashed my foot into his face. There was a sickening crunch followed by a pained grunt.

Good. I hope I broke the bastard's nose.

I was up on my feet sprinting away before he could get his hands on me again. I had no clue what he would do if he did. My body delighted at the idea of him catching me and having his way with me, ignoring the fact that murder was also on the table. Thank the Gods that dumb idiot wasn't in control.

Weaving through the trees, I scanned the forest for a hiding spot. If it wasn't broad daylight, I would have considered climbing one of the trees, but their sparse leaves wouldn't hide me.

Wetness hit my cheek. I swiped it away only to feel it again. Rain fell in a light mist. I growled under my breath. Not again. It'd be impossible to keep running at this speed with the rain making the dead leaves underfoot slippery. The rumble of the Enforcer's feet hitting the ground was the final decision maker.

I spotted a fallen trunk with an opening wide enough for me to fit through. Sucking in a breath, I wiggled inside on my back, the rough bark scraping my skin. It smelled earthy and a bit like mold. Insects skittered over my skin. I shivered in disgust and did my best to brush them away with the little space I had to move.

Outside, the rain patter came down harder.

Leaves crunched just a few feet away. I held my breath.

"Oh, Little Thief," the Enforcer said, much too close for comfort. His voice was unnaturally deep and tinged with amusement. I was still dealing with the predator. "Come out now and I promise to be gentle. If not, when I find you, I'm going to fuck you raw."

My whole body lit up, totally on board with the latter.

I bit down on my knuckle. The pain helped distract me from how badly I wanted to accept his offer. Even after what I had just witnessed, it didn't dim my attraction. Self-recrimination and shame burned my cheeks. I hated myself for wanting him.

Why? Why of everyone in the lands did my body have to react this way to him?

"Raw it is," he said with a smile in his voice. His footsteps retreated. Quietly, I exhaled.

I waited for him to return, but he didn't. Hours passed, as I listened to the rain beat down on the forest. My muscles ached from laying cramped inside the log for so long. At one point, the trunk flooded with cold mud and water, drenching me. I wrapped my arms around myself to stave off the chill.

The light streaming in dimmed into a golden glow as the sun set.

I hadn't heard a peep from the Enforcer. He could have easily used the bargain bond to yank me to him, but he hadn't. Which meant he was enjoying this. Enjoying the hunt.

Footsteps sounded nearby.

"Should I bury my face in that lovely cunt before or after I fuck you?"

The exhaustion and cold were forgotten as my stomach clenched. Images of the Enforcer with his head between my legs as I pulled on his hair flashed across my mind before I could stop them, and my stomach tightened further.

"Hmm. I think I'll lick your pussy first. Then I'll flip you over and fuck you face first in the mud."

I sucked in a sharp breath.

"You'd like that, wouldn't you?" he said in a rough voice, sounding just as affected by the idea as I was.

His bare feet appeared through the rain, right at the base of the trunk. Breath stuck in my lungs. I held as still as possible.

Several tense seconds passed.

He moved away and I exhaled in relief.

Hands suddenly wrapped around my ankles, and I was dragged out of the trunk. I slammed into the mud. Lord Taran had me pinned under him in seconds with my hands restrained above my head.

"Found you," he whispered.

I thrashed under him, trying to dislodge his weight. "Get off me, you bastard!"

He pressed me further into the mud, his hips settling heavily between my thighs. He wasn't going to let me go.

I headbutted him.

Pain cracked across my skull. He reared back with a curse. I slammed a fist into his ribs before he could recover and pulled myself out from under him. Just as I'd managed to get to my feet, he swept them out from under me.

I landed in the mud, and he leapt on top of me. I punched at the side of his head, but he blocked the attack and pinned that arm to the ground. I tried kicking his face next, but he imprisoned both legs between his thighs.

Before I could clock him with my only free limb, he grabbed it, and wrenched it down. I was trapped.

I panted in his hold, catching my breath as he kneeled over me.

"I love it when you fight me," he groaned. I could feel his cock grow impossibly hard against my legs where he held them. "No one else would dare."

"You're a sick bastard."

A dark laugh. "Perhaps."

Jaw tight, I glared up at him. "Let me go."

Rain streaked down his face, some of the cold droplets dripping onto my stomach. He stared at me with that dark, unblinking gaze. "Never."

"Enforcer," I warned.

His smile was blade-like.

I had to remember this wasn't Lord Taran anymore. This was the killer.

I tried to slam my face into his again. This time he expected the attack and moved out of the way before it landed. He yanked both arms over my head, holding them with one hand and wrapping the other around my throat.

Warmth pooled in my belly at being held immobile.

Why was I enjoying this?

Did I like being dominated?

I didn't have enough experience to know. The Enforcer was the only male I'd ever met who could overpower me like this and fuck did I revel in it.

He tightened his hold on my neck, not enough to harm,

but just enough pressure to keep me pinned as he moved closer and dragged his nose up the column of my throat. He groaned. The masculine sound sent pleasure shooting straight between my legs.

"What are you doing?" I said, bewildered.

"You smell so good when you're aroused." His voice was thick and gravelly.

Horror struck when I realized how he had found me. He had said all those dirty things, knowing what they would do to me and tracked my scent.

My stare hardened. He was playing with me, like a beast toying with its next meal.

"Either kill me, or get the fuck off me."

"I don't think you want me to do either of those things." His fingers tightened on my neck. "I think you want me as much as you hate me. I think you want me to fuck you right here in these woods."

I shivered under that pitch-black stare. Not out of fear, but anticipation because I wanted him to do just that.

The glare I sent him in response felt weak even to me. I was tired of fighting this. Here, half-naked in the rain and mud, with this virile male staring at me like he wanted to devour me, all my scruples went out the window. I didn't give a fuck why I shouldn't.

He saw the second the fight left me.

"Make me feel good."

A feral expression came over his face. "Fuck."

He tried to slam his lips down on mine, but I held him back. "No kissing."

Something flashed across his expression too quick to catch. He flipped me. I ended up pressed face first into the cold mud with his weight at my back. A hand moved underneath me and easily found my clit. Electricity lit up my whole body like an ashtray had shocked me. I twisted my head to the side, moaning.

I placed a hand on top of his and shoved it down my underwear. "Harder," I demanded.

He groaned at the wetness he found, then roughly stroked me with the pad of his finger. Toe curling pleasure ripped through me.

His lips touched the shell of my ear. "Did you ever think hate could feel this good?" he whispered, furiously playing with my clit as he ground his erection against me.

Dark, mocking laughter followed when I didn't answer. "You want this. Want me. Admit it."

"No." My protest ended in a breathy moan when his finger entered me. He rolled his hips against my ass in time with his strokes. The friction in my center built and built with every movement.

"Tell me you want me," he growled in my ear.

I was too absorbed in the pleasure he was giving to answer but managed to shake my head.

"My cock is so close to your pussy." He rolled his length against my ass. "I could have it inside you in a second. All you have to do is admit you want it."

Fuck. I did. I wanted him inside me. But I couldn't admit that with words like he wanted. Saying it out loud made it too real.

"I said to make me feel good," I hissed through my teeth.

He wrenched down my underwear with his free hand while his other continued to work my center. My insides clenched. The head of his cock pressed against my entrance. Panting, I angled my hips up to give him better access.

Yes, right there.

He pressed me back into the ground with his tip so close to where I wanted it, slipping it through my folds. I moved my hips in time with his. The delicious friction increased the tension mounting in my core. His mouth moved to my neck as we continued moving against each other.

"Tell me you want me to fuck you dirty in this mud. Say the word and my cock is yours."

I couldn't. I couldn't acknowledge what was between us. If I didn't voice it out loud, I could pretend I wasn't me and he wasn't the Enforcer. I could pretend we were just a man and a woman who were insanely attracted to one another.

I was wound so tight all it would take was a few more—

Abruptly his weight vanished along with his fingers.

"What the fuck?" I whipped around to glare at him.

He crouched off to the side, water dripping down his heated gaze.

"Come back here," I demanded. Everything tingled and ached. He couldn't just leave me like this.

"Ronan," I panted, using his name for the first time.

He sucked in a sharp breath, fighting himself. "Not unless you admit you want me," he said in a strained voice.

"Why does it matter?"

His jaw tightened. He glanced away, but not before I caught the glint of vulnerability in his eyes. "It just does."

I understood what this was about. He wanted, maybe even needed, to hear I wanted him—Ronan Taran. Not the Enforcer. Not the dangerous myth.

Too damn bad. We weren't lonely for the same reasons. If he didn't want women fucking him for his deadly reputation, then maybe he shouldn't murder innocents.

I rose onto my knees and yanked up my underwear, glaring at him through the rain. My hand came back stained with a pinkish liquid. The rain had washed away most of the teenager's blood, but it had set into my undergarments.

I vomited.

Acid burned up my throat as I heaved over and over again.

"Vera?" the Enforcer came closer.

I threw out a hand. "Stay back."

I retched up all the berries and roots I had eaten this morning. My stomach clenched on itself when there was nothing left to throw up.

By the time I finished, the adrenaline from the chase and subsequent fight fled, leaving me completely drained. I sagged into the mud.

"Are you okay?" Lord Taran asked softly. The rattling timbre to his voice was gone meaning so was the killer.

But the killer wasn't really gone. It and Ronan were one in the same. He had told me that the first night, but somewhere along the way I had forgotten that, and I had let those same hands that murdered the teenage boy give me pleasure.

I gagged and wiped my mouth.

"No," I said dejectedly.

I didn't have the energy to be angry anymore. There was only a bitter sadness that I couldn't save that teenager. And how could I? Five days from now I would walk right back into the Crone's lair, and I'd let her do all the horrible things she did to me as a child. I couldn't protect myself from her any more than I could protect that teenager from the Enforcer. It was laughable to think otherwise.

"I don't understand why you are so upset," he said in a quiet voice. "Did you know him?"

I trained my gaze on his. Water misted down on us, and the evening was growing steadily darker.

I couldn't quite put my finger on what it was, but there was something about the cover of night that held a measure of safety to it, lent itself to a degree of vulnerability I wouldn't dare during the day. Maybe it was simply, the darkness allowed me to hide.

"I don't have to know him to know what it's like to be

helpless," I said. "And maybe—maybe I just wish I had someone like me to protect me when I was younger."

"Who did you need protection from?"

The scars on my back itched.

I dropped my gaze. "It doesn't matter now."

"It does to me."

My head snapped up. "Why? Why does that matter to you, but not that teenager's life?"

"Because I didn't have a choice."

"Corthshit. You said it yourself. You're the judge, jury, and executioner."

"He stole, blatantly, in front of everyone. If I'd spared him, it would only encourage others to follow his example," the Enforcer said simply.

"You're not even sorry, are you?"

His eyes spit fire. "Do you think I enjoy killing unarmed civilians? That I do it for sport? Do you think I'm not *haunted* by all the blood I've spilled? That I don't see each and every one of their faces when I shut my eyes?"

"Then why do it?"

His jaw clenched. "Because someone must."

"Why does it have to be you though?"

A sigh left him at the same time the anger sizzled from his gaze. He scrubbed a hand down his face, looking world-weary. "You're looking for answers I can't give you. I am who I am, Little Thief. I am no hero. I accepted that a long time ago. You need to as well."

As awful as killing the teenager was, I could understand his motivations. I didn't agree with them, but I could under-stand them. The Enforcer's greatest weapon wasn't the sword he carried, it was the fear he inspired.

If he had shown mercy after the teenager's defiance in front of all those miners, it would have made him look weak.

"Did you kill that boy back at the train?" I blurted out.

My breathing stalled as I waited for his answer. That boy was no criminal. He was just curious. There was no need for him to die.

I didn't need the Enforcer to be a hero. I was far from one myself, but I *wouldn't* stand for a child being harmed.

And I desperately wanted Lord Taran not to be that kind of man. I wanted, no needed, some sort of validation that this strange connection I felt with him wasn't bad. That of all the wrongness in my life, this was the one thing that was right.

Silence.

My stomach sunk.

It was all the confirmation I needed.

"You really are a monster." I whispered. "Stay the fuck away from me."

18

I didn't speak a single word to the Enforcer over the five days it took to hike to the Crone's offering site. I nodded, shook my head, and grunted when it was necessary, but I didn't give him anything more than that.

He might not *look* like the terrifying monster all the stories depicted him as but looks were deceiving. The Crone had taught me that.

Her name was misleading. She enjoyed the shock value. Those coming to her for help expected some decrepit old hag, and while that's exactly what she was under all the magic, she appeared as a young, beautiful female.

I knew the real her though. There wasn't enough beauty or enchantments in the world to hide a heart blacker than night in the Darklands.

And now I knew the real Enforcer too.

If seeing him run a sword through a teenager hadn't been bad enough, the knowledge that he had killed that little boy disillusioned me completely.

He had murdered a *child* over a stupid piece of gold.

It was inexcusable. It placed him firmly in the same box as the Crone in my mind.

Things had become much bigger than a vest. The godstone—whatever it was—could not fall into the hands of the Enforcer. It would make him even more powerful than he already was. How many more innocent children would die then?

No. I would kill him first, find the godstone, and deliver it safely into the hands of the Rogues.

Since it was much faster to cut diagonally through the woods, the Enforcer opted not to cross the river and return for our things before coming here, so killing him would have to wait. I didn't have a good counter argument and I still hadn't figured out exactly how I was going to get the iron dust in his system. I only had one opportunity. I couldn't waste it.

I was able to retrieve my clothes, dagger, and chains after our little adventure through the forest.

"What is this place?" Lord Taran asked, surveying the area.

The Crone's offering site was once a place of worship for the Gods. Weather-worn columns covered in vines kissed the tree canopy. They lined a stone path, now crumbling and broken up by thick roots and grass.

I ignored his question and carefully traversed over the uneven ground. Some patches of the earth remained softened from the recent rains causing the rocks to shift underfoot. Beyond the columns was a circle of massive stones set into the ground. The stones were flat and just as tall as I was.

I stepped over one and blew off the top layer of dirt covering its surface, revealing a face carved into the rock. It was a female with long flowing hair. The end of her beak-like nose was partially worn away, but its sharp lines remained. She held a clay pot overflowing with water. The goddess' name was carved below her image.

Brigidis, Goddess of Healing.

Without looking, I knew what the other stones would say.

Ogmas, God of Language.

Belenus, Goddess of the Sky.

Cerna, God of Knowledge.

Anu, Goddess of Nature.

Taranis, God of War.

Dagdan, the Original God and Chieftain.

"You can't ignore me forever." The Enforcer's breath whispered over my neck. I had heard him come up behind me but was too busy pretending he didn't exist.

I shrugged and moved away, but he grabbed my hand and spun me toward him.

"I—" He started, then stopped. Tight lines bracketed his mouth. "I don't like this."

And I was supposed to care because?

I stared at where his hand gripped my wrist, then glanced back at him with a raised brow.

He released a frustrated sigh, dropping his hand.

I walked past the worship circle to the meadow beyond.

Someone had left a fresh offering for the Crone. The loaf of bread and woven doll stuck out among the small white flowers. Butterflies delicately balanced on the flowers' leaves, their wings fluttering in the gentle breeze. The rustling of the surrounding trees whispered softly in the background adding to the meadow's tranquility.

The beauty and peacefulness of this place only made its purpose more nefarious. Desperate souls entered. Some never returned. Those who did came back changed. They came back missing what was most important to them.

I pulled out my knife and cut open my hand before squeezing it into a fist and dripping blood over the white flowers. When it hit the soil, the liquid activated the spell over this area. The ground bubbled and hissed, spitting out steam.

It wouldn't be long now.

I swiped up the bread with a disbelieving laugh and plopped down on a log. Who was dumb enough to think they could tempt the Crone with stale bread?

Before eating, I unwound the chains wrapped around my torso and set them beside me on the trunk. It was a pain in the ass carrying them like that but well worth it when night fell and I didn't have to worry about falling asleep.

The Enforcer entered the meadow seconds later. He sat beside me, putting his thigh flush with mine. Prior to revealing what a child murdering bastard he was, I would have either let myself enjoy his touch, or shoved him away with a threat.

Now, he got nothing from me, not even my anger.

In my peripheral, I watched him discreetly smell the air.

He had done that often over the last five days. Little touches here and there to trigger my arousal scent. None of them worked. One of the perks of seeing his true colors. That annoying pull I felt between us was completely severed. He could touch me all he wanted. I didn't feel a thing.

He growled under his breath and slid over. I snickered.

His gaze latched onto mine. "Is this really how it's going to be for the rest of our journey?"

I tore a chunk out of the bread and shoved it into my mouth, staring passively. It was hard to chew, but a welcome change from all the berries and roots we'd been eating.

He ripped the loaf out of my hands and chucked it far into the trees.

I opened my mouth, ready to tear into him until I caught the eager gleam in his eyes. He *wanted* me to yell at him.

I sucked in a deep, calming breath and forced myself not

to react. Gods, was it hard, but I wasn't letting him get a rise out of me anymore.

His mouth bunched up. He didn't like that.

"Fight me," he demanded. "Yell at me. Make me bleed if you want. Anything, but this endless silence."

I stared flatly.

He jerked me toward him and slammed his lips down on mine. Despite my best efforts, arousal spiraled through me.

He tore his mouth away and inhaled deeply. "I knew you were still attracted to me," he said triumphantly.

. . . And that arousal dried right up.

He was just using me for his ego. Using me for the godstone.

I shoved at his shoulders with a snarl.

But he wouldn't move. He stayed in my space. "Whatever you are thinking. Stop."

A vortex of wind appeared at the center of the meadow. I was grateful for the timing. That was our ride.

"Vera, wait." He grabbed my arm as I rose from the log.

I glared down at him, nostrils flaring. "What?" I bit out, too upset to be silent.

His gaze shifted between mine. "Talk to me."

"Why do you even care?"

"I didn't realize how much I loved the sound of your voice until you wouldn't speak to me."

Damnit, that was . . . Nope. I was not going to let that confession get to me.

"Maybe you should have thought about that before you murdered that teenager and little boy." I jerked my arm out of his grip and stormed over to the vortex, grateful for the anger. It didn't leave any space for fear. Once I stepped inside her domain, there was no going back. The Crone would take from me, regardless if I used the Eye.

"Would you rather I lied to you?" he called out. "Pretended to be something other than what I am?"

"You're an honest child murderer," I shouted back. "I'll give you that."

"I did not murder that boy."

I whirled around. "Corthshit."

His gaze was open. I detected no hint of deceit.

"You already admitted you had." I resumed walking toward the vortex.

"No, you made an assumption."

Oh, for the love of Gods.

"We don't have time for this!"

I was already losing my bluster to face the Crone. If the vortex disappeared before I reached it, I didn't know if I would have the courage to offer my blood a second time.

I raced toward it. The Enforcer's footfalls thundered behind me.

We both threw ourselves into the vortex at the last second. Air whipped around us, pulling at our hair and clothes. When the vortex dissipated, we stood inside a seemingly innocuous patch of woods, but I knew we were close. I could feel the Crone's presence like a greasy worm wriggling in my chest.

I palmed a rock and threw it behind me. It crashed into something mid-air, and a pulse of pink exploded across the tree line in the distance. A magical barrier. It kept the Crone's home hidden from view.

Slowly turning, I faced my childhood home. Tucked away in the trees was the two-story stone cabin with a wrap-around porch. If not for the evil witch living there, I might have called it quaint.

The sight of it brought a tremor to my hands. I clicked my talons nervously together.

This place held so many memories. None of them good. Being back here made me feel things I hadn't felt in a long time. It made me feel small. Weak. Like I was a helpless child again.

I don't know how Lord Taran knew what I was feeling, but somehow he did. He was attuned to me in ways I wasn't even attuned to myself.

He wrapped his hand around mine and squeezed.

That single touch communicated the thing I needed to hear the most.

You aren't alone.

I'd never admit this out loud, but I was grateful for his company. I could go back to being angry at him after this was over, but right now, I needed him. He was an anchor in a turbulent sea intent on drowning me.

I squeezed back.

I dropped his hand and moved deeper inside the Crone's territory.

A foul scent hit my nostrils. It was a nauseating smell; a horrible odor of death that burned my nostrils and lungs with every breath.

I choked and drew the tunic over my nose and mouth, but it did little to keep the smell from invading all my senses. The stench seemed to be a physical thing, permeating every molecule of air.

The second thing I noticed was the loud, incessant buzzing of swarming insects hovering over a graveyard. It was littered with bodies in various states of decomposition. The Enforcer stopped and stared at a body cavity with black organs spilling out, maggots feasting on the rotting meat.

The body twitched.

His horrified gaze swung to mine. "Is it still alive?"

"They all are." For now. Until the Crone bled them dry.

His jaw clenched, but otherwise he seemed unaffected by the mass grave before us. With a sword like the one on his back and scars like his, he had to be accustomed to death. Still, it was impressive he wasn't gagging at the smell alone. This place had been my home for fifteen years, and *I* was choking on the stench.

"Who are they?" he asked.

I glanced down at the bodies with a pitying stare. "Beings who were too selfless for their own good."

Visits to the Crone were for one of two reasons—either they wanted something for themselves, or for someone else. For those that came for a loved one, the Crone preyed on their love and desperation.

"I remember one time, a mother came to the Crone for a spell that would waken her comatose son. He had suffered severe injuries from a beast attack but had managed to survive. She asked the mother what her son's life was worth to her, if she was willing to trade her life for his." I lifted my gaze from the bodies and found Ronan's gaze rapt on me.

Ronan? When had I started calling him Ronan?

I blamed it on being back here. It was hard to think straight with the terrors of my past all reaching for me at once. As the years had past, the memories had grown fainter, the pain duller. It was easy to forget until something triggered one, like the broberie feathers. Now all those memories were roaring back with a vengeance.

"For a selfless person like that mother, their most trea-sured possession *is* the person they came for, but they have something of equal value to offer the Crone—their pure hearts. Apparently, they taste the juiciest."

Ronan's face twisted in disgust. "She eats them?"

"In a way. She feeds off their life force."

I gave the bodies a final glance before continuing toward the cabin. To the left, I saw a square slab of wood. My feet stalled as my heart crawled into my throat. It was used to cover an abandoned well I was all too familiar with.

When I had refused to cooperate as a child, and let her

carve me up for spells, the Crone loved to toss me inside. She left me to rot in the dark for days, sometimes weeks at a time until I became more agreeable.

I could still feel the cold mud seeping between my toes, smell the damp mold. I would scream for hours until my throat was raw and the only thing to soothe it was a handful of moist dirt. I remembered feeling through the mud for grubs to alleviate the gnawing hunger.

But the thing I remembered the most was the endless pitch black and the fear that I would die alone in the dark. Cold and forgotten.

I kicked the board off the well and peered inside. The shaft of light cut through the dark, illuminating the moldy, stone walls all the way to the bottom. It was bone dry.

It appeared so innocuous in the sunlight. Different. Or maybe I was different.

"What's this?" Ronan's voice pulled me from my thoughts. He stood beside me, staring into the well.

"The Crone used to throw me in there and leave me in the dark as punishment," I said mechanically.

I convinced myself the only reason I shared that was so he would know what kind of evil we were dealing with.

When he remained silent, I glanced up. He was holding himself still. I sucked in a breath at his expression and for the first time, I felt the thinnest thread of fear toward him. His face was savage, with a murderous intent glinting in his steel gaze. He was seconds away from exploding.

"I'm going to kill her."

He unsheathed his sword and started toward the cabin.

"She can't die." I had tried. Many. Many times.

Ronan's volatile gaze jerked over his shoulder as he stopped. "I saw you offered her your blood." His teeth gnashed together. "Is that what she wants from you?"

She already took my most treasured possession. My

innocence. But I had something equally valuable to offer.

The Rogues had all sorts of theories on the origins of my beastly features.

Bet her dad was a fisherman and fucked a mermer. They've got claws and fangs like hers and lure men into the sea.

No, my bets on the mom.

They were all wrong.

"No. She's the one who cursed me." I raised my hand, showing my talons. "She turned me into this *thing* so she could have endless material for magic."

His blond brows slammed together. "She wants . . . pieces of you?"

I swallowed around the lump forming at the back of my throat. "Yes," I choked out.

He charged toward me and grabbed my hand. "We're leaving. She's never getting near you again. We'll find another way."

I dug my heels in as he towed me behind him. "Ronan, stop. There isn't another way."

He swung to face me.

Even if I had never agreed to his bargain, I would have ended up here at some point to learn the godstone's location. I survived fifteen years with the Crone. I could survive one more visit.

Every line of his body was rigid. I could tell he wanted to grab me again and carry me away. I didn't understand it.

"This was always the plan," I said. "What's changed?"

"Everything," he said so quietly, I wasn't sure I heard him correctly. Resolve washed over his features. "We will get access to the All-Seeing Eye, but I will be the one who pays the price. Not you."

"I—"

"Don't argue with me." He released a controlled breath. "If you do, I'm not going to be able to stop myself from throwing you over my shoulder and taking you away from this vile place."

"Okay." I wasn't sure what else to say.

Hand in hand, we hiked to the cabin.

In sharp contrast to the outside, the interior of the Crone's home was full of life. Vines grew along the wall with red blossoming flowers; trees stretched from floor to ceiling; insects scuttled between floorboards.

Somehow, despite the gag inducing stench just outside the door, the inside smelled like honey and berries. I glanced over my shoulder at Ronan and found him taking it all in with a dumbstruck expression.

The Crone was noticeably absent. I wouldn't be surprised if the witch was building a web somewhere so she could trap us and eat us for dinner. Her appetite for death was equal to her love of flesh.

A stair creaked and my eyes shot to the top of the staircase to find the death witch smiling down at us.

The Crone, the death witch, Balor's lover—she had an infinite list of names she'd amassed over her long life. But she didn't appear more than a few years older than me. Long, golden curls spilled down a blue satin gown with puffed sleeves. Her bow lips were painted red, her cheeks brushed pink. Black coal lined two amethyst eyes, making them even more startling.

"Hello, Vera." A voice like a velvet wrapped blade dragged down my spine, causing me to shiver. "Back so soon?" She asked her question with a wide smile, but there was a sharp undercurrent to her words I might have missed if I didn't know to listen for it. She was in a dangerous mood.

That was expected. I had managed to run away from her. None of her victims ever had. I threw a look over my shoulder that warned Ronan to let me do the talking.

"What a pleasant surprise, child. I've missed you dearly."

She descended the stairs, gingerly holding the edge of her dress. Every gesture was delicate and full of grace like she was a queen, and not a life sucking witch. I had already grown tired of her game by the time she reached the bottom.

All of this was a charade for the fae behind me. He had never witnessed her true form. The Crone wanted to be renowned for her beauty.

"Oh," she purred. "And who is this delectable male you've brought along?" She licked her lips, staring at Ronan.

"Cut the crap. I'm here to make a trade."

Her nails dug into the railing as a tinkling laugh rang out through the quiet space.

"Impatient and surly, just like your father."

The statement caught me off guard. She'd never spoken of my father before, and I was never willing to pay the price for an answer. This was punishment for not playing along.

"I need to use the All-Seeing Eye," I said.

This time the smile she flashed was genuine.

"That will cost you," she said with absolute glee. The Crone would relish extracting her price. She always did.

"You're not touching her." The menace in Ronan's voice shocked me into glancing over my shoulder. He dug through a small pouch attached to the leather belt around his waist and withdrew a brooch with a wolf's skull carved into the ivory.

"I offer you my most treasured possession, and in return you will allow us to use the All-Seeing-Eye."

The Crone's smile was serpentine as she beckoned him forward.

He moved past me and held out the broach to the Crone but didn't release it as her spindly fingers ran over the surface.

"You were very close with your mother. This is the last

piece you have left of her. I accept." She took the broach.

His mother.

The Enforcer has a mother . . .

Of course, he did. He mentioned an uncle before too. I had just never thought about it. In my mind, he had appeared into the world fully formed, wielding his sword.

They *were* close.

His mother was dead.

My gaze locked on Ronan's face. I could only see his profile, but it was enough to notice the distress lines tightening his eyes as he stared at the broach in the Crone's grip.

A soft pang hit my heart.

I was wrong about the Enforcer. He wasn't like the Crone. She loved nothing and no one except for herself.

His mother obviously meant a great deal to him, and he was giving up the last thing he had to remember her by for *me*.

I couldn't let him.

My body would heal, but he would never be able to get that piece of his mother back.

"I'll give you a piece of my wing as payment," I announced.

The Crone's greedy eyes flicked my way. The scales on my wings were highly potent for spells. I knew she wouldn't be able to resist the offer.

"I accept."

"Wing?" Ronan's voice rang out as a sharp barb cut its way through my chest. I clenched my hands at my side. If I didn't need the Crone to use the Eye, I'd stab out her black heart for forcing me to reveal that to the Enforcer.

The Crone's expression was the picture of innocence. "You didn't know? Oh, my daughter here is quite unique."

"I'm not your daughter," I ground out.

She flicked a dainty hand in the air like the distinction

was inconsequential. It sure as fuck was an important difference to me. She had raised me, but that didn't make her my mother. She couldn't bring life into this world, only death.

"You need to leave," I warned Ronan.

I didn't want him to witness what was about to happen.

He faced me, black flickering in his gaze. The killer was fighting for control. "No," he snarled. "She's not touching you."

"Send him outside the barrier," I told the Crone. "Or no deal."

She flicked out her hand and Ronan was dragged out of the cabin, but not before he sent me a venomous glare that promised I would pay for going back on our agreement.

He'd get over it when I returned his mother's broach.

The door slammed in his face.

I bared my fangs. "If you hurt him . . ."

She flashed a knowing smile. "No reason to fuss. He is waiting for you outside."

Like I would ever take the Crone at her word. I marched over to the small window adjacent to the door and peered through the dirty glass to see Ronan pacing in the distance like a rabid animal.

"Give me the broach," I said, still watching him.

"No. The broach was offered and accepted, same as your wing. I can bring him back inside to use the Eye with you if you'd like?"

What she really meant is she'd bring him back inside to see me get tortured.

I'd figure out a way to get it back before I left.

I shook my head, then faced her. "Let's get this over with."

The Crone dropped all pretense of politeness. A knife appeared in her hand. "Oh, I'm going to enjoy this. It's been too long, daughter."

19

Tension tightened my body. I said nothing. Did nothing.

"You know how this goes. On your stomach."

Phantom sensations of pain jolted over my back like electric pulses. My muscles tightened, preparing for what was about to happen, but I still couldn't make myself move.

Another flick of the Crone's hand and an invisible force dragged me to the ground. My knees hit the hard floor, then my chest.

The Crone planted a heel on my spine. "I miss the times I didn't have to use magic on you," she said with a sigh.

She meant the times I was too young and naive to know what she was doing was wrong. When I was old enough to know better, I fought her tooth and nail. Sometimes I won. Those were the times she threw me in the well.

Cold air hit my back when she wrenched up my tunic and I shivered. The knife sank into the fleshy meat between my shoulders and my vision blurred. I bit my tongue hard, and my mouth flooded with the coppery taste of blood. The pain was a welcome distraction from the fire in my back.

With every drag of the knife, it felt like the Crone held

an open flame to my skin, but I refused to make a single sound. I wouldn't give her the satisfaction.

Despite my resolve, a scream tore from my throat when she cut into muscle. I dragged in deep breaths through my nostrils, fighting not to pass out.

There was a deafening roar outside. The cabin walls shook like a giant had them in its grip. Hung baskets crashed to the ground, scattering roots and herbs over the floor. Leaves rained down from the trees.

A loud, put-upon sigh came from the Crone. She moved over to the entrance and yanked open the door.

"You can't punch your way through the barrier, Enforcer," she called out. "It's impenetrable."

The shaking abruptly stopped.

"Where's Vera?" he shouted. The rattling timbre was back in his voice. The killer had taken over. "I heard her scream. If you hurt her . . . Not even the Gods can save you." The last part was said in a low snarl.

"Not even the Gods you say?" the Crone murmured in amusement. "My daughter is alive," she told him.

"Vera!"

The Crone glanced over at me, annoyance clear in her expression. "Calm him before I am forced to."

I worked my throat, swallowing thickly as I unstuck my tongue from the roof of my mouth. "I'm okay," I called out in a scratchy voice.

"Are you—"

The Crone slammed the door shut and returned to me.

Ronan shouted something, but it was too muted to make out. The walls shook one last time, making his extreme displeasure clear, before he fell silent again.

"Where were we?" The Crone picked up the knife she had set down. Her gaze moved over my back. "This would be easier if you would just draw your wings out, darling."

This being torture.

If I knew how to draw out my wings, I would have flown from this place long before I was fifteen.

The Crone kneeled beside me. "Ah, there." Each muscle on my right side tensed as she unfolded a wing, relieving the pressure in my back, but not the pain. My talons dug into the ground, gouging the wood as the Crone skinned off scales. It sounded like a soft brush moving over wood as she worked.

Though I refused to acknowledge the things in my back, they were very much a part of me, as evidenced by the scalding pain that followed every slice of the Crone's knife. I could hide my wings from everyone else but her. She was the one who had put them there in the first place.

I sucked in the smell of honey, desperate to focus on something other than being skinned alive.

"So beautiful," the Crone murmured.

My back was in too much agony to twist and witness the fresh patch of scales she had peeled off.

"My beautiful daughter."

Her words ripped off the flimsy patch I had been using to keep my rage at bay for what she had turned me into. The same patch kept me together whenever someone flinched at my smile or skirted away from my ungloved hands, or the seven years I'd spent as an outcast with the Rogues. All because of the evil witch behind me.

So, against common sense telling me not to anger the only person who could give me access to the All-Seeing Eye, I bared my teeth, snapping, "There's nothing beautiful about me. You cursed me. Made me a monster. Just like you."

"Cursed you?" Her lips smacked together in displeasure. "I gave you a gift, my child. I made you strong. I made you unstoppable."

I stared at my outstretched hands. They seemed normal until the fingers ended and the black talons began. The same talons that had destroyed endless walls and floors and turned strangers, even friends, fearful. They weren't a gift; they were a curse.

"You turned me into a half-beast."

Silence.

I don't know why I wasted my breath arguing with her.

"Am I paid in full?" I gritted out, staring at the ground, feeling her stare burn holes in my head. She was quiet for several moments before her footfalls retreated, heels clacking over the wood.

"Yes," she said from somewhere in the cabin, likely putting my scales into a jar for later. She needed them for spells for her customers, because without any customers, she'd have no one to trick into becoming one of the rotten corpses outside. And without any bodies to drain, she'd turn back into her true self; a withered bag of bones.

No one knew the Crone's true age, or origin. I had seen her—the real Crone—only once when an exceptionally long rainy season made the river impassable for potential customers, and all her current victims were sucked dry. The memory of it would haunt me forever.

I remained on my stomach as my back knitted itself together. It would take days to heal, but at least the bleeding would stop.

"Come darling, your prize is this way." The Crone appeared at the bottom of the staircase, crooking a finger before stepping up the stairs.

I rolled my shirt back down, wincing at the burn of fabric touching the open wound. My arms shook with the effort of pushing myself up. The painful pull in my back had me clenching my jaw so hard it clicked, but I managed to peel myself off the ground and make my way to the staircase, leaning heavily on the railing to drag myself up one stair at a time.

My breath came in fast bursts by the time I reached the top. The Crone waited in the upstairs hall with a patient smile. Her lavender eyes were bright, like she was enjoying my pain. Figures. She sustained herself on others' deaths. I imagined pain was a tasty snack.

With a great deal of effort, I straightened my spine, meeting her gaze before marching over to where she stood. I lifted my chin. "I'm ready."

"Use it swiftly. The longer you use the All-Seeing Eye, the more it takes."

I narrowed my eyes, suspicious she would offer me any warning without something in return, but her expression gave no answers.

A door behind me swung open, leading into a dark space. She swept an elegant hand toward it.

"The Eye awaits you."

The floor creaked below me as I stepped inside the dark room. I shivered, feeling another presence in the space with me. The shadows seemed to shift around the room. The door slammed shut, and I jerked forward. The lock snicked, trapping me inside.

No one knew how the Crone acquired Balor's All-Seeing Eye. Some said the Lord of the Beasts cut it out and gave the Eye to her as a sign of his devotion and love. Others said she seduced him and cut it out herself before banishing him back behind the wall. Whatever happened between the two, Balor had not been seen since the Dark Wars over five hundred years ago.

His severed eye had become the stuff of legends; an eye with the ability to see all—past, present, and future. But like with all magic, its power had a cost. I wasn't entirely sure what that cost was, only that like the Crone's price, I'd pay it.

Short of death, nothing would stop me from finding the godstone.

A faint slice of sunlight slipped through a broken beam in the ceiling. Dust motes floated in the light showcasing how filthy the room was. There was no furniture inside, only a large, covered object at the very back suspended in the air with rope. I moved toward it and ripped off the cloth covering.

Dust stirred, making it hard to breathe for a moment before it settled to the ground. The movement pulled painfully at the injuries on my back. I stood still, pinching my eyes shut as a wave of dizziness crashed over me. When the pain dulled enough and I was sure I would not vomit, my eyes moved to the object I'd uncovered. It was a monstrous eye hung in a gold frame.

It stared right at me.

My heart beat hard in my chest as I took a slow step back like I was standing in front of a deadly beast.

The giant gold iris moved, tracking me.

"Closer," a disembodied hiss bounced off the walls, echoing in the small space. When I didn't move, an invisible force dragged me forward until I stood in front of the Eye. A rock felt lodged in my throat as I stared into it.

The Crone had heavily spelled this room when I was a child. If I came within a foot of the locked door, my head throbbed, and I grew nauseous. It was a space I avoided at all costs when I was younger.

How did this work? Did I speak to it, tell it what I wanted to see?

"We know what you seek." That eerie voice sounded all around like there were hundreds of Eyes. Icy fingers dragged down my spine, but I hid the accompanying tremor. Just like with the Crone, I knew not to show vulnerability to a predator; especially a predator that could read my thoughts as if I'd spoken them aloud.

Its statement registered, and I wanted to smack myself. Of course, it knew what I wanted; it had already foreseen this meeting.

Before I could have any more idiotic thoughts, black tendrils shot out of the eye, wrapping around my wrists and ankles. They were cold and slimy like a treachna's tentacles.

I was about to fight against its hold, but the pupil started spinning, distracting me from my terror, until it was nothing more than a vortex of black and gold. It was captivating, pulling me in with every spin. If not for the tendrils holding me in place, I might have stepped closer.

The room around me dissolved in a kaleidoscope of colors, replaced by a bleak landscape. Everything blurred at first, making it difficult to understand what I was looking at. The image focused. I stood in a dark desert.

Moonlight illuminated a rocky plateau to the left. The rest of the scene was flat, with nothing but sand. The structure was vaguely familiar, but I couldn't put my finger on why.

There was movement on the plateau's western side. The image shifted and zoomed closer. On the other side of the rock structure, dark silhouettes carried something. A chest maybe?

Beyond them was something I recognized—a square pit. That was the opening to the ore mines. The object was in Mayhem, or at least it would be ten days from now based on the first quarter moon in the background.

The scene continued to play out and the figures managed to haul the object to the edge of the mortal-made hole. They carefully removed the wood planks boarding it up.

A figure stood off to the side, watching, but was too far away to make out more than their silhouette.

Words were exchanged, but they were muddled. The other figures and whatever object they carried between them disappeared through the opening, leaving just the one. Suddenly they moved, jerking their head over their shoulder

"Hello, Vera."

The image vanished, and I was left standing in the dusty room. The tendrils released me. Shock slammed into my lungs. I dropped to my knees, sucking in air. My heart felt like a fist with every beat. That voice . . . Where had I heard it before?

My brain was too foggy with fresh panic to make sense of things. They had seen me. That should have been impossible.

"You desire more," that ethereal voice spoke.

My head snapped up, brows furrowed. "No . . . I have what I need." I rose to my feet.

Hisses and clicks sounded all around. "We see all. Even your deepest desires."

Before I could respond, those tendrils grabbed me and the Eye sucked me in again.

20

This time I found myself in a bright, airy room. Large wildflowers were painted on the walls in warm colors, stretching toward the ceiling. A cool sea breeze and ocean sounds drifted in through an open window. At the center of the room was a white cradle, but it was empty.

Creaking sounded, followed by humming. My eyes shifted to the corner to see a large male cradling a sleeping baby as he rocked in a chair. He murmured softly to it, gazing down at it with the tenderest expression. The baby appeared so tiny and fragile compared to the giant arms holding it.

The male lifted his head and two startling gray eyes collided with mine. My breathing stuttered.

Ronan.

He stared past me.

A gorgeous female walked right through me into the room. Glossy, chocolate waterfall curls fell to the middle of her back. She had olive skin, and wore a gold circlet on top of her head that had a pair of wings with a draoistone at its center. She had matching blue crystal earrings and a collection of gold bangles encircled both of her wrists. Her dress had a high, white gossamer collar leading to a lavender bodice

"There you are," Ronan said. A huge smile split his cheeks.

An ugly feeling coiled in my stomach.

Who was she? He had never smiled at me like that.

The Eye ripped the image away before I could get any answers.

Cold shock rippled through me. The tendrils released me, and I stumbled backward, struggling to catch my breath.

"Why did you show me that?" I demanded. "I didn't want to see that."

"You did," it hissed.

"No—"

A presence entered my mind. It felt like someone was poking me in the brain with a stick. I shook my head like I could dispel the feeling, but the prodding continued. Pain flared briefly and then it was gone, taking the presence with it.

"Our deal is done."

I shivered at that chilling voice. Our deal was done? My gaze shot to the Eye.

"That was you?"

It didn't answer. It didn't need to.

"What did you take?" I rushed out.

"Knowledge for knowledge."

A rock settled in my stomach. "What does that mean?"

"You will learn soon enough," it said ominously.

"What did you take?" I shouted.

The invisible force shoved me out of the room, then slammed the door in my face. I pounded on it, shaking it in its frame. "Tell me what you took!"

Pain pinched my back and I stopped, abandoning my search for an answer.

What knowledge had I just lost?

I moved back from the door with a sigh. There was no way of knowing, and I probably wouldn't find out until it was too late.

"Did you get what you needed?" the Crone asked from someplace behind me. My entire body stiffened. Subtly, I angled myself sideways, not wanting to have my back to her.

I wondered how long she had been standing in the hall.

"Yeah," was all I offered, staring at the door.

"You're looking for the godstone."

I said nothing. I wasn't in the mood for chitchatting.

"You are not the first one to come seeking answers about its whereabouts, darling."

That got my attention. I whirled around, ignoring the sick pull in my back. "Did you allow someone else to use the Eye to find it?"

"If they paid well enough." Her smile stretched. "That isn't the only thing they are searching for."

"What do you mean?"

She curled her hands in front of her dress, looking prim and delicate. "What is the information worth to you?"

My back was still bleeding from my first payment. The information might be valuable, but I couldn't afford a second round.

"Can you not be a soul sucking witch for once in your life and help me?"

Silence.

Irritation flared in my gut. Not at her, but at myself. I should have known better than to ask a monster for compassion.

Ignoring her presence, I rested enough to gain the strength to walk down the stairs without flinching. If I showed any sign of weakness, the Crone would pounce on it like a predator on wounded prey.

My gaze drifted to a familiar door at the end of the hall, partially opened, and before I knew what I was doing, I stood in front of it, pushing open the door to my childhood bedroom.

"It is just as you left it," the Crone said. I didn't dare turn around and allow her to see the spectrum of emotions crossing my face—the same emotions my childhood memories brought dragging and kicking to the surface, despite my best efforts to bury them—confusion and pain, followed by anger.

The walls were a bright yellow, a color the Crone had let me choose when I was six. She had bartered a small spell with a customer to have the paint brought here simply because she knew it would make me happy. That same night, she ripped off a talon to see how potent it would be for her spells.

I let the Crone do it willingly because I was too young to understand the concept of cruelty. Her torture was all I had ever known, and I stupidly thought that was just how someone showed their love.

I still didn't know much about love, but I envisioned it was unconditional; it was accepting, supportive. It should make me feel like I could fly, not pin me down and rip apart my wings scale by scale. The Rogues didn't love me—they tolerated me at best—but I could live with that because anything had to be better than this, than the Crone.

I stepped into the room, drawn inside by a morbid curiosity, despite the raw emotions clawing at my chest, desperate to be free, desperate to be acknowledged. A tall dresser sat against the wall on my left, displaying tiny treasures I had collected from the forest as a child; acorns, twigs, and a heart-shaped rock.

The sight of the rock caused a surge of disgust. I had given it as a gift to the witch behind me. She had accepted it with a laugh, asking why I would give her such an ugly thing, and when I explained that I wanted to show I loved her, the Crone laughed even harder.

"That's very stupid of you, darling. You should not love someone who can never love you back," she had said.

Why had she kept that rock, put it on the dresser? It certainly wasn't there when I'd left this awful place. I curled my hands around the hideous thing, the evidence of my stupid naivety, desperately wishing to crush it to dust. But I knew the Crone watched behind me, so instead, I put the rock back in its place like it was as meaningless to me as it was to her.

"There's no dust," I noted out loud. The room showed no signs it had sat vacant for the last seven years.

"I wanted it ready in case you returned." The Crone stepped into the room, her heels clacking on the floor as she did.

I finally looked at her. "Why did you let me leave?"

When I was younger, she allowed me to come and go through the barrier as I pleased because I would always return. No matter what she did to me, I came back because this place was all I knew.

Once I grew older and wiser, she used the barrier to keep me here, but on the day Ness showed up, it was mysteriously down. Part of me had always known that wasn't a coincidence. The Crone would never be so careless.

She had let me go.

"Because you wanted to," she said mildly.

My brows furrowed, cutting lines into my forehead. It couldn't be that simple. Nothing ever was with her.

"Liar. We both know you never loved me or gave a damn what I wanted." My voice cracked at the end, and I hated myself for it. The Crone didn't deserve to know her actions had any effect.

The pain that followed my admission had nothing to do with my back. It was a pain born of years of neglect, years of trying to prove I was worthy of her love, only to find out in the end, my worth was just as spell material. My value to her began and ended there.

I had spent so many nights on that bed, crying myself to sleep, wondering why I wasn't good enough.

My talons twitched, eager to tear this room into shreds. I wanted to set it ablaze and burn away every awful memory it held.

The Crone stalked further inside the room, the predator buried beneath her glamour and makeup emerging. "Love," she spat. "What a foolish, worthless emotion. I gave you something far more useful."

"Oh yeah?" I swallowed the emotion sticking in my throat. "What?"

"Strength. I gave you the power to save these lands or raze them to the ground and still you pine for your pathetic notion of love."

I was too astonished to speak at first.

"You're a monster." And delusional.

Power? What power? My freakish abilities to control beasts, or burn people at random? I would have taken a caring maternal figure over that any damn day.

Her expression turned to ice, her cool facade back in place. "Every monster was a child once. Monsters aren't born. They're made in the dark."

I frowned. I had no idea what to do with that.

"There is tea waiting downstairs," she said at my silence. Only the Crone would torture me one moment and offer me tea the next. She was a study in opposites, death and beauty, torture and civility.

With the pain in my back, I didn't have the energy to argue, much less walk, and the longer I stayed here, the less time I spent with Ronan in my condition. He was already upset with me. He would be more so if he saw me like this.

I waited for the Crone to go down the stairs before following. She sat down on a couch woven from twigs and branches. I took a high-back chair opposite of her with flowers blooming across the fabric. Between us was a moss-covered stump with a delicate tea set laid out.

"Please, drink." She gestured toward a rose-colored teacup.

The Crone had drugged me before as a child when I refused to let her chop off bits and pieces for her magic; before she had discovered my fear of the dark. She certainly wasn't above poison either. I might be tired, but I wasn't stupid. "You first."

Tinkling laughter. "Oh, how I've missed you. You were always so clever."

I didn't respond, watching as the Crone reached for my cup and lifted it to her lips. When she returned it back to its tiny plate, I made sure it had less liquid than before.

"Go on, take a sip," she urged.

Still, I hesitated. A delighted smile spread across her red lips.

"The tea is safe. That large fae would have my head if I poisoned you."

"You can't be killed, at least not with your victims outside."

She lifted her teacup to her lips, humming. "That is true, but that fae would come close. I cannot recall the last time I felt that kind of power."

I didn't like the hungry gleam in her eye. If he was as powerful as she claimed, she could feed on him for years. A knot formed in my stomach at the thought of Ronan becoming one of the rotting bodies outside.

"Touch him and you'll regret it." The threat popped out of my mouth. If anyone was going to hurt him, it would be me. I hadn't suffered his company this long just to let someone else take my kill. That's . . . why I was feeling protective over him. Right?

Right. No other reason.

She grinned at the warning, though I had no idea why.

Since the Crone was still alive and my mouth was as dry as the Red Desert, I finally took a sip of the tea.

The Crone took a sip of hers as well, licking her lips with a forked tongue when she finished. I'd always wondered what she was, but in all the time I'd lived with her, I could never figure it out. She guarded her secrets well.

The saucer clinked as she placed it back down.

"Tell me, does the creature stir in his presence?"

The question was asked with an air of indifference, but I knew the Crone's every tick. She sharpened her gaze as if she very much cared to know.

My eyes tightened at the corners. "What does that have to do with anything?"

The Crone smiled like she knew a secret I didn't.

I didn't like where this was going. Her possessing knowledge I did not have would only end poorly for me. She would weaponize it and find a way to use it against me. It was time to go.

"I'm leaving," I said with finality.

Her eyes flashed; no doubt she was furious she couldn't force me to stay.

I saw the ivory brooch sitting on a table as I walked to the door. Against common sense, I stopped and turned back to the Crone. "What would it take to get the brooch back?"

I wasn't stupid enough to steal it outright and give her cause to hurt me further.

The Crone cocked her head to the side, studying me with open curiosity. "You like him."

"Answer the question," I gritted out.

She tapped a finger against her lips, making a contemplative sound. "One more visit with me at a time and date of my choosing."

She never bartered because she held all the power. I either had to accept her terms, or leave the brooch. I didn't let myself think twice about it.

"Deal." I swiped up the brooch and jabbed its pin into my thumb. I squeezed it until blood beaded the surface and dripped on the floor with a sizzle.

"Oh, and darling, a word of warning."

I pocketed the brooch and waited.

"The Mortal Lands is a dangerous place for the Enforcer."

Glancing over my shoulder, I narrowed my gaze on her. Did she know what I had planned? No, I didn't think so. She had mentioned the godstone wasn't the only thing people were searching for.

"Someone's looking for him, aren't they?"

She smiled coyly.

"Who?" I demanded.

"His enemies."

"He's been everyone's enemy for the last five hundred years," I said slowly. "Why now?"

Even with the iron dust, he wasn't an easy target. I would know.

The answer hit me.

"The godstone. It can kill him."

"You're starting to understand."

My gaze slitted further. "Why are you telling me this?"

"You care for him," she said simply.

"You don't know what you're talking about."

I didn't care for him. I wanted to kill him and if someone wanted to as well, they would have to get in line.

I stormed out of the cabin and the stench of fetid, rotting bodies hit me again. I leaned over the railing and gagged before making my way to the barrier. My back ached something fierce as I walked. The Crone had used some magic to dull my pain while inside.

How kind of her after skinning me alive.

The barrier opened and I stepped through the gap as my legs shook and sweat beaded my forehead. Warm blood soaked through the back of my tunic. I took another step and collapsed. Before I hit the ground, strong arms swept me up.

"I've got you," Ronan whispered.

I was cradled against his hard chest. He faced the cabin with me in his arms. "I will kill you for this!" he roared.

The Crone's laughter was the last thing I heard before the pain took me under.

Consciousness became elusive, like I was back in the depths of the river and no matter how hard I kicked, I never reached the surface, but I could see it. Ronan peered down at me, his face distorted by the ripples in the water.

Words drifted down, garbled and distant. I couldn't make them out, but the tone was soothing like he was trying to comfort me. I wanted to tell him I was okay, but my lips wouldn't work.

Something yanked on my leg and dragged me deeper into the abyss.

A cool cloth glided over my back when I finally surfaced. The sensation felt wonderful against my feverish skin, but there was an undercurrent of pain with every glide. I groaned; the sound muffled from where my mouth pressed against a piece of fabric beneath me.

"You're awake," Ronan rumbled.

His touch was delicate. Hands that butchered and maimed weren't capable of such gentleness. I had to be delirious or dreaming. Everything had a purple haze to it.

I was sweating profusely. My clothes clung to my sickly skin. A shiver racked my frame. How could I be cold and hot at the same time?

My throat burned.

"Water," I rasped. "I need water."

"Here." Ronan helped turn me onto my side. He brought his hand to my mouth and I sucked down the water cupped in his palm. It was a little gritty with dirt, but I was too thirsty to care. When the cool water hit the back of my scorched throat, I groaned.

He brought me more. I wish he was this caring when I was awake. It was nice to be cared for, even if it was just a dream. I always had to go through this alone as a little girl.

"Thank you, my gentle giant," I murmured between sips.

A hand came to my forehead. He withdrew it with a curse. "You're burning up."

"Why hasn't the wound closed yet?"

I don't think dream Ronan was talking to me, but I answered anyway. "It's the magic, silly. She spells her blades."

Magic inflicted wounds were nasty and took the longest to heal. But I would. I always did.

The giant became very still. "She—she used a spelled blade on you?"

My head moved up and down.

He spoke to himself again. "How is that even possible? Only my House has that ability, and even then, we use it sparingly because it is considered a form of torture."

I blew out a raspberry. "It's the only kind she has, dummy."

Dream Ronan wasn't very smart.

He pressed a cool cloth to my head. "You've got pretty lips," I said. They were pink and plump, but rugged too with the scar.

"Do I now?" he murmured in amusement. "I'm going to put you back on your stomach so you can rest more."

"I don't want to rest." I wanted to keep talking to dream Ronan. I liked him much better than the real one.

He brushed a sweaty clump of hair from my face. "You must." His lips brushed over my temple.

I gave him a dopey smile. "I like you."

He didn't smile back. "You won't in the morning."

I frowned. That wasn't true.

"Get some sleep. I'll watch over you."

21

————————

S oft dawn light prodded at my eyelids. I groaned, throwing an arm over my face, but it was too bright to fall back asleep. Reluctantly, I opened my eyes. Rays of morning light streamed down, softening the harsh gray of the trees. I peered around, trying to figure out where I was. The last thing I remembered was collapsing into Ronan's arms after the Crone butchered my back.

It still ached something fierce, but it didn't feel like it was bleeding anymore so that was a good sign.

Carefully, I sat up and spotted Ronan.

He sat, leaning against a tree. The hard glint in his eyes dried up the greeting on my tongue.

He was shirtless. Thick chest muscles and tattooed abs made me swallow hard. I yanked my gaze away, glancing down at the soft fabric beneath me. It was his tunic. The bottom portion was missing.

"How long have you been awake?" I asked.

"All night," he said gruffly. "How are you feeling?"

"Fine."

His eyes sparked with fire at that response. "Fine? No,

you're not fine. The woman who raised you shredded your back."

I rubbed my tired eyes, then sighed. "What do you want me to do? Cry about it? What good would that do?" It had taken me a long time to accept that was just who the Crone was. Being upset that an evil witch did evil things, well that was just stupid.

His mouth set into a grim line. I didn't know what he wanted from me, and I was too exhausted to figure it out.

"Are you hungry?" he bit out.

My body required a vast amount of energy to heal a magic wound. "Yes."

He moved over to where he had a small fire going. A bird was being spit roasted over the flames. "Wing or breast?"

"Breast."

I left him to cook and brood as I took in our surroundings. There weren't any landmarks to orient myself and I didn't hear any running water. I did spot the chains I had left at the offering site, so I knew Ronan had passed through there when I'd been asleep, which made sense. The Crone would have conjured another vortex to return us there.

"Here," Ronan grunted, impatiently waving a piece of cooked bird in my face.

I snatched it out of his hand. It was too early for this grumpy corthshit. I took my annoyance out on my meal, ripping into the juicy meat as he returned to his tree. It was cooked just enough to lock in the flavor without drying out the breast. I devoured it in seconds, sucking the juice off my fingers.

I found Ronan's hungry gaze rapt on my mouth when I was done. His foul mood hadn't diminished. He appeared furious and aroused at the same time.

"Whatever's got your panties in a twist, spit it out." I wasn't going to deal with this for the next four days.

"We agreed I would pay the Crone's price."

His mother's brooch was burning a hole in my pocket, but I wasn't sure this was the best time to return it. It might only make him angrier.

"I understand you're upset that I went back on our agreement—"

"Upset?" he interrupted in a quiet voice. "No. I'm *furious.*"

My own anger flared in response to his. "You should be thanking me for trying to save your precious brooch," I snapped.

It's not like I had a jolly time letting the Crone tear up my back. I had half a mind not to give the brooch back at all to the ungrateful prick.

"I saw—" his teeth gnashed violently together. "I saw the scars on your back. "I want to kill her, choke her with my bare hands."

Ice slithered into my veins. I froze. "When did you see the scars?"

"I caught a glimpse of them when I chased you through the forest, but I had been distracted by other . . . things. I saw them up close when I tended to you. Do you not remember?"

Fuck.

I hadn't been dreaming.

I shrank away from his gaze, feeling over my back. How much had he seen? Was my wing still visible? It was one thing knowing about it and another to see the grotesque thing.

The skin surrounding the wound was incredibly tender and I dropped my hand with a hiss.

"Did you see anything else?"

"The scars were enough," he snarled. "There were hundreds."

The weight of his stare burned over my face. It felt invasive, crawling over my skin like spiders. I couldn't stand it.

"Stop looking at me," I snapped. "I don't want to talk about it."

I should never have let him come to the Crone with me. I should have sucked it up and faced her on my own. All my secrets would be safe if I had. Now he knew too much. He knew things about me no one else did. Things I never wanted another soul to know.

"Most of them were old. You had to have been just a child."

Shame wrapped around my bones like barbed wire. My jaw burned from how tightly it was clenched. He had no right to know those things. He had no right to voice the Crone's abuse out loud. Speak truth into it. Force me to acknowledge what happened to me.

Anger swelled in my lungs. My ribs worked in great heaves. "Say another word and I'll break your fucking neck."

"Look at me."

I snapped my burning gaze at him and immediately wished I hadn't.

Two gray flames seared my retinas with their intensity. They peeled back layers of my skin, flaying me open. There was no hiding from that gaze. I was naked before it, all my shameful secrets dragged out into the daylight for him to see.

He was witnessing all my broken pieces, but there wasn't an ounce of judgment or disgust in that gaze, only fury on my behalf.

My anger dissipated into panic. I couldn't stay here. I needed to run. Hide and re-armor.

"Little Thief," Ronan said sharply. "Don't you dare run from me."

My breathing hitched. I had to.

I bolted.

He tackled me before I could get far and wrestled me to the ground. I jerked my hands where he had them pinned over my head. "Let me go," I growled.

His eyes blazed. "No. I'm not letting you hide from me. You have nothing to be ashamed of."

I screamed like a banshee, thrashing in his grip. Pain spread over my back, but I ignored it. "Get off me!" I sank my fangs into his forearm.

"That's it," he whispered. "Fight me. Get angry."

He released my hands, and I swung a fist into the side of his head. He didn't move. He took the blow without flinching.

"Do it again. Hit me as hard as you need to."

I pummeled his chest with my fists. Each time they crashed into him, I pictured the Crone's face. I pictured all the times I was helpless to defend myself against her; all the times I begged and pleaded with her to stop.

I let myself feel all the rage I couldn't feel in those moments.

She was supposed to take care of me. Instead, she hurt me.

I hit him over and over again as tears streamed down my cheeks, as I screamed at the top of my lungs.

Ronan took every punch, holding my gaze. He let me hit him until his chest was black and blue and I couldn't feel my arms.

There was so much rage simmering inside me. I didn't stop fighting until I expelled it all. When the ball of fury burning my insides was nothing but an ember, I sagged to the ground, chest heaving.

I shut my eyes and caught my breath. There were shooting pain over my back. It had probably started bleeding again. My knuckles were torn and aching, but they would heal quickly. What a shame my healing abilities could only fix external wounds. They were nothing compared to the damage imprinted on my soul.

I kept my eyes closed even after my breathing had evened out. I couldn't meet Ronan's gaze, but I felt it moving over my face.

He brushed a piece of hair out of my eyes and tucked it behind my ear. My emotions were too raw in that moment to handle that gentle touch. No one had ever touched me like that. No one had ever touched me like I was worth something. Except him.

I burst into tears.

"Oh fuck," Ronan said in a guttural voice. "Please don't cry."

That only made me cry harder. He made a panicked sound, snatched me into his lap, and stroked my hair. His movements were uncertain like he wasn't used to giving comfort. This battle-hardened warrior was undone by a crying girl. His reaction was . . . ugh. It was adorable.

He held me tightly as I fell apart. It took several minutes before the sobbing dissolved into hiccups, and then silence. When I wrangled myself under control, awkwardness filled the air. I was clinging to Ronan's neck with my legs wrapped around his waist after having sobbed in his arms.

Discomfort settled over me. I tried to get off his lap, but he grabbed my hips. "Don't go," he whispered.

I had to put my hands on his shoulders to balance myself as I leaned back to look at his face. "What are we doing? What is this?" I gestured between us.

His gaze turned uncertain. "I don't know. I only know I don't want it to stop."

My chest tightened. "Why? You don't even know me." I had made certain of that with every prying question I'd dodged.

"I might not know all of you, but I know enough." That gentle gaze shifted between mine. "I admire you, Vera. I understand why you guard children so fiercely even if they aren't your own."

I seized onto that opening like a lifeline. I would have done anything in that moment to get away from him. To get away from that emotion shining in his eyes.

"I guard them while you murder them in cold blood."

Yes. I needed to remember that. Remember what he had done. I had put aside my anger while at the Crone's, but nothing had changed. He was still the enemy and he still had to die. I felt the armor slowly reforming over my heart and breathed in relief.

He released me with a growl, and I scooted off his lap. "I know what you're trying to do. It won't work and you want to know why?"

I stared.

"We are the same in many ways. We shut down if someone gets too close to seeing the real us because we're terrified they won't like what they see. I *like* what I see when I look at you. I admire your strength and bravery. Even your stubbornness. And I think . . . I think you like what you see when you look at me too."

"You murder *children*."

His expression didn't shutter like I expected. It remained soft and open.

"I told you the truth. I did not harm that boy."

"You really expect me to believe that after I watched you run a sword straight through that teenager?"

"I did not harm him. I swear it."

He was looking me square in the eye, but I still didn't believe him.

"Liar," I growled.

"I know you want to believe I am. You want to believe I'm

awful because if I am, then you don't have to acknowledge what's between us."

He scooted closer, with that earnest gaze locked on me. "Tell me you feel this. You feel this inexplicable pull between us. Tell me your thoughts wander to me so often it's impossible to focus on anything else. Tell me you're constantly thinking of excuses to touch me. Tell me the thought of parting ways after this is over tightens your stomach."

I drilled my eyes into his. Ronan's gaze was bare, completely naked to me. It shined with sincerity. He meant every word.

It was too much to digest in that moment on top of everything else.

"I don't know what I feel right now," I said. I needed space to think. To process.

If my response disappointed him, Ronan didn't show it.

"Are you okay to walk?"

It would be slightly uncomfortable with my back still healing, but I preferred discomfort over whatever this emotion was in my chest.

I nodded.

"We should get moving then."

I now knew the bottom half of Ronan's tunic was missing because he had used it as a cloth to tend to me, and Gods, I wish he hadn't. It left a portion of his abs and the delicious 'v' leading below his waistline visible.

My eyes kept drifting to it as we walked.

"Like what you see?" Ronan asked. I jerked my head up to see a smirk on his lips. An odd pang hit my chest at the sight. I rubbed over my breastbone trying to figure out what the strange sensation was.

I crashed to a halt mid-step. It was longing.

I *missed* his playfulness. It had almost been a week since the last time he teased me.

Balor's balls. When had I started keeping track? I quickly averted my gaze and continued walking, prompting a soft chuckle.

If I was really determined to keep my distance, I should have gone back to thinking of him as the Enforcer, or Lord Taran, but I couldn't bring myself to do it. Those names felt too impersonal now.

The soft trilling of bird songs accompanied our hike along with the slight rattle of the chains I carried. Dappled sunlight spilled through the canopy. Not much undergrowth grew in this part of the forest leaving a clear path for us to travel.

Our peaceful surroundings were at odds with my turbulent thoughts. I couldn't reconcile how the same man who had run a blade through that teenager's chest was the same one who had tended to me so sweetly; the same one who had held me tightly as I fell apart in his arms.

The Crone was an evil woman who did evil things. That was clear cut. I understood her motivations, even if I hated her.

I didn't understand Ronan. He had made it clear he took no joy in his Enforcer duties. Even more than that, all the killing was taking its toll. But Lord Taran wasn't a man who did something unless he wanted to, so why be the Enforcer at all?

Because someone must.

But why?

Careful, Vera. This is a slippery slope.

I knew that insidious voice was right. My last defense against the Enforcer was his secrets. If I didn't know them, I could make my own assumptions. I could justify using the iron dust.

It was already going to be difficult to use because I *did* feel the same connection he felt. There was this invisible rope tethering us together. I had felt it since the train and had done a good job of ignoring it at first, but it had only grown stronger the longer we were together.

I found my gaze constantly seeking him. Every time he was near like now, my whole body was aware of his every movement, and I itched to close the space between us. I itched to erase that hollow stare put there by the numerous women that fucked him, but never saw him.

They didn't see the way his eyes lightened and crinkled at the corners when he was in a playful mood, or how the scar on his mouth reddened when he laughed.

Godsdamnit. When had *I* started to notice those things?

Oh, you're fucked.

Shut up.

22

I tabled those thoughts for now. We had been lucky enough to only skim the boundary of the air beasts' territory on the way to the Crone's offering site, but to reach the river again, we had to pass straight through their nesting grounds. I needed to be alert and aware.

The woods became deathly silent as we traveled farther east. It was an empty quiet that saturated the air, devoid of any signs of life. No birds chirped, no rodents scurried, and most unsettling of all, there was no forest song from the rustling of leaves and branches. There was nothing.

But as night fell, the things creeping in the shadows stirred. It was a new moon, which meant there wasn't a drop of moonlight to guide our way.

I was grateful Ronan had given me space for most of the day. Besides teasing me earlier, he had been quiet as we walked.

"You need to put away your draoistone," I told him.

The blue gem was producing an annoyingly bright glow that would attract every beast in the vicinity for miles around.

He removed the stone and shoved it into his pocket. Then it was pitch black.

Every cracking twig and rustling sound sent my heart racing. I purposely brushed against Ronan's side more than once to remind myself I wasn't alone in the dark. If I wasn't alone, I was okay.

"Little Thief, you're shaking."

Was I?

I stopped walking, peering down at my hands. They were trembling.

"I might be the tiniest bit scared of the dark," I admitted. He already knew my worst secrets. I didn't see any harm in sharing that one too.

I couldn't make out Ronan's face in the blackness, but I saw the moment he connected that fear with the well. His entire body coiled tight. He didn't move for a full minute before a breath hissed out between his teeth.

He intertwined our fingers. The warmth of his rough palm against mine felt like a soft feather whispering down my spine. I shivered at the delicious sensation, which Ronan mistook as fear.

He squeezed my hand. "You're okay. I've got you."

He did, didn't he? He had me when I was on the brink of drowning in the river. He had me after the Crone ripped open my back. And he had me now, when a silly fear from my childhood was getting the best of me.

Every time I needed him, Ronan was there. Without me even having to ask. I had never had that before.

I glanced up at him with a grateful smile.

"Have I told you how beautiful you are?" he murmured, gazing down at me.

My breathing stuttered. "No."

"You are the most alluring female I've ever seen."

What about the woman from the Eye's vision? She was stunning.

"Do you have a lover back home?"

I screwed up my face. I had not meant to ask that.

By the dark starry night, was I jealous?

"No."

"A child?"

"No. Where are these questions coming from?"

Why was I so relieved? What had gotten into me?

I told you, you're fucked.

"I think I might be running another fever."

Yes, I was sick. That's what all these strange emotions were. Just a product of my injury. Once I was healed, everything would go back to normal between the Enforcer and I.

Ha! See? I was even able to use his job title again. I was not fucked.

Yes, you are, because you don't want things to go back to normal between you two.

Pfftttt. What do you know?

Everything. I'm your subconscious, you idiot.

Ronan felt my forehead. "It doesn't feel like you're running a fever." He stopped us, and grabbed my shoulders, his concerned gaze moving over my face. "Do you feel ill? Is it your back?"

There was a sharp crack on our right, and we jerked apart. I pulled out my dagger at the same time he unsheathed his sword.

I peered into the forest, heart thrashing in my chest.

"Do you see anything?" Ronan whispered.

It was impossible to make out anything other than the thin silhouettes of the trees in the pitch black.

"No," I whispered back. "Beasts have night vision. If one is stalking us, we won't see it until it's too late."

"You aren't feeling well. Let's set-up camp for the night."

With the distraction of the beasts, I was actually feeling much better. It gave me something else to focus on.

"No, it's too dangerous. We can stop when it's daylight out and sleep then."

"I'm fine," I added at his narrowed look.

As if to punctuate my point, a wail pierced the air. I clutched my ears to shield them from the ear-splitting sound. The cry was so drenched in desolation and despair, my heart clenched.

"Banshee," I explained. "They'll burst open your eardrums, but otherwise they're harmless." The wailing sounded far off, which meant we were safe for now.

"I'm familiar with banshees, Little Thief," Ronan said lightly. Right, he had probably fought his share of beasts during the Dark Wars. "Just be glad it is not a sloaugh."

I shivered at the name. Those things would drown us in grief, showing images of our dead loved ones on repeat while it devoured us whole. We would be too distracted to realize what was happening until it was too late. Air beasts were the nastiest sort. It was impossible to defend myself against grief and sorrow.

"You promise you're okay to keep going?" he asked.

"I promise."

"Okay. Stay close," he said, creeping forward with his sword at the ready.

"*You* stay close," I sassed back, wielding my dagger. I was perfectly capable of protecting myself.

He shook his head, smiling at that.

Growling and snarling joined the wailing in the distance as we continued forward.

We came across two large puddles, however given the recent rains, I didn't give them much thought as I splashed through one and Ronan the other. Faster than we could blink, we were both entombed in a case of solid ice up to our shoulders.

Ronan frowned down at the frozen liquid imprisoning him and attempted to move. The ice crawled up his neck an inch.

"It is a callitech's trap. The harder you struggle, the more the ice grows," I warned.

Callitech were air beasts with the ability to turn their victims to ice, and depending on their mood, either shatter them, or devour them.

There was a faint purple light emitting somewhere between the trees. A pair of eyes waited in the shadows with a long, slender silhouette hovering slightly off the ground. Several silhouettes branched off the main one.

It was a crua—an air beast who controlled shadows and used them as minions. The sneaky bastard had stalked us here knowing we would be caught in the callitech trap. Crua's were a second-tier beast and callitechs a third tier, which meant the crua was likely following the callitech's orders.

"There's a crua over there," I whispered. Ronan twisted his head as far as the ice would allow.

"What is it doing?" he asked.

"It's waiting for its master, the callitech, to return. They'll share us."

Ronan was unphased by the information. "Why are our heads not frozen?"

"To keep us fresh. It means the callitech is away from its nest. It didn't want us to die before it returned."

All we could do was wait for the air beast to arrive and kill it before it killed us. The ice quickly infused my limbs, and my lips became numb. My teeth chattered. Gods, how I hated the cold.

Thankfully, we didn't have to wait long before it

returned. The air around us turned frigid. Even before I saw the figure flying through the trees, I knew the callitech was nearby.

It crashed through the branches and lowered in front of us. The callitech had a woman's figure. Its skin was blue, and I knew it would be frozen to the touch. Its long hair was frozen stiff. White claws stuck out from its limbs.

The moment the callitech dropped to the ground, the area around its clawed feet froze. It melted the ice around Ronan first. He fell on his knees, blue-lipped and shaking, but the callitech didn't attack. The crua did.

Five shadow minions surrounded Ronan, stretching to match his height as he rose from the ground. He unsheathed his sword and struck at the closest minion, but it moved like smoke, vanishing and reforming around his blade.

A feral grin split Ronan's face. "I see you're not going to play fair." He dug out his draoistone and slapped it on his arm. "Then neither will I."

His draoistone flared brightly casting a blue glow over the surrounding woods. A rock and several branches rose from the ground. Ronan twisted his hands in the air and manipulated their matter. The rock flattened and elongated into a hammer. The branches were filed down and sharpened into spears.

He struck out with his sword and the newly formed weapons all mimicked his movements. As he slashed and stabbed at the shadow minions, so did the other weapons.

Even more impressive—as the shadow minions' attacks moved out of sync with one another, so did the hammer and spears. Ronan was fighting five opponents at once, controlling four different weapons at the same time with his mind alone, but he couldn't kill them. None of his weapons were gold.

Ronan flung his hand toward me. I felt a vibration on my thigh. The dagger rattled in its sheath before bursting through the ice. The cage around me shattered as the dagger flew into his hand.

I fell to my knees, gasping for breath, and tossed the chains I held off to the side.

Flashing me a roguish smile over his shoulder he said, "Sorry. Need to borrow this."

He melted the gold from the dagger. The handle fell to the ground with a clink. Mid-air, he reshaped the gold like he was kneading bread. He pulled it apart and sent pieces to each of his weapons battling the minions and his sword. The gold attached itself to the ends and resolidified, leaving each weapon with a gold tip.

Ronan reshaped what was left of the gold back into a dagger and reattached the handle. He tossed it to me.

I caught it, and frowned down at the dagger with a blade the size of my pinky finger.

"What am I supposed to do with this?" I called. "Pick the beast's teeth?"

Ronan's head swung my way, but he didn't stop parrying the minions' movements with his sword. He fought them without looking.

Okay, he was just showing off at this point.

"You'll figure it out." He winked and turned back to his battle.

The playful action made my stomach flutter and frustrated me at the same time.

Just as he took down those shadow minions, ten more rose in their place. The crua couldn't keep this up for much longer, and I couldn't let Ronan have all the fun.

I charged into the fray.

In my peripheral, I saw Ronan smirking as I thrust my

toothpick dagger into the closest shadow. I missed. I was a foot away and I missed.

"Stop distracting me," I growled. I put my back to his so neither of us would have a weak spot as we fought.

"I like distracting you," he purred. I heard a wet thunk of something getting chopped off.

"You're awfully chipper for someone who got rejected this morning." I stabbed at a shadow, but it shifted before I could hit it.

"Oh, but you didn't reject me, Little Thief. The fact that you didn't was very telling."

"This is not the time for this conversation," I growled.

He laughed lightly. The sound made my insides tingle.

I threw the dagger at the crua. Its form blurred and shifted to avoid it, and it would have, if my aim had been even remotely accurate. I had thrown the blade too far to the left, right where the crua moved to. What was going on with my aim tonight? Ronan. It was his fault. If he would stop flirting with me, I could focus.

The blade sunk into the crua's torso with a wet sound. It shrieked, and lost its hold over half of the shadows, leaving one in front of me and four with Ronan.

The shadow charged, the crafty thing turning solid long enough to knock me to the ground before returning to its airy form. Ronan rammed his sword through its chest and the shadow vanished. He had already taken down the remaining shadows.

I stared dumbfounded. "How did you do that?"

"Their hearts can't change states like the rest of them," he explained, then offered me a hand up.

I smacked it away, growling, "It was my kill, and you stole it." I shoved to my feet. "The callitech's mine. You take the crua."

"You mean the beast you stabbed and is already half dead?"

I smirked. "Think you can handle it?"

Ronan scowled like a petulant child who had their toy taken away. I snatched one of the gold-tipped spears from the air, fighting a smile.

Both beasts moved deeper into the woods realizing their catch wasn't as easy of a meal as they thought. We stalked after them and split up.

The callitech released a blood curdling scream and a jet of frigid air blasted from its mouth. I threw the spear up, blocking my face from the worst of it. I gritted my teeth and forced my feet forward despite the wind gale shoving me back.

The wind blast stopped, and I darted behind a tree knowing something worse was imminent. There was a sick stretch in my back from all the vigorous activity, but I was too high on adrenaline to feel any pain.

Spears of ice shot toward me. One sunk into the trunk, right above my head. I stared at the three-foot-long ice spear sticking out as my chest heaved. Just another inch, and it would have lodged in my skull.

I jerked to my feet and rushed forward, weaving between the trees to make myself a harder target. A blast of ice grazed my right shoulder. It froze my skin there and fissured out, freezing the rest of my arm.

Fuck. I couldn't afford to be hit there again. Even the slightest bump could shatter my arm and I didn't think my healing abilities extended to limb regeneration.

I used another tree trunk as a shield, plotting my next move. All I had was the spear and my throwing arm was frozen. I had to get close enough to stab it. Rushing forward, I sprinted as fast as I could, leaping over another stream of ice and landed a foot away from the callitech. I thrust the spear at it ... And missed.

Its clawed hand seized the spear. Ice slithered over the surface before the entire thing shattered.

I leapt back as it opened its mouth, and I knew. I just knew this attack would be fatal.

The callitech shrieked and a tornado of ice blasted from its mouth. My inner darkness stirred, unfurling in my mind. Liquid fire barreled through my veins as my power exploded out of me. Flames shot out of my palm. The fire and ice slammed into each other mid-air and locked into a battle, neither able to overpower the other.

I grit my teeth, shoving my palm forward, willing more heat into the flames. The callitech pushed back at the same time and my feet slid back in the dirt.

"Burn, you fucker." I willed all the power I could into my unfrozen hand and inch by inch the fire was able to eat away the ice. The flames slammed into the callitech when its icy shield was gone. The beast screamed shrilly as the fire engulfed it and melted its flesh.

Its screaming cut off and it collapsed to the ground. A plume of sparks flew up from its burnt corpse. The flames on its body sizzled into smoke at the same time the fire in my palm vanished.

I dropped my arm. Ragged breaths left me as I plopped to the ground. Fuck, that had been close. Why couldn't I hit it? Maybe I was just off because my body still needed time to heal. I caught my breath as my arm and shoulder thawed, then glanced around for Ronan. He had been quiet while I was fighting the callitech. Too quiet.

I peered around and froze at what I found.

Ronan kneeled on the ground several yards away. His face was colorless and twisted in agony like someone was carving out his heart. Tears slipped down his cheeks. His mouth was moving soundlessly.

But none of that is what chilled the blood in my veins. It was the sight of the sloaugh beside him. The skeletal beast had a hunched back covered in a tattered, black shroud. There was a bony protrusion where a nose should have been, and its eye sockets were empty.

The beast was feeding on his soul. Ronan was sweating and much thinner than he had been just minutes ago. It was killing him.

23

I crept forward and snatched up the discarded rock hammer nearby. The sloaugh was too distracted by consuming its meal. Its head jerked up just before I swung the hammer into its neck. It snapped and the sloaugh went limp. I bludgeoned its head for good measure.

When I was certain it was dead, I dropped the hammer and rushed over to Ronan. Whatever hold it had over him didn't dissipate with its death. That devastated expression remained.

I kneeled before him and cupped his cheeks. "Ronan," I whispered. "Come back to me."

His expression didn't clear. Worry pierced my breast. I shook him urgently. "Ronan. Snap out of it."

Blinking slowly, he came to, and I blew out a relieved breath.

"What happened?" his voice was rougher than normal.

"Sloaugh." I pointed to the dead beast's body. His eyes roved over the corpse, then back to me. Those steely eyes were penetrating as they settled on my face. His stare was weighted and intense. "What?" I asked, on the point of squirming.

"Why weren't you affected?"

"I—" My mind blanked. I had no clue.

It didn't occur to me that I was unaffected until he pointed it out. The sloaugh was close enough, it should have affected both of us. The answer hit me, followed by a piercing pain in my chest. I didn't have any loved ones for the sloaugh to use against me.

Not yet, that annoying voice whispered. *But you will soon. Fuck. Off.*

I clenched my jaw, struggling not to let any of my thoughts show on why I wasn't affected, but Ronan and his damn perceptiveness seemed to sense them anyway.

Understanding flitted across his features. "I saw my mother," he said.

Well, now was as good of a time as any. I dug through my pocket to retrieve his mother's brooch and held it out to him.

He stilled.

Ronan stared at the brooch in my outstretched hand for a long moment as if he wasn't sure it was real before he gently lifted it from my fingers. He cupped it delicately in his palm, scarcely daring to blink.

He was silent for a while, lost in whatever memories the item stirred. His gaze eventually shifted to me. His throat worked. "Why did you steal this back for me?"

The thick emotion strangling his voice brought tears to my eyes. I quickly blinked them away and decided not to correct him on how I had gotten possession of the brooch.

"Any mother who inspired a devotion like yours had to be a wonderful woman. I couldn't let her memory be desecrated in the hands of the Crone."

He stared at me, hard, long enough it became uncomfortable. Those eyes glowed with some foreign emotion I had not seen on his face before. It was an emotion I was too much of a coward to examine.

He jerked me forward and fused his lips to mine.

The kiss was urgent. Frantic. Not at all like the confident way he'd touched me before. His hands clung desperately to my sides like he was terrified I'd run, and he'd never seen me again.

This wasn't the cocky, dirty-talking Enforcer. This was a man on the verge of losing something.

And godsdamnit that made me feel things I didn't want to.

I gripped his face and kissed him back just as frantically. I poured all the anger, confusion, and desire he stirred into it.

His hands threaded through my hair, angling my head to give him better access, and he plunged his tongue inside, tangling it with mine.

I moaned into his mouth.

He tore his lips away, panting, "Tell me you feel this. Tell me you crave me as much as I crave you."

Our breaths mingled as I stared into his eyes, eyes I had seen wracked with grief moments ago. I searched his gaze. I wasn't sure exactly what I was looking for.

I meant what I said earlier. I didn't want to use Ronan like all those other women had. It wouldn't be right to toy with his feelings like that. I'd been there with Ryder and it was awful. He had made his feelings for me clear. If I gave in to him, I had to be certain I returned them, and the only thing I was certain of right now was how confused I was.

"I need more time. Time to get to know you."

"You want to get to know me?" he asked with a strange note in his voice.

"I do."

His gaze shifted between mine. "I will tell you anything you want to know."

"About me," he added. "Some secrets are not mine to share."

"Like what really happened to that boy?"

"He is alive and well," he said firmly. "I give you my word."

I blew out a breath. He was asking me to trust him. I didn't, but I wanted to try.

"Okay. Let's walk and talk. Other beasts will scent the dead bodies and come scavenging."

He stood and offered me his hand. I caught sight of the magnificent bulge in his pants.

"Little Thief," Ronan said in a strained voice. "I only have so much willpower. *Please*." He jerked his hand and I took it this time. Once I was on my feet, he released me and reformed my dagger into a normal sized blade.

He held it out to me once he finished.

"Thanks."

Note to self: Ask more about his impressive powers.

I returned to where the callitech had imprisoned us in ice and retrieved the chains. Ronan appeared out of nowhere, grabbing them, and wrapping them around a shoulder.

I was about to protest when my gaze caught on one of the pink cuffs dangling over his arm.

"Did you take those from the brothel after . . . " I trailed off. It shouldn't have mattered if he had been with someone then. I was adamant on hating his guts in Gold City, but I still needed to know.

"Firstly, I don't need to pay for sex. And secondly, I haven't been able to look at another woman since you."

He said the latter part so matter of factly it eased the tightness in my chest.

I stared up at him, considering him long and hard. "What would have happened if I had taken your hand then?"

Would we be in the same place as we were right now? Or would I be in Mayhem, with only flashes of memories of our time together?

His gaze heated. He took a step forward, putting our chests flush and dipped his head. "I would have had you screaming and writhing underneath me in pleasure for days."

I ignored the dip in my stomach. This was important.

"And then you would have taken my memory and sent me home?"

His lips grazed my ear. "No. I would have locked you up, and never let you leave."

I drew back with a scowl. "So I could be your fuck toy?"

"No, so you could be mine. You were always going to be *mine*."

Not his prisoner. Not his tool. *His*.

"I—I don't know what to say to that."

"You don't have to say anything." He took my hand before putting away his draoistone. "Ask your questions."

"So," I cleared my throat as we set off into the night.

Ronan glanced down at me as we walked. I realized he did that every time I spoke to him; gave me his full attention. No, that wasn't right. I had noticed it before. I just never wanted to acknowledge it.

"Let's start with your mom," I said. "Tell me about her." It was only fair since he had met the woman who raised me.

He straightened, talking into the night. "Ríona Taran battled as fiercely as she loved her children. She was a mother first and a warrior second. You remind me of her in some ways."

I groaned. "Just what every girl wants to hear. That they remind you of your mother."

He chuckled softly, squeezing my hand. "It's a high compliment. Even after I became lord of House Taran, she never hesitated to put me in my place." I heard the smile in his voice as he continued, "I remember this one time, she dragged me into the kitchen by my ear in front of all my men."

I burst into laughter imagining this giant of a man being dragged around by the ear. "She did not."

Ronan grinned down at me. "She did. Ríona Taran was fearless, and she never let me get away with anything. Just like you."

"She sounds wonderful."

He smiled wistfully. "She was." When his expression turned heavy, my chest constricted. I was great at shooting people, but not so great at comforting them. Before Ronan, I had no example of what comfort even looked like so I did what he would have done for me.

I dragged him closer, and locked our elbows, putting our sides flush together, and let my voice fill the silence.

"I spent fifteen years in this forest. The Crone would never tell me who my real parents were, not without paying dearly," I said. "I decided early on, I didn't want to know anything about the people who had left me with such an evil woman. She can't leave her little section of the forest, not without a life source to feed off of, which means my birth parents had brought me to her. I don't know how she turned me into this half-beast. It had to be a very powerful spell. That's why I don't have a fae brand. I wasn't born in the Faylands."

If I had confessed that to anyone else, I would have been too afraid to look at them after, but not Ronan. Not once had he made me feel ashamed of who I was or where I had come from.

I glanced up into his eyes.

262

His soft gaze touched over my face. "Is that why you sleep in chains?"

"Yes."

"I saw the Callitech. Is that part of the curse?"

Instinct made me want to recoil and hide, but I forced myself not to. "It is."

I couldn't help the breath clenching in my lungs as I waited for his response.

"I am sorry for everything she did to you," he whispered.

I smiled mournfully. "I am sorry you lost your mother."

We fell into a companionable silence for a while as we walked.

I should have peppered him with more questions, but Ronan's heat seeping into my side relaxed me into a sleepy stupor. All the excitement from the battle leaked out and exhaustion weighed at my eyelids, but sleep would have to wait until daylight chased the beasts back into hiding.

The persistent ache returned to my back. I couldn't wait for the damn thing to heal fully.

"You look like you're about to fall asleep on your feet," Ronan remarked.

"No," I said slightly slurring the word.

"You're a beautiful, stubborn fool. Come here."

He tried to put an arm under my legs and scoop me up, but I pushed it away.

"You are not carrying me." I wasn't some fragile flower in need of saving. He should know that by now.

"Then let's stop for the night. We are far enough away from the beasts' remains and I don't hear any others nearby."

It wasn't smart to sleep while beasts roamed around us, but the idea of shutting my eyes was too enticing.

"Okay."

We found a set of fallen logs to lay down between. A

beast could easily climb over either of them to get to us, but it was more secure than sleeping out in the open.

Ronan unsheathed his sword, laying it above where he'd rest his head. He slid the chains off his shoulders next and I gestured for them. He hesitated before chucking them off into the night.

I heard them land somewhere with a soft chink, but it would take forever to find them in the dark.

Irritation chased away the fatigue. "What is with you taking things that aren't yours and throwing them?" I growled. "You're going to get them back."

"No. I want you to sleep in my arms without them."

"Absolutely not." If he wouldn't go find them, I would. I moved away.

He grabbed my arm, sitting up. "Please."

Cold trepidation slithered into my veins."Why?" Didn't he understand what he was asking? The kind of danger he would be in?

"You had this wide, dreamy smile when we woke up in the cave together. I want to see it again. Every other morning you have woken up exhausted and half panicked."

I shook my head and went to search for my chains, calling over my shoulder, "We can sleep the same way we did in the cave."

"No," he grunted at my back. "I cannot stand to see you chained up like some animal."

The distress in his voice brought my movements to a halt.

"I believe this will work, but I need your trust," he continued.

I blew out a long breath. Doing this required giving him my complete faith, and I had never given that to anyone before.

For some insane reason, I wanted him to be my first.

"Okay." I marched back to him, hands flexing at my sides. "But if you wake up missing a limb, remember you wanted this."

Still, I hesitated.

He smiled up at me, and my breath caught in my throat. It was nothing like the smiles he'd given me before. It was a face-splitting grin that lit up his eyes.

It was beautiful.

For a span of time, all I could hear was the *thud, thud, thud* of my heart as we stared at one another.

He opened his arms to me and inwardly I groaned. That wasn't fair. How was I supposed to say no to him when he was like this?

Huffing, I lowered beside him. He wrapped his arms around me and released the most contented sound I'd ever heard.

I'm so fucked.

That was my last thought before I fell asleep.

24

When I woke the next morning, the sun was already high in the sky, and the dirt beside me was cold. I stretched out with a huge yawn. My body felt invigorated, and other than some soreness in my back, it was almost healed.

I hopped to my feet, bouncing on my heels, with a restless energy in my bones. I felt like I could fight ten callitechs, and I hadn't even had breakfast.

My sleep had been peaceful. Ronan had held me tightly all night. Being in his arms had calmed whatever monster lurked inside. I didn't know why, or how, but it only made it harder to fight what was happening. I could get addicted to this feeling, to this lightness in my chest.

It scared the shit out of me.

Good things didn't happen to me, and I couldn't squelch this growing dread that the moment I gave in to whatever was between us, the Gods would remember that, and rip it away.

Maybe this connection between Ronan and I wasn't good; maybe that's why it was happening. Our issues weren't magically resolved because I'd gotten one good night of sleep in his arms, and he'd agreed to tell me more about himself.

I still didn't know what happened to that boy, and even if he was safe like Ronan said, that didn't mean all the other children were.

He wasn't going to stop being the Enforcer, and I wasn't going to stop being me.

You're getting ahead of yourself. What if after learning more about him, you realize you don't like him as much as you think?

I doubted that, but I had to know. I had to know who he really was.

Was Ronan the merciless killer, or the playful man with a heart-stopping smile?

Once I knew, I would decide.

Ronan appeared. I let myself look at him as he walked over. His shorn blond hair was longer than when we'd started our journey, and he had a slight beard growing. A thin coat of dirt speckled his skin. It wouldn't have worked on anyone else, but it only made him look more rugged, and highlighted the color of his eyes.

I was just as dirty.

His gaze hooded, appraising my figure, as he reached me. He moved closer and I took a step back. I hadn't washed since his camp, and probably reeked.

"I need a bath," I said when he tried to get close again.

He jerked me toward him and dragged his tongue up my neck. "Don't ever feel self-conscious with me," he whispered. "I *crave* you. Clean or dirty. I'd happily bury my face between your legs right now if you'd let me."

I pushed him away. "That's disgusting." But also strangely attractive?

"Where were you?" I asked to distract myself from the ache between my thighs..

"Foraging." He opened his palm; pale grubs were wriggling around in it.

Face screwing up, I pushed his hand away. "Please tell me you aren't going to eat those." Food was food but I drew the line at worms.

He pinched one between his thick fingers and slurped it vulgarly into his mouth. The suction sound made my stomach tighten.

"I know what you're doing."

"Mmm." He did it again, groaning exaggeratedly once he'd finished. The satisfied, masculine sound had my thighs clenching together. He wanted me to know what that mouth would do if I let him use it on me.

This was some disturbing form of seduction but fuck it was working, because he was the one doing it. All he had to do was look at me a certain way, and my whole body reacted.

I stomped off to find food I wouldn't gag on.

You'd gag on his cock.

Ronan with his hand wrapped around his thick, tattooed member flashed across my mind. Arousal flooded me.

Not. Helpful.

Damnit. I didn't know how long I was going to be able to resist him. I needed to interrogate him so I could make up my mind.

When I returned with some mushrooms, I was determined to do just that. He had already eaten all the grubs. Disgusting.

"You'll eat grubs, but not moldy bread?"

"I had a choice then. I don't now."

Because I was an idiot, and ran into a raging river in the middle of the night without any of our things, rather than admit I was attracted to him.

"Want a mushroom?" I asked as I lowered on the log across from him.

"No."

I bit into one, chewing methodically as I stared. "How do your powers work?"

"I can turn anything into a weapon, and wield it expertly."

I swallowed. "Anything?"

He nodded. "I can rip a man's bones from his body and reshape them into a weapon."

A shudder tripped down my spine. "That's impressive and disgusting. Why use your sword then?" I stuck another mushroom in my mouth. It was chewy and dry, but still better than eating grubs.

"I only use my powers when I must. Any victory feels cheap otherwise."

"Oh, and stabbing your sword through teenagers doesn't?" The question popped out before I could stop it. "I didn't mean that," I said quickly.

"You did," Ronan replied in an even tone.

I wanted to listen with an open mind, the same way Ronan had always done for me. He never judged or criticized anything I told him.

"Doesn't mean I needed to say it. I understand why you killed him, even if I detest your actions. Rehashing it won't bring him back. "

His gaze snaked along my face. "Would it help to know I forced Gold City to accept the children and their parents waiting outside the gates the day we arrived?"

My jaw unhinged, displaying a mouth full of half-chewed mushrooms. I snapped it shut and swallowed. "You did?"

He nodded.

That was why he had spoken with Lucinda? I had

thought it was odd how small the line outside the gates had been when I snuck off to the church.

"Why are you just admitting this to me now?"

"You weren't ready to hear it before."

That much was true. I wouldn't have believed him.

"Did you do that for me, or you?"

"You," he said without hesitation. "I wouldn't have taken that kind of risk for myself."

"What risk?"

"What do you think would happen if word got out that the Enforcer has gone soft? That I'm saving families?"

They'd stop fearing him.

"Will . . . that happen?"

"No. Lucinda enjoys living too much to betray me."

I considered him long and hard. Ronan had done that after I'd pulled a gun on him in the alley. While I was plotting his death, he had purchased a new wardrobe, chains, and saved those children. All for me.

"Why? Why would you do that? We hardly knew each other then, and I had tried to rob you."

I never understood his behavior toward me in the beginning. Once he had me bound to him through the bargain, it was like he became a different person. He went from threatening my life to holding a doctor at sword point to ensure I got the treatment I needed.

Ryder was my friend, and he hadn't even *talked* to the Mayhem doctor on my behalf.

It couldn't be about sex. All the man had to do was hold out his hand to get a woman in his bed. He didn't need to go through any of that effort if that was all he was after.

His hard stare imprisoned me. Storm clouds rolled through his gaze. "That, you aren't ready to hear." He stood. "We should get moving."

I didn't get up, shoving the remainder of the mushrooms in my mouth, as I stared up at him through slitted eyes.

He grinned. "You look very intimidating with your cheeks stuffed like a chipmunk."

I tried hard not to laugh, but the sound escaped anyway, and a mushroom caught in my throat. I spluttered, hitting my chest as I forced it down.

"Don't make me laugh with my mouth full," I rasped, once I'd swallowed it. "I almost choked."

A crooked smile. "I can have you choke on something else."

"Ronan."

He sighed. "I promise to tell you soon."

"Fine." I'd let it go. For now. There were other things I wanted to know about him first. I dusted off my hands, and we set off east again.

We still had a two day hike before we reached the river.

"Tell me about the killer," I said as we walked.

Ronan glanced over with a furrowed brow.

"The thing that happens when your eyes go black and you get extra growly," I explained.

He laughed softly. "That is called my battle-mode."

"You're going to have to give me more than that."

Pulling his gaze away, he explained, "The shift happens during intense activities like fighting or sex. In battle-mode, I operate purely on instinct. It shuts off the mind so the body can do what needs to be done."

Like murder.

My stomach dropped at the unpleasant reminder.

"Is it true you slaughtered an entire village once, women and children included?"

"Yes."

I stopped.

Ronan paused, and took a measured breath, before

271

casting his gaze to me. "You said you want to know me. Some of what you hear you will not like. I won't blunt my words to spare your feelings. This is who I am. I am not a good man."

"If that was true, you would have killed that little boy."

His eyes widened. Mine did too.

I believed him about the boy. I didn't realize it until just now.

Even more than that, I believed he was a good man despite what he was telling me. I wanted to see the best in him, even if he couldn't see it himself. That was new. I never saw the best in anyone.

He started walking again. I followed as his voice filled the silence. "I am no hero, but I can say I was a different man back then than I am now. I was younger, and unbendable in my sense of duty to eradicate any threat to the fae. I swung my sword with an unwavering belief that I was doing the right thing."

"How is a child a threat to the fae?" I asked lightly, trying to understand.

"That little boy back at the train picked up a piece of gold without thought. He should have been terrified of it. His mother failed to instill a fear of the fae in him, and a fearless boy will grow up into a fearless man, and that is a very dangerous thing. Fearless men question things. They start rebellions."

"Then why spare him?"

"Because as time passed, the criminals I executed started to look more like desperate mortals. It no longer felt like justice." His gaze sought mine. He looked *haunted*. "It felt like murder. A little piece of my soul died with each life I took. But I couldn't stop. I had to rely on my battle-mode more and more to fulfill my duty."

"Why couldn't you stop?"

His lips thinned.

"Let me guess. That's not your secret to share."

He jerked his head, and I gestured for him to continue.

"For anyone else in my House, it would take a great deal of concentration to transform into their battle-mode. It is buried deep, and only called on when absolutely necessary because a Taranis fae in battle-mode can do unspeakable damage. And things," he said. "My battle-mode is close to the surface. I can slip into it without thought, and it is getting harder to control. I tread a very thin line between man and monster, and everytime I use my battle-mode, I get closer to crossing it. Once I do, there is no going back."

My chest swelled with empathy. "I understand what that's like," I whispered. "I know what it's like to be a monster, but desperately not want to be."

Ronan grabbed my arm, and jerked me to a stop. "You are not a monster, Vera," he said, sternly.

I lifted my eyes to his. "Then what am I?"

"You are a bright beacon guiding me home."

I sucked in a sharp breath at the unexpected answer.

My heart became a pattery mess, beating out of sync.

I stepped closer and slid both hands up his arms to rest on his shoulders. Ronan held very still. I rarely touched him first, but I was finding myself doing it more and more.

"You're going to have to give me more than that," I breathed.

He removed one of my hands, and pressed a kiss to it, before holding it over his heart. It raced beneath my palm.

"I was lost in the darkness for so long until you blazed into my life like a wildfire." His gaze was eager as it looked into mine. "You stared me down so fearlessly that day outside the train, your eyes spitting venom on that little boy's behalf. Leaving you was hard, and then when I saw you again . . . I knew I was done for."

My gaze shifted between his. "Why haven't you asked me for the godstone's location?"

This all began because he was using me to find it. Was he still using me?

He still needed me to find it. Is that why he had offered his mother's brooch to the Crone, so he could use the Eye instead of me?

Is that why he was being sweet now? To get me to tell him?

"I knew you would tell me when the moment was right," he said.

I don't know what I wanted to hear, but it wasn't that. I pulled away from him.

Disappointment weighted his lips. I started walking.

"Why are you fighting this?" he called. "Why are you fighting me?"

I spun around, hands fisting at my sides. *Because I'm terrified none of this is real. I'm terrified you're just using me like everyone else.*

"Because it's all I know how to do. I've spent my whole life fighting. I don't know how to stop."

A small smile spread. "Fight me then. Push me away. Yell at me. Hurt me if you need to, but I'm not going anywhere," he said. "I've never lost a battle, and I am not about to start."

25
_____

It was another three days before we made it out of the forest, and a fourth to reach Coldwater. Things had changed between us after our conversation. We were more relaxed around one another, offering laughs and smiles as easily as breathing. Both our guards had fallen, and no matter how much I lectured myself on the danger of that, I couldn't put mine back up. He was winning this war, just as he said he would.

Ronan had shared secrets with me I was certain no one else knew. I understood now what he was trying to tell me that first night by the river. He was both Ronan Taran and the Enforcer. He was the merciless killer, and the man who took a risk just to do something to make me happy.

Even if he couldn't say it, I also understood that if it was up to him, he wouldn't be the Enforcer at all.

Ronan had offered me two choices when we'd first met. Bargain, or death. They weren't good choices, but choices nonetheless. I think he was in a similar situation. I think Ronan acted as the Enforcer because his other option was even worse.

He had flirted and teased me mercilessly the entire way

to Coldwater, and touched me at every opportunity—long lingering touches and stares that made my stomach flutter. None of it was sexual. He hadn't mentioned sex after the grubs. He was leaving it up to me.

Ronan didn't understand exactly *how much* he was leaving up to me.

We had bathed in the river, and collected our belongings on our way out of the forest. I had clean clothes, a full stomach, the iron dust, and the godstone's location; everything I needed to get out of this bargain, and get my vest.

The godstone would be in Mayhem four days from now. I had to make a decision soon.

"This counts as a town?" Ronan asked, disrupting my thoughts.

"In the Mortal Lands it does."

I could throw a rock from one side of Coldwater to the other. It was a little community built to serve the gold mines and its workers. This town ensured the workers were fed and drunk when they weren't in the mines.

Many of those miners lingered in the streets, glaring at Ronan with openly hostile expressions.

"Are you sure it's a good idea to stay in a town full of miners when you murdered one of their own not long ago?" I whispered as we walked down the narrow street bisecting Coldwater. It was the only way in or out of the town.

"They know better than to try anything," he said loudly, ensuring they heard. Most dropped their gazes and returned to their business, but not all. A handful crossed their arms and widened their stances, as if daring the Enforcer to make them look away.

"Mortals usually are not this brave. They are behaving strangely," Ronan said lowly, only for me to hear.

"What do you mean?"

Ronan ducked into an alleyway, pulling me with him

before he explained, "Five hundred years ago when the fae laws were first enacted, and I was given the duty of enforcing them, it took many deaths at the end of my sword before the mortals fell into line. Since then, the laws are broken only a handful of times each year, but it has been happening more and more as of late. And that—" he gestured toward the street—"No mortals have ever dared to make their disdain so public. Then there was the mortal outside Gold City. Something is happening."

"The Crone mentioned that people came to use the Eye. She wouldn't say who, but they were looking for you."

A savage expression came over his face. "Let them come."

"What if it's the same people who stole the godstone?"

He laughed. "I think we are giving the mortals too much credit. Even if they were in possession of the godstone, they would stand little chance against the fae, even less against me."

I didn't share his amusement. My stomach tightened.

Ronan sensed my change in demeanor immediately, perceptive ass that he was. "What is it?"

"I . . . I don't like the idea of anyone trying to hurt you," I confessed.

Hypocritical given what I carried in my bag, but still true.

His gaze softened. "Do not worry, Little Thief." He brushed a thumb over my cheek. "I am very hard to kill."

"Just be careful. If you get into trouble, the bargain magic will pull me into it," I said, trying to play off my concern. His grin told me he wasn't buying it.

Before he could say anything else, I dragged him out of the alley to the saloon next door.

"Where are we going?" he asked.

"To get a hot meal."

He allowed me to tug him through the swinging doors.

The noise died down at our entrance. Wary eyes stared from gold-dusted faces. Ronan's look warned them not to cause any trouble. The saloon's occupants had more sense than the mortals we had encountered outside. Their attention quickly returned to the mugs of poitín at their tables.

Except for one.

He caught my eye while Ronan's attention was elsewhere, and made a lewd gesture with his hands. My face screwed up in disgust. I drew a talon over my throat, and the miner quickly looked away.

I guided us over to the bar where a female worked behind it. She wore a blue corseted dress with her breasts on the verge of spilling over the top and a high bun with two strands of curly hair framing her delicate face.

We took the only two available stools at the end of the bar, only Ronan chose to stand beside me instead of sitting. Probably because the stools were small, and it was unlikely he could fit more than one ass cheek on it.

The female barkeep sashayed over to our seats, and leaned over the bar, giving Ronan a generous view of her breasts.

"It's been awhile," she purred.

I glanced between them. Did she . . . ? Did they . . . ?

Ronan stiffened beside me. It was subtle. I wouldn't have even noticed if he wasn't pressed against my side.

Son of Balor. They had slept together.

I dug my talons into my palms to keep from reaching over the bar, and doing something violent.

"We'll take whatever your house special is tonight," I ground out before Ronan could say anything.

"What's your poison?" the barkeep asked him, still completely ignoring me, and leaned further across the bar. If the barkeep moved any closer, I would stab her.

Hands grabbed my hips, and pulled me against a hard

chest. I had to widen my legs to give Ronan space to stand between them. Tilting my head back, I met his gaze. The swirling gray of his eyes was hypnotizing. I almost lifted myself off my stool for a closer look.

He dropped a quick kiss to my lips. "Are you thirsty?"

It was hard to concentrate with all his intensity focused on me. It was like the force of a lethal hailstorm had been compressed into the skin of a man.

Electricity crackled over my skin. A breath shuddered out of me.

"Little Thief," he whispered, a wicked smile playing on his lips. "If you keep staring at me like that, I'll eat you for dinner."

"Water," I croaked.

His smile widened minutely before his gaze returned to the barkeep.

"Two waters and two house specials," he said coolly.

Ronan's stare returned to me, dismissing the other female completely. The barkeep turned away from us with an irritated huff.

"How is your back?" he asked.

Ronan already knew. He had checked on it constantly over the last four days, but I still reassured him. "All better."

He ran his hand up and down it, causing raised bumps all over my skin. Why did his touch always feel so wonderful?

He leaned down and his lips touched the shell of my ear. "Good. I have plans for you tonight."

I shivered as my thighs clenched. My body was very much on board with whatever those plans were.

The barkeep returned a short time later. She plopped my plate down with a loud thud. It was some sort of meat with egg yolk drizzled over the top and smelled wonderful.

Some of the yellow liquid sloshed over the edge with the rough handling.

I glared at the barkeep as Ronan's plate was gently set down in front of him.

"Enjoy handsome." She winked and strolled down to the other side of the bar.

I glared at her back. "How many mortal women have you fucked?" I couldn't hide the jealousy from my voice.

Ronan stared intensely. "None that matter."

He leaned close. "What about you?" I could feel the tension in his body.

"None that matter."

He flashed that heart-stopping smile.

"Good. I don't have to kill anyone."

I shouldn't have enjoyed his jealousy as much as I did, but it was nice to know he felt as possessive over me as I did him.

We both dug into our meals. I had just finished mine when a mortal appeared beside me, slurring his words as he called for the barkeep. A rancid smell hit me, like his teeth were rotting in his mouth. When the barkeep didn't come fast enough, he slammed a hand on the bartop.

"Lucccyyyy! Get me a fuckin' drink!"

The barkeep I now knew to be Lucy appeared, scowling. "This is your last one, John." She filled a mug and slid it over to him, but before she could walk away, he reached across the bar, and snatched her wrist. "Whyyy don't me and ya goooo upstairs?"

Lucy tried to tug her hand free. "Let me go."

I was seconds away from intervening when John finally released her, and she hurried away. As if just noticing he wasn't the only one at the bar, the smelly mortal turned toward me, swaying. It was the same one who'd made the lewd gesture.

He raked his eyes over me. It made my skin crawl.

"Whattt's about you? Fancy a round upstairs?"

Ronan went still beside me.

I had dealt with plenty of drunken fools in Mayhem, and did what I always did to scare them off. I smiled wide, putting every fang on display, but the mortal didn't tuck tail and run. The challenge only made him bolder. He edged closer, leaning in. I drummed my talons on the bar's wooden top.

The mortal stopped short at the sound, but still didn't leave. "Aw, honeyyyyyy. That ain't enough to stop me. All we need is some glovessssss, and a sack over your head and you'd make a fine whore."

In a flash, Ronan had his hand wrapped around the drunk's throat. He slammed the drunk's spine against the bar, snarling, "What did you just call her?"

All the noise in the saloon cut off.

Even as drunk as he was, the mortal realized the danger he was in. He blanched, stammering out an apology. "Enforcer-r, Sir, I—didn't realize—"

"He's not worth the effort," I told Ronan, placing a hand on his arm. The mortal wasn't. If I fought every mortal that talked to me like that, there'd be hardly any left.

He pinned me with a hard look. "But you are."

Ronan fisted the front of the drunk's shirt, threw him to the ground, and planted a boot on his chest.

"I—I'm sorry. Have mercy!" The drunk screamed as he tried to wriggle out of Ronan's hold. With the drunk's mouth open, Ronan shoved his fingers inside, and snatched a hold of the drunk's tongue, turning his screaming into incoherent babbling.

He turned toward me. "I'll hold. You cut."

His offer warmed my chest. He knew I hated anyone fighting my battles for me, but I didn't mind so much when

Ronan did it. He knew I could hold my own. He didn't fight for me because he thought I needed him to. He did it because he wanted to.

"You go on. You're really sexy when you're violent."

He flashed a panty-melting smile.

Then he ripped out the drunk's tongue.

The mortal howled, thrashing as blood spurted from his mouth. His hands flew to his face. Gurgling noises bubbled out of his throat.

Ronan tossed the tongue to the ground. It hit the floor with a wet splat. He cleaned his fingers on the drunk's shirt, and straightened.

"Anyone else have anything unkind to say about my woman?"

His woman? A fluttering sensation filled my stomach.

The saloon was deathly quiet, the patrons scarcely daring to breathe in Ronan's presence. He stood seething as he glowered down at the bar's occupants.

When he had calmed enough he asked, "Lucy, do you have rooms above the saloon?"

Lucy had flattened herself against the shelving behind the bar. "Y—yes. How many beds?"

Ronan looked to me. This was my decision. I didn't have to think about it. "One."

26

This room wouldn't pass as habitable in most cities. The once brown wallpaper was yellowed, and curling away from the walls as if it didn't want to be here anymore than I did. A red bedspread lay across the half sunken mattress. It was peppered with holes as if various rodents had gnawed on it, and stained in some areas with something I didn't want to think about, let alone sleep on. Then, there was the rusted tub in the adjacent bathroom filled with brown water that had sat stagnant long enough it started to collect flies.

There went my hope of washing. It was safer to bathe in beast-infested waters than that tub.

Boots thudded behind me. I felt Ronan's heat at my back as he peered inside the bathroom.

"This is unacceptable," he growled.

I turned and laid my hands on his shoulders.

He grabbed my hips, and pulled me against him, nuzzling the top of my head. The tension riding him from the disgusting state of our room eased.

"I think I saw a clean spot on the ground in the corner," I joked.

He pulled back, his lips quirking, and kissed my fore-head. "I will return shortly."

I gripped him tighter, and tried to coax a real kiss from him, but my distraction attempt failed. I didn't want to wait another second for this.

"Don't go. I've stayed in worse."

"No. You deserve the world," he growled. "Go stand in your clean corner, and try not to touch anything."

He stalked out of the room.

My thoughts turned to what had happened in the saloon in his absence.

He had ripped out a man's tongue for insulting me. It was violent, and a little unnecessary, but gratifying all the same. Endearing even. If Ronan was only after the godstone's location, he wouldn't have done something so extreme. His action spoke volumes. It cemented what I was finally allowing myself to believe. He cared for me as much as I cared for him.

My woman.

I didn't mind being his. In fact, I could get used to the idea. I moved to the center of the room, and kept my hands close to my sides until Ronan returned.

He brought a small army with him.

Lucy and several males I didn't recognize rushed inside the room like a beast was on their heels. I moved out of the way as the bed was stripped, and replaced with brand new linens. The disgusting tub was removed. A much larger one was brought in, and filled with hot water.

When they were finished, the mortals hovered near the door as Ronan surveyed their work. He didn't appear satis-fied, but still sighed, and said, "I suppose this will have to do. You may go."

"Why aren't we staying in Gold City again?" I asked as soon as we were alone.

We could have been halfway there already if we'd purchased some horses when we arrived.

Ronan's jaw clenched. "Lucinda insulted you. I will not be spending my silver there anytime soon." His gaze drifted to mine. "I am sorry you had to hear that. I should have removed her tongue like I did the mortal's."

So, he had been paying attention when I mentioned hearing that part of their conversation.

I waved off his concern. That was then. "She probably wouldn't have allowed the families inside if you had."

"I still should have said something," he said looking distraught.

I strode over to him, stood on my tiptoes, and kissed him. He returned my kiss with fervor. Our lips moved together in slow, sensuous movements that had fire igniting in my belly. He grabbed my hips, and backed me up until my spine hit the wall.

I arched into him as he deepened the kiss, grinding against him. Heat coiled in my center at the hardness I felt. He groaned and pulled his lips away, kissing over my collarbone, and up my throat.

You smell so delicious," he rasped in my ear.

He continued his tortuous movements, sucking on my throat as his hands moved up my tunic.

Rippppp.

He tore the shirt and the undergarment beneath it in half.

My exposed breasts heaved under his stare.

I should have been annoyed he ruined a perfectly good tunic, but I was too turned on to care.

He teased the tight bud of my nipple between his fingers, and I moaned. "You're so fucking beautiful," he murmured, then he pinched it.

The biting pain made my back arch. "Oh that hurt you

bast—" My complaint ended on a gasp as he took my breast in his mouth. His tongue swirled over the sensitive tip, melding the pain with pleasure. He sucked it once, releasing it with a low groan. The tip glistened with his spit.

His mouth kissed down my stomach until he reached the waistband of my pants. He wrenched them down, and I rushed to kick them off.

I went to remove my underwear, but he grabbed my wrist. "Allow me."

He kneeled, and stared up into my eyes as he stuck his thumb into the sides, and slowly dragged them down my thighs. I shivered at the feel of his rough palms moving over my skin.

When the fabric hit my ankles, I stepped out of it, and then I was naked before him.

He stared at my center, licking his lips.

My whole body felt like it was wrapped in live wire. It tingled and burned for his touch.

"Ronan," I breathed.

I saw the strain in his body. He was desperate to put his hands on me, but he shook his head. "You know what I want to hear," he whispered, hungry gaze still fixed between my legs.

"I want you, Ronan Taran."

He released a deep groan, and pinned my hips to the wall. His tongue lashed my clit. I squirmed beneath him as he continued to lick it with rough strokes. He tightened his grip as his tongue slipped inside.

I arched into it with a muffled cry. "Yes."

He pushed a finger in, thrusting it in time with his tongue. His facial hair scraped over the soft skin of my thighs. Electricity lit up my insides. The slurping sounds he made as he feasted on me were vulgar, and only heightened my pleasure.

286

He hooked his finger inside, and hit a sweet spot with every stroke. My body coiled tighter and tighter.

His fingers worked faster as he sucked my clit into his mouth.

My legs started to shake. I would have slipped down the wall if his hand wasn't holding me up.

"Ronan, fuck, I'm going to—" I exploded on his tongue. I cried out, my entire body arching with my release.

He moaned, and lapped every drop.

When he drew back, his mouth glistened with my pleasure. He licked his lips. "You taste as good as you smell," he rumbled.

He tried to lick me one last time, but I pushed his head away, and sank to the ground. I was too sensitive there.

I stared at him, chest heaving, as I came down from my orgasm. He leaned his head against mine. Our lips were a breath away.

"Thank you," I whispered. "That was . . . " Mind blowing. Unlike anything I'd experienced before. "Satisfactory."

He chuckled darkly. "I'm not through with you yet."

"You're not?"

He pulled back, looking offended. "You think I'd be done with you after just one?"

Every other guy I'd been with had.

His expression darkened like he could read my thoughts.

"Get in the tub," he ordered. "I'm going to bathe you, and then fuck you so thoroughly you forget every man that came before me."

Any other time, him ordering me around would have been met with a glare, but when it came to sex, I liked when he was bossy. I couldn't let him know that though. He was too used to getting his way. If I gave him even an inch, he'd take a mile.

I put my lips to his ear, rubbing his erection through his

pants. His hips bucked as he hissed between his teeth. "Good luck," I whispered, then pulled away.

I was taunting him. He didn't need luck.

I sashayed toward the bathroom, giving him a generous view of my ass.

"Little Thief," he growled. "You are playing with fire."

I smiled though he couldn't see it. "Fire happens to be a specialty of mine."

An animalistic growl vibrated the room. The sound of clothes hitting the ground quickly followed. A small yip left my mouth as I was lifted into the air.

Ronan carried me into the tub. Water sloshed over the edges. It was double the size of a normal tub, but with how tall we both were, it just barely fit us comfortably.

"Where did they find a tub this size?"

"They keep some nice furniture in storage for when Gold City's council visits to check on the mines."

Interesting.

He positioned me with my back to his chest, cradled between his muscled legs. An iron bar pressed into my bottom. I moved against it, hoping to entice Ronan into forgetting the bath altogether.

He hissed out a breath. "Stop. Moving."

"What if I don't want to?" My voice was unrecognizable. It was rough, and seductive like a mermer trying to lure its victim into the sea.

"Then you'll get nothing at all."

I didn't believe him, but I played along anyway, and stopped.

"Good girl," he crooned in my ear, and my belly coiled tight despite the orgasm I'd just had. It wasn't healthy to be this attracted to someone.

His muscles rippled underneath me as he reached around for a bar of soap. He dipped it under the water creating a soapy lather in his hands. He worked it into my hair, digging his strong fingers into my scalp.

My whole body tingled. A shiver skipped down my spine, and gooseflesh pebbled my skin. I shut my eyes, and relaxed into his touch. He massaged my head and neck, easing the tension I carried there. My muscles melted under his skillful hands.

When he touched a particularly hard knot, and kneaded it away, I moaned deeply. Ronan's hands froze a moment, his cock pulsing against my bottom. It grew impossibly harder. Wordlessly, he resumed massaging my scalp, though his movements were far less smooth than before. He took shallow breaths through his nostrils, fighting to maintain his composure.

I tipped my head back, smiling warmly at the male determined to take care of me despite the fierce need riding him.

"Lean forward and wash your head," he ordered, his voice rough.

Plunging my head into the bathwater, I scrubbed away all the residual foam coating my hair. Ronan had a fresh lather waiting for me when I popped up to the surface.

He washed my back and shoulders, then pulled me against his chest, and glided his hands down my front. His roughened palms scraped my breasts, and the delicious feeling sent a jolt of desire straight between my legs.

He lightly pinched a nipple, and I arched back, gasping.

"So responsive," he murmured.

His fingers brushed down my stomach, leaving a trail of fire in their wake. My breath came in fast bursts as my body clenched in anticipation. His hands smoothed down my thighs, washing me forgotten. My skin tingled. Tension built.

He slid his hands back up, the tips of his fingers lightly grazing my entrance as they moved past it.

"Please," I begged. Though I wasn't quite certain what I was begging for.

His lips came to my ear. "Please what? Tell me what you want."

"I want you to fuck me."

He snatched my chin with his other hand, and forced my head back.

"Eyes on me. You stop, I stop. Understood?"

"Yes," I hissed.

He stroked my clit. I gasped as my hips bucked forward, but I didn't break eye contact. Ronan's heated gaze crinkled at the corners telling me he was pleased.

He grabbed my hips, and twisted me around to face him. I ended up straddling his waist with his cock pressed against my entrance.

I rolled my hips against him, and we both moaned.

His fingers dug into my sides, preventing me from doing it a second time. He was shaking with restraint.

Why was he holding back?

I searched his gaze. The emotion glimmering there stilled me.

"I want to be gentle with you," he said in an uncharacteristically reserved tone. "When I'm rough, it triggers my battle-mode, and I go somewhere else. I don't want to go anywhere. I want to be here with you."

My chest pinched. This beautiful man.

"Okay," I said softly. "We can go slow."

"I'm." He paused, exhaling roughly. "I can't touch you. I won't be able to control myself if I do." He moved his hands to the edges of the tub.

Biting my lip, I stared at this muscled, dangerous man

holding onto a tub for dear life because he wanted to make love to me.

I lowered my lips to his. The kiss was brief, but tender. I pulled away, raising my hips, and gradually worked myself down on the head of his cock. He was huge. It would be painful to take all of him, but I didn't care. I wanted this man more than air.

The stretch was sublime as I lowered a little further. Ronan moaned. I leveraged a hand against his chest to work myself lower. His knuckles were white from how tightly he was gripping the tub.

Pain flared as I continued taking more of him. I paused a moment, until the sharp sensation stopped.

It happened again when I moved, and I grit my teeth.

Ronan's eyes tightened. "Are you okay?"

I nodded. "You're just." I hissed out a breath. "Big."

"Here, how's this?" He moved a thumb to my clit, rubbing it in circles. My muscles immediately relaxed as the pain mixed with pleasure, and I sank lower.

"Much better," I breathed.

Inch by inch I moved down until I took all of him. We both moaned when I bottomed out.

Ronan didn't take his eyes off me, as he continued touching me.

I started to ride him, watching him carefully. When I went too fast, I saw his jaw tighten as black flickered in his gaze, and slowed my movements.

"No," he panted. "Don't stop."

He grabbed my bottom with both hands, and ground me against him. My clit brushed his stomach with every roll of my hips, ratcheting the fire building in my core higher and higher.

"Ronan," I moaned.

"Say my name again," he demanded.

"Ronan."

"Fuck." He gripped my hips, and started hammering into me.

Water spilled over the edges as I gripped his shoulders. Each thrust of is cock hit me just where I needed it.

"Yes, right there."

Black swallowed his gaze. I snatched a hold of his chin. "Stay with me." Every nerve ending was on fire. I was so close.

I gripped him tighter when his eyes didn't change. "I want to come for Ronan, not you. Give him back," I panted.

The black disappeared.

Ronan's arms hugged me to his chest as he continued pistoning his hips. The adoration shining in his gaze as he held mine was my undoing. He slammed me down on his cock, and I shattered.

He jerked his hips once, twice, then he followed. The sound he made in my ear as he found release was the sexiest thing I'd ever heard.

We didn't move, clinging to each other as we came down. It took several minutes for us to catch our breath.

Eventually, he pulled back, and peppered kisses over my face. His lips tickled my skin, and I pushed his face away with a laugh.

We stared at each other. He stroked a thumb over my lips, gazing at me with the same expression he wore when he looked at his mother's brooch.

Like *I* was his most treasured possession.

"Come to the Faylands with me when this is all over," he breathed.

My gaze shifted between his. "Do you—Do you really mean that?"

"Yes."

I stared at him, pursing my lips. As much as I wanted to

accept his offer, there was a hard limit for me. I understood he couldn't stop being the Enforcer, even if I couldn't understand why, but I couldn't be with someone who hurt children.

"I have one condition."

He laughed, and brushed a damp tendril from my face, tucking it behind my ear. "Of course, you do."

"No more killing anyone under eighteen."

Ronan frowned. He was quiet for a long moment. I held my breath, dreading he would say no.

"I can't make you that promise," he said carefully. "But, I can promise to spare as many of them as I can."

"Okay," I whispered, nodding. "That's a start."

"So you'll come home with me?"

"Yes."

He flashed his heart-stopping smile. I smiled just as widely back.

"Come here." He slipped out of me, and clutched me to him, stroking my hair.

A warmth blossomed in my chest as he held me. My brows dipped at the strange sensation. I'd never felt anything like it.

The closest thing I could compare it to was the first morning I'd stepped out of the Rogue compound, free of the Crone, and the soft dawn light had hit my cheeks. That sunshine felt like hope, like a beautiful, new beginning.

We were both quiet for a while, just enjoying each other's company until Ronan broke the silence. He traced a finger down my arm, asking, "Is there a meaning behind all this ink?"

My head dipped down, brows crinkling. I knew I didn't have any ink tattooed on my skin like him but felt compelled to glance down anyway. There was nothing there. "What are you talking about? I don't have any ink."

Ronan froze under me.

"No," he whispered. "It can't be . . ." his voice trailed off.

"What?" I glanced up at him.

He shook his head. "Nothing. I must be seeing things. I am more exhausted than I thought."

He relaxed, and pulled me back to him. More time passed in silence until Ronan's stomach rumbled loudly. I laughed. "I guess that meat and yolk wasn't enough."

"I will go see if there are any leftovers in the kitchen." He started to move out of the tub, but I stopped him.

"I'll go. You relax." At his belligerent look, I added, "Let me take care of you this time."

He smiled. "Hm, it is very hard to tell you no when you say things like that."

"I learned from the best." I brushed my lips over his, then rose from the tub, and dressed. Something else in my saddlebag caught my attention, and I curled my fist around it.

"Be quick," Ronan growled from the bathroom. "I'm not done with you yet."

"Seriously?" I was exhausted.

He chuckled softly as I stepped out of the room.

Downstairs, I tried to remember the direction I had seen the barkeep come from when she brought our food. There was no way I would ask her to make something for Ronan, knowing their history. Plus, the nightgown I'd thrown on wasn't appropriate attire for the saloon, but I had been too lazy to put on real clothes.

Loud voices spilled down the small hallway where I stood. The miners would be drinking well into the night. I went in the opposite direction.

The saloon wasn't large. It didn't take long to find the kitchen, which was locked to keep thieves like myself out. Using a talon tip, I carefully popped the door's locking mechanism. The old lock gave out easily, and I swung open the door.

A floorboard creaked behind me. I spun around, bumping into the door frame, readying an explanation.

"Hey, V."

It was Ryder.

27

I pulled him into the kitchen, leaving the door cracked open until I found something to light the lantern on the wall. The kitchen was half the size of the room I shared with Ronan. It could barely fit two people comfortably.

Ryder leaned against the door frame, crossing his arms as he fixed me with a cool gaze. He wore his black and white srphy vest and loose trousers. His silver hair was longer, covering his brow line. There was a hardness to his gaze that hadn't been there before.

"I got your message." His eyes dragged over me, taking in my swollen lips and sheer nightgown. "You certainly have the situation handled, don't you?"

I mimicked his stance, folding my arms over my chest knowing he could see my breasts through the thin material. Orin had gotten word to the Rogues after all. To be honest, I had completely forgotten I'd asked. Gold City seemed so long ago. So much had changed since then.

"Oh, fuck off, Ryder. Don't think I've forgotten how you threw me to the wolves in Mayhem."

He blinked slowly, taken aback by my heated response. Weren't expecting that were you, asshole?

"You threw yourself. I warned you what would happen, V."

"You should have had my back."

"I convinced Boone to give you another chance to earn a vest. What else should I have done?"

I scoffed, turning to sift through a small wall of cabinets behind me. "Yeah, real opportunity you gave me. Someone tried to blow me up and took the weapon for themselves."

I didn't know if he knew what the weapon was actually called. I wanted to keep that information to myself for now.

"You knew there were risks," he said. "If I was able to find intelligence on it, so could others."

"Did your intelligence also tell you that it was never going to Gold City?" I snarked over my shoulder. Most of the shelves were empty, but I spotted a jar of white jam. It had to be from the Faylands as I had never seen berries that color before. I faced Ryder.

"It was," he said adamantly.

I slammed the jar down on the counter. "No," I gritted out. "It was going to the Enforcer."

I watched his reaction carefully. Did he really not know?

He blinked rapidly, lips compressing together. "What are you talking about?"

"The godstone belongs to *him*."

Ryder went very still as he processed the weight of that statement. "V, I swear I didn't know," he said after a moment.

I knew him well enough to know his surprised response was genuine. That didn't mean I was going to forgive him for sending me to my death anytime soon. My collision with the Enforcer had turned out better than I could have imagined, but I could have just as easily been killed.

He sucked his lips between his teeth, scrutinizing me. "If you stole from him, how are you still alive?"

Seriously? I basically just told him he had sent me to die

and instead of offering an apology, or asking if I was okay, his only concern was how I survived?

My hands fisted at my sides, but he couldn't see with the counter between us.

"Weren't you listening?" I growled in frustration. "I *didn't* steal from him."

"Then why are you here and not whoever did?"

"Because I was the one stupid enough to get caught." I leaned back against the cabinets. "How did you find me anyway?"

Ronan and I hadn't been in Coldwater for more than a few hours.

"Same way I heard about the weapon."

"And what way is that exactly?" I asked, drumming my talons against the wood. His gaze flickered to my hands. He wasn't quick enough to cover his shudder. I itched to hide them behind my back, but I shoved away the urge. I refused to hide in the shadows anymore. "I'm curious to know where you're getting your false information from."

Ryder jerked his gaze up. Tight lines bracketed his mouth. "What are you implying?"

Tap. Tap. Tap. I continued hitting my talons on the cabinets.

He gathered news for the Rogues. I wasn't sure how, only that he provided the information and it had never been wrong before. So why of all the times, when my life depended on it, did his sources not know the godstone belonged to the Enforcer?

I knew he was telling the truth about believing the weapon was bound for Gold City, but things weren't adding up. There was something he was leaving out. I could feel it.

Tap. Tap. Tap.

"How is it you found me here so quickly, but somehow missed the most important piece about the godstone?"

He chose his next words carefully. "The fae hide their secrets well and I didn't find you quickly. You were last seen entering the Deadwood Forest. This is the closest town to it. I've been waiting here for you for days."

My tapping stuttered to a stop. "You . . . have?"

"Yes. Orin heard the Enforcer threaten you. I tried to find you as soon as I could. I—I was worried about you." The last part was a whisper.

That admission helped to relieve some of my simmering anger, and I felt a little guilty for my accusation. Our relationship had become *complicated* since he became the Rogue's second. He straddled the line between doing his duty to the Rogues and his friendship with me and though he often neglected our friendship in favor of them, I should have known better than to think he'd send me to my death.

His gaze flattened as it moved over me. "But it looks like I was worried for nothing."

My relationship with Ronan wasn't any of his business, but I did feel like I owed him some answers given he'd come all this way.

"I made a bargain with him," I explained. "I'm helping him find the weapon."

A dark veil descended over his face. "Did the bargain include sex? Is he forcing you?"

"What?" I scowled. "No! Of course not. He wouldn't—"

Ryder flicked up a brow.

"I know he's not known for his decency," I said slowly. "But he's not the monster everyone thinks he is."

Rage flashed. "Are you seriously defending *the Enforcer*? The fae's dog who murders women and children in cold blood?"

"He's good."

Barbed laughter rang out. "And I'm king of the fae."

"He is."

"Oh, so you're spending time with him of your own free will?"

I released a frustrated sigh, knowing how the truth sounded. "Not at first, but that was before I got to know him."

He stared in mock pity. "Are you really that desperate?"

A thorn burrowed into my chest. I shoved off the cabinets and leaned over the counter. "Fuck. You."

His anger evaporated. He raised his hands. "V, I'm sorry. I'm not trying to hurt you. But you have to see he's just using you."

"And the Rogues aren't?"

"They are," he admitted. "But at least you would get a vest out of it. What do you think happens once he gets the weapon back? He'll invite you to his home? *Make you his wife?*"

He said the last part, like the very idea was ridiculous. Like it was crazy that someone might actually care about me. I didn't feel guilty about my accusation anymore.

I thrust up my chin. "He asked me to come to the Faylands with him."

"You don't have a fae brand," he said gently. "What's to stop him from selling you to one of the fae lords?"

My jaw ticked.

I almost told him that Ronan was a fae lord, but I caught myself. That wasn't common knowledge.

"He wouldn't do that."

"Has he seen what you can do?"

I saw the Callitech. Is that part of the curse?

My lips thinned.

"Exactly," he said. "The Enforcer probably recognizes how powerful you are, and doesn't want to risk losing you. You're just a tool to him."

I leaned forward, my talons gouging the wood slab separating us. "You're wrong."

When he saw he wasn't going to convince me, an icy smile crawled over his face. "And you're an idiot."

Fire licked through my veins. I was so tired of being mistreated. I didn't understand how badly I had been until Ronan came along and showed me what kindness really was. Maybe his words were finally starting to sink in. I deserved more than the crumbs the Rogues offered.

I launched myself over the counter and wrapped my hand around his throat. I slammed his spine into the wall and leaned into his face. "Say that again. I dare you."

Ryder was intelligent enough to keep his mouth shut, though his eyes glared daggers at me.

"Back in Mayhem, you might be somebody, but here in this room, you're no one, and friend or not, I won't hesitate to slit your throat if you speak to me that way again. Understand?"

His head bobbed.

I shoved away from him and returned to the other side of the counter.

He backed up slowly, rubbing his throat. He stared at me like I was a stranger. Maybe I was.

"You didn't come here because you were concerned about me. You were concerned about the weapon," I growled. "The Enforcer might be many things, but he isn't fake like you. He doesn't smile at my face one minute, then stab me in the back the next."

He stiffened. "I have always been kind to you. When everyone else stared and whispered, I was there for you. I tried my best to balance being Second and a good friend to you. I didn't always do a good job. I recognize that. But I never stopped watching out for you. I am here, right now, trying to do just that. Do not continue on this path with the Enforcer."

His version of kindness and mine were very different.

"This isn't about me. This is about your vendetta against the fae."

"It used to be your vendetta too. The fae are selfish, evil creatures. They leave our lands plagued and infertile. They leave families to starve, or be slaughtered by the beasts."

"He's not like them."

His gaze searched mine. "If you're willing to risk your entire future with the Rogues for him, you better be sure."

"I am."

He smiled sadly. "Then I guess this is goodbye."

"I guess so."

We stared at each other. Seven years of history lingered between us.

He had been the closest thing I had to a friend when I'd showed up at the Rogues' compound as a scrawny teenager. I had been quieter then. More reserved, waiting for them to hurt me like the Crone had. Ryder had taken me under his wing and brought me out of my shell. We were thick as thieves, always getting into trouble together, until Ryder was made Second in command.

Our friendship had deteriorated over the last two years, but I would always be grateful for the good times we shared.

We were on two different paths now.

"What will you do about the weapon? If the Rogues manage to find it, I can't stop the Enforcer from coming after you."

"Does he know the Rogues want it?"

"No."

As much as the Rogues had let me down over the years, they had given me a home when I needed one most. If they still chose to go after the godstone, knowing it was the

Enforcer's, then that was on them. But I wouldn't implicate them and have a hand in their deaths.

He nodded. "Thank you for that."

"Take care of yourself, Ryder."

"You too, V."

He left.

The kitchen grew uncomfortably quiet in his absence. I slid down against the cabinets, and stared at the vial in my hand. The silver filaments sparkled in the low lantern light.

Was this the right choice?

I had come down the stairs with a full heart, certain it was. But my conversation with Ryder had left the tiniest seed of doubt.

What if Ronan was like other fae, and he was just showing me what I wanted to see?

Even if he wasn't, what if I went to the Faylands, and he grew bored of me and cast me out? What would become of me then?

I was placing a great deal of faith in a man I hardly knew. No. That wasn't true. I knew Ronan. He had shared pieces of himself with me that few others knew. The connection between us couldn't be faked. He cared for me. I was certain of it.

I pinched the vial, and twirled it between my fingers.

This was my last connection to my past. Once I got rid of it, there was no going back. I *knew* I didn't want a life with the Rogues anymore, but a part of me clung to it anyway because it was familiar. Safe.

The Rogues couldn't hurt me. I had sealed my heart off from them years ago. But Ronan? I sucked in a breath. He was in too deep. There was no cutting him out. He had the power to destroy me. Could I really trust him?

Fuck, I wanted to.

I wanted to trust him with every broken part of me.

A clock chimed in the distance. I snapped my hand shut around the vial. I had been gone long enough. Ronan would come looking for me soon, and if he caught me holding this . . . I shuffled to my feet, and lifted the lantern off the wall.

I scoured the space for a good hiding spot where no one would find it. There was a small gap between the wall and one of the cabinets. I shoved it there, then searched for something Ronan could eat with the jam.

I found a slightly burnt pastry, tucked it under my arm alongside the jar, and slipped out of the kitchen.

Just as I relocked the door, pain exploded across the back of my skull.

28

I stumbled into the doorframe. The jar slipped from my fingers and crashed to the floor. I teetered backwards and fell on top of the glass shards. They sliced into my back, right through the thin nightgown.

A boot slammed down on my chest. It punched the air from my lungs.

Everything was spinning. I couldn't think past the pounding in my skull. Warm liquid dribbled down my ear. My head was bleeding, badly, based on the amount of blood I felt.

"Quick, tie her up." It was a male voice.

"With what?" a female hissed.

The whistle of a belt being pulled from its loops sounded. "Use this."

My hands were bound together. I tried to fight their hold, but I was so dizzy and disoriented all I succeeded at was making myself more nauseous. What had they hit me with?

"Fuck, the wound is sealing."

"Use the hammer this time. The guy said it was spelled. Should knock her ass out."

The hammer crashed into the side of my head. It whipped to the left. Stars exploded across my vision. Blinding pain followed. I fought hard not to pass out. I knew if I did, I'd never wake up.

Someone cursed.

"I said to hit her. Not bash her skull in. We need her alive."

A hand hovered over my mouth. It reeked of urine. "She's got a pulse. We're fine."

My arms were yanked over my head as I breathed raggedly through my nostrils. My head felt like it'd been split in half. I could feel air touching over the wound, and I fought a shudder. I probably had a damn whole in my head.

They started to drag me.

"Faster," one of the men snapped. "He can't find us yet. Not until we're ready."

"You sure he'll come after her?"

"Yeah. He ripped out John's goddamn tongue just for insulting her. He'll come."

Another male grunted. "You help then. She's heavy."

They dragged me faster. I groaned at their rough pulling. Every bump and jostle sent blistering pain over my skull.

I tried to lift my head and see where we were going, but it was too heavy, or I was too weak. Even if I could move my head, my vision was distorted. Everything was fuzzy shapes. I urged my eyes to blink rapidly to get rid of the haze, but my eyelids were made of lead. They fluttered shut.

Maybe I'd take a little nap first and then I'd free myself . . .

No! A voice screamed in my head. *Stay awake. You have to stay awake.*

I was losing so much blood. I could feel it seeping out of my head. How much could someone lose before it was fatal?

306

They had used a magic hammer. By the time my healing abilities stopped the bleeding, it might be too late.

Fire blasted through my veins and my eyes shot wide. The darkness was awake. Those purple eyes watched me from the shadows.

Was that you? I asked, but it gave no answer.

My attention returned to my attackers. The hands pulling me had my wrists in a bruising grip. They smelled of sour sweat and ale. No. I hadn't survived the Crone and years of battling the beasts just to be taken out by some smelly bastards.

I slitted my eyes. I couldn't hold them open all the way, they were too heavy, but as long as I didn't let myself fall asleep, I'd be okay. I was going to survive this.

Wood floor became earth. Rocks scratched my back as I was dragged roughly over them. We had left the saloon.

The dragging stopped. I heard clinking, then rattling. Warm air whooshed over my face, followed by the heavy scent of manure. They dragged me again. The ground they pulled me over was still hard, but something crinkled beneath me.

Straw. It was straw. I was in some sort of barn. Stables maybe? No, I didn't hear any horses.

My healing abilities started to stem the flow of blood—just barely—but I couldn't risk them knowing yet. They'd hit me again, and if a third blow to the head didn't kill me, it would knock me unconscious. I forced myself to remain limp as they secured me to some sort of wooden block.

Their footfalls retreated. I heard one of them pacing, straw crunching underneath their feet with every pass. Slowly, the sickening pain in my head eased enough for me to catch my breath. I listened to them argue.

"Where are they? Weren't they supposed to meet us here?" The male's voice was panicked.

"They'll be here. They really want the Enforcer dead with what they're paying us. We just have to sit tight. We did our job. They'll take care of the rest."

My sluggish mind struggled to keep up with their conversation, but I did understand one thing; they wanted to kill Ronan.

No.

Fury shot through me. It flooded my veins with energy.

Ronan was mine.

The darkness moved. Those purple eyes burned fiercely in the recess of my mind. I frowned as foreign feelings of possessiveness added to my own.

Ours. He is ours.

My teeth gnashed together as liquid fire surged through my veins. The bindings on my wrists burned away. More energy pumped into my blood. The darkness was lending me its strength, replacing what the blood loss had stolen. The power coursing through my muscles was invigorating. I felt invincible.

My vision cleared. I saw two males and one female. I didn't recognize any of them.

I rose from the ground.

"You're not touching him." My cold voice sliced through the quiet.

All three heads swung my way. I showed them the ball of fire sitting in my palm. They paled, realizing the danger they were in.

"What are you?" one of the males whispered.

I flashed my terrifying dagger smile. "I am the last person you should have ever fucked with."

Common sense kicked in and all three raced for the barn doors, but I was faster. I moved in a blur, putting myself between them and their only means of escape. "Which one of you hit me?"

"Jimmy! It was Jimmy!" The female shrieked and pointed a finger at the male in the middle of their trio.

My lips curled into a vicious grin. "Oh, Jimmy," I sing-songed.

Jimmy collapsed to the floor with a shrill scream, covering his head with his hands. I scowled. "I haven't even done anything yet."

He screamed again. I threw the ball of flame at his face just to get him to shut up.

It blazed through the air . . . And landed six feet away from its intended target, setting a pile of hay aflame.

My gaze darted between my hand and the fire. What in the Darklands?

I willed another fire ball into my palm. It hit the roof this time. I stared in shock as the flames ate up one of the beams.

What in the ever-loving night was happening?

I never missed.

A whimper escaped Jimmy. He was on the ground sniveling and crying. I changed course and threw my fist toward his face, nearly tripping on my own feet in the process. My hand ended up crashing into his shoulder instead.

He jerked back with a howling cry. Based on the new angle of his shoulder, I'd knocked the thing clean out of its socket. He passed out a moment later.

The female tried to dart past me while I was distracted. I threw out my arm at the last second and the idiot ran right into it. She went down, and I pressed a boot against her throat; not hard enough to cut off her air supply, but a warning I could. Blood trickled from my forehead as a wave of dizziness hit me. I shook my head, and forced myself to focus.

"Who wants to kill the Enforcer?" I demanded.

"Everyone in the Mortal Lands, you stupid bitch," she wheezed out.

I pressed down harder. Her face reddened as she gasped for air.

A gun cocked a second before a bullet tore into my calf. Sharp pain shot up my leg and it buckled, but somehow, I managed to stay upright. I glanced over my shoulder. The second male had a gun trained on me.

I tried to conjure more fire. My palm sizzled and spat out a wisp of smoke. *Come on you stupid flames. Work!*

I wavered on my feet. My strength was fleeting. Whatever was in that bullet was zapping my energy. It was too much, even for my cursed abilities to overcome.

"He warned us about you, half-beast. Gun is loaded with gold bullets. You won't be using those nasty powers of yours anytime soon."

Since they had kidnapped me in only my flimsy nightgown, I had no weapons.

Fangs and talons it is.

I slowly turned to face him, breathing shallowly through my nostrils. My whole body felt heavy. The strength the creature had lent me was fleeting. Yeah, attacking wasn't going to go well. I could barely keep myself upright.

"Move an inch and the next bullet goes into your skull," he hissed.

I raised my hands.

Smoke burned my nose. I cast my gaze to the two fires I had started. They had tripled in size. The fumes from the flames drifted up through the rafters, but there was nowhere for it to go. The barn was filling with smoke.

My eyes started to water, and I broke out into a coughing fit. "This whole place is going to be on fire in minutes. You stay here, you're gonna die. Let me live and you'll still get your shot at the Enforcer."

The mortal adjusted his grip on the gun. "I leave, I don't get paid."

Flames licked up the columns of the barn and razed over the hay strewn across the ground. The fire drew closer and closer to where we stood.

"He really worth dying over?"

"The money they're offering is."

"Who's they?"

Part of the roof collapsed and crashed down behind us. I took advantage of the distraction, rushed forward, and threw my body weight into the mortal. We hit the ground near a pile of burning hay. The fire singed my hair and nightgown, but I didn't let it stop me from trying to wrestle the gun free from the mortal.

My movements were weak and sluggish, but I managed to knock it out of his hands. It slid over the ground into the flames.

The mortal headbutted me. There was a sickening crack. Blood gushed from my nose. Gods, it'd be a miracle if I had any left after this.

I reared back, clutching my nose with one hand and slashed his stomach with the other. The mortal howled as I staggered to my feet and limped toward the gun.

He shot past me, clutching his stomach. I raced after him as fast as my injured body would allow. My lungs burned with every breath. I coughed, choking on the smoke as my eyes watered.

When my vision cleared, I saw the mortal was inches away from the gun. I put the last of my energy reserves into tackling him. We rolled around in the flames, both reaching for the gun.

The mortal got to it first.

I jerked back, but I was too slow. He pressed it to my temple.

I froze, heart slamming against my rib cage.

"You can't stop what's coming half-beast." He cocked back the hammer.

A sword rammed through his chest.

Shock rounded his eyes as blood gurgled out of his mouth. He slumped toward me, but something kicked him sideways.

Ronan loomed over me. His lips were peeled back in a snarl. Black thunderclouds engulfed his gaze. Leashed violence vibrated his body.

"Hello, Killer," I whispered. I reached for him with shaking arms. He lifted me off the ground, and rushed me out of the burning barn.

As soon as he'd taken me a safe distance, he lowered me gently to the ground, kneeling over me. He scanned my body for injuries, but I was covered in so much blood and soot, it was impossible to find them.

"Where are you hurt?" That rattling timbre held a frantic note.

I smiled up at him, cupping his cheek. He leaned into my touch. "Are you worried about me, Killer?"

"Yes," he growled. "Is all this blood yours?"

"Yes."

He held himself very still. His muscles swelled, straining against his skin.

"Why does that bother you so much?" I whispered, searching his dark gaze.

"Because it's yours."

Now that the threat was over, the energy carrying me through the fight and dampening the pain fled and the blood loss caught up to me. Lethargy seeped into my bones, weighing down my muscles like they were made of stone.

I dropped my hand, sagging to the ground.

My eyelids drooped.

"Little Thief, I need you awake." It was Ronan's voice this time, not the killer's. He shook my shoulders gently.

I unstuck my tongue from the roof of my mouth and croaked, "The bullet. There's a bullet in my calf."

"We need to get you to a mortal healer."

"No, mortals—" I struggled to take a breath—"you dead."

"Shhh." He brushed aside the blood-soaked hair sticking to my forehead. "You're safe now."

"I c—can—"

"Take care of yourself, I know." He smiled down at me. "You are the most stubborn creature I've ever had the pleasure of knowing."

I tried to smile back, but it was more of a grimace.

His arms reached for me again.

I protested weakly, hating that I would have to be carried away from the battlefield, but there was no way I could walk on my own. I consoled myself with the knowledge that it was no ordinary fight. Those fuckers had used a magic hammer on me.

Ronan hugged me close to his chest. "I know you are strong, fierce, and more than capable of fighting your battles, but you don't have to do it alone anymore. You have me."

I smiled, and let the darkness take over, knowing I was safe. Just as I drifted off, a cold realization hit me.

I knew what the Eye had stolen.

29

A figure scowled at me from the corner. I shot up in bed, glancing around for my weapons. The sudden movement caused a surge of dizziness. I froze, clutching my head, then hissed at the sharp pain that followed. I dropped my hands.

"Why is my head wrapped?"

The figure moved closer without responding, and I jerked back, tensing for an attack, but all he did was pour me a glass of water. His movements were stiff and agitated. He set the glass down on the nightstand beside the bed with an irritated thud.

"Drink."

My forehead crinkled as I stared at him. He had dark hair pulled into a bun and icy blue eyes glimmering with hate. The fae looked vaguely familiar, but my brain was too lethargic from sleep to place why.

"Do I know you?" I croaked.

His eyes narrowed. "Are you hard of hearing? I said drink."

I bristled at his tone. All vestiges of sleep were washed away by his rudeness. "Why don't you make me, Fairy?"

The fae dragged in a long breath through his nostrils as if he was fighting for the patience not to strangle me. His surliness caused a flash of recognition. This was Ronan's steward, Finn. I hadn't forgotten his dickishness.

Smirking, I tipped the glass over.

"Why you ungrateful, filthy—" Finn lunged, but stopped himself at the last minute. He straightened away from me, muttering, "By the Gods, how does he stand you?"

My lips twitched. I didn't know why I enjoyed provoking him so much. I leaned casually back against the bed frame fighting to reign in my amusement before I asked, "Where is your lord by the way?"

Ronan had to have been the one to tend to my wounds. Finn would have let me bleed out.

The last thing I remembered was Ronan carrying me back to our room above the saloon after I had failed miserably at fighting off those mortals. It was like I was fighting for the first time. Because I was. That's what the Eye had stolen from me. I knew something was wrong after the battle with the callitech, but I thought I was just having an off day.

After my fight with the mortals, I had no doubt. My fighting knowledge, gained from years of training with the Rogues, was gone. Just... Gone.

An ache started in my chest.

I had worked so hard to become strong. To learn how to defend myself so no one could ever hurt me again like the Crone had. Now, I was weak and useless. Ronan had to carry me away from the battle like I was a child.

Finn's voice distracted me before my thoughts could spiral further.

"He used a scrying mirror to demand I travel all the way from the Faylands and abandon my duties, so I could come

315

play nursemaid for the likes of you while he seeks revenge on your behalf. You have been out for two days."

"Revenge how?"

"He's out slaughtering the town."

My brows shot to my hairline. "What? Why?"

That was an extreme measure, even to me.

"They all played a part in your kidnapping. It seems Ronan killing that teenager back at the mines had a disastrous effect. Someone wants him dead, and they used that incident to further their agenda."

Worry churned in my gut. The mortals had failed to use me to lure Ronan to his death, but they were merely pawns. Whoever wanted him dead was still out there. "Who?"

"He is attempting to find that out now."

"Are you sure it is a good idea for him to be out there alone?"

Finn laughed tonelessly. "Lord Taran would be offended by your concern. Every House Taran soldier is worth fifty regular ones on a battlefield. *He* is worth an entire army."

After seeing how he fought in the forest, I didn't doubt Finn's statement in the slightest. "Why did he send for you?"

"I am the only one he could trust to watch over you. Even still, I had to swear an oath to protect you before I could convince him to leave your side." His nose wrinkled in disgust. "You're an ugly sleeper by the way. You drool and snore like a fat farm animal."

My gaze narrowed. "Watch it, Fairy. I swore no oaths."

He didn't respond to my threat. Instead, he stared at me —hard.

"What?" I hissed after I had enough.

"I have known him for five hundred years and in all that time, I have never seen him act this way with a female before," he said. "Did you bewitch him?"

I laughed at such an insane question, until I realized he was serious. "Do I look like a witch to you?"

He squinted, pursing his lips. "Hmm, no, you look like your mother bedded a beast."

Shocked laughter burst from my mouth. "Are you always this blunt?"

"I am always this honest."

If not for Ronan's warning regarding harming his people, I would have punched Finn in his pretty face for that remark.

Instead, I glared.

He glared back.

A game of wills ensued. Both of us refused to blink.

Finn lost and a triumphant smile lit up my face. He scowled. "My Lord might be smitten with you now, but it will pass. Has he told you about fae mates?"

I had only heard of fae mates once, when a fae came seeking a potion to cure his mate's infertility. It was the only time I saw the Crone turn down a customer after accepting their offering.

"No," I hissed as my stomach sunk. It wasn't hard to guess where this was headed.

"A mate is the other half of a fae's soul. The highest blessing. Mate pairings are chosen by the Gods."

A heavy disappointment weighed down my shoulders and chest, but I forced it away. Ronan and I might be attracted to one another, even strangely drawn to one another, but in no reality would the Gods have chosen a half-beast like me for him.

"What makes you think I'm not his?" I snarked anyway.

A cruel smirk. "You're not fae. If you were his mate, you wouldn't be in this filthy room. You'd be at his House, being introduced to his people."

So what if I wasn't his mate? It didn't make the connection I shared with Ronan any less real.

"He invited me to the Faylands."

"To be his Lady?"

To be his. At the time it sounded romantic, but what exactly did that mean?

"No," I growled.

"Fae mate for life. He will toss you aside as soon as he finds her. She is his destiny, a gorgeous, strong female hand-picked by the Gods just for him, to carry on his powerful bloodline." He smiled coolly. "You're just a means to pass the time."

His bloodline . . .

The image of Ronan holding a baby as he smiled at the beautiful dark-haired woman flashed across my mind. She was his mate.

I assumed the Eye had been showing me the present, or the past, but after Ronan's surprised reaction to my questions, I had pushed what I'd seen to the back of my mind. Now, I understood. It had been showing me the future. When in the future, I had no idea.

"I might be dead long before he finds her."

"That is true, but she is out there somewhere. He can never be yours. Not fully. His heart belongs to her."

Something ugly unfurled inside me. It bubbled in my chest, dark and acidic.

"I want you to leave."

He smiled, mockingly, knowing his words had hit their mark.

The acidic feeling spread, burning its way through my heart.

"I said leave!"

That taunting smile remained in place as he slipped from the room.

I retrieved the glass I'd knocked over and poured myself more water, hoping the cool liquid would ease the hot sting in my chest. It didn't.

I set the cup down with a hard thud, then stormed inside the bathroom, intent on taking a bath, when I caught my reflection in the mirror. What an ugly picture I made. My skin was pale. Bruises ringed my bloodshot eyes, and the light cloth wrapped around my head was soiled with blood.

Even healed, I could never live up to the beauty of Ronan's mate. She was stunning. I bet she was strong too. I bet he would never have to carry her away from a fight.

I slammed a fist into the mirror, shattering it. Ronan returned hours later after I had picked up the mirror pieces and hidden them under the bed.

He stormed in with a savage expression, gripping his sword. All my thoughts slammed to a halt at the sight of him. He was shirtless and covered in blood. His chest was a work of art; tattooed, swollen muscles smeared in red, blood he had spilt for me.

My thighs rubbed together beneath the blanket.

Our gazes collided.

"If you keep staring at me like that, I'm going to take you right here in this filthy room," he growled.

I licked my lips. "Do it."

His gaze was hot enough to burn this entire saloon to the ground.

"You don't know what you're asking." His jaw clenched. "I can't—I can't be gentle with you right now."

"I don't want gentle." I wanted him to take me and erase any shred of doubt he was mine. I threw off the blanket, letting him see the sheer nightgown I wore. "I want you," I whispered.

He sucked in a ragged breath.

My fingers brushed over my thighs, lifting the hem of my nightgown.

The knuckles gripping his sword turned white.

I opened my legs.

The sword clattered to the ground.

"Take me, Ronan."

He lunged.

He grabbed my ankles, dragged me to the edge of the bed, and tore my nightgown in half.

My breasts heaved as he stared down at me in just my underwear. His eyes glazed with need. They flickered between gray and black.

He raised a shaking hand, then dropped it with a harsh breath, and tore himself away. "No. You're still healing."

"Ronan."

"No," he growled. "I was digging a bullet out of your leg not even two days ago. You need rest. Your head wound hasn't sealed yet either."

He marched into the bathroom, and shut the door before I could argue with him.

The room grew cold in his absence. I shivered in my ruined nightgown, on the verge of tears.

He doesn't want you, Finn's voice whispered through my mind. *He wants her.*

I removed the nightgown, and changed into a new one as a tear slipped down my cheek. I swiped it away.

If my conversation with Ryder had cracked the door to doubting my connection with Ronan, Finn's words had blown it wide open. I knew Finn had only told me about mates to get under my skin, but the Eye had no prejudices against me. Ronan had a mate out there, and it wasn't me.

He reappeared after a time, freshly bathed, wearing new clothes and a stern expression.

"Care to explain how the mirror broke?"

I swallowed the emotion clogging my throat. "No."

He opened his mouth.

"Please let it go." I slumped back against the wall. "I don't feel well."

He rushed to my side, and felt my forehead. "You aren't running a fever. Is it your head? I'll change your bandage."

I was too tired to argue. Carefully, he unwound the cloth, and examined the wound. "Another day and you won't need the bandages anymore." He replaced the wrappings with new ones.

As soon as he finished, his expression turned thunderous. His hands clenched at his sides. "I wish I could slaughter them twice over for what they did to you."

You might care now, but you wouldn't have looked at me twice if you had your mate, I thought bitterly.

I should tell him what the Eye had shown me. That he finds his mate, and they have a beautiful baby together. Tell him how happy she makes him. But I couldn't because I was rotten and selfish, and I wanted him to myself.

"Finn said you were out getting revenge. Did you learn anything about who wants you dead?"

"No, unfortunately only three had direct contact with whoever it was. Two of them were killed in the fire, and the third is missing."

The female. I cursed myself for letting her get away.

"Did you . . . kill everyone?"

"The children were spared per our agreement. Finn is on his way to my House with them as we speak."

"Your House?"

"Yes, I am a man of my word. I will spare those I can."

"By making them your slaves?" My voice came out more heatedly than I intended.

Ronan frowned. He lowered beside me on the bed. "What is wrong?"

He tried to pull me into his lap, but I shifted out of his reach. "Nothing. I just don't like the idea of you saving children just so they can end up being enslaved like the halflings."

"My halflings aren't slaves. They are free and paid handsomely for their service."

Any other time, his statement would have elated me, but right then it only served as a reminder that this wonderful male wasn't mine. He could never be. He belonged to someone else.

Ronan studied me when I didn't respond. I couldn't meet his gaze knowing what he would find, but he didn't allow me to hide for long. He placed a finger under my chin and forced me to look at him.

"Did Finn say something to you? I know he can be rather abrasive at times."

I pulled my chin from his grasp, dropping it to my chest as I mumbled, "He only told me the truth."

"And what truth is that?"

That your heart can never be mine.

A rock lodged in the back of my throat. My chest tightened. The answer he sought was too painful to acknowledge. I pinched my eyes shut against the onslaught of tears threatening to spill.

When I opened them again, I sensed he wanted to reach for me, force me to look in his eyes, but thankfully he let me have my space. He remained patiently beside me until I gathered myself enough to respond. "It doesn't matter."

He stroked a hand down my hair. "It matters to me," he said softly.

I sucked in a sharp breath. He was so much easier to handle when he was being his demanding, assholish self, but when he was like this . . . Fuck, I'd rip out my own heart if he asked. In a way he was, asking me to come to the

Faylands despite knowing he had a mate somewhere out there.

"The godstone will be in Mayhem tomorrow," I whispered, turning on my side. "We should get some sleep. We need to be up early."

He grabbed my shoulder and gently turned me toward him and lowered his lips to mine. It was gentle, tender . . . loving. Two days ago, I would have eaten up his attention. Now, it only twisted the knife deeper. I was an interloper, accepting kisses that didn't belong to me.

I tried to pull away, but he tightened his grip, frowning. "Something is wrong."

I smiled. It was thin and forced. Focusing on his chest, I explained, "I'm just tired. Almost dying will do that to you."

We both knew why I couldn't meet his gaze, but thankfully Ronan didn't call me on it. He held me a moment longer before releasing me but didn't let me go far. He pulled my back flush against his chest and wrapped his arms around me. His body heat soaked into me, but it couldn't stop the ice spreading in my chest.

I had given him a partial truth. I was tired. Bone tired.

Tired of never being good enough.

Tired of always being chosen last.

I was a fool to think things with Ronan could be any different.

30

"Vera, wake up," Ronan whispered.

I groaned and turned on my side, huffing, "It's the middle of the night."

It had taken me some time to doze off after our conversation. Ronan had gripped me tightly the whole time. His comfort helped soothe some of the fear and worry Finn's words stirred.

Truthfully, I felt better than I had before.

So what if Ronan had a mate out there somewhere? The Eye had given no timeframe on the scene it had shown me. He might not find his mate for another thousand years for all I knew.

But I still couldn't stop the niggling thought that he wasn't mine. Even if he found his mate after I was gone, my entire relationship with Ronan would be haunted by the knowledge that I was just a placeholder until someone better came.

I wanted to be someone's forever, and I knew I couldn't be his.

He shook my shoulder. "Little Thief, please. You must wake up."

The urgency in his voice pierced through my sleep induced haze. I shot up in bed and looked over at him. Ronan was fully dressed with his sword peeking out behind his back as he hovered over me. I rubbed my eyes. "What is it?"

"I am being summoned. You must hide."

"What? Why?"

He grabbed both of my shoulders and stared at me with an intensity that made me shiver. "Please just promise me you'll hide."

"Okay, I promise."

"Good. Now dress quickly. You won't have much time before I have to pull you behind me."

Ronan vanished.

"Fuck." I flung off the covers and raced over to my saddlebags, determined not to show up wherever Ronan's enforcer duties had taken him half naked again. The bargain magic snapped me out of the room just as I finished tying my boot laces.

It dropped me inside an expansive room with black floors and white pillars. Flames flickered along the walls encased in crystal sconces. At the end of the room, the ceiling rose to a soaring height with a circular skylight cut into it. Moonlight poured in through the glass, shining down on the massive throne beneath it. The throne was made of metal and positioned on top of a platform raised several feet in the air, about as tall as Ronan. The height was intended to make anyone standing below it feel small and insignificant.

There was a body sprawled headfirst over the set of steps leading down from it. I was about to go over when I heard male voices. I dove behind the closest pillar as Ronan and an unfamiliar fae came into view.

They stopped in front of the platform. The fae ascended

the staircase, carelessly stepping on the body in the process. Whoever it was didn't move or make a sound, which meant they were likely dead.

The male fae was dressed in all black with white-blond hair down to his chest. Sharply pointed metal epaulets, jutting upward like the peaks of the Fayette Mountains, sat on top of a pair of broad shoulders. Armored plating covered his chest and forearms. He drew aside the gold mantle flowing behind him before he sat on the throne.

"I assume that is the law breaker?" Ronan gestured toward the body.

"Correct. I already did your job for you. You are welcome," came the other male's magnanimous reply.

Ronan's jaw tightened. "If you wanted to speak with me, your highness, a scrying mirror would have sufficed."

Your highness. Fae lords only paid deference to one fae.

This had to be King Desmond. My hand slid to the dagger on my thigh. I'd love nothing more than to stab it into the fae king's eye for discarding one of his halflings so heartlessly.

"Perhaps—" He lazily shrugged a shoulder "—but where is the fun in that old friend?"

Ronan crossed his arms, cocking a brow. "So, this is a friendly visit then?"

"That depends entirely on you. Do you have the godstone?"

"There . . . has been a delay in its retrieval."

"A delay?" King Desmond asked sharply.

"Yes." Ronan turned and peered into the shadows. His gaze zeroed in on my hiding spot in an instant like he could sense me. He turned and faced the fae king. "Do you trust the ears listening right now?"

Whatever was about to be said . . . Ronan didn't want *me* to hear it.

Bastard.

King Desmond rose from his throne. "Follow me. There is another reason I summoned you."

They disappeared through a side door, and I debated for a moment whether to follow them. It was the middle of the night, which hopefully meant most of House Dagda was fast asleep, and safer to be near Ronan than caught alone inside the throne room like some thief.

I cracked open the side door and peered down both directions of the torch lit hallway. Seeing it was clear, I crept forward, staying close to the walls as I followed the sound of their voices. Their conversation was too faint from this distance to make out, but the low murmurs were enough to guide me in the right direction.

They descended a spiraling stone staircase at the end of the hall, and I waited for them to walk down it before following.

The air grew colder the deeper I went, the stairs leading into the heart of whatever this place was. A cacophony of hissing and low snarls reached me when I neared the bottom, and my entire body went on alert.

I had followed them into a dungeon. Rows of cells lined either side of the stone walls with gold bars. Each one contained a familiar and terrifying sight. Beasts.

My heart jackhammered in my chest as I took in the menagerie of bloodthirsty creatures. There was a variety of every kind; air, land, even water.

A growling failin paced in its cage, a heavy gold collar around its neck secured with chains bolted to the floor. An ashray peered at me from its large glass tank. The king had even managed to capture a banshee.

It had the figure of a woman, but was completely translucent, like peering through a frosted window in winter. It wore a black shroud and dress with a corseted bodice and tattered seams. Its skin was milky white, the same as its long hair. It floated slightly off the ground, even with the chains holding it down.

What in the lands was the fae king doing, housing all these dangerous beasts, right under his home no less? It was the equivalent of storing a room full of explosives in a hot space.

Voices sounded down the corridor. Ronan and King Desmond rounded the corner where they had disappeared out of sight. They were coming toward me.

"My staff gives them a dose of liquid gold twice a day to keep them docile enough for containment."

"What are you planning on doing with them?"

There was a beat of silence. "Studying them for now."

"And later?"

I backed toward the staircase without hearing the king's response. I made it a quarter of the way up before I heard footfalls coming down the stairs.

Trapped. I was trapped.

I raced back down and frantically searched for a hiding spot, but there was nothing except for the beasts and their cages.

Ronan and King Desmond's voices grew louder. They would be here any minute.

My heart crawled into my throat realizing I only had one option.

I had to go into one of the cages.

Fuck, fuck, fuck.

Panicked, gaze skipping down the rows, I saw two purple eyes—attached to rippling fur and forearm size fangs—fixed on me. The failin was the only beast large enough to hide behind.

If it didn't eat me first.

Using a talon, I quickly picked the lock on its cell. I

opened the door a slither, fully expecting it to charge. It sat back on its haunches, watching me with the focus of a predator, but it didn't move.

"Good wolf. Stay right where you are."

I exhaled a shaky breath then opened the cage even further.

The failin still didn't move.

Gripping my dagger, heart threatening to rip out of my chest, I slowly crept inside the cell, inching along the wall, and kept my back away from the beast. I quietly closed the door, shutting myself inside.

Gods, of all my idiotic ideas, locking myself inside a cage with a massive, feral wolf had to be the most moronic of them all.

The failin rose to its full height, blocking out all the light in the cell. I froze, my heart hammering so loudly, I worried Ronan and the fae king could hear it down the hall. My skin felt feverish against the cool stone at my back. Something dripped down my forehead. I realized I was sweating.

Voices carried down from the staircase.

"One shot each. That should subdue them until morning."

The failin moved in front of me, sitting between me and the cell door. It blocked me from view as three fae appeared, their draoistones casting a blue glow over the dungeon. When one of them approached the cell where I hid, the failin growled menacingly, snapping its teeth. It spikes along its spine raised.

An argument ensued between the three about who would be the one to enter the cell and administer the dose.

"What is going on here?" A male voice snapped. King Desmond.

Double fuck.

Even though the failin's mass was more than sufficient to

329

block me from view, I curled further in on myself and threaded my shaking hands through the failin's fur.

"M-My king, this beast is stronger than it should be. Its last dose was only four hours ago, but something has set it off into a rage. It is not safe to enter."

"Morel, who is in charge here? You or the beast?"

"I am?"

"Either you open that cage and administer the dose, or I'll lock you in there as its next meal."

"I'll do it." This came from Ronan.

There was a brief pause before the cell door clanked open.

Ours. Do not harm him, mutt.

The failin calmed instantly. Ronan's gaze flickered to mine as he reached over the beast's neck with a syringe. He must have known I was in here. That's why he volunteered.

His expression was thunderous as it took in my huddled form. He gripped the syringe in his hand so tightly I feared it might shatter. If I survived this, he was definitely going to kill me.

"It's okay. I'm okay," I mouthed, hoping he could read my lips. "It won't harm you."

He plunged the needle into its fur, then quickly backed out of the cell, slamming the door shut behind him.

I held my breath, waiting for them to leave. Three sets of footfalls receded, continuing further into the dungeon, which meant two remained.

"I must be going, My King," Ronan said.

"Remember what we spoke about." King Desmond's tone was filled with warning.

There was a brief pause before Ronan said, "You'll have the godstone."

A whoosh of air told me Ronan had vanished, but King Desmond remained. I could feel his weighted gaze staring into the cell. I pinched my eyes shut, silently praying for him to leave.

A creak. Keys jangling.

The cell door opened.

No, no, no.

The failin was too weakened from the gold dose to do more than issue a faint growl. Boots scraped over stone as he moved inside. All he had to do was glance around the beast and he'd see me.

"Why did you behave for the Enforcer?"

A stretch of tense, heart pounding silence passed where I had no idea what the king was doing on the other side of the failin.

Relief flooded me as I felt a tug on the bargain magic.

"What are you doing in here?"

Cold terror choked my lungs. My gaze locked with the king's just as I was catapulted out of the cell and back into the room above the saloon.

Ronan jerked me to him. Steely arms banded around my back, holding me close. It took me a second to catch my breath and I squeezed him back just as tightly, pressing my ear to his chest. The steady rhythm of his heart helped to calm my own.

"Thank the Gods." Ronan nuzzled my hair. He took in several slow inhales, breathing me in.

Surrounded by his warmth and intoxicating scent of leather, amberwood, and something distinctly Ronan, the trembling in my limbs eased.

Abruptly he pulled away, holding me by the shoulders. He looked me over for injuries.

"What were you thinking?" he asked sharply once he finished.

"I'm fine."

His gaze snapped to mine. "Fine? No. Fine people do not

lock themselves in cages with beasts. You could have been killed." He nearly shouted the last part. His chest was heaving.

"You told me to hide," I said carefully. "I was trying to keep my promise. Trust me, if there had been *any* other option, I would have taken it."

My explanation did little to ease his agitation.

"How are you still alive? Why didn't it attack?" he asked.

I hesitated, not because I didn't want to tell him. I wasn't sure how to put it into words.

"I can conjure fire, but I'm sure you already put that together after the callitech's trap. But that's not all I can do. I hear this voice inside my head sometimes. It ordered the failin not to harm you when you entered the cell."

His jaw hardened. The tendons in his neck muscles grew taut, bulging out of his skin. "You've done this before?" he gritted out. "Given a beast an order and it listened?"

"Yes . . ."

"Fuck," he whispered harshly.

"What? What is it?"

"Nothing." He dismissed me, turning away as he removed his sword and stripped off his pants and boots with rough movements.

I placed a hand on his back. "Ronan, please talk to me."

He paused long enough to twist around and kiss my palm. "It's late, my Little Thief," he murmured. "We'll talk in the morning."

I laid stiffly beside him in bed all night. I couldn't sleep for most of it, but I drifted off into a restless sleep for a few hours.

I woke to Ronan packing.

Yawning, I watched him stalk around the room, swiping up his discarded clothes. "Where's the fire, big guy? The godstone isn't going into the mine in Mayhem until tonight."

The thieves wouldn't go through all the trouble of moving it there just to move it again tomorrow. We didn't have to rush.

He said nothing. Wouldn't even look at me. He continued stuffing his saddlebags.

Worry twisted my stomach. I rose from the bed, and stayed the hand buckling his bag. "Hey."

He pulled away and gave me his back.

"Ronan?"

Silence.

Frustration leaked into my voice as I reminded him, "You said we would talk in the morning. It's morning now."

He stiffened. A heavy sigh left him as he turned toward me. His eyes were black, his face empty.

The pit of my stomach sunk like it was being pulled underwater by a grundylow.

"I no longer require your assistance," he said tonelessly. Faster than I could track, he had a blade poised at my palm, and used it without warning.

I jerked back with a hiss, but he wouldn't release me. "What the fuck was that for?"

He slashed his hand and pressed it on top of mine.

A burning sensation started. It traveled down, growing hotter as it went. By the time it reached my toes, my skin felt like it was melting. It stopped just as quickly as it started.

My wild gaze flew up to his. "What did you do?"

He moved away, and grabbed his saddlebags, slinging them over his shoulder.

"Your end of the bargain is fulfilled. You are free to go. I will retrieve the godstone on my own." He wouldn't look at me.

"Free to go?" I echoed dumbly, then shook my head. "What are you talking about? We're going to get the godstone, and then go to the Faylands together."

He glanced over his shoulder at me with those dark eyes. "No."

My throat tightened. I spoke loudly over the pulse pounding in my ears. "No? No, I won't be coming with you to find the godstone, or no I won't be coming with you to the Faylands?"

"Both."

The single word fell between us like a hammer blow. It slammed into my chest knocking me back a step.

"You—You asked me to come to the Faylands with you only two nights ago."

"Ronan was thinking with the wrong head when he made that offer. It was a mistake."

My pulse slowed, turned sluggish in my chest. The same chest this male was twisting a knife through. "Let me talk to Ronan," I demanded.

His eyes flickered to gray, but that indifferent mask didn't slip, not even at the devastation I knew he saw written on my face.

"Why are you doing this?" I whispered.

"Oh, don't look at me like that, Little Thief. This was always a short-term arrangement."

I shook my head as if I hadn't heard him correctly, but I knew I had. I swallowed around the hard lump in my throat. "Is this because I told you what I could do?" I asked in a small voice.

"Yes. I can't bring a beast hybrid back home with me."

Hot tears burned at the edges of my eyes. I dropped my gaze, brokenly whispering, "I'm not a beast." But the claim felt weak even to my own ears.

"The only thing capable of controlling a beast is a more powerful one."

"You've known about my curse long before this and it never bothered you."

A sigh. "You're not getting the hint so let me make it very clear for you. This was a transaction. You help me find the godstone and you get to live. Seducing you was a fun challenge, but I've had you and I have the godstone's location. I have no reason to keep you around."

"This was more than a transaction. You—"

"I was kind to you, yes. But that's all it was. It's not my fault that you're so starved for affection, you mistook my acts of decency as more than what they were."

"You said I was your beacon."

"I would have used whatever honest deception I could to get into your pants. I told you, seducing you was a fun challenge. No woman has ever held out against me as long as you did. You should be proud of yourself for that."

Lava filled my veins. How *dare* he. My fists clenched tight. I wanted to knock out his teeth.

"Fuck. You," I spat.

"You're broken, Vera. I am not the man to fix you."

Tears burned my eyes. I grabbed the closest thing and hurled it at his head.

He ducked in time and the lamp shattered against the wall.

"Get out! Get the fuck out! I never want to see you again."

He moved to the door and stopped with his hand still on the knob, hesitating. I didn't look up even though I felt his gaze on me.

"Go!" I screamed.

The door shut and I slumped to the bed. Ice wrapped around my bones, and seeped into my blood. A numbness took hold.

I didn't know how long I sat there, staring at the now vacant space, before my feet moved on their own accord and carried me out the door. Somehow, I was dressed, and my saddlebags were in my arms. Down the stairs I went, not seeing anything, not feeling anything.

I found myself outside the kitchen and heard banging inside. Ronan was there sifting through the cabinets. The noise stopped and I assumed he found what he was looking for.

Suddenly, he was running out of the kitchen. I slipped into a closet a second before he would have seen me. Once his pounding footfalls retreated down the hall, I darted inside the kitchen.

A bowl of cold beef broth was set out on the counter. I moved, and blinked down at the vial in my hand. My gaze shifted between the food and the iron dust.

I sprinkled it on top of the soup and stirred.

Then I ran.

I ran until I reached outside, and nausea rolled through me. I bent over emptying my stomach. There wasn't much as I had been asleep the last two days. Acid burned my throat as I dry heaved.

What had I done?

I straightened, swiping my mouth, and rushed back into the saloon. I wanted Ronan to hurt like I did, but I didn't want him dead.

Never dead.

The kitchen was empty when I returned.

So was the bowl of soup.

31

Bodies littered the streets of Coldwater. Flies buzzed around their corpses. Most were given a quick death with their throats slit. True to Ronan's word, none of them were children.

Gold City would not be pleased that the Enforcer had killed twenty or so of their workforce in the mines, but they also valued their trade with the fae far more than their own people.

The town was eerily quiet as I trailed behind Ronan. After I had found the kitchen empty, it wasn't difficult to guess where he would go next.

He disappeared into the stables and returned with a horse. I ducked behind a building to avoid being seen, but I shouldn't have bothered. Ronan's gaze was clouded, the lines around his eyes tight. Usually, he was hypervigilant as he moved, his body alert to the subtlest of sounds around him. I could have stood directly in his path, and I wasn't certain he would have seen me.

Ronan mounted the horse and kept glancing over his shoulder at the saloon. He stared at it for a long moment before he shook his head and urged his horse into a trot.

I watched him go, embracing the surge of anger and betrayal at how easily he abandoned me. He had shown me the worst pieces of himself, and I had accepted each and every one of them. But the moment I had shared my ugliest parts, he left.

Hot tears filled my eyes, but I refused to shed a single one for that bastard.

I should have known better. When was I going to learn? People didn't see something to love when they looked at me. They saw a monster to use as they saw fit and discard when it was convenient.

Nothing Ronan and I had shared had been real. How eagerly my lonely heart had devoured his lies. The organ beat hollowly in my chest. I wanted to claw the useless thing out.

He disappeared in the distance. Good riddance.

Someone out there wanted him dead. That was his problem. What did I care if the bastard lived or died? He had tossed me aside like I meant nothing. Ronan deserved whatever was coming. Besides, he was an immortal, powerful fae. He would be hard to kill, even with the godstone.

My pulse stuttered in my chest.

No . . .

He wouldn't be immortal once the iron dust kicked in. He would be weak and very killable. I might as well have handed whoever wanted Ronan dead a loaded gun.

A persistent itch started in my legs, demanding I follow, keep him safe. I clenched my jaw and ripped my gaze away from the horizon.

No.

The fucker didn't deserve my concern. He was lucky I didn't finish the job and take the godstone for myself. I could. But that would be pointless. Even if I still wanted a vest, I couldn't be a Rogue anymore, not with my fighting abilities gone.

I stormed toward the saloon, intent on figuring out my next move.

Every step I took away from him was agonizing and only spiked my anger more. My mind conjured images of Ronan lying limp, his once fierce eyes, glassy, staring up at the sky. A sharp, piercing pain slammed into my chest, robbing me of breath. I froze mid step and struggled to breathe. It felt like a giant was sitting on me. Nausea followed and I bent over, dry heaving.

I spent a good minute getting my body back under control. My mind and heart were at war. My mind wanted to let the bastard fend for himself, but my stupid heart couldn't stand the thought of living in a world where he didn't exist.

Godsdamnit.

Snarling, I spun and stalked inside the stable. I would make sure the idiot didn't die, and then I would wipe my hands of him.

I chose a horse for myself before freeing the rest as there was no one left in the town to care for them. I rode hard to catch up with him, then slowed and followed at a safe distance. The entire time, I glared at him hard enough, hoping he'd burst into flames. Unfortunately, he never did.

Ronan's posture was odd as he rode. The high and mighty Enforcer's shoulders slumped slightly forward with his head hung. For a moment, a foolish part of me thought he might feel remorse for what he had done, but I shoved the stupid idea away. If he truly regretted his actions, he would have come back for me.

At nightfall, he stopped to set up camp while I hid from sight in a small outcrop of trees. I sat on my bedroll, watching him from afar. He had a small fire going. The flames cast shadows over the planes of his face, but I was too far away to make out his expression.

My talons twitched at my side, desperate to sink into his flesh. It would be so easy to gut him as he slept. I might not want him dead, but I would love nothing more than to make him bleed. Let him feel just an ounce of the pain I felt. The idea soothed the fury clawing at my insides enough for me to relax.

When my eyelids began to droop, I removed the chains from my saddlebag and secured them to a tree, then to myself. I had found them the next morning after he'd thrown them, and kept them just in case I needed them again. Looks like I was right.

Deep down, I had always known what I had with Ronan was too good to be true. I should have listened to my gut.

The icy metal against my wrists felt foreign and uncomfortable and stirred bittersweet memories of the wonderful nights I had slept chainless in Ronan's arms.

Shivering in the cold night, my burning anger dissipated leaving a black chasm in my chest. Bleak, endless loneliness consumed me. Under the cover of darkness, I allowed the flood of tears I had been holding back all day to fall.

I had spent my entire life alone. I had accepted that being used by the Rogues was the best things could ever be for me, and I never complained. Compared to my time with the Crone, life with the Rogues was good. It wasn't great, but I could learn to be happy.

Then Ronan crashed into my life. He offered me things no one had ever offered before; showed me I didn't need to settle for a mediocre life with the Rogues. He had given me hope that I could have more. Be more.

Then he'd cruelly ripped it all away. All his promises had been empty. He had abandoned me like I was nothing. Less than nothing. I wasn't sure if I was angrier at myself for allowing him the power to hurt me, or him for using it.

Never had I felt so . . . worthless.

This was my fate, to always be alone. It was time to accept the fact that I was unlovable.

Great big sobs wracked my body. I covered my mouth to keep any sound from spilling out. I fell asleep that way. Chained and alone.

Soft light pierced through the cloud cover early the next morning, waking me. With swollen, red rimmed eyes I stared up at the sky. It was a dreary gray. Head lolling to the side, I glanced over at Ronan's camp and ensured he was still there. He was starting to stir, which meant he would be departing soon.

Sighing, I sat up. My eyes felt like they had been scrubbed with sandpaper. The sharp pain in my chest had dulled to a persistent ache. I quietly removed the chains, then splashed my face with some water from my canteen. The cool liquid stung at first but removing the layer of tears crusted on my cheeks made me feel more like myself. I rose and packed up my camp, a new sense of determination coursing through me.

Once Ronan had the godstone safely in hand, I would let him go. It wouldn't be easy, but I had survived much worse. I would survive this too.

Our journey resumed at a brisk pace. We rode for hours until Mayhem appeared on the sandy horizon like a mirage. Over the course of the day, I watched as the iron dust took effect. Ronan's movements were sluggish and slow. He had difficulty staying upright on his horse.

The consequences only grew worse as I entered behind him into the city. He weaved unsteadily through the streets wearing a large cloak and hunched shoulders to disguise himself, though his massive frame still drew unwanted attention. Wary eyes watched his teetering gait.

Ronan lost his balance and crashed into a vendor's stall. Those observing on the sidelines gasped. The stall's owner flew at Ronan as he struggled to his feet, screaming obscenities.

The Enforcer tossed some silvers at him and resumed stumbling through the street like a drunk giant. Everyone flocked to watch him go, drawn by curiosity.

As I squeezed through the crowd, my eyes connected with a familiar face, and I froze. It was the female who had attacked me in Coldwater. She noticed me at the same time, eyes widening a second before she bolted. I shoved through the crowd, sprinting after her.

She wasn't as fast, but she was clever. She darted down alleyway after alleyway, then changed tactics unexpectedly and cut back through the market to the other side of the street. I dashed down the alleyway after her.

Something slammed into my face with a sickening crunch.

I crashed to the ground as blood spurted from my nose. I clutched it, glaring while the crazy mortal discarded a thick piece of wood, and took off again. I leapt to my feet and rushed after her, putting all my strength into my legs. I couldn't let her get away again.

The mortal took a sharp right at the end of the alley and disappeared. This time I was ready when I caught up to her and she tried to crack my skull open with a rock. I ducked under the swing and charged, tackling her to the ground.

My hands wrapped around her throat. Blood from my broken nose dripped onto her face. "Who wants to hurt the Enforcer?" I demanded, squeezing.

The female gasped, clawing at my hands.

"I said." I slammed her head against the ground. "Who wants to hurt the Enforcer?"

I loosened my grip just enough for her to speak.

She smiled coldly. "You're too late," she rasped. "He's walking right into our trap. The Enforcer is as good as dead."

Something crashed into the side of my face. My head whipped sideways from the force of the blow. The mortal had managed to get her hands on a huge rock. I slumped off of her, head spinning. She got behind me as I struggled to shake off the haze, and wrapped a scarf around my throat. A foot braced against my back as she wrenched the scarf as tight as she could, cutting off my air supply.

I wheezed, clawing at the fabric, but I couldn't get it away from my neck enough to breathe. Everything blurred and spun. I could feel my eyes popping out of my head.

She pulled harder.

My throat burned. I was seconds away from passing out.

I shredded the scarf with my talons, tearing into my throat in the process. The second the pressure lifted, I flung my hand behind me, and raked my talons through the air. They snagged on flesh, and the mortal cried out.

She raced away, limping, as I struggled to remain conscious. Bright lights burst behind my eyes, and everything went dark.

When I came too, my head and neck were throbbing, but mostly healed. My nose was too, crookedly. I snapped it back into place, cursing shrilly at the burst of pain.

I was still on the ground in the alley. I had no idea how long I was unconscious for.

My chest seized.

Ronan!

With my heart in my throat, I stumbled to my feet and flew out of the alley, skidding to a stop on the street. Franti-

343

cally, I scanned the crowd for the Enforcer's lumbering form, but I couldn't see him anywhere.

No, no, no!

What if I was too late?

The mines. He's going to the mines.

Panicking, throwing elbows to create a path, I hurried to the other side of the city. There were only two exit points, the front gate, and a lesser known, smaller gate at the back of the city. I barreled through it, bursting with speed. I ran faster than I had ever run before. My darkness stirred, lending me its power and strength.

Sand flew up around me as I raced across the desert to the ore mines.

Please be okay. Please, please be okay.

I saw the plateau the Eye had shown me in the vision.

Almost there.

The entrance was nothing more than a square cut into a hillside, its roof supported by a log frame. Its darkened interior gave no indication of how deep the mine was or how many guarded the godstone.

I ran down the dimly lit tunnel in silence until loud grunts and meaty thunks filled my ears. I slowed, unsure what I was walking into. The landscape of the tunnel transformed and opened into a bright cavern.

At its center was Ronan facing off against ten robed assailants.

I sucked in a reverent breath at the grace and power in his movements. Even poisoned, Ronan was the best fighter I had ever seen. He wavered on his feet, but still managed to land a hit every time he struck.

A loud ringing filled the air as Ronan's sword clashed with two figures. The others stood with their weapons raised, ready to strike as they slowly encroached him. One of them pulled a gun and fired.

Ronan wasn't fast enough to avoid it and the bullet buried into his abdomen. I grimaced. That had to hurt, but the Enforcer didn't slow for even a second. He spun on his heel, slamming his boot into the attacker's chest. The figure flew back and crashed into the wall. He didn't get up.

I started forward, flexing my fists at my sides. I might be a shit fighter—courtesy of the Eye—but I wasn't going to let Ronan fight them on his own.

I didn't get more than two steps before something cold pressed into the back of my head.

"Don't. Move."

I knew that voice.

"Ryder?"

I tried to twist backward to confirm, but the barrel shoved harder against my skull.

"This is your last warning, V."

He kicked out my legs and shoved me to my knees.

My arms were wrenched behind my back as soon as I hit the ground. I was too stunned to react at first, then I thrashed violently in his grip. "Ryder, what are you doing?" I hissed. "You're not really going to shoot me."

"I will if I have to." He sounded nothing like the Ryder I knew. His voice was cold and distant.

The gun cocked and I froze.

Ronan's whole body tensed at the sound. His gaze clashed with mine. So many emotions flashed across his eyes, it was too quick to follow. He stared at where Ryder held a gun against my head and all the gray bled from his eyes, leaving only black.

He seemed to grow in size—muscles bulging and red veins appearing as if too much mass packed under his skin to fit properly. His midnight gaze fixed on us, and a shiver coursed through me.

This wasn't Ronan anymore. This was the killer.

"You don't touch her!" His roar shook the walls.

He released an animalistic snarl, and charged through the ten robed figures surrounding him like paper.

Some leapt forward, grabbing hold of his arms and his legs to stop his pursuit, but it did little. He waded through them, coming toward us.

I felt the gun at my head tremble. Ryder was scared. "The gun is full of gold bullets. One more step and she is dead," he snarled.

Ronan froze.

I kicked out at Ryder's shin, but he dodged the attack. He gripped my hair, and wrenched my head back, shoving the barrel of the gun under my chin.

"Surrender, or she dies."

"Ronan! No!"

We both knew he would be killed if he did.

Ronan's dark gaze met mine as he lowered to his knees.

He placed his arms behind his head as the ten figures surged behind him. He didn't fight as they collared his throat and arms in iron shackles.

"Ronan, get up!" Hot tears slid down my cheeks. "Please," I begged. "Fight them!"

He didn't move, holding my gaze the entire time.

32

I was stripped of my weapons, bound, blindfolded, and handed off at gunpoint. I fought and kicked for all I was worth as they dragged me somewhere, but I couldn't see my captors, and there were too many of them.

Metal clanged. I was shoved hard and fell. My knees hit rock. Hands gripped my shoulders, yanking my arms behind me. Something cold snapped around both wrists. A door slammed shut. Then it was quiet.

I shuffled forward on my knees. I didn't get far before the cuffs on my wrists jerked me back. I stood, feeling around me with an elbow. It hit something hard, and I recoiled at the sharp pain.

A wall.

Carefully, I leaned forward and rubbed my face against it, pushing the blindfold up off my face.

I saw I was in a cell. The space was small and dark. A torch was the only source of light, casting dancing shadows in the light breeze sweeping through. The breeze was good. That meant I was above ground at least, but I didn't have a clue where.

My arms were cuffed behind me and attached to chains

bolted into the wall. I walked to the edge of the cell. Through the bars, I saw Ronan in his own prison across from me. His head and hands were secured in an iron stock. He had to lean forward at an awkward angle to accommodate its bulky weight.

His head lifted as soon as he felt my gaze on him. "How are you feeling?" he rasped.

I stared at him for a long moment and then burst into laughter. It sounded as crazed as I felt. How was one supposed to feel locked inside a cell after someone they once considered a friend held a gun to their head?

He laughed a little himself, though he sounded much saner. "Right."

Our laughter died off leaving only the crackling of the torch.

Ronan continued to stare at me, and the longer he did, the darker his expression became.

"You shouldn't have come."

"Yeah," I scoffed, bitterness filling my belly. "You made that pretty clear."

"Then why did you?" he asked softly.

I ignored him, moving away from the bars to sit against the back wall. I tipped my head against the stone hoping he would drop it, but I should have known better. The bastard was just as stubborn as me.

"Vera? Why?"

My rage returned with a vengeance. I glared, jaw clenched so tight it was on the verge of cracking. "Because I was worried about you even though you don't fucking deserve it," I snapped.

He flinched and had the decency to look ashamed. "I'm sorry. I didn't—"

"Save it. I don't want to hear whatever corthshit is about to come out of your mouth."

348

My gaze returned to the ceiling. He was right. I shouldn't have come. Ronan had made his feelings clear, and I had still followed him like a pathetic, lovesick idiot. Now we were both locked in here.

A weighted silence stretched between us. I was the one to break it.

"Why did you surrender?" I asked.

Those ten men were no match against Ronan, even weakened. If it hadn't been for me, they wouldn't have been able to imprison him. One minute he had thrown me away like trash and the next, he had surrendered. For me. I couldn't make sense of it.

My gaze drifted over to him when he remained silent.

He was staring at me. His gun-metal eyes were sharp and penetrating, swirling with that same foreign emotion I refused to acknowledge when I'd returned his mother's brooch. Only this time, the strength of it was tenfold. That gaze saw all the pain I carried, all the bitterness.

And worst of all, he saw the one emotion I was desperate to hide. It was the same emotion reflected at me.

"You know why, Little Thief."

I sucked in a breath as his words pierced the icy shield of anger I wore around my heart. It was my turn to stare hard. "I don't believe you."

Guilt flashed. "That's fair, but it doesn't make it any less true."

"Look me in the eyes and say it," I demanded.

He shifted closer, his chains clanking over the ground. He gripped the bars, staring me dead in the eyes.

"Vera, I—"

The door to the jail opened. Both of our heads swung toward it as Ryder entered. He donned the black robes of the House of Night, his Rogue vest nowhere in sight.

It took a second for my mind to catch up to my eyes. I

349

hadn't seen any other Rogues in the mines. Just Ryder and the robed figures. I had been too worried for Ronan to fully process what I had seen, but the pieces fell into place in that instant.

"You're one of them. A Nighter."

"Yes."

I tried to launch myself at the bars, fangs bared, but the chains stopped me shy of my goal. "Traitor!"

He was unimpressed with my outburst. There was no trace of the Ryder I had spent the last seven years with. He appeared so much older than twenty-one in that moment. The boyish charm was gone, locked behind a callous stare and cruel smile.

"No, *you're* the traitor," he said coolly. "The fae are the enemy. The Enforcer even more so. He's the weapon they use to keep the Mortal Lands under their thumb, and you chose him over the Rogues."

"And you chose the Nighters so I guess that makes us even," I spat.

He shook his head. "The Nighters aren't the enemy. They might have extreme views, but they hate the fae as much as the rest of us and are willing to do something about it. That makes them allies."

"How long? How long have you been sneaking around behind Boone's back with them?"

"Boone knows. It took some convincing, but unlike you, he sees the larger picture. How do you think we knew to cut the rope?"

Boone had told him about my connection to the Crone . .
.

"Lovely woman. I see why you're so fucked in the head," he continued.

His words sliced right into my chest. I strained against the chains. "Fuck you," I bit out.

Ryder leaned a forearm against the cell and stared at me. He was close enough to strike, but that is exactly what he expected me to do. I had to bide my time.

"Tried that once. Wasn't great," he said with a mean smirk.

My body shook with the violence I wanted to unleash on him. He was provoking me. I wouldn't give him the satisfaction. Not until the time was right.

"You didn't come to Coldwater for me. You already knew where the godstone was because the Nighters had it. You were looking for the Enforcer. You used The Eye. It showed you he'd be there, didn't it?"

"Imagine my surprise when I saw you two looking cozy in the saloon. I knew he'd let you live when I got your message, but I wasn't expecting that. I tried to warn you to stay away from him. You didn't listen."

"So you used me to lure him out instead."

"Yes, but those three idiots kidnapped you too soon. They were supposed to wait until my back-up arrived."

He moved away from the bars seconds before I was going to attack, with a smirk, and I bit down my frustrated curse. He was toying with me.

"You were right when you called us glorified soldiers for the fae. Both the Rogues and the mortals serve the fae in some way. As long as they live, none of us will be free."

I stared at him. The pieces were all coming together.

"You can't touch the fae while he is alive." My gaze briefly met Ronan's. He was listening to our conversation in silence. "You sent me after the godstone knowing I would never be able to steal it. I was meant as a distraction for the Enforcer."

"Yes. I saw the way he reacted to you outside the train."

"How were you able to tell all those lies?"

"I never lied. If you'd managed to retrieve the godstone, we would have given you a vest. I knew it belonged to the fae. Gold City demanded they be the ones to return it to them, but none of us knew it belonged to the Enforcer.

He had sent me on an impossible mission. I was never going to get the godstone and he knew that. Even worse . . . "You knew I was stealing from the fae. You sent me to die."

Ryder shrugged. *Shrugged.* That's how much my life meant to him. "Change requires sacrifice. I did try to save you in Coldwater."

I ignored the latter part of his statement. It didn't cancel out sending me to my death in the first place.

"That's easy to say when you're not the one doing the sacrificing."

His lip curled. He advanced on me, but not close enough for me to strike. "You think I haven't sacrificed? I had four sisters and a mother before I came to the Rogues. Do you want to know what happened to them? King Desmond gave them to some of his visiting dignitaries as entertainment. They were beaten and raped, but that's not the worst of it. No, what the bastard did after—" Ryder glanced away as a harsh breath shuddered out of him. "House Dagda halflings that can't perform their duties properly are killed. He had their throats slit and thrown away like trash. My youngest sister was only fourteen."

A girl. His sister was just a girl.

I swallowed around the hard lump in my throat. Despite what Ryder had done, despite what he was going to do, I couldn't help the swell of pity I felt. He didn't deserve it, but he had it anyway.

"I'm sorry," I choked out.

Ryder shook himself and all traces of his despair vanished, replaced by rage. "Don't be. The fae will get what's coming to them."

"And me? We've been friends since I was fifteen. We

grew up together. I thought that might have meant something."

"It does, V, but there is so much at stake. If you could prove you're one of us, we would give you everything you've ever wanted—a vest, a place with the Rogues."

"How do I prove that?"

I already knew, but I wanted him to say it.

"Kill the Enforcer."

My gaze drifted to Ronan. He was pale and sweating in his stocks, but even weakened, he was still the strongest male I had ever laid eyes on. His tunic, dirty and torn from the fight back in the mines, revealed the hard, muscular planes of his chest and arms and the scars there. Arms that had held me close through the night and laid waste to those who had attempted to harm me. Arms that made me feel beautiful and desired.

I had spent my entire life trying to prove I was worthy.

Not with Ronan.

I never had to prove anything to him.

He accepted me just as I was—stubbornness and monstrous appearance and all.

I didn't want what Ryder offered anymore. I only wanted Ronan, even if he didn't want me back.

Fuck, I was an idiot.

I was in love with the bastard. Just the thought of something happening to him made me sick to my stomach.

"No." My voice rang out, firm and strong. "And if anyone else tries to harm him, I will burn this entire city down, with you and every other rotten soul inside it."

Ryder released a mocking laugh. "You can barely control yourself, let alone your powers."

I shrugged. "Guess you're going to have to kill us both then."

"Thanks for making that easy." He tipped his head

toward Ronan's cell. "We were going to use the godstone to kill him, but that would be too clean a death. Now he gets to die just like the rest of us. It's beautiful, really."

I lunged. There was enough force behind it that I ripped one of the bolts from the wall. Ryder was expecting me. He snatched a hold of my throat through the bars and squeezed.

He leaned into my space. If not for the bars between us, we would have been nose-to-nose. "You chose the wrong side, V," he snarled. "You did this to yourself."

"Get your fucking hands off her," Ronan's vicious voice rang out.

Ryder's face broke into a cold smile. "He doesn't know does he?" he whispered, then squeezed harder, choking all the air from my lungs. I gasped trying to free my hands from behind my back.

Ronan thrashed in his cell. "Let her go!" he roared.

Ryder released my throat with a flourish of his hands. "Interesting you still want to defend her after she poisoned you."

There was a beat of silence before Ronan growled, "You're lying. She wouldn't. It was you and the Nighters."

A pit opened in my stomach.

Ryder stared at me with an evil smile. "She got the iron dust from us. I was there. Go on, V, tell him I'm lying."

My pained gaze met Ronan's.

His face fell.

"No," he whispered. "It's not true. Tell me it's not true."

I couldn't.

Ryder's grin grew. "I'll let you two talk." He left the jailhouse knowing he had won.

The truth spilled out of me as soon as he was gone. "I got the iron dust while we were in Gold City, but I swear I wasn't going to use it, not after I got to know you. I was just angry and as soon as I realized what I had done, I tried to stop it, but it was already too late. I followed you here to make sure nothing happened to you. Please, I'm so sorry, Ronan. I would have never let anything happen to you."

He stared and stared. The ensuing silence was like a thunderclap in my ears, reverberating through my bones.

"Please, say something."

Nothing. There was no anger in his gaze. No sadness. There was nothing and that made it so much worse. An ache started in my chest as tears spilled down my cheeks.

"Ronan, *please*."

He stared right through me like I didn't exist.

"I'm so sorry."

Silence. Silence. Silence.

R onan slumped forward in his stocks, breathing heavily. His condition was getting worse. He couldn't keep himself upright anymore. The iron dust in his system and the energy he'd exerted fending off those Nighters had caught up to him. He was sweating and shaking and the injuries he had sustained during the attack weren't healing.

Worry lanced through my stomach. I focused on it and beat back the swell of emotions. If I allowed myself to succumb to them, to feel the pain, guilt, and devastation, I would be no good to anyone. Ronan might not want anything to do with me, but he needed me right now.

I crept forward on my knees as far as the chains would allow. With one of the bolts loosened, I was able to make it all the way to the bars. Pressing my face against the cool metal, I peered through and whispered, "Ronan."

He tried and failed to lift his head. My stomach tightened painfully. I did this. I reduced this powerful, fierce fae lord to *this*.

I blew out a breath and shoved away the tears pricking at the back of my eyes. Feeling sorry for myself wasn't going to save him. After all this was over, I would let the consequences of what I had done sink in. I'd let myself cry, but first I had to make sure he was alive to hate me.

The Nighters would be back soon and I was greatly outnumbered. Even if I hadn't lost my fighting skills to the Eye, brute force wasn't going to work, but burning my way out might.

Closing my eyes, I tried to focus on my center and call on my power, but nothing happened. I squeezed my eyes tighter. Still nothing. *Fucking of course.* The one time I really needed it, the stupid thing didn't work.

My gaze flitted around my cell, stopping on the bolt freed from the wall. If I could free the other, I could reposition my hands and pick the lock on the cell, then do the same for Ronan. I had no idea what I would find outside the door, but I knew for certain if we remained here, we would both die.

Bracing both feet against the back wall, I leveraged my weight against it and pulled the bolted chain as hard as I could. The metal barely moved. I tried again and again until I was breathing heavily with little progress to show for it. The chain fell to the ground with a hard thud.

Frowning, I stared at the bolt freed from the wall.

How had I done it the first time?

I remembered charging the cell door to get to Ryder so fast the thing ripped out of the wall. Maybe I just needed to do that again. I moved into position against the back wall and shoved off, sprinting as fast as I could. When I neared the bars, I threw my body weight forward and slammed into them. Metal grinded against stone, and I glanced over my shoulder to see an inch of the bolt sticking out of the wall.

I smiled despite the pain blooming in my chest from the collision with the bars. This might actually work. I repeated the process over and over again, driving the bolt further out of the wall each time. Just an inch more and I'd be free.

I lined up against the wall again, ready to run when a new figure entered the small jailhouse alongside Ryder.

The newcomer wore a failin skull and a red robe. On their shoulder, they hefted a double-bladed battle axe. The material of the two blades was unlike anything I'd ever seen. It was pure black with veins of electric blue glyphs running over the surface. A wave of power slammed into me, strong enough that it squeezed the air from my lungs.

I pressed myself as close to the back wall as I could to get away from the uncomfortable sensation.

This was the Nighter's leader. He had given me the iron dust.

Ryder gestured to the newcomer. "V, I want you to meet Bale."

The figure stared down at me through the narrow slits of his mask.

"Hello again." That masculine, cultured voice poured over me like honey, ringing with familiarity.

"You're the one from the vision."

Bale's mask shifted higher like he was smiling beneath it.

"Let her go," Ronan growled. My gaze shot to his cell. He had to grip the bars to keep himself upright. "It's me you want. She has nothing to do with this."

I stared at him, shocked. After everything, he was still trying to save me. A tight knot formed in my chest.

"You know what this is, Enforcer?" Bale lifted the axe on his shoulder and turned toward Ronan, ignoring his plea. The blue veins moved over the axe's surface like srphys.

I slid down the wall, lowering myself in front of the loosened bolt. Ryder's gaze cast my way briefly before returning to Bale. With their attention on Ronan, I started working on twisting the bolt the rest of the way out.

"This is going to usher in a new era. One where mortals

are no longer lambs for the slaughter and the fae are brought to their knees." Bale pointed the battle axe at Ronan. "You'll be the first."

Ronan's face took on a dark edge. He spat out a glob of blood, a side effect of the iron, and flashed a chilling smile. "That is only one weapon, and you are only mortal. You can't take us all down, even with your iron dust."

"That is true, but something can."

Ronan froze.

His face paled.

"No—"

"Yes."

I didn't understand.

"V, did you know that iron dust isn't the only thing that can kill a high fae?"

My fingers froze on the bolt as Ryder glanced back over his shoulder. His question finally registered over the wild pounding of my heart at almost being caught. "What are you talking about?"

"Why don't they come for their runaway halflings? If high fae are so powerful, why lock the beasts behind the wall? Why not just slaughter them?"

I didn't understand what he was getting at. Suddenly the answer slammed into me like a fist to the gut. I had always found it odd how close the sloaugh had come to killing Ronan. If I hadn't been there . . .

It should have been impossible.

"The beasts can kill high fae," I answered and looked to Ronan for confirmation. His jaw tightened. He wouldn't meet my gaze.

"Very good," Bale said. "We are going to destroy the wall and free them."

The godstone could destroy a fae, and they had created the wall imprisoning the beasts. If the godstone could kill them, there was no reason it couldn't destroy their magic too.

"It won't work," Ronan gritted out. "Your plan will fail. It will take years to destroy the cumulative power of all the fae magic creating that wall."

"Ah, but the fae's magic grows weaker with each passing year. If it didn't, the beasts couldn't escape at all, could they?" Ronan's jaw clenched so hard I thought it might shatter.

Bale glanced at me. "Perhaps the fae aren't as powerful as you think."

Ronan looked pained. He didn't respond.

"My plan will work if the fae magic is weak enough. Fortunately for me, I won't have to wait another millennia for you all to die off. The Blood Moon will suit my needs," Bale continued. "Or, who knows. With the Enforcer out of the way, we might even accomplish our goal sooner than you think."

A rock formed in the pit of my stomach. The Blood Moon was only four months away. With no sun for a day, the fae would be at their weakest, and so would the magic creating the wall. The beasts would rampage the Mortal Lands and slaughter millions. This Nighter was trying to free the beasts for good.

"You're insane! The beasts won't just kill the fae, they'll kill everyone," I hissed.

"Not everyone," Bale remarked. "Lord Balor and I have struck a deal. Those I deem worthy will be saved."

I returned to unscrewing the bolt with renewed vigor. We had to get out of here.

Ronan scoffed from his cell. "The Lord of Darkness would never bargain with a mortal, not truly. He is using you."

"Lord Balor will keep his word." The Nighter sounded

certain. Either he was an idiot, or there was something we didn't know.

Bale hefted the battle axe over his shoulder. "It is a pity neither of you will be alive to see it."

I tugged hard on the bolt, ripped it out the last inch, and charged the bars, grabbing a hold of Bale's robes. I dragged him to me before he could pull away and pressed a talon to his neck.

"Open this door, or I'll slit your throat," I snarled.

Ryder started toward us, but Bale raised a hand, stopping him. Sharp teeth flashed. That was my only warning before a scalding pain exploded over my hands. I reared back with a curse.

There were third degree burns on my palms. "How?" I whispered, my gaze darting up to Bale.

"I already told you. I see what others cannot."

"That doesn't explain—"

"Guards!" Bale called out, cutting me off.

Robed figures swarmed inside and yanked Ronan and me from our cells. There were too many to fight even if my fighting skills weren't shit at the moment, but that didn't stop me from trying.

I thrashed and kicked out as my arms were wrenched behind my back. I managed to kick someone in the gut before my ankles were shackled and I was dragged out of the jailhouse.

I stumbled blindly into the outside world as my light deprived eyes struggled to adjust. The guard at my back shoved me forward, barking, "Walk faster, fae lover," and the force of it sent me tumbling into the dirt face first.

I bared my teeth, growling as I was wrenched back to my feet. The smart male moved away too quickly for me to tear a chunk out of his throat.

Six masked Nighters in black robes passed, supporting Ronan's dead weight between them.

"Where are you taking us?"

"Don't worry. You and your little lover boy will be reunited soon enough."

We were walking to our deaths.

I stopped abruptly and slammed my body weight into the guard behind me before bolting for Ronan. I didn't get more than a step before a force barreled into my back and knocked me to the ground. The guard pressed my face into the dirt hard enough I couldn't breathe. He held me there just on the cusp of suffocation before loosening his hold to signal something.

I heard a pained grunt and shifted my head to the side. A fresh track of blood trickled out of Ronan's back from where one of the guards had stabbed him.

I thrashed, growling and snarling. "Touch him again and I'll kill you!"

The guard restrained me with embarrassing ease. He laughed. "Tough words for someone chained up." He jerked me to my feet. "Too bad you chose the wrong side. We could use someone with your spirit."

I twisted around and spit in his face. "You and every Nighter are disgusting."

The guard punched me in the gut. Air wheezed out of my lungs from the force of the blow. I doubled over, clutching my stomach. "What in the lands are you? Mortals don't have this kind of strength," I hissed between my teeth.

He snatched me by my hair, forcing me to arch my back. "We're more alike than you know," he whispered, then shoved me forward.

"I'm nothing like you lunatics. Bale's plan is insane. You have to know that."

The guard didn't respond. I should have known better

than to waste my breath reasoning with one of them. Anyone who wanted the beasts freed had lost all sense.

I squinted into the bright day to figure out where we were headed. Several yards ahead, a crowd gathered below a wooden structure with two looped ropes swinging in the breeze.

They were taking us to the gallows. The Nighters intended to execute us publicly. Bale stood on the raised platform.

As we were dragged past the edge of the crowd everyone pumped their fist in the air, chanting, "Kill. The. Beast. And. The. Fae."

Their words bounced around in my skull. Of course, the town would be glad to see me dead right alongside the Enforcer. I had been and always would be a beast in their eyes.

The guards pulled us up the stairs. "So glad you could join us," Bale said in greeting. He dismissed us, turning to the crowd. Ronan blinked, coming to momentarily as a noose was placed around each of our necks.

"I give you the Enforcer and his beastly companion," Bale announced. The crowd broke out into a deafening uproar.

"No longer will you have to live in fear. With the Enforcer dead, the Mortal Lands will finally rise against the fae's tyranny. We will storm the Faylands and take what is rightfully ours. They live like kings while we starve and break our backs to meet their demands for gold. No more!"

Masked Nighters appeared below tossing something into the crowd. The mortals eagerly snatched the offerings.

Iron dust.

They were giving them iron dust.

Another chant started, the crowd lifting their vials into the air.

"Kill. The. Fae. Kill. The. Fae."

Bale's satisfaction emanated off him in waves. The senti-ment he stirred would quickly travel across the Mortal Lands and soon enough, mortals would storm the fae's border.

The fae would be too distracted fending off the mortals now equipped to kill the most powerful among them when Bale unleashed the beasts. It would be a swift victory come the Blood Moon with the fae fighting a battle on two fronts.

"Idiots! Can't you see he's using you?" I screamed at them, but my warning fell on deaf ears.

No one listened. No one cared. They couldn't see past their hatred for the fae.

Frantically, I scanned the crowd for anyone who might be able to stop this madness. Rage filled me as my gaze caught on Boone. Ryder stood beside him along with several other Rogues. They all lifted vials into the air and joined the chanting.

"Kill. The. Fae."

The dirty, traitorous scum. They would all pay.

"Any last words?" Bale asked.

Ronan turned to the Nighter, chin lifted, and head held high despite the noose tight around his neck; despite his muscles shaking with the strain of supporting his weight.

He wouldn't cower.

He wouldn't beg.

His gaze shifted to me, those gray eyes stoic and unafraid. "Spare her."

Those two words were a battering ram to my composure. Tears spilled down my cheeks blurring my vision. I shook my head, skin scraping against the coarse rope around my neck.

I deserved death for what I had done, but not Ronan. The infuriating, demanding fae lord was kind and compassionate beyond measure. He loved and gave without reserve. Beneath the Enforcer facade was the best, most honorable man I ever had the pleasure of knowing.

Despite everything I had done, he was still trying to protect me with his dying breath.

He had to live.

No matter what happened, Ronan would live.

Determination coursed through me, shutting out everything else. The creature stirred, sensing my intention. Those purple eyes flared brightly in the recess of my mind where I kept the darkest part of myself hidden and locked away.

I can save him, a disembodied voice sounded in my skull. *But you must free me.*

A sickening fear took hold of me. I had spent my nights in chains to prevent that very thing. I knew if the creature was ever freed it would cost me dearly. Possibly even my life, but if it meant saving Ronan, I would gladly pay it.

Burn it all down if you must, but he lives.

The creature arched its back, stretching out its limbs. Smoke billowed out its nostrils as its massive head tipped forward, mimicking a nod.

Deallll. He lives, it hissed, its forked tongue peeking out.

For the first time, I opened the cage door and set it free.

The creature lunged for the surface and my whole body jerked. Scalding, agonizing pain came next. Fire licked up my spine and consumed my insides. My talons and fangs swelled to monstrous proportions as something hard and grotesque formed over my skin.

I felt someone's burning stare on me and lifted my gaze to find Bale's eyes filled with absolute bewilderment.

"That's not . . . You're not . . . You are an impossibility. I thought you were all dead."

The creature trumpeted a warning call, loud enough to

shake the platform where we stood. A jet of fire blasted from my mouth, dissolving the noose around my neck.

I stepped down from the wooden box.

"You are misssstaken. I am very much alive." My voice came out multi-layered and ancient, echoing through the air. "I am the last dragon."

34

I roared, a torrent of flames bellowing from my mouth. The scene around me dissolved into chaos. Bale leapt off the platform into the crowd of stampeding mortals, his followers not far behind.

Everyone was screaming. The dragon lapped up their terrified sounds like a delicious treat.

A choking rasp snapped my attention to Ronan. The bastards had kicked his block out from under him, but his neck had not broken. He was strangling to death. I rushed forward and burned through his noose. He fell toward me, gasping for air. I caught him under the arms and pulled his dead weight down the stairs, racing against the flames consuming the gallows.

The structure crumbled just as I managed to fling us to the ground. I patted out the flames eating at his clothes and skin, then laid him on his back and brought my face to his mouth. Warm air brushed my cheek and I slumped back in relief.

He was alive. Barely.

Strangulation marks ringed his throat. I stared at the

nasty red band as a tide of fury rushed through my veins. If his neck had broken. . . .

The dragon's rage added to my own.

How dare they touch what is oursssss.

Icy panic flooded me as the dragon took full control of my body.

No! He's safe.

He won't be safe. Not as long as this city breathessss. It all burns.

An itch started in the center of my back, making it twitch. That itch quickly turned into a stabbing sensation. My shoulder snapped forward with a crunch and dislocated itself. My bones started popping and I arched off the ground, screaming soundlessly. The pain was overwhelming. My right leg twisted at an unnatural angle, and the bone snapped just like it had under the rock.

My body was on fire, every cell inflamed. Flesh melted off my bones. I could smell it burning. The scent of it made my eyes water. I clenched my jaw and tried to focus, trying to take control back, but the dragon refused to be caged again. It was like trying to punch through the walls of Gold City. It did nothing, but leave my mind battered and bruised.

Limbs extending, I rose and rose until I could see over every building in Mayhem. Wings punched through my back.

"Vera," Ronan whispered, reaching for me. He didn't hesitate to touch my scaled skin, even though I knew what he saw—a massive dragon hovering over him.

The beast nuzzled him with its massive snout, then we launched into the air, our powerful wings carrying us high into the clouds. We circled once, then dove toward the city beneath. Streams of fire shot out of our mouth, leaving a trail of burning buildings in our wake.

We shot back up into the sky and stopped to gaze down at the destruction we had caused. From this distance, the people were mere ants, running through the streets. Their terrified screams drifted up, riding on the plumes of smoke billowing off the buildings.

A quarter of the city was on fire.

That won't do. It all burnssss.

No, no, no.

I grit my teeth, trying to stop the dragon, but I had no control. I was merely a passenger.

My stomach dropped as we dove down, spiraling toward the city.

The screams grew louder. I could hear the crackle and popping of the fire as it ate away at the buildings. More flames burst from our giant maw. This time we circled the entire city, setting it all aflame before returning to the sky. Ants raced into the desert as their city burned behind them.

We swooped down and caught several of the mortals between our talons. Those gathered scattered like insects, running and screaming, terrified they would be next. The beast tossed the mortals into our mouth, devouring them and spitting out their bones. Nausea and repulsion flooded me.

A small figure raced by, yelling hysterically. A child. It was a child. My gaze darted toward the city in the distance and my heart stopped. There were children in there.

Panic seized me. I needed to shift back. Now, before the beast did more damage. I poured all my mental energy into wrangling control back from the dragon. I kicked and screamed, beating at the darkness inside me, but it wouldn't go back inside its cage.

Give me back my body, reptile!

No.

The dragon flapped its wing, readying to launch back into the air for another attack. My heart jackhammered in my chest. I was completely powerless to stop it.

"Vera!"

Ronan stood between us and the fleeing mortals. He swayed on his feet. His face was charred on one side. There were patches of burnt flesh all over his face and his tunic was torn, hanging in threads from his chest.

"Put out the fire, dragon, and shift back," he demanded.

The dragon snarled, snapping its teeth inches from his face, but Ronan didn't flinch or step back. "Dragon. Do it NOW!" he roared.

The beast reared back on its hind legs, trumpeting a deafening warning call. Still, Ronan didn't move. Its front paws slammed to the ground kicking up a cloud of sand and shockingly, it obeyed.

It flapped its wings, creating a powerful gust of wind and didn't stop beating until every last flame was extinguished.

Ronan approached with his hands raised. When the beast didn't attack, he drew closer and pet its muzzle, crooning, "Good girl. Now I need you to shift back."

The dragon chuffed, blowing a plume of hot air at him.

"*Dragon.*" His low voice was filled with warning.

My joints started to crack. Bones broke and reformed. The shift was just as painful as it had been the first time. When it finished, I fell to my knees, crying out in agony. It felt like I'd been run through with a battering ram.

Ronan was there, cradling me in his arms. He held me tightly against his chest whispering soothing words in my ear until the pain subsided.

I pulled away from him, stood, and offered my hand. We needed to leave, get somewhere safe, before someone came and finished what the Nighters had started.

He accepted it and rose, but he was unsteady. None of his wounds were healing with the iron dust still in his system. His eyes rolled in the back of his head a second before he collapsed.

"Ronan!" I lunged for him, shaking his shoulders. "Ronan, we need to go." He wasn't waking up.

"Fuck."

I grabbed him under the arms to pull him, but it was difficult. He was heavy. I fell a few times, grunting before I managed to get a good grip under his arms and started dragging him back to the city. It was a slow process.

Mortals ran wildly around me, some still screaming even though the immediate danger was over.

A large gap existed where the city gates stood only an hour before. I pulled Ronan inside and spotted an abandoned cart. I gently laid him down before rolling it over to him and tried to lift him onto it, but he was too heavy to lift by myself. I managed to only get part of his torso on before my arms gave out and he slipped over the side.

I darted forward and eased his fall to the ground, then frowned at the cart. There was no way I could get him loaded on my own.

"Need some help darlin'?"

My head whipped around to see Marty standing behind me. Ash coated his face, and his silver hair was a mess. He held out a blanket toward me. Slowly, he walked forward with it outstretched and draped it over my shoulders before backing away.

I realized I was naked. My clothes had burned away during the shift. I twisted it and wrapped it around my body like a dress.

"Thanks," I mumbled.

My gaze briefly darted between the two males before I stepped protectively in front of Ronan, eyes narrowed. "How do I know you're not aligned with the rest of the crazies that want him dead?"

His gaze turned apologetic. "If I had an inkling of what the Rogues had planned . . . " He blew out his cheeks. "I would never have allowed them to go through with it. I got to the gallows too late. "

I believed Marty might have tried to save *me*, but I couldn't say the same for Ronan.

I widened my stance. "He's a fae."

Marty moved quickly for his age. He brushed me aside and grabbed one of Ronan's arms before I could stop him. "They ain't all bad," he said. "And besides, I just saw you burn down half a city to save him, hun. I ain't stupid."

My stomach tightened. "So you . . . know what I am," I said at his back.

"I always knew you were special, darlin'." He grinned at me over his shoulder. "Now come on. This bastard's heavy. We need to get him somewhere safe."

I grabbed the other arm and together we loaded him into the cart.

"We'll take him to my place."

I nodded and we each grabbed a handle and started into the city.

As we moved through the streets, my stomach sank. I saw the destruction I had caused firsthand. Buildings were nothing more than burnt rubble, smoke still drifting off them. Charred debris littered the streets.

Something soft landed on my eyelashes. I wiped it away and my hand came back black. I glanced up to see flakes of ash raining from the sky. It coated everything in gray snow.

A sickening barb twisted through my gut when my eyes landed on the first dead body. It was frozen in time, hands outstretched as if they were begging for help in their final moments. I had to look away. I didn't care much for mortals, but that was a horrific way to die. Even the beasts gave them a quick death.

The closer we moved into the city center, the more dead bodies I saw. A pair of corpses caught my eyes. They were clinging to one another. I peered harder and realized it was a mother and her small child.

I dropped the handle of the cart and vomited.

A hand stroked my back as I emptied my stomach onto the street. "We've got to keep moving, darlin'," Marty said once I finished.

I ignored him, staring at the small doll clutched in the little girl's tiny hands. She couldn't have been more than three or four. Her entire face was burned off. She wasn't the only one. The more I looked, the more tiny bodies I saw.

My stomach heaved again. Acid burned my throat when there was nothing left to throw up. I straightened as I wiped my mouth.

My gaze drifted back to the mother and child. "I did this, Marty," I whispered. "I'm a fucking monster."

Dark thoughts consumed me. How could I have done this? I was no better than the Crone. I was pure evil. I—

A stinging slap hit my cheek. "Snap out of it, sweetheart. Your man needs you."

My hand shot to my face as I spun toward Marty. "Did you just . . . slap me?" I asked incredulously.

He flashed a grin. "Worked, didn't it? Get your ass moving."

I shook off the darkness threatening to devour me whole and picked up my end of the cart. We continued our way through the streets, stopping once we reached a familiar building.

Marty's saloon. As far as I could tell, it was untouched by the fire. Relief flooded me at the sight. I couldn't bear it if I had burned down Marty's livelihood.

We carried Ronan into a small room above the saloon.

"Now what?" I asked, gaze lingering over Ronan's motionless body.

"Now we wait. Ain't nothing else we can do for him. He's gotta wake up on his own."

35

I sat by Ronan's bedside through the night, scarcely daring to blink as I watched the rise and fall of his chest. I was terrified that if I took my eyes off him for even a moment, I would lose him like I had been so close to doing back at the gallows.

The bruised ring blemishing the skin around his neck haunted me. As did the patches of melted flesh and scorch marks all over his body. His tunic—a bloodied, tattered mess—hung off his muscled chest and exposed the black lettering just beneath his collar bone.

I am the sword and shield.

Tears stung at the edges of my eyes. I had reduced this powerful fae lord, the same one who struck fear into the hearts of every mortal, to the pale, unconscious figure on the bed. The guilt was unbearable. It threatened to consume me, and I would let it. I would let the acidic tar filling my chest devour me from the inside out just as soon as I saw Ronan awake.

I stroked his cheek and pressed a feather light kiss to his forehead.

"I am so sorry," I whispered. Words wouldn't heal the

damage to his body, or his trust, but I felt compelled to say it all the same.

This wasn't all my fault though. If he hadn't treated me so cruelly back at the inn, I would have never used the iron dust. If he loved me as he claimed, why had he done that?

He owed me some answers and I owed him some too. I would explain everything and make him see reason when he woke. He would be beyond angry, understandably, but I'd tell him my side of things, and he'd forgive me. He had too.

Shortly after midnight, Ronan's open wounds began to stitch themselves back together and the discoloration on his throat bled away. A shaky, relieved breath left me. The iron dust was working its way out of his system. He would be immortal once more.

I finally left his side to see if I could scrounge up something in the kitchen knowing he would be starving when he woke. Marty was gone and the kitchen didn't have much beyond raw ingredients. I was unwilling to submit Ronan to my atrocious cooking skills, so I settled on a loaf of bread with some butter.

He was still sound asleep when I returned. I placed the food on the bedside table, then returned to my post at his side. When the first rays of sunlight peeked through the open curtains, Ronan groaned, shifting in the bed. I bolted upright where I had drifted off in a chair and reached for his hand.

His eyes opened and pure joy slammed through me. That steel-gray gaze was the most beautiful thing I had ever seen. I smiled, squeezing his hand.

"You're awake," I whispered fervently. "Thank the lands, you're awake."

His gaze was unfocused for a moment as it shifted around the room. "Where am I?" he asked in a rough voice.

"A friend's."

He moved to sit up, but I stopped him with my free hand. "Careful. You're still injured."

Ronan took stock of his body, then his gaze drifted to our joined hands. He pulled his away, then slowly sat up against the headboard.

I kept the smile plastered on my face despite the arrow spearing through my chest.

"Where is my sword?" he asked gruffly.

My smile faltered, disappointed I couldn't give him better news. "With the Nighters, wherever they escaped to."

I planned on storming their hideout below the church at the first opportunity, but I knew it was unlikely I would find much.

He frowned in response. I caught myself reaching toward him, wanting to comfort him, but pulled my hand back.

"I am going to find them and the godstone." My vow disrupted the awkward silence stretching between us.

Ronan rose from the bed without a response. He was unsteady for a moment as he got his bearings. They returned quickly, and once again, I stared at the male I had seen back inside the tent. The strong, formidable Enforcer of the fae laws.

His gaze dipped to his ruined clothes before scanning the room and finding the ones I had stolen off the largest mortal I could find on our way to the inn.

"They might be a little small," I explained, then turned my back to give him some privacy while he dressed. We had seen one another naked, but that was before.

My lips quirked when I refaced him and saw the pants ended mid-calf, busting at the seams. He didn't bother with the shirt.

Ronan moved toward the door. My brows furrowed. "What are you doing?"

"Leaving."

I shot to the door, placing myself between it and him. "You need to rest. I . . . I brought you some food."

He glanced at the food with a heavy frown. "Then I'll do it in a place with people I trust."

I flinched, suddenly realizing how stupid I had been. He would never accept any food I offered him again.

He tried to move around me. I matched his steps, holding up my hands. "Please, let me explain."

"Your actions have spoken plenty." A hint of bitterness had entered his tone betraying his indifferent expression and my chest tightened.

He brushed past me to the door.

"Ronan, please," I called at his back.

He spun on me with a snarl and leaned into my space. "Was this your plan all along? Abuse our connection? Take advantage of my feelings for you so you could kill me?"

I reared back. His accusation stirred up all the rage and pain I couldn't feel when he had abandoned me back in Coldwater.

"*I* took advantage of *you*?" I laughed coldly. "That's rich coming from the male who made me all those pretty little promises and then when I finally opened up to you, you treated me like I was worthless."

His fists clenched. The scar running through his lips appeared whiter against his steadily reddening face.

When he said nothing, I scoffed. "That's what I thought."

"I was trying to protect you," he roared. Then in a calmer voice said, "Do you know what you are, Vera? You're a dragon. The same creatures I hunted to extinction during the Dark Wars because they were too powerful to lock behind the wall. They are the only tier five beast to ever exist. They can bend every other beast to their will. If the fae

378

find out what you are, you will be hunted down and slaughtered, or worse."

There was a lot to unpack there, but one thing snagged my attention. "What's worse than death?" I asked.

"King Desmond adding you to his zoo."

Ronan had hurt me because he wanted to protect me ... I wasn't sure how to feel about that. "I didn't know," I whispered. "Why were you going to give the godstone to that monster anyway?"

"He threatened my people if I didn't."

My gut twisted itself into a thousand knots. "I—I swear I never would have—"

"You would have." His words cleaved the air.

Hot tears threatened to spill at how certain he was. "You really think so little of me?"

Silence.

"You're a hypocrite. You threatened to kill me when we first met," I reminded him. "You forced me into a bargain. You were using me. Of course I wanted to kill you. But that was before I got to know you. After I did, I wasn't going to use it. I was just so angry. I immediately regretted it. I followed you here to protect you "

That penetrating gaze skewered me. "You're wrong," he gritted out. "I never needed you."

"What?"

"The bargain was a ruse."

I was too shocked to speak for a minute. "What are you talking about?"

"I knew where the Crone was. I could have killed you and found the godstone on my own."

"I don't—I don't understand."

"When I saw you back at the train, you had this look in your eyes. This pain. It called to me. Leaving you there, not knowing if I would ever see you again was . . . difficult.

When I saw you again, I knew it was fate. I couldn't let you go a second time. I wanted to know you. I had to know what put that sadness in your eyes."

"You just . . . wanted to spend time with me?"

"Yes," he said harshly. "I knew you'd never willingly let me get close to you. The bargain was the perfect idea. I could explore this pull I felt between us and find the godstone at the same time."

I swallowed thickly, trying my damndest to keep the flood of tears at bay. This whole time . . .

He tore his gaze away. "If I had known what the Crone was going to do to you . . ." He sucked in a sharp breath. "I would never have allowed her anywhere near you. She was able to hurt you again because of *me*. I couldn't—" emotion choked his voice. "I wasn't going to let anyone hurt you ever again. Even if it meant you hated me."

I stared imploringly. "Why didn't you just tell me?"

His overly bright gaze anchored to mine. I saw the pain beneath his anger and it *gutted* me.

"If I had, and I asked you to stay behind, would you have?"

"No." Nothing would have stopped me from coming with him. I couldn't even after how horrible he was to me back in Coldwater.

Fuck. I had messed up. I had really messed up.

"At least let me fix this," I rushed out. "Let me come with you and explain to the fae king."

"Haven't you already done enough?" he whispered.

I lowered my gaze as hot, fat shameful tears spilled down my cheeks. I allowed myself only a second of self-pity before I lifted my watery eyes to his.

"I made a mistake," I choked out. "I was just upset."

Ronan's face twisted like he was in pain. This time he was the one to look away.

"I've hurt people. Slaughtered thousands, but you, Vera?" He glanced over at me. "I could never. Even if the Gods themselves commanded it, I would sooner run a blade through my own chest than see a single drop of your blood spilled."

I felt sick to my stomach. I wanted to vomit.

"I am not a good man. I know that. Everyone, even my own people fear me, and for good reason. You were the first who wasn't afraid. The first person to really see me. Not the Enforcer, but Ronan Taran. I didn't feel like a monster when I was with you, but you used me. You made me think—" A ragged breath shuddered out of him. "You made me think you cared for me, all the while you were plotting my death. I should have known better. Everyone wants to fuck the monster, but no one wants to love him."

Tears slipped down my cheeks. "Ronan, I lo—"

"Don't." He looked tormented.

"But it's true," I breathed.

"No. People don't poison the ones they love. If what you claim is true, you could have disposed of the iron dust at any time, but you kept it. You were always going to use it."

I opened my mouth to explain that wasn't true, but he stopped me with a shake of his head. "I won't believe a word that comes out of your mouth."

"I'm sorry," I whispered brokenly. "I'm so sorry."

He was quiet for several moments after that, several long moments where all I could hear was the pulse pounding in my ears. I wanted to beg and plead for his forgiveness, but I knew it was far too late for that.

"I'll need a sword, or a dagger. Whatever you can find is helpful."

I sniffed, swiping at my cheeks, and cleared my throat. "Of course."

Ronan was still weakened by the iron dust. He needed

one to protect himself. I left to pilfer one off the many corpses now lining the street.

I found a wicked sharp dagger with a black handle and returned, proud I could be of some use.

I knocked once on the door just to be courteous before entering.

The space was empty.

Ronan was gone.

36

I might have caught up to Ronan if I had left shortly after I returned with the dagger, but his departure said everything he couldn't. He was well and truly done with me. Instead, I laid in the bed for days where his scent lingered until there was nothing left of him in the room. Just me and my guilt.

Our conversation haunted me every waking hour. He had pushed me away to protect me and how easily I had let him because I was eager to believe he had just been using me. Thinking back on that moment, I could have done things so differently. Why hadn't I fought, gotten angry, demanded he allow me to come anyway?

Because deep down, a part of me believed what he had said. Because experience had taught me that my only value was my use.

What good did a fae lord have for a beast hybrid that brought nothing but death and destruction?

I never needed you. I wanted to know you.

My stomach shrank in on itself.

Ronan had never used me. He took an extreme measure to spend time with me, but he was right. I never would have spent time with him without the bargain. What he had done was crazy, but also endearing. He hadn't noticed my frightening features that scared everyone else away that day outside the train. He had looked past that and seen *me*; seen the pain I worked so hard to hide. And he wanted to know the cause of it.

I had seen him too, past all the myth and bloodshed. Thinking back on our interactions, there were so many moments, where I caught hints of his vulnerability. He expected me to use him for his body like all the women who had accepted his hand.

Everyone wants to fuck the monster, but no one wants to love him.

He too, thought he was unlovable because that's what he had experienced. My betrayal had only reinforced that belief. And fuck, that broke my heart more than any of the rest. That I made him feel unloveable.

Hysterical laughter bubbled up my throat. We were two broken souls that somehow fit perfectly together.

Except we didn't. Not anymore. Ronan had left. He had a beautiful mate out there, waiting for him.

Another reason I didn't follow him. He deserved better. He deserved to smile so hard it made his cheeks ache. I couldn't give him that, but she could. As much as it pained me that I couldn't be the one to make him smile like that, I wasn't going to stand in the way of his happiness.

That decision didn't lessen the gnawing ache in my chest. It didn't ease the emptiness once full of Ronan's heated looks, his playfulness, and demanding ways. That was all gone now. I would never get to experience it again.

Ronan and his mate, whenever he found her, would be off having beautiful babies, and I would return to the Crone as penance for all the pain and destruction I had caused.

A knock sounded, interrupting my melancholy. I didn't answer, but the door swung open anyway.

Marty stood on the other side. He took in my disheveled state and my red rimmed eyes, with a frown. "Some of those corpses outside look better than you."

"Watch it, old man, or you're liable to become one of them," I said, but there was no heat to it.

He chuckled. "Still got some fire left. There's hope for you yet."

I found myself smiling despite my mood. Marty always had a knack for that—making me smile even when it was the last thing I wanted to do. He perched on the edge of the bed where I clung to a pillow that no longer smelled of Ronan and folded his hands.

"Sitting in this room crying ain't going to do you no good, darlin'."

I averted my gaze, shrugging. The alternative was returning to the Crone, not just as penance, but also because I had nowhere else to go. I knew I would have to leave eventually, but I could barely get out of bed.

"You love him?" Marty asked.

I had just stopped crying. His question threatened to start the tears all over again. "I don't want to talk about that."

"Too bad. I ain't leaving until you do."

I glared. He grinned.

I released a harsh sigh. "Yes, I love him."

"Then what in the lands are you still doing here?"

"He hates me."

"Fine line between love and hate, darlin'."

"I poisoned him with iron dust, Marty. He almost died because of me. He deserves better."

He snatched the pillow out of my hands and thumped me over the head with it.

I scowled, blocking him from doing it a second time, hissing, "What was that for?"

"For being birdbrained. I watched you spend seven years fighting to be a Rogue and you didn't even like any of those bastards and you're telling me you ain't even willing to fight for the man you love? If that's true, he does deserve better than you."

I dropped my head into my hands. "I don't know," I whispered.

"What's there to know? The only people who don't fight for the ones they love are goddamn cowards and you've never been one of those a day in your life."

Feeling Marty's eyes on me, I lifted my head and stared into his discerning face. It was aggravating because I knew he was right but fuck, for once I wanted to be a coward. For once, I wanted to take the easy way out. I was so tired; the kind of exhaustion that seeped into your bones and no amount of sleep could get it out.

I scrubbed my face and moved off the mattress, needing to get away from that knowing stare. Outside the small window, I saw most of the city was in shambles. Some of the buildings were still smoking. People moved between the streets, carrying cart loads of dead bodies to bury out in the desert.

"Why are you here?" I gritted out, flinging a hand at the window. "I did this. I destroyed the city. Burned it to a crisp. You should be angry with me. Hate me even." I glanced back at him, snapping, "If you had any goddamn sense, you'd fear me at the very least. Maybe you're the birdbrained one."

Marty didn't rise to my anger. He stared patiently at me from the bed. "I am five hundred and three years old."

My brows flew together. "What?"

"You wanted to know my age." He waved a hand. "Well, there it is."

I turned toward him, leaning against the window. The glass was warm against my back. "I thought halflings live to three hundred at the most."

His lips tipped up into a smirk. "They don't make 'em like me anymore, darlin'."

I believed that. Marty was one of a kind.

"You didn't answer my question," I said.

He scowled and I couldn't help but laugh. "I'm getting to it, if you'd quit running your trap."

I raised my hands in surrender, a teasing smile on my lips, but remained silent.

Glowering at me, he continued, "I was the first halfling to ever come to these parts. The Rogues didn't exist at the time. I had no idea what I was running to when I left the Faylands."

"So why did you?"

"Had a daughter. Wanted a better life for her than the one I had. You and Delilah, you'd have been fast friends."

Had a daughter . . . My smile fell. "What happened to her?" I asked gently.

"Beasts got her."

My chest squeezed painfully. I couldn't even fathom how hard that must have been. "I'm sorry," I whispered.

Marty waved me off. "Everyone's got a story like mine. This world ain't right, but you already know that." He rose from the bed, staring pointedly. "You ever stop being afraid of yourself, you might just be the one to save it."

I laughed bitterly. "I just burnt half this town to the ground. This world needs to be saved from me."

A dark look stole over his face. In all the years I'd known him, I'd never seen him look so serious before. "These lands could use a good burning. Sometimes to save something, you gotta kill it."

I turned slowly. My gaze drifted briefly to all the corpses below. "I've done enough killing to last a lifetime."

"What you're looking at ain't nothing compared to what's to come. The Nighters started something here that's not going to stop just because your man lived. If you ain't willing to fight for him on your account, do it for him. He's going to need you."

I sighed, shaking my head. "He doesn't need me. He's the Enforcer." And I could barely protect myself at the moment, let alone him.

Marty gave me one of his 'don't be stupid' looks.

"What?"

"The Nighters gave iron dust to every mortal in this city. If one of them doesn't manage to kill the Enforcer, the Nighters will see to it."

"You think they will go after him again?"

"I know it."

A harsh exhale left me. "Fuck."

Going after Ronan was no longer a choice.

I packed my things while Marty watched. When I finished, I pulled him into a hug.

"Thank you," I breathed. "For everything."

Marty squeezed me tight. "Take care of yourself, alright? I've already lost one daughter. I can't bear to lose another."

Tears pricked at the edges of my eyes. I released him and patted his cheek. "Don't worry. I don't go down easy." I moved to the door.

"Don't forget to check the stables on your way out. There's a surprise waiting for you," Marty called after me.

I smiled at him over my shoulder. "I will, there's just one more thing I've got to do first."

Marty flashed a knowing smile. "Give 'em hell."

I kept my head straightforward as I walked through Mayhem. If I allowed myself to take in the destruction I'd caused right then, I would never make it to my destination. Once my business was finished with the Rogues, I'd take it all in.

Unfortunately, their compound had escaped the fire relatively unscathed. There were scorch marks on the roof, but otherwise, the structure was intact, probably due to the stone fortifications Boone had added during renovations. The buildings in the surrounding vicinity weren't as lucky; they were nothing more than charred husks.

I opened the door to my room and found everything just as I left it, except now a thin coat of dust had settled over the sparse furniture. The room was bleak and colorless. There were no personal effects of any kind. Just four gray walls. Standing in it now, it felt more like a prison than a room.

I had never settled in here, too afraid of being booted out at any moment. This room was never really mine, just like I was never really a Rogue. I didn't belong; I never had, and for once, I was grateful for that because if I had been one of them, I would have never met Ronan.

Without bothering to take anything, I shut the door behind me. I couldn't stomach standing in that cold, lifeless room where I had spent so much time dreaming of becoming a Rogue a second longer. I wasn't even fully sure why I was here at all. The Rogues had all betrayed me—sent me to my death *twice*.

Maybe it was because I had spent seven years here trying to make a home for myself, and it had all been a waste. Maybe I needed closure.

Hushed voices sounded from somewhere below in the compound.

I continued the rest of the way down the stairs and found a group of Rogues gathered at the bottom. Their conversation died the moment they saw me. Tension sucked the air out of the hall. Some Rogues stared in shock, some in fear. I felt like a ghost haunting their compound.

"What are you doing here?" Boone snapped.

My lips curled into a nasty smile. Now, I understood why I was here.

It wasn't for closure.

It was for revenge.

37

"Where's Ryder?"

The backstabbing coward was nowhere to be found, just like the godstone and Nighters. Marty had asked around for me.

When none of the Rogues answered, I uncurled my talons and advanced on them.

Duke held up his hands, backing away. "We—We don't know, Vera. I swear."

Boone held his ground as the others continued backing away, an inch at a time like they were worried I would attack at any sudden movement. Boone crossed his arms, projecting a calm he didn't feel if his body posture was anything to go by.

"Ryder is gone and so are the Nighters." His smile was downright smug. "They're in the Spirit Lands. You'll never get to them without a pooka."

A pooka was the only beast with the ability to access the Spirit Lands—the spirit realm that ran parallel to this world and held the souls of all those who had passed. They were as rare as they were elusive, and the only beast the wall couldn't contain.

How in the fuck did the Nighters get their hands on one?

That was a question for another day. At the very least, that was one less thing I had to worry about. If the Nighters were hiding in the Spirit Lands, that only left the mortals to go after Ronan.

I rushed Boone. He wasn't expecting it. I shoved him against the wall and pressed my forearm against his throat before he could blink. I tore the gun out of his holster and shoved the barrel under his chin.

I heard the other Rogues close in. I cocked back the hammer. "Come any closer and I'll put a bullet in his skull."

Boone's chin quivered even as he challenged, "You don't have the guts."

Genuine, amused laughter careened up my throat. "I burned half this city and its people to the ground, and you really think I don't have the guts to kill *you*?"

His bravery soured. He trembled, looking so pathetic in that moment.

"I can't believe I ever looked up to you," I said shaking my head. I jerked him away from the wall and pressed the barrel against his back. The other Rogues watched with tense expressions. They wanted to help their leader, but were also too terrified of me to try.

"Give me all the silver in your pockets," I ordered.

They exchanged glances. I snapped my teeth at them. "All the silver now, or I let my dragon out again for its next meal."

The Rogues paled and burst into action. They turned their pockets inside out, flinging the contents at my feet.

"You too," I told Boone.

He didn't listen, and I shoved the gun harder against him, snarling, "Now."

"You're going to regret this," he warned, digging into his pocket.

"The only thing I regret is not doing this sooner." I was going to rob these fuckers blind. There wasn't enough silver in the lands to make up for all the corthshit they'd put me through, but this was a good start.

"Take off your clothes," I barked once Boone emptied his pockets.

"No," Boone growled. "Take our silver and go."

"It's adorable you think you have a choice," I said with fake sweetness. I rammed the butt of the gun into his head. "Take off your fucking clothes."

The other Rogues rushed to strip off their garments. Boone took his time, but he obeyed all the same.

When they were all butt naked and trembling, I ordered everyone but Boone upstairs. They stampeded up the steps, leaving their leader to my mercy.

I shoved Boone forward. "Go. You and I are taking a little walk."

I took him to the armory where I had him load up a bag of gold bullets and a dagger to replace the one I lost to the Nighters. The blade wasn't close to the quality of the one Ronan had given me, but it would have to do for now.

Next, we went into the kitchen and filled another bag with food. Once we finished, I directed him back to the hall to collect all the clothes, vests, and silver strewn on the floor.

I deposited the two bags by my feet, gun trained on Boone's chest.

"This isn't the last you'll see of me," he warned. "Word travels fast in the Mortal Lands. You'll be hunted."

"It's in your best interest to persuade whoever is still left in this city to keep the dragon attack under wraps. Get the word out it was a fire."

Boone was a respected leader in the community. If anyone could do damage control over the clusterfuck my dragon had caused, it was him.

He crossed his arms, trying and failing to look intimidating while standing buck naked. "Why would I do that?"

"The night the city burned wasn't a full moon. What do you think will happen when word gets around that a beast who can burn a city to the ground isn't contained behind the wall?"

"Mass hysteria," he admitted begrudgingly.

"But just to give you a little extra incentive, if I hear a single word about a dragon attack, I'll come and finish this city. We clear?"

"Yes," he bit out.

I hefted the bags over each shoulder and turned toward the exit, taking Boone's gun with me.

I stopped mid-way and glanced back. "And if you, or any other Rogue, come for the Enforcer, I won't let the dragon give you a quick death."

Jaw clenched, Boone jerked his head.

I exited the Rogue compound, carrying my stolen goods. Putting Boone in his place had felt good. Putting a bullet between his eyes would have felt even better. If I didn't need him for damage control, I would have. If what Ronan said was true about the fae, I needed the dragon that was undoubtedly seen by everyone in this city to remain a secret.

I could have taken out the other Rogues, but there would be a full moon in three days. If I killed them, it would leave innocent lives unprotected from the beasts, and I had already taken enough from them as it was. This whole city didn't need to die for the actions of a few.

Mortals lingered in the streets, putting their city back together. They were too busy cleaning up the wreckage to notice me. I shifted the bags on my shoulders and started toward the stables.

It was eerily quiet as I walked except for the faint squeaking of the cart wheels as they carried bodies out.

Rubble from the fallen buildings littered my path. I passed the doctor's office. There was nothing left of it but skeletal remains.

The further I walked, the more destruction I saw. The entire city was washed in a gray pallor and the air was somber. It was like walking through a graveyard.

My stomach tightened. I had reveled in the fear my dragon caused with the Rogues, but on the other side of that fear was this. This wreckage. I didn't delight in any of this.

A cart passed by carrying bodies. My gaze caught on a child and the sight punched me square in the chest. Sharp, nauseating pain shot through me.

I . . . I had murdered *children*.

The bags slipped to the ground. I followed. Suddenly, they were all I could see. Their tiny bodies were everywhere, buried amongst the rubble with no family left alive to bury them.

Self-disgust pooled in my stomach like acid.

How could I have done this? How could I have let this happen?

Stinging tears filled my eyes. Nausea punched up my throat and I vomited onto the street.

I knew freeing my dragon would have disastrous consequences, but I could never have imagined how deadly they would be. Not even the beasts wrought this kind of carnage.

I *was* a beast. Not half, not similar in appearance. I was one. I had no idea how the lands the Crone had managed to turn me into one, but I'd be sure to ask when I saw her again.

Gods, this was all so fucked.

Deranged laughter burst from my mouth. I laughed and laughed in between bouts of vomiting until my throat felt raw.

Then the laughter devolved into sobbing. I cried for the

children I'd killed. I cried for the love I'd lost. I cried for the little girl I once was who'd been robbed of the chance at a normal life.

Gazes darted my way as I wept in the middle of the street. I knew I looked like I'd lost my mind and maybe I had. There was only so much a person could deal with before they cracked.

I sobbed until there were no tears left to cry, and then I did what I did best. I got back on my feet and carried on.

After grabbing a cart and shovel, I loaded every child I could find. I brought them out into the desert and gave them a proper burial.

I dug their holes deep beneath the sand so no beasts could get to them. Even though I didn't hold much esteem for the Gods that had abandoned these lands long ago, I prayed over the graves, pleading with them to help these children find the peace and comfort they were denied in life.

I forced myself to look into each of their eyes before I covered the graves. I wanted the image of their melted faces seared into my heart until the day I died. I would remember those faces. I would remember what I had done to those children.

"I will never release my dragon again so long as I live," I vowed to them. "No child will ever suffer the way you did."

It was such a weak and pathetic offering for what I had done, but it was all I had to give.

I had been bluffing when I told the Rogues I would let my dragon out. I would *never*. It was going to rot in the darkness of my mind for all of eternity.

Patting down the sand over the last gravesite, I numbly headed back into the city. If not for Marty's warning about the risk to Ronan's life, I would have returned straight to the Crone; allowed her to torture me for the rest of my days as penance for what I had done to those children. There was nothing I could do for them now, but I could still protect Ronan. I owed him that.

I made my way to the stables. True to Marty's word, there was a surprise waiting inside for me.

A single horse stood in a stall. Its coat was black with a scar running down its left flank. And those eyes. Those eyes stared right at me like it knew who I was.

I held my breath. No, it couldn't be. I was seeing things.

"Ness?" I took a shaky step toward the horse and reached out my hand. The horse chuffed and leaned into my touch. My heart felt like it was going to explode. It was her.

I burst into tears and launched myself at her. I didn't deserve this. I didn't deserve to have her back after everything I had done, but fuck I was so grateful I did.

I felt like I had been thrown in the sea with anchors around my legs and she was the only thing keeping me from drowning.

I clung to her neck, tears trailing down my cheeks.

"It's really you." I nuzzled her neck. "You came back for me."

I held her tight for several minutes, my heart beating a wild staccato in my chest. I feared if I let her go, my precious mare would vanish.

Eventually, I pulled back. "Are you ready to go on another adventure with me, girl?"

Ness reared back, neighing loudly, stomping her hooves on the ground.

I had missed her so damn much. I sniffed, swiping at my eyes, and gave her the biggest smile. "I know. I know. The last adventure didn't go as planned. You'll like this one much better, I promise."

When Ness still didn't seem convinced, I said, "You know they say the Faylands have hills of yummy, delicious

397

grass for as far as the eye can see. No more prickly bushes."

Ness threw her head down once in agreement.

It was settled then.

"I'm coming for you, Ronan."

∼

Thank you so much for reading! I hoped you enjoyed Vera and Ronan's story as much as I enjoyed writing it. Want more of them?

Their story continues in...

Nights of Steel and Shadow

Coming March 3, 2023

Pre-order on Amazon

Want exclusive access to updates, arcs, and giveaways?

Join Shannen Durey's Newsletter

ACKNOWLEDGMENTS

This story and I went through some tough times together. It was originally published as a clean, young adult fantasy romance, but when I sat down to write the sequel, my heart just wasn't in it.

I took a chance and decided to completely rewrite the story, telling it the way I wanted this time, and not the way I thought others would like. I read every book on romance structure and writing explicit sex scenes I could find. Then I put on my big girl pants and wrote the word cock over and over again until the idea of others reading that word in my book didn't make me cringe.

I overhauled the story, threw in a lot of spice and angst, and fell back in love with Vera and Ronan again.

Rewriting this story has been wonderful and terrifying at the same time. I decided to take a leap of faith and follow my heart with no idea where I would land, but I don't regret a thing. I poured so much love and work into this rewrite and I cannot be prouder of the result.

E.H. Demeter deserves the biggest thank you. She has been my cheerleader and biggest supporter from the start. Thank you for always believing in me, even when I couldn't. This book wouldn't exist without you.

To my beta readers, I cannot thank you enough for feedback. It was absolute gold and helped make this book the best that it could be.

And last, but not least, a big thank you to the supportive

community on Tik Tok. Your kind and supportive words gave me the courage to put this story out there, the way I wanted to tell it.

THANK YOU!